EVENINGS
AND
WEEKENDS

EVENINGS AND WEEKENDS

Oisín McKenna

4th ESTATE • *London*

4th Estate
An imprint of HarperCollins*Publishers*
1 London Bridge Street
London SE1 9GF

www.4thestate.co.uk

HarperCollins*Publishers*
Macken House
39/40 Mayor Street Upper
Dublin 1
DO1 C9W8, Ireland

First published in Great Britain in 2024 by 4th Estate

1

A catalogue record for this book is
available from the British Library

ISBN 978-0-00-860417-2 (hardback)
ISBN 978-0-00-860418-9 (trade paperback)

Epigraph extract from 'Peanut Butter' in *I Must Be Living Twice/New & Selected
Poems* by Eileen Myles. Copyright © 2015 by Eileen Myles. Courtesy of
HarperCollins Publishers.

Set in Adobe Garamond Pro and Arno Pro Italic

Printed and bound in the UK using 100%
renewable electricity at CPI Group (UK) Ltd

This book contains FSC™ certified paper and other controlled
sources to ensure responsible forest management.

For more information visit: www.harpercollins.co.uk/green

For my mam, Fiona, and dad, Ricky.

'summer as a

time to do

nothing and make

no money.'

'Peanut Butter' – Eileen Myles (1991)

2019

1

A WHALE GETS STUCK IN THE THAMES. IT'S A RARE whale, a big whale, a northern bottlenose whale to be precise. Five metres in length, twelve tonnes of shuddering blubber and bone; thrashing, frantic, wildly distressed, its body half-beached next to shopping trolleys and syringes on Bermondsey Beach. By Friday, it becomes a sensation. People on Twitter give it a name. They photoshop its image over screenshots from *The Simpsons*, *The Lord of the Rings*, and *Harry Potter*, at first a hilarious meme, then an annoying fad once brands begin using it to sell their products on Instagram. It's suddenly important to have an opinion. Callers to daytime talk shows wish the whale well and suggest schemes for rescuing it. Crowdfunds are set up, bake sales planned, and thousands of pounds are raised within hours, though some argue that certain causes – food banks, police bail funds, refugees crossing the Mediterranean, injured British army veterans, people in need of gender-affirming care, and generally, Syria – are more deserving of your money. Battle lines are drawn, arguments lost and won. Blame is attributed to some combination of carbon emissions, single-use plastics, the European Union, English nationalism, eco-fascism, the volume of fossil fuel required to keep the internet turned on, and anyone who still buys cheap clothes from high street shops. The exact ratio of factors is yet to be agreed, but one thing is certain: the whale is bad news. It points its finger in accusation. No one is innocent in the whale's unblinking eyes. You, declares the whale, are morally, spiritually and ecologically bankrupt. The whale is alive, but only just about.

It's a tense summer. It's June. Dehydrated office workers spew from Tube stations with frayed nerves and anxiety. On every beautiful day, people feel compelled to look out their window and say, 'It's very worrying, isn't it?' as if it were tasteless to comment on the warm sun and blue sky without remarking on the mass extinction of humans and whales within the same breath. The air is warm and damp. No bedsheet is un-drenched, and everything, everywhere is sticky with sweat. The hours of each day are rationed between unbearable heat and biblical rain, and even though it has only been this way for three weeks, it is impossible to imagine that things have ever been any other way. People move slowly, if they move at all, and no one has thought a coherent thought all month.

. . .

ED SEYMOUR, A COURIER, IS DELIVERING A BOX OF pastries to an office in Canary Wharf, dripping with sweat and chirpier than he's been in weeks. He's cycling along the riverbank – not the fastest route, but so calming to watch the river glisten – when he spots the whale on the opposite bank.

He steadies himself and rubs his eyes like a crazed cartoon character. Ed Seymour, a good man, a normal man, a man with a pregnant girlfriend, is certain that he's hallucinating. He thinks the whale is the latest in a long line of imaginary creatures he's encountered recently, sometimes friendly, sometimes threatening, but, crucially, never real.

It is not the first time that Ed has hallucinated this year. It is not the second, third or fourth time either. Nine weeks ago, Ed learned that his girlfriend Maggie was pregnant, and his life would change forever. While this change was not necessarily unwelcome, it was certainly unplanned, and shocking enough for Ed to call his friend Callum, a small-time drug dealer, and ask if they could meet at the pub. Callum, on learning the news, consoled Ed in the only way he knew how: he passed a tab of acid under the table. Ed didn't want to get high, exhausted by the news of the pregnancy and the fact that his friend only knew how to express love through the sharing of drugs, but seeing that Callum was trying to express love all the same, and at thirty years old still keen to be seen as one of the boys, he wearily complied, at heart a people pleaser. Ed placed the tab beneath his tongue and twenty minutes later the walls turned pink and fleshy. They expanded and contracted like the walls of a lung, and Ed became spindly like a frail little bronchiole.

Now, he grips his handlebars, struggles to breathe, and wonders if he's going to die. He's had this thought more than once since January, when his dad, a labourer, passed away at fifty years old and Ed became aware that a life could end. Ed had always known about death in a theoretical sense, but now that he had encountered death in the flesh – his dad's seizure, the chill of his hands – it was no longer abstract or hypotheti-cal. It was real, wrenching, unacceptably painful, so painful that it should quite literally be impossible. Death could happen to anyone at any time, even people like Ed's dad, big people, solid people, people with the weather-beaten resilience of a surviving Stone Age monument. Even those people die. Even Ed will die. So when he glares at the whale and his heart beats from his chest to his ears, he thinks: this is it. The end. I'll never meet my baby.

He takes out his phone and almost calls Maggie, primed to say his last goodbye, but remembering she's at work, and also, is pregnant, feels the news of his upcoming death would be both inconvenient and distressing. He managed to care-fully conceal the acid trip from her – not the first secret he's kept over the years – even though there's no one who could have calmed him down from those panic attacks like Maggie could have done (taking him somewhere quiet, holding him, prompting him to breathe to the same rhythm that she does).

She was amazing at the funeral. She made sure everyone knew where the toilets were, and that there was coffee (normal and decaf) and which sandwiches had no butter and which had no mayo, and sometimes she told little jokes to break the tension. She could always tell when things were getting too much, and then she would put her hand around his hand, and squeeze it, and stroke it with her thumb, and she would quietly say: I love you so much.

That night at home, she cradled his head and kissed his hair, and he felt tiny as a baby.

Anyway, he calls emergency services instead, and when they answer he instantly blurts out a stream of unintelligible gibberish. He tells them his heart is racing and he thinks he's dying and there's a whale half-beached on the banks of the Thames but the whale does not actually exist.

'Calm down, sir. I'm going to need you to start again.'

He tries to breathe like Maggie would have told him to.

'I think I'm hallucinating. I've seen a whale on the banks of the Thames.'

The voice on the other end laughs.

'You're not hallucinating, sir. The whale is real.'

'It's real?'

'It's been on the news. The whale is real.'

Ed is mortified and relieved. He apologises, hangs up, and after taking a few breaths to calm down, takes a picture of the whale to send to Maggie. He says that he loves her and he can't wait to see her later. He wishes her luck for her last day at work.

Then, he remembers that he is meant to be delivering pastries to a professional networking event, and partially on account of the scenic route, partially on account of the time lost to the whale, is now half an hour late. When he arrives, the professional networkers are muttering about their belated pain-au-chocolats and hungry tummies. It's only 10 a.m. and he's already lost out on earnings: he normally would have completed two or three orders by this time. He'll take on more jobs today. No more scenic routes or toilet breaks. He's got a baby on the way, and he can't sleep at night for fear of how they're going to pay for the nappies and the food and God knows what else.

. . .

MAGGIE DOESN'T NOTICE THE MESSAGE FROM ED UNTIL later the same day. She's on her break, her last one ever, in the kitchen of the Greenwich café where she's worked as a waitress for the past eight years. It's 4 p.m. In an hour, she'll clock off for the final time. She notices Ed's text, ignores it, and holds her phone up to Renée so that they can watch a news clip together.

Renée squints at the video and slowly shakes her head.

'No. No. I just don't see it, babe.'

Maggie laughs, incredulous, and says, 'But they're literally identical!'

'I honestly don't know what you're talking about.'

They're watching a marine biologist, Valerie, give an interview to the news.

Valerie has been tasked with the return of the whale to the sea. She explains to the reporter what the rescue operation will entail. She is confident and clear.

But here's the important thing about Valerie: she looks exactly like Princess Diana. Or perhaps: *somewhat*. The precise likeness is contested, but suffice to say, someone posted a clip of the interview to Twitter, and within the hour: a new discourse.

Hundreds, then thousands, posted their take. They're nothing short of identical. They're literal opposites. The marine biologist does not, in fact, look like Princess Diana, and instead, looks like Lady Gaga, or Marine Le Pen, or, most bizarrely, Saint Hildegard of Bingen. A new subgenre of conspiracy theory emerges: Diana never died. She has been living the humble life of a marine biologist this entire time. First claimed ironically, then sincerely, then an impossible-to-interpret blend of the two. It's not just that she looks like Princess Diana, say the theorists: she speaks like her too. She says,

'Well, the Thames isn't very deep for a whale of this size', with the exact same intonation that Princess Diana said 'Well, there were three of us in this marriage' in her famous 1993 interview with the journalist Martin Bashir. All over London, people re-watch the interview and are struck by Diana's magnetism. A gay icon, they say, a fashion icon, an icon of the twentieth century, Diana, Princess of Wales, we love you. Then: the pun, held back at first, but it can't be helped: *Diana, Princess of Whales*, posted by dozens, hundreds, thousands within the hour, each claiming to have been the phrase's true creator, and proclaiming all instances in which it is uttered uncredited to be flagrant violations of intellectual property. Then: the perfunctory debate on the digital commons – everyone has been here before, the old points rehashed – and Maggie wonders: does she truly believe that Diana, Princess of Wales and Diana, Princess of Whales are all that alike? But then, this is beside the point. The point is that it's funny to say that she does.

How to explain all this to Renée?

Maggie puts her phone away and Renée returns to the chopping board. Hands deep purple with beetroot, she tells a story of her six-year-old son.

'Jackson wants to be a marine biologist now. Can you imagine? I don't have a clue where he gets it from. I know the sea is interesting, but he's barely ever seen it.' She chops rapidly while she chats, and Maggie remembers a joke from the internet about how the ocean is queer (expansive, unknowable, subversive). She starts to tell the joke to Renée, but doubts herself; they are of different generations, different cultural touchstones. She remarks simply, 'The sea is gay, you know.'

Renée stares. Maggie is mortified. Renée is a serious woman, mother of Jackson, future marine biologist. Maggie is a woman who says things like 'The sea is gay, you know.'

Renée laughs, perplexed. 'What are you talking about – the sea is gay?'

'Lots of gay kids like the sea.'

Renée sighs, ignores her, and rinses the beetroot from her hands. She says, 'It won't be long now until you've got a little marine biologist of your own. How are you feeling?'

Maggie breathes in. 'I feel great,' she says.

She pauses for a moment, lets her smile linger.

She goes on, 'Like, I'm scared too, obviously. But no morning sickness, so that's been a relief. And we're all set for the big move. Just wish I didn't have to leave you lot!'

'Oh you won't miss this place. You'll miss London though.'

'It's only half an hour on the train. Basically a London suburb.'

Renée smiles encouragingly and says nothing more.

It's almost twelve weeks to the day that Maggie and Ed had sex for the first time in months. A surprise even to themselves. They had returned home from a day in Brighton, a little drunk on beer and sun, a little more daring than normal. The city throbbed, unseasonably hot, its skin was flushed. Maggie throbbed too. His breath in her ear. The tips of their noses touching. A little sore at first, then, the imperceptible shift from *gentle, go slow* to *fuck, that feels good*, both wanting deeper, longer, more. They both came at once. He flopped on top of her, then onto the mattress, and his dick flopped onto his thigh too, sloppy with semen smeared down its side. It was cute. She smiled at it, and he smiled at her smiling.

Then: the missed period.

Then: the peeing on a stick.

Then: confirmation from the doctor. Undeniable. She was pregnant.

There were other events too. There was a mother on the street, and for the first time thinking: *Could that be me?* There were conversations with Renée, one of the first people Maggie told of her pregnancy, desperate for someone older and kinder to tell her what to do.

Subtle at first, barely noticeable, but by the time the doctor confirmed it, she had decided: it was fantastic, miraculous, the best thing that could have happened to her.

She was thirty years old: would this be her only chance?

And Ed? Ed will be an *excellent* dad. He does impersonations of cartoon characters. The baby will love his Homer Simpson, and the way he sings absent-mindedly in the style of Frank Sinatra. Sure, they will become a teenager and be embarrassed by the Frank Sinatra crooning – *You're such a loser, Dad* – but Maggie will say in response, *Don't be so hard on your poor dad, he works very hard for you*, which will be true, because Ed *will* work hard, *does* work hard, and he wakes up early on birthdays and Sundays and sometimes even Tuesdays to cook her favourite breakfast. That's the life in store for you, little baby! Special breakfast from your dad on an otherwise uneventful Tuesday, and when you grow beyond your teenage years, you'll look back on his embarrassing singing with absolute affection.

Of course, the money. The slow slog towards the back wall of their overdraft. Even at their most frugal – no holidays, no takeaways, no new clothes – they can't afford their life in

London, and that's without a baby. How much did nappies cost? And food and cleaning products and childcare? They would make it work, they said. They would move further out. Leyton, Romford, Dagenham. A baby couldn't have survived their flat in Hackney in any case. Ed can barely survive it himself. The damp in their bedroom has affected his breathing, his work, their sex life. The carpet has rotted through, and Ed's breathlessness has become chronic.

So they improvised. They were grasping for anything to hand. It felt as if they had been put on the spot and ordered to agree the course of their life within seconds. *Basildon!* they blurted out under pressure, faces grimaced, shoulders hunched into a shrug as if to say: will this do? Is this the right answer? *Baby!* they went on, then the more uncertain . . . *baby?* and finally, looking at each other, nodding seriously: *baby*, they confirmed. Full stop.

She'll get a job at the restaurant where her cousin works, Ed will work at one of the distribution centres in Tilbury.

'I've never been to Basildon,' calls Renée now, hauling boxes from the freezer.

'It's nice. Got a shopping centre. Leisure centre. Not too far from the sea. The rent is literally five times cheaper and the house is three times the size. We'll be close to my mum, and Ed's mum, so we'll save a fortune on childcare, and Ed's a homebird at heart anyway.'

'That's not too bad so. And as you say, it's close enough so your mates can visit. What's the name of that boy? The nice one. A bit quiet until he has a few drinks in him. I'll never forget when you brought him to the staff Christmas party and he did Cher at karaoke.'

'Phil.'

'He didn't even need to look at the screen. Knew all the words by heart.'

Maggie laughs at the memory, and then sharply inhales.

She's leaving next week and she hasn't even told him yet.

At 5 p.m., it's time to leave.

She makes her way to the kitchen. She mutters under her breath, 'It's my last day.'

She tries to take it all in as if it were a film.

To Renée, she always thought she'd say: Renée, you're the best person I've ever worked with and I love you. To her manager, she thought she'd say: Adrian, you're a tyrannical bully and that's why you can't retain staff in this overpriced hellhole. But lingering at the little party Renée has organised in the kitchen, she doesn't say much at all. Renée has made a platter of cheesy olive bites; everyone sips an aperitif; they all say 'Cheers!' Somehow, it has passed into café folklore that Maggie adores the cheesy olive bites. Her love for them has become a popular joke. Someone will say 'Maggie, will you take the bins out?' and someone else will say 'Only if you give her a cheesy olive bite!' Maggie can't account for where the joke came from, or why it's a joke at all; she feels ambivalent at best about the cheesy olive bites and is almost certain that she's never stated otherwise. But still, it was kind of Renée to make them. She gives her a hug, tells her she's an angel. She says her goodbyes, and leaves.

Outside, she sits on the bench where she used to smoke. Tourists huddle for pictures with Canary Wharf in the background, and an *Evening Standard* flaps at her feet, a grainy picture of the whale and a sensational headline. This is my last day, she says again.

She takes a breath and drafts a text to Phil, typing quickly and pressing send before there's time to entertain her doubts. *Are you free in the morning? Got some big news.*

. . .

THERE HAS BEEN A LONGSTANDING COMPETITION between Maggie and Phil, so palpable and real that it seems frankly absurd that neither of them has ever acknowledged it out loud.

When they were eleven, for example, a shopping trolley showed up on the estate where they grew up. No one knew where this shopping trolley came from and no one ever found out. It was summer and summer was a time during which un-explained phenomena could randomly occur without anyone ever needing to understand their backstories.

This particular summer was a long summer. A hot sum-mer. It was the summer they were friends with Kyle Connolly, and Kyle Connolly had smoked a cigarette. He hadn't enjoyed it, so he never smoked another, and this gave him a sense of mystique; to have done something so transgressive, and to have been above even that! An unspeakable glamour. He had snogged one girl in Majorca, one girl in Chelmsford. He wore a silver studded belt.

Maggie and Phil competed viciously for his affection.

Someone would say, 'Let's play the shopping trolley game,' and Maggie and Phil would power walk towards it, never ad-mitting they were trying to overtake each other, and never breaking into a run so as not to appear desperate. Kyle trailed behind ambivalently.

The shopping trolley game was this: one person sat in it, someone else pushed as fast as they could. Maggie and Phil always wanted to be the one to push Kyle.

That summer, Kyle and Phil played another game too, a game they kept secret from Maggie. Like the shopping trolley, this game was another of summer's great inarticulable mysteries. Even if Phil wanted to tell her, he wouldn't have known what words to use. The game had been Kyle's idea. He had suggested it vaguely, giggling, through gestures and broken sentences. Phil didn't know where the game came from, but he knew that it was nice and that he wanted to keep playing. The game was this: Phil would go to Kyle's house, they would close his bedroom door, they would take off their clothes, and Kyle would lie on top of Phil beneath the duvet. They would stay that way for twenty minutes – eyes open, arms dead-straight by their sides, chests swollen with held breath – and they wouldn't move an inch.

One day, Maggie walked in. She had waited for her friends for hours. When they didn't come, she called to Phil's house, then Kyle's house, then she ran up the stairs, two steps at a time. She exploded into the room and saw them in bed. It was very bewildering.

'What are you doing?' she said.

'Nothing,' they responded, panicking, scrambling for white lies. They didn't really know what they were doing, but they understood intuitively that it was wrong, and by extension, that they were bad. It was critically important that no one ever knew.

Maggie said, 'I have to go have lunch now,' even though it wasn't even midday yet. She ran out the door and the boys wordlessly agreed to never play the game again.

The next day, she told Phil, 'I don't care about yesterday and I'm not going to tell, as long as you let Kyle push me and *only me* in the trolley for the next three weeks.'

Phil agreed that this was a reasonable deal.

For the next three weeks, Maggie rode through the estate like a queen.

2

IT'S 5.30 P.M., AND PHIL IS STUCK IN A MEETING WHICH
should have already ended. He clicks his pen. He unclicks
it again. He barely tries to conceal the impatience in his
cough. The windows here don't open. The sun is hung at
such an angle so that no matter where you sit you have to
shield your eyes from the glare. This room, which normally smells of air conditioning and the burning dust of an
overheating overhead projector, today smells disconcerting-
ly organic: sweat, coffee breath, a brief but truly shocking
whiff of unacknowledged fart. Outside, there is London.
Every now and then, its sounds – its traffic, its birdsong, its
shouts – puncture the ambient din of the office; the rum-
bling air vents, the sad old PCs growling on their desks, a
high-pitched beep which happens at the same time every
week and for which no one has any explanation. Everyone is
on their phones. Phil receives a series of texts in succession:
his housemate Debs is planning her outfit for the party tomorrow and wants to know if her new dress makes her look
like Theresa May.

Alan, Phil's manager, has been practising gratitude. To thank the team for their work, he scattered fun-sized packets of Haribo across the table at the start of the meeting ('Sweeties!' he announced in the manner of a children's entertainer, or indeed, in the manner of an actual child). The empty wrappers, sugar-crashes, and ceaseless drone of conversation recall the cranky close of a sixth birthday party, waiting to be taken home by parents who won't stop conversing with the other adults. No one has been paid for their time since 5 p.m.

Phil daydreams. Specifically, he daydreams about Keith, the book he plans to give to him this weekend, and the inscription he plans to write in the book.

'Keith,' he'll write, 'before I met you, I never knew that the earth beneath London was made out of clay – one of many deep things I learned from you.'

He turns the phrase over in his mind, omitting a word here or there.

'Keith,' he'll write, 'before I met you, I hadn't known that the earth beneath London was made out of clay. It's not the only deep thing I've learned about from you.'

The book is about geology, specifically the geology of London, the minerals in the soil, the plants that thrive, the taste of the tap water, the tough clay that Keith turns over in his allotment on Sunday mornings while Phil struggles with the strimmer.

Sometimes, especially now that it's summer, Keith takes off his shirt while he works, and sweat dribbles down his back towards the waistband of his pants.

Sometimes, he kisses Phil like that, half-naked, mucky,

drenched in sweat, and Jacinta, the old woman in the neigh-
bouring allotment, wolf-whistles, says, 'Good on ya, lads!' and
jokes about how it's been too long since she herself had a good
roll around in the grass. Then, they usually listen to Jacinta's
funny but long-winded anecdotes about the disputes that
plague the allotment committee, while Phil dreams of getting
Keith to himself.

Phil bought the book because Keith is interested in the
soil and the trees and the birds and the buildings of London.
Really, that's what he's referring to when he says 'deep things';
time and again, Keith has shared a morsel of knowledge about
the city and this morsel of knowledge has been enough to
make the city seem strange and entirely new.

He senses a shift in the room; Alan is no longer the only
person speaking. He tunes back in to the conversation; it seems
that each member of the team has been asked to describe an
event that happened this week which they're proud of. It's
nearly 6 p.m. now – an hour after the meeting was supposed to
finish. Everyone outlines some difficult task they completed,
some breakthrough in personal or professional development.
Phil tunes back out.

Of course, when he says 'deep things' he is referring
to deep things of an emotional nature too, like caring and
being cared for, feeling kinship, taking pleasure from food
and landscapes and having a body that dances, a body with
nerve endings and erogenous zones, and he supposes, too,
that one of the deep things he's referring to is his own asshole – not *explicitly*, as such, but if Keith were to interpret it
on that level, he certainly wouldn't be against it – and while
Keith has only fucked Phil on one prior occasion, it was an

experience so explosive that it allowed Phil a brief but truly life-changing glimpse into just how much pleasure a human body can feel.

'Phil.'

Phil jolts; Alan is speaking to him, everyone glaring.

'It's your turn, Phil.'

'Yes, it is, it's—'

'To say what you're proud of.'

'Of course, yes.' Phil is so checked out of the room that he's barely conscious of what he says at all. He says, 'I'm proud of the way the team gelled this week. Our channels of communication felt open. I think we're finally ready to be vulnerable.'

Alan nods profoundly as if Phil were a contestant on a TV talent show who has just revealed a tragic backstory, and Phil reaches for his phone to make a note of the mental edits he's made to the book's inscription. This is when he notices the message from Maggie.

Big news? That seems like a foreboding thing to say.

Maggie and Phil have spoken every day since they were kids. They're so accustomed to each other – dependent, really – that they begin to feel unlike themselves when they've been out of touch for too long. He replies: *Yeah I'm free tomorrow*, even though this is not true and means he'll have to postpone plans with his mother until later in the afternoon.

He has a big weekend ahead; Keith after work, Maggie in the morning, his mum in the afternoon, the party tomorrow night. Any second now, the meeting will finish, and the hottest weekend of the year will burst into being. In one brief moment, he'll race to his desk, shut down his PC, and sprint, panting, towards the sun; then, only then, will his real life begin.

. . .

ROSALEEN CLIMBS INTO THE DRIVING SEAT AFTER WORK. She is fastening her seatbelt when her phone pings with a message from Phil. *Hi mum, something came up tomorrow, can we do 2pm instead of 12? Thanks xx.*

She mutters, 'For Christ's sake,' feeling a brief but potent flare of guilt at having taken the Lord's name in vain, even though she's not had a drop of faith in the Lord or his name since she left Ireland at eighteen years old.

She blows through her lips. She's always guilty these days. Her sense of guilt has taken on a new lease of life since she sat in the doctor's office last week and he told her about the lumps in her breasts and armpits and back. A renewed interest in the Lord, too.

She replies, tells him it's fine, feeling guilty at having felt it wouldn't be.

It's been ten days since her diagnosis, five days since she tried to call Phil to tell him about it, and three days since she decided it would be better to meet in person instead.

He's only postponed by two hours, but he's hard to get hold of, her youngest son; he postpones by two hours, then by four, then several days, then several weeks, and the doctors can't say for sure yet whether she's got several weeks or several years left.

She was careless like that at one time too. She used to spend every waking minute with Pauline Duffy from number

47, until her mother threatened to have her sent away if she continued to go gallivanting with Pauline and her famously loose morals.

She reverses from her parking spot and switches on the radio. It's the six o'clock news; the whale in the Thames. An expert is being interviewed, a woman named Valerie, who says the whale is bewildered, injured, and unable to find its way back out to sea.

'The Thames,' she says, 'is much, much shallower than the deep oceans a northern bottlenose is used to swimming in. We're doing everything we can to support her, to console her, to gently guide her out of the river and back towards those deep oceans, but at this point, myself and my colleagues are extremely concerned for the whale's well-being.'

Rosaleen gasps.

'That's terrible,' she says aloud to no one. She imagines telling Pauline about it.

The outskirts of Basildon whizz by outside. To a passerby, Rosaleen's nondescript: a brown-haired woman, a careful driver, but on the inside, all sorts of things are taking place.

For example, the malignant growth of cancerous cells.

For example, delight at the glass of wine and pair of slippers that await her at home, and displeasure at her work uniform which feels almost unbearably stuffy. Every day, she drags her arms through its sleeves, the bright red shirt, the dull blue cardigan. Every day, she ties the sheer neckerchief around her neck, every day thinking the same thing, which is that it's ridiculous to have to get dressed up for this job; she works in a call centre, and the customers don't see or care whether she wears a neckerchief or not. Every day, she sits at a computer, one of hundreds, in a room where posters promote the company's four key behaviours (Empowerment, Accountability, Go The Extra Mile, and Do The Right Thing). She takes calls from disgruntled customers who wish to cancel their TV, broadband, or phone services. Every day, she says 'I'm sorry to hear that' or 'Let me be the first to apologise' or 'What I'm going to do is: I'm going to pop you on hold, just for a sec, and if it's OK, I'll have a quick chat with my team lead on how to take this forward.' Every day she has a coaching session with her team lead, who says he believes in her, who says she has what it takes, who speaks as if she were Rocky about to enter the ring, not a middle-aged woman trying to convince an irate granddad in Cardiff that his quality of life will, in fact, be significantly reduced without access to the Wedding Channel, the Murder Channel, or Sky Atlantic.

She pulls into the driveway. Across the road from her house, Joan Seymour – Ed's mum – sits on the pavement as usual. For as long as Rosaleen can remember, Joan has dragged the contents of her living room – armchairs, rug, cabinet, the lot – onto the pavement every night and sits there like she owns the place. It used to drive Rosaleen crazy. What was the point in having a house if you were going to live outside? Who did Joan think she was?

But she regrets having felt so bitterly towards her now. Joan's husband, who died this year, used to sit there with her. She still drags his chair out as if he were around to sit in it.

Rosaleen is worried for her, yes.

But also, she's tired.

She thinks of saying hello, but instead makes a show of pretending not to see her. She hums tunelessly while digging through her handbag, but her guilt – still churning in her gut from taking the Lord's name in vain – gets the better of her.

'Hiya, Joan,' she calls out. 'You alright?'

Joan grunts.

'It's a lovely evening,' continues Rosaleen. 'Would you like some company?'

'Go on then.'

Rosaleen crosses the street, heat rising off the tarmac. Insects buzz in the balmy air.

There's nowhere to sit except for Peter's chair or the arm of Joan's – both insensitive and overfamiliar in their own way – so Rosaleen stands, unsure what to do with her hands; she puts them in her pockets, then behind her back. She gazes around for something to offer a comment on, and now, quite frantic, blurts out breathlessly, 'I love your chair, Joan.'

'Are you going to sit down or not?' replies Joan without lifting her head.

'Me? Oh no, I'm fine, thank you—'

'He's dead, you know.'

'Sorry?'

'My husband. He's dead. So you can sit in his chair.'

Joan lights a Marlboro Red.

She gestures to Rosaleen impatiently, 'Sit down, will you? He's not here to sit in it.'

'Alright,' says Rosaleen, sitting in the chair as if it were about to break.

'I don't believe in ghosts, Rosaleen. Don't believe in heaven. Peter's gone for good. I'm not precious about that. I'm not under any illusions. Don't care who sits in the chair.'

'Well, everyone grieves differently, don't they?'

Joan speaks slowly, languidly, stares into the distance the whole time. She says, 'Men are always dying before their wives. Did you know that? Suicide. Cancer. Heart attacks. Strokes. I've seen it in the papers. Daytime chat shows. Journalists. Talking heads. They say things like "feminism has gone too far – the vote was good, but dead men are bad" and some bloody *dietician* will say that a turn away from red meat is long overdue. They say to talk about your mental health. They say to check your testicles for tumours. They demonstrate how to do it with these educational, disembodied, baby-blue plastic scrotums.'

All of a sudden, Joan cackles at this detail, before continuing, 'Of course it was lung cancer that got Peter in the end. Asbestos. He hadn't even looked at a fag in decades.'

Rosaleen looks around. She rubs her hands as if she's cold.

'Hey, how's your boy?' she stutters. 'How's Ed? Still going strong with Maggie?'

Joan puffs on her fag.

'They're moving back to Basildon.'

'They're not!'

'She's pregnant.'

'She's not! Is she? Phil never told me that. Neither did Callum.'

'She's twelve weeks now. Only started telling people.'

'That makes sense I suppose.'

'I'm looking forward to having them around. A little baby too.'

'That'll be nice for you. Phil's up in London and we barely see him, or Callum. Callum's got the wedding coming up, so I suppose we can't blame him, but those two boys, they never tell us anything. They barely even talk to Steve, and he won't talk to them either.' Rosaleen hesitates and digs her nails into her hands, before deciding to offer a joke. 'I swear to God,' she says. 'I feel like an interpreter in this family. I feel like a switchboard operator.'

Joan laughs. 'It was the same with Peter and Ed. I was always the middleman.'

'I'm sure they were grateful for it.'

'He's a good lad, Ed. A daft lad, but a good one.'

'You're lucky.'

A breeze pulses through the palm tree – the first breeze of the day.

'I am,' concedes Joan with a sigh that shakes her voice.

. . .

CALLUM, ROSALEEN'S ELDEST SON AND ED'S BEST FRIEND, is getting married in six weeks. It's all Rosaleen can think about. Although the cancer has dislodged it from the front of her brain, it's only done so partially. She pictures herself at the meal, standing up from her chair, clinking her knife against a wine glass. She'll clear her throat, calm her nerves, and smile serenely towards the room full of family and friends. 'Callum,' she'll say. 'Before I had you, I never knew just how many creatures could live beneath the earth of one tiny back garden.'

She'll say it because it's true. As soon as he could walk, Callum would traipse around the garden, digging for earthworms and centipedes and all manner of larvae. He'd place them in the cupped palms of his hands, walk up to the back door – gently so as not to disturb the sleeping creepy crawly – and he'd say, 'Look at what I found!' an expression of sheer wonder on his face. He was an adventurous child. He could make even the most mundane situations fantastical. He and his best friend Ed Seymour used to transform living rooms and kitchens into pirate ships and haunted shopping centres and the tombs of ancient Pharaohs. She was so proud of him then. He was a delight to her. Of course, she loved both of her sons equally, but it can't be denied that Callum was the only one who had a drop of confidence as a child.

When she told Callum about the cancer, he wanted to make it better. He said he'd pay for private healthcare. He wasn't going to let her languish on an NHS waiting list for the next five years. They'd get a second, third, fourth opinion. Also, he said, she needed a new TV. Sick people needed to watch TV. They also needed cake. Would she like some cake right now, he'd said, because he could go and get it? Black Forest gateau, lemon drizzle: anything.

How he'd planned to pay for private healthcare was beyond her (he had a job in recruitment, but it didn't pay *that* much) and she was happy with the TV she had. She tried to explain that she hadn't told Phil yet, so Callum needed to keep the news to himself for now, but he was so upset that she's not sure if he even heard her. This is why she needs to tell Phil sooner rather than later. If she doesn't, then someone else will get there first.

3

ED SEYMOUR FINISHES WORK AT 6 P.M. AND CYCLES home through the Docklands and the City.

Before this, he worked in a call centre for six years, then was made redundant, then was on Universal Credit, then they threatened to cut his benefits and he became too anxious to sleep or eat or even talk, so now he does this.

When he goes for walks with Callum, or when the Basildon lads get the train into London, Ed can take them to vantage points on the Heath, Primrose Hill, or Hilly Fields, and point to the city's skyline. He can say, 'I've worked in that building. And that one. And that one,' and everyone laughs because they know Ed's got no qualifications, earns fuck all, and that's why it's funny for Ed to claim to work in those places: that's the whole joke.

Now, he's tired, sweaty and buzzed on caffeine.

It's been a long day, and it'll be a longer weekend. They've barely started packing.

He watches punters heave outside each pub. They spill halfway across the street and get in the way of endlessly honking buses.

Everyone is drunk. Everyone is laughing out loud at jokes they can't hear.

Everyone is smoking, especially the non-smokers. It's too hot to think about ageing or illness or death, and it's too hot, too, to wear a shirt or drink a glass of water or have dinner or go to bed or show up to work on time or show up to work at all. Everyone is downing their drink, getting another, downing their drink, getting another.

Everyone is looking for something to happen.

There's the high reek of exhaust fumes and uncollected bins.

There are men with ties loosened, tongues loosened, men loose and loosening. Tops off, tops lost, tattoos in cursive fonts. Silver chains, gold chains, topless in the station. Bare necks and freshly faded scalps: burnt the bright pink of boiled ham. Broad backs – freckled, blanched – and the soft fat around a man's side bulging over his too-tight tracksuit bottoms.

And Ed: stalled at a red light, staring a moment too long.

His belly trembles. He licks his lips without thinking.

And suddenly, he's sad. Overheated, and a little feral.

He doesn't want to go home. He wants something to happen.

June, as usual, has burst in without warning, and everyone but Ed is making the most of their one life.

Every day, he cycles from Hackney to Whitechapel, from Whitechapel to Canary Wharf. Every day, he runs red lights, cycles on pavements, darts in front of traffic to deliver an order on time. Every day, he nearly dies; every day a passing driver calls him a cunt; every day someone tries to fight him. Every day, he thinks of the vast amount of money needed to make this baby possible, and every day, he pushes through his breathlessness to the point of choking. He knows of couriers who have collapsed on the job. He knows of customers who have stepped over their convulsing bodies to collect an order without calling an ambulance.

His day never recovered from the morning's panic attack. The feeling of near-death lodged in his lungs and all afternoon he carried the sense that there's not enough time left.

He wants more from his weekend than this. He wants more from his life.

He glances again at the too-tight tracksuit bottoms.

The light turns green. He carries on.

He reminds himself that it's Maggie's last day at work, and he wants to make a dinner to celebrate, a dinner that will communicate love in a way that words fail to do. It's not that he doesn't tell her he loves her – he tells her all the time – but the words 'I love you' are famously inadequate for describing the depth of the feeling. Sometimes only gestures suffice.

So he locks his bike, whizzes through the supermarket, and emerges with bags of veg, alcohol-free prosecco, two fat steaks. Boiling and sweaty, he realises he's bursting to pee.

He dashes across the road to Liverpool Street station. He sprints past the pub – the sloshed post-work boozers all shout '*Wheyyyyyyy!*' at a glass that's smashed on the floor – and through the dense flow of commuters, eager to get back to their various suburbs and livid when anyone gets in their way. The station boils with colour and noise. There's the coffee counters, stale baguettes stuffed with hardened cheese and sliced ham, pigeons' coos drowned by the ding-dong that proceeds an announcement. A hen party stumbles towards the exit, waving bejewelled bottles of pink prosecco above their heads, ready for Shoreditch and its earthly delights. Ed's jealous of the hen party, the drinkers, the people with places to go.

That'll be Maggie tomorrow, he thinks, getting loud and rowdy at Holly's hen-do, although of course she won't be able to drink, and doesn't really like Holly or Holly's friends, and is only going because Holly is marrying Callum, and Callum is Ed's best friend.

Either way, he bolts toward the gents. He makes it just in time, the station's noise muffled as the door slams. He finds a urinal, drops his bags, unzips: ahhhhhhh.

Relieved of needing to pee, he washes his hands beneath the hot tap, enjoying the smell of the soap, the heat of the water, when he notices a man linger over his shoulder.

City boy, slicked-back hair, suit too tight around the thighs, standing at the urinal. Reeks of cologne. Older than Ed, but only by a little.

The man cranes his neck; he glances at Ed; he raises his eyebrows so marginally that it would be indiscernible to an untrained eye, but Ed knows an invitation when he sees one.

The man slowly walks into a toilet cubicle.

Then, he casts a glance back at Ed.

Ed looks away, pretends not to notice. He takes his bags and heads for the exit.

But stops.

He looks back at the cubicle, door not yet closed.

Fuck's sake, he whispers. He shakes his head in disbelief.

He checks his phone: no word from Maggie.

She's probably gone out with Renée and that lot.

She probably won't be home for hours at this stage.

He inhales. He closes his eyes. It's too hot to think and too hot to go home.

He's thirty years old.

A partner, yes, a dad-to-be, sure, but his own dad died the year he turned fifty.

How many years does Ed have left? How many more chances? Ed could already be more than halfway through his life, and his life in London is on the brink of ending entirely.

He was never young. Never went to university. He went straight from childhood to adulthood with no in between. He's wasted too many hot days already.

Right now, every single person in London is cackling into the mouth of the heatwave weekend, screaming *Let's have it*, except for Ed. Next week, Ed will move to Basildon, and he'll stay there, like his dad, for the rest of his life. He'll be a good man, a good dad, and he'll love the baby and Maggie no matter what.

His blood is boiling. He makes a snap decision.

He turns back.

He approaches.

He's at the cubicle door, and his ears are ablaze with the feeling of being alive—

Wait. A noise. He spins around.

Someone pulses into the toilets.

It takes a split second to register, but it's someone Ed knows. *Oh fuck*, he thinks.

'Oh fuck,' he says aloud.

No time to think.

'Hi,' he blurts out.

. . .

ON A BENCH IN GREENWICH, MAGGIE THINKS THAT SHE should go home to Ed. They have packing to do, and packing has not been going well. She started last week with the best of intentions, even devising a *system*. She would sort her old papers into four categories – financial, professional, administrative, sentimental – and had bought colour-coded binders in service of this system. It had been working well for a time, but soon the integrity of the system came into question; so many documents seemed to belong to multiple categories, or none at all, and everything was so contingent on everything else, that the next thing she knew, she was emptying out her wardrobe and her cupboards and the big blue IKEA bag under her bed, and everything she owned – unopened bank statements, half-empty pouches of dried-out tobacco, scraps of paper on which she had scrawled illegible notes – had ended up in a heap on the living-room floor. She had ten years' worth of accumulated crap to pack, and just yesterday, she had to take a break in order to watch a ten-minute YouTube video on how to mindfully eat an orange that her GP had recommended for managing anxiety and other unpleasant emotions.

She starts making her way towards the DLR; she thinks about getting a takeaway; she reviews her position on whether it's OK to drink a small amount of alcohol during pregnancy.

She thinks of her flat, which she'll leave next week.

It's the best place she's ever lived.

It's also uninhabitable.

Both are true at once.

It's big, sturdy, ex-council, in the centre of Dalston. Impossibly cheap, her rent the stuff of mythology. When she tells people she lives in Hackney, she always adds, *I only pay five-hundred pounds a month!* lest anyone misconstrue that her glamorous East London lifestyle is facilitated by family wealth, which of course, it's not. It's facilitated by a shared willingness to live in a flat so damp that Ed's childhood asthma has erupted again after two dormant decades, and a resignation to the landlord's refusal to do anything about it.

And so, she pictures herself in Basildon. She'll be a person who owns houseplants. They will crowd her kitchen, hang from her shelves, and climb her walls. She will consider whether they need more or less water, more or less light. There will be so many plants that she will need to hack her way to the kettle with a machete every time she wants a cup of tea. She will tell a joke in which she describes her kitchen as a *rewilding project.* Her Instagram algorithm will flood her feed with ads for *Monstera, Pothos,* English ivy. These websites will have very attractive branding, and she will develop a low-level but not entirely harmless addiction. In London, all she does is sip overpriced coffees from paper cups and pay more rent than she can afford to pay. In Basildon, she will have houseplants, and also, a baby, and therefore, will not regret her decision to leave. She and Ed will walk along the estuary with the child in between them. They will swing the child upwards so that the child can imagine themself to be a rollercoaster, or motorbike, or dragon. All together, they will say *Weeeeeeee!*

She thinks sometimes that she has no business with a baby.

Last week, the doctor rubbed jelly across her tummy and pointed out the baby's organs. Maggie watched herself as if she were material for a film – Maggie, at the doctor's office, Maggie, being part of a narrative arc – but she couldn't feel excited. All she could do was shudder in shame at how ill equipped she was to give a stable future to herself, let alone anyone else. Her sister says the world is about to end. By the time the baby reaches thirty, she says, the polar bears will be dead, and everyone will be living in a brutal police state if the state hasn't collapsed entirely. Her mother, likewise, a one-time radical, is a fatalist in matters of work, love and money. When Maggie told her she was pregnant, she was quiet, and then said gravely, 'Raising a baby is hard, love. And you know I've never been sure about Ed.'

But Maggie has no doubts about Ed, or rather, she does have doubts, but those doubts seem insignificant. He isn't perfect, sure, but he is someone she loves, her boyfriend, even if they have less sex than they used to, like an old married couple, resigned to a life of celibacy and the smell of each other's unabashed farts. Of course, he is someone whose habits grate on her from time to time; the way he says everything in a silly accent, as if to undermine he is saying anything at all; even the most mundane of statements like 'Would you like some coffee?' or 'Where is the olive oil?' or 'Let's watch the Kardashians tonight' he says by raising his voice, fluctuating between highs and lows like a wacky cartoon character. Worst of all, he does imitations of the automated announcements every time they get public transport. 'This is the 149 to Edmonton Green' he says. 'This is a Central Line train to Epping' he says. 'MIND THE GAP' he exclaims, and it enrages her. She doesn't know why. It's petty, and she knows it's petty, and she doesn't want to feel that way, because she loves him too, for his kindness, his slowness, his impersonations of politicians and celebrities.

She taps in at Greenwich DLR and waits for a train. The evening is beautiful, balmy and thick. From her vantage point on the platform, London's skyline looks like a watercolour painting. The sky is pale blue, lilac, browny-yellow. The air quivers with rising heat.

Everyone on the platform is on their way to nights out. Maggie feels glum. It's as if the people of London have converged on the city's parks, beer gardens, and street corners to revel in the great collective joys of being alive, *everyone but you*, they seem to say, *you loner, squanderer, you who stares longingly at the laughing groups of youth in London Fields*.

This, she thinks, is the crux of it. The crux of it is that she wants to go to a party.

She remembers a music festival. Their first time on ecstasy. Ed couldn't stand still: he wanted to rush from one stage to another and pick her up and spin her around. For months and years after that, she thought of that music festival as the most romantic thing that ever happened to her: all the orange and pink lights and jungle and him holding her from behind.

The night after she told him she was pregnant, he got high with Callum and came home tripping. This, in itself, was fine. What *wasn't* fine was that he never wanted to get high with her. Sure: she was pregnant. Not the right time. But she'd been asking him to go dancing for a year before that. Always, an excuse: work, money. No problem. But why did those excuses evaporate in Callum's company? What did Callum have that she didn't?

Before the pregnancy, she would leave her flat on a Friday, and the weekend yawning ahead of her would always seem like the big one. The life-changer. She'd hold court in the Spurstowe smoking area. Friendly acquaintances would stop at her table to pass on their gossip. She would see and be seen,

know and be known, and even the hot bar staff who stared forever into the middle distance would pause from their reverie
to compliment her sunglasses. At a certain point, the night always turned. Typically, she teetered before taking the plunge.
The music would get louder, a glass would shatter, cocaine
would appear from nowhere. Rumours, then, would gently
start to simmer: a rave on the Marshes, fabled at first, the
night too swollen for the pub alone to contain. The music too
loud to talk any more, queens off-shift from Superstore doing
a turn on the bar, and, finally, a critical mass for the Marshes:
everyone flinging themselves out onto the street, then onto
their bikes: a convoy of women and gays, running red lights
and giving each other backies, and fuck it, she'd always think,
this is too good to miss, and off she'd go down Mare Street,
Well Street, Lower Clapton, Lea Bridge Road, and it never
mattered if she didn't find the party, or found it, hated it, and
left in search of cheesy chips. Finding the party was never the
point. The point was travelling towards it.

She admits that she doesn't want to leave. Every time
they've gone to view a new flat, she's calculated its distance
from Dalston Superstore. It's ridiculous. She's been acting as if
Dalston Superstore were the very centre of the universe, as if her
priority in life were to have easy access to Dalston Superstore
at all times of day and night. She doesn't even like Dalston
Superstore. It's too narrow. It's impossible to stand anywhere
without being in the way. But now that it's being taken away
from her, that little corridor seems like heaven on earth.

In Hackney, she'd been part of a scene. People knew who
she was. She mingled in the queer world, the art world, the
world of nightlife, so much so that everyone assumed she had

an art career of her own, even though the demands of her full-time café job stamped that dream out years ago. She doesn't make art any more. She just socialises in proximity to it.

And now that she's leaving Hackney, she can't even claim that. Yesterday she made a snap decision. She moved her old sketchbooks, her art supplies, from the 'keep' pile to the 'maybe' pile and from the 'maybe' pile into the communal bins of the estate. She hadn't looked at them in months, and every time she thought about them, she felt embarrassed.

There was a highchair on sale in Lidl this week. There among the hand blenders, the tents, cheap and lovely in the supermarket's middle aisle. It was bright red and their baby could have sat in it. It was only thirty pounds and mashed up bananas could have oozed from the baby's mouth and plopped onto its hard plastic, and yet: Ed said he could get one from a cousin. She pressed him – which cousin was he referring to? – but Ed didn't know; it just seemed like a thing that would happen. When he stays up late, staring at spreadsheets and murmuring, 'How are we going to afford it?' she tells him they'll find a way. That's what everyone says: once the baby is born, you just find a way. 'The only people who say that are bankrolled by their rich parents,' he says. She kisses his neck, and says that things will be fine.

The train comes. She squeezes on.

They pull into the next station and her phone vibrates with a message from Ali, an invitation to karaoke at the pub in Stoke Newington, a blowout before she leaves the city. She considers this. Of course she shouldn't go. Her flat is a mess, half packed up and so much work still to do, and karaoke at the pub in Stoke Newington has never been a good idea.

She has a pounding headache. Is it the pregnancy? Is it the air pressure? The atmosphere is taut with electricity. The air, muscles tense with the rage of a barely restrained punch, is just about holding back the inevitable rainstorm. She thinks of the old-timey women who could forecast the rain by the cramp of a foot. She tries to experience a moment of matrilineal kinship with them. Her headache gets worse. She glugs on her water.

Still, she gets off the train. She gets on a bus, and travels towards Ali's flat.

Why? It's because of the summer. It's because of the mania that grips London during a heatwave. It's because the grass is yellow and no one can sleep, and the city is desperate, tetchy, and horny. It's because everyone is alert, primed for something huge to happen, and she's afraid this could be the last spontaneous act of her life.

. . .

EVERY DAY, PHIL TYPES 'HELLO, I HOPE THIS EMAIL finds you well' multiple times before 10 a.m. He opens, but doesn't read, various tabs, Word docs, PDFs. Every day, he makes a to-do list. Every day, he meets with the team. Every day, he says: I'll give you an update on the projects I've been working on. He explains: It's a quick rundown of the actionables and measurables. We're on track to meet our Q3 KPIs, which were devised in line with our mission, goals, aims, and objectives. As a result of our interventions, the majority of our respondents said that they felt *more connected* now than they did when the interventions were commenced, and six out of ten experienced a sense of well-being, wellness, good mental health, or contentment, on *at least* one additional occasion per fortnight. He pauses, sombrely, after select phrases. He gesticulates, casually, and smiles like a person smiles at their buddies.

Before work every day, Phil goes to the gym. His face contorts. His forehead dribbles with sweat. He lowers himself down for the final rep – his muscles buckling under the weight – clenches his jaw, drives back up, and places the barbell back on its rack with a crash.

He once messaged Maggie, *all I want is a corbyn government and a massive ass!!*

She replied, *ah! The two great dreams of our time!*

Every day, he browses the Instagram pages of professionally hot men, always on holidays, in Mykonos, in Sitges, in tiny speedos, with tattooed legs, heads shaved not because they are balding but because it accentuates their conventionally handsome bone structures. He understands that he is being duped by the forces of capitalist advertising but can't help but speculate that if he looked like those men, then he too might always be on holiday, unconcerned about money, free, happy, in peak emotional and physical condition, in a state of total enjoyment for the rest of his life. He can't afford to go to Sitges or Mykonos, but clings to the more modest dream of being pictured in his speedos at the men's pond on Hampstead Heath. That's the extent of the fantasy: first to be seen, then, to be envied, and over the past months he's reduced his food intake to such a degree that he often feels dizzy.

Every day, he rushes through Liverpool Street station to get a westbound Central Line, and glances at the weight loss ad above the escalators; a before picture of a man with a belly spilling over his Lycra shorts, an after picture of the same man, now with ripped pecs and abs. According to the ad, this could be you in just six weeks. It's been there since Phil first moved to London a decade ago, and he often gazes at the man's bulging veins, visible from the top deck of the 149 like the Great Wall of China is visible from space.

He's unleashed from the meeting at 6 p.m. and is about to leave when Alan asks what he's up to for the weekend. Phil explains that there's a party happening in the place that he lives, and Alan, a glint in his eye, takes this as a cue to wistfully recount his early nineties halcyon days, when he was nearly never not high at an acid house rave.

'Best years of my life,' he says. 'You must be getting up to all sorts at those parties.'

Alan winks, apparently trying to draw Phil into a sort of complicity.

'I suppose so,' says Phil, pretending to laugh, but not sure what the joke is.

'Hey, I know what it's like. I know what people get up to.'

Alan taps his nose. He holds one nostril shut and snorts a line of imaginary cocaine. Phil nods and smiles, picking up on the hint – Alan is trying to let Phil know that he too has done drugs and, therefore, is cool. Phil cringes for them both, while Alan says, 'I'm only joking. Those days are behind me. I've three kids now, a marriage, a divorce. Lost my hair, and the clubs from back then are shut now anyway. Enjoy it, kid. It doesn't last long!'

Phil pretends to laugh again.

Then, he hastily wishes Alan well for the weekend, and practically skips down the stairs and out the door, relieved to be away from him, and from the work week in general.

Outside, it scorches. A flurry of party-planning texts in the house group chat, excitement stacking on top of itself. Debs decides against the Theresa May dress: she's going to Oxfam to find something else and is leaving in fifteen minutes if anyone wants to join.

Phil rolls up his sleeves, pops open his shirt buttons, and untangles his earphones. He jams them into his ears and opens Spotify, keen for something to soundtrack his walk to the station. Something ecstatic, cathartic, romantic, blissful. Something to encapsulate his life at this precise moment in time. At this precise moment in time, he is a young person in the city, finished work for the weekend, and on his way to have sex with a man he adores. What phenomenal luck! What greater pleasure! What deeper joy can this life provide?

Annoyingly, his phone won't connect to 4G, so his euphoric post-work strut down the street is largely soiled by having to open and close Spotify multiple times in the hope that when he next presses 'play' the music will stream forth into his ears, which it doesn't.

Well, never mind: there are a dozen things to occupy his thoughts. Who will he see at the party? What will he wear? Maggie recently asked him to describe his personal style in two words. *Action Man*, he said. *Wait, no: Bruce Springsteen.* Masculinity feels like dress-up: he grows out his facial hair and feels like a sort of drag king. Last time he went to Keith's allotment, Jacinta laughed, exclaiming: *You look like a mountaineer!* and Phil practically shuddered in pleasure. *Mountaineer*, he thought. *That's exactly what I'm going for.*

Without music, he'll listen to the city instead. He listens to the road rage of the drivers who impotently beep and beep again, the clatter of drills on the building sites, and in the pause between drilling, the blissful blast of a Top 40 banger that belts from a car window.

A piece of grit flies into his eye; the sweat in his armpit prickles; his work clothes really are too hot for this weather. The air is so thick that his breathing feels strained, and he's just reached the station when he notices a message from Keith. *Hello gorgeous. I'm sorry to do this but something has come up and I'm gonna need to postpone until a little later in the evening. Not sure what time yet but I'll text when I'm free. Hope you've had an ok day xx*

Phil sighs audibly and mumbles, 'For fuck's sake.'

It's no big surprise.

Phil's relationship to Keith could typically be described like this: housemate whose dick he occasionally sucks when they both happen to be drunk, horny, and at the same location. Until recently, these conditions arose only occasionally, and they agreed it was better that way; Phil and Keith are good friends and had no wish to spoil their friendship by introducing troublesome obligations to each other. But for the past month or so – really since the heatwave began – they have spent most nights together. They have said things like 'You make my life better' and 'I'm obsessed with you' and they often bail on their friends to stay in bed and show each other clips of their favourite Stevie Nicks performances on YouTube.

But still, Keith is in an open relationship with Louis, a proper boyfriend, so wouldn't be available even if Phil did want to get serious, which, as it happens, he doesn't. Phil insists that at twenty-eight, he's smack in the middle of the best time in his life and has no desire to limit its horizons by getting too attached. All he wants is to roll onto his front, let Keith climb on top, and gnaw lightly on his tightly clenched fist until pain turns pleasurable. Is that too much to ask? he wonders as he descends the station escalator. Is that not a fair thing to want?

Admittedly, yes, Phil has only been fucked by Keith once – the rest of their encounters made up of drunken fumbles and oral sex – and before that, he hadn't been fucked in years, not since one particularly bad night in Burgess Park. His body and mind are usually shy. They shut down on the precipice of deep and vivid feeling. When faced with something hot, unknown, frightening, desirable, his body and mind try to reject it, no matter how much it would improve his life and love and happiness to have it. All of which is to say: Phil has a problematic relationship to bottoming. When anyone has tried to fuck him in the past nine years, his body has entered a state of alert, in pain before even being touched. After sex, he becomes sad and ashamed, wanting to wipe the cum from his chest hair straight away, fish around the side of the mattress for his pants, and sleep in his own bed by himself. His body acts as if it were automated, inanimate, his relationship to his own sex life that of an external narrator. But with Keith, things are different. Keith has yanked Phil's consciousness out of his mind and placed it back in his shuddering body. Keith, in short, makes Phil feel real.

He shoves himself onto a rush hour train to make his way back east.

The Central Line at peak times is like an oven, especially in summer; he's crammed shoulder to shoulder with fellow commuters, each person gasping for their fair share of air.

Everyone is pretending they're not really here. In front of Phil, a woman googles *why is the central line so hot* and repeatedly refreshes the page even though there's no WiFi. People flap dead air around with battered *Evening Standards*.

There's a man opposite Phil. Office worker, tight suit, salty droplets dribbling towards his mouth. He's got a beard. His neck strains against his shirt collar.

He's chewing on gum and his chin is cocked.

He glances at Phil, and Phil glances back.

They both look away.

Phil thinks of the classic gay literature in which men are always shagging strangers they meet on the Tube. He wonders if anyone still does this, and if so, would he like to do it?

Furtively, he looks back at the man.

The man is already looking.

They hold eye contact for more than a second.

In his head, in the cubicle of a Victorian public toilet, Phil sucks the man's cock, his nostrils clogged with the pong of centuries-old piss and half-dissolved urinal cubes.

The train stops at Liverpool Street. The commuters scramble into new shapes to allow other passengers onto the platform. The man grazes Phil's hand as he disembarks.

Then, he looks back. He grins. He nods his head as if to say *come on*.

Phil freezes. He instinctively smiles.

There are seconds until the doors slam shut.

He disembarks.

He's propelled through the station by the tsunami of power-walking City workers. The man moves a few paces ahead, but it's crowded, and Phil loses sight of him.

He bolts up the escalator, two steps at a time, and spots him on the other side of the concourse, making a beeline for the men's toilets and disappearing through the door.

Phil stops.

He thinks about Keith. What would he do? He'd push through the toilet door and see what happens.

He thinks, too, of Burgess Park – panic, pain, boredom – and his heart beats hard.

His ears get hot.

He wants to follow the man. He wants for this to be a sort of healing. Fifty years from now, he wants to look back on his summers in London and think that he rinsed them for all they were worth.

He walks up to the toilet door and takes some deep breaths. He thinks of the film he saw at seventeen in which a man is brutally murdered while cruising on Clapham Common.

He almost turns back.

He almost sprints towards the exit, but instead, he pushes through his fear, and he swings through the door, and he stands at the edge of the men's toilets – fluorescent lights, smell of piss – to find the man from the train is nowhere to be seen, but another man is here, a frozen face, a man who had been standing at the door of a cubicle and was about to go in.

Phil freezes at the sight of him.

It's Ed Seymour.

Ed Seymour, who Phil used to sit beside in class, best friend of Phil's brother, son of his mother's neighbour, boy-friend of Maggie, the love of her life, who claps Phil on the back whenever they meet, calling him 'mate' 'man' or even 'Big Phil' as if Phil were a prepubescent nephew in need of positive male role models, and Ed, a benign uncle, probably overcompensating, probably trying to blot out the things that he and Phil did together – at fourteen, at seventeen – things they don't speak of aloud, not to each other, not to Maggie.

'Oh fuck,' says Ed. 'Hi.'

They look each other right in the eye.

The cubicle door inches open. The man from the train pokes his head out and looks from Ed to Phil and back. Phil almost laughs: he and Ed had been pursuing the same man.

Ed ignores him.

'Hey, Big Phil,' he says. 'Great to see you, buddy. What a place to run into you! What are you doing here? I mean, it's a toilet, so obviously you're here to use the toilet.'

The man from the train, recognising a lost chance, bolts through the door and leaves.

A millisecond passes. Phil thinks about Maggie.

'I've just finished work,' he says. 'On the way home.'

'Nice,' Ed says. 'The weekend, eh? The big weekend. A summer scorcher.'

'I'm seeing Maggie tomorrow.'

'Maggie?'

'She says she's got big news.'

'Big news? Yeah. Big news.'

There's a pause.

'Well,' says Phil eventually, sucking his lips and searching for something to say to make this feel normal, 'we're having a party at our place tomorrow. Maybe see you there?'

Ed looks dazed. 'Maybe,' he says.

'Great,' says Phil. He turns and walks out the door before Ed has time to answer.

On the street, the sun is blocked by the high-rise buildings.

Phil stands on the pavement to try to calm down. He feels overheated and manic, his blood pumping from following the man, and seeing Ed, and from thinking of Burgess Park.

What was Ed doing in there? Does Maggie know he picks up guys in train station toilets? Is this part of some new arrangement between them? Surely not. Couldn't be.

He'll have to tell her about it.

Won't he?

Surely that's the right thing to do.

Maggie is Phil's best friend – of course he'll tell her about it.

He breathes heavily. He checks his phone several times. He can feel a question brewing in his mind, a painful question, a question he is embarrassed to ask, but if he really had to phrase that question with words, the words might be: if Ed has wanted to fuck men all along, why didn't he want to fuck Phil back when he had all those chances?

And if Phil tells Maggie, does he have to tell her what happened years ago too?

He peers down the street, cooler now that he's outside and in the shade, and decides to walk home from here, thinking, ambivalently, of the first time Ed Seymour sent him a text.

He looks to his phone then and notices a message from his brother's fiancée, Holly.

He grits his teeth. This only ever means one thing.

Callum's gone AWOL, she says. *You haven't heard from him, have you?*

4

HOLLY, IN HER ROOM, WAITING FOR CALLUM TO TEXT back. A familiar scene. If her life could be summed up in a single tableau, this would be it. Phone clutched, gin half-drunk, cig half-smoked. She refreshes Instagram: a picture of the marine biologist who looks like Princess Diana, then a picture of Princess Diana herself. Diana died when Holly was six. It was the first time she was old enough to be aware of events in the world beyond home and school. Too young to really understand, the death of Diana and every other news story she learned around that time seemed to merge. Princess Diana and Mother Teresa had seemed like the same person, their deaths the one death, their stories a component part of the war in Kosovo, war in Northern Ireland, Tony Blair becoming prime minister, and Geri leaving the Spice Girls. It all suggested that adult life was perilous and brutal and to be approached with much caution.

Callum's mother might be dying.

Holly panics when she thinks of it. She wants to hurry to him, and through sheer force of will make everything better.

Here! she could say, gesturing towards his favourite snack. *It's a cheese and marmite toasty with the cheese slightly burned around the edges!* Or *Look!* she could cry: *I'll drive us to Cornwall and bring a bag of magic mushrooms.*

She hasn't seen or heard from him since yesterday, and she normally hears from him every two to three minutes. He can't stop drinking, which is nothing new, only now, rather than see his drinking as dangerous and problematic, his friends see it as a necessary way of processing grief. But soon, Holly will marry Callum. She will have his children, all being well. She, too, enjoys a drink. But even Holly can see that things have gone too far.

It's her hen party tomorrow. She wants to enjoy it without worrying that her fiancé has landed himself in an alcohol-induced coma. Should she text Ed? Phil? Should she text Callum's mother? She doesn't want to disturb a dying woman on her Friday evening; she's already caused enough grief. Last weekend, at dinner with Callum and his parents, Rosaleen turned to Holly and said: 'You've probably heard my news from Callum,' and Holly turned and replied: 'At least you've an excuse to miss the hen!' Oh God. What a stupid thing to have said. She had meant it in a funny way; the fact that Rosaleen hadn't wanted to go had been an in-joke between them anyway, but that was the thing with words: you only knew they were the wrong ones once you'd already said them, and by that time it was too late.

Above all, Holly wants to be liked. At school, she was always telling other girls how pretty they were, how she wished she had their hair. She wanted love enormously, so much so that she felt demeaned by it. Certainly, she thought it was old-fashioned to need love as much as she did, but the world was hard. She was afraid all the time, and she only sometimes felt beautiful, and yes, to enjoy her own company would be a fine thing, but getting a boyfriend seemed easier, and what was so wrong with the path of least resistance? Life was short: she had things to do. She walked up to Callum one night on the grassy lane between her estate and his, and said: 'Will you go for a walk with me?' 'Yes,' he said, and so they did.

She texts Rosaleen now: *we'll miss you tomorrow.*

She waits, bites her nails, sends a follow-up: *you haven't seen Callum, have you?*

. . .

THERE'S A PROGRAMME ABOUT A COUPLE WHO GIVE UP everything to live off the land. Rosaleen watches with her husband, Steve. The couple are ready to say goodbye to the supermarket, the city, their jobs and commute. They will sew their own soft furnishings, tend to their own tomatoes, and milk their own goat. 'Oh it's not for me,' says Rosaleen to Steve.

'I wouldn't mind it,' he replies.

'You wouldn't know the first thing about living off the land.'

'Could learn.'

'We're too old.'

'I suppose.'

It's 9 p.m. Rosaleen and Steve have sat on the couch for the past two hours, Rosaleen nursing a wine, Steve drinking a beer. She stands up every now and then to check if Joan Seymour is still out there, which she is, and Rosaleen occasionally wonders if she should invite her in but can't figure out how. Joan, would you like to come in? or Joan, we're doing nothing. Will you join? Or Joan, this is our house – you're welcome in it. Time and again, she almost figures out the correct phrasing, but when mumbled aloud, it sounds ridiculous.

She looks at Steve, his eyes fixed on the screen.

'That's mad,' she continues to press, laughing. 'Why would anyone choose a life of hardship? I'm at the stage of my life where I want things to be easier, not harder.'

Steve nods and hums as if to concede that she's right, or at least that he doesn't want to talk any more. She sinks back into the cream leather couch, which wasn't chosen because it looks good, but because it supports her back, it reclines, it's got a footrest. She's at a stage of life where she wants comfort. She wants to explain this to Steve, to remind him that she didn't always have it so easy, and growing up she slept in the same room as her six sisters, and you'd feel the mice brushing up against your feet at night, and mice shocking you awake never ceases to be an unpleasant sensation. It's not that she decided to have a more comfortable life than her parents; it was the times themselves that had changed, and of course she moved from Ireland to England, as so many people did then. She couldn't have afforded to stay. She means that economically (she had no job or qualifications) but she couldn't have afford-ed it in the spiritual sense either, meaning that her soul, her life force, had been hammered flat with a mallet while growing up in Dublin, and she wouldn't have survived another year's hammering. That meant leaving her mother, who hated her for leaving, and Pauline – her loose morals – who died shortly after without Rosaleen getting to say goodbye.

Her friends and sisters used to mock her when she visited. They'd swish around, curtsy, put on a posh English accent whenever she spoke. She used to equivocate, tell them it rains even more over there, say it's too grey and too busy, Brits have no sense of humour, and Irish dairy products are truly world class (as if she'd have chosen a measly bit of Irish butter over free NHS GP visits). She'd say there's nothing like a pint of Guinness in Grogan's and she misses her mother's cooking, making herself two-dimensional, a caricature of an Irish emigrant, a character from a Barry's Tea advert, and she never told anyone in Ireland that London was exciting. She never told them that she liked the crowds, the way they surged around and made so many things seem possible. Even if nothing ever actually happened, it never stopped feeling likely, inevitable, that your life was about to change, if you turned a street corner, struck up a conversation, got off the Tube a few stops early to see what the buildings looked like in Willesden Green or Clapham Common.

She looked at London then as if she were a video camera and the footage would be broadcast directly to a television in Pauline's front room. Everything she ever did, felt, or said, every place she ever went, she did with a view to telling Pauline about it one day.

She remembers feeling at the time that England could belong to her just as much as it belonged to anyone. She remembers feeling that the word *England* could be big, up for grabs, that no one got to own it. It could fit more inside of it than simply the white, the rich, the royalists. There were other Englands – at Notting Hill Carnival, Ridley Road Market, the Irish pubs in Stoke Newington and Willesden and Tottenham

– and they had just as much of a right to call themselves *England* as any other place did.

Her accent soon changed. There were Ts left out, the long, broad vowels. She'd raise her voice at the end of a sentence, as if asking a question rather than making a statement.

Then, after a few years in London, she met Steve, and off they went to Basildon.

She remembers: there's ice cream.

'There's ice cream,' she says.

Steve, needing no further instruction, stands up and goes to the kitchen.

When he was young, Steve used to think he'd live alone in the wilderness. Imagine that. He used to think he'd walk into a forest, and no one would hear from him again. She feels guilty for saying they were too old to live off the land. There it is again: her guilt.

What had been loose about Pauline's morals anyway? She wore red lipstick, she was good at doing cartwheels. Both mortal sins; red lipstick because it smacked of sex, cart-wheels because your skirt might go up around your head and the other girls might see a flash of your knickers. Then, it wouldn't be just you who was going to hell: it would be the onlookers too. Knickers themselves were sinful in a general sense: to say the word *knickers*, to think the thought *knick-ers*, certainly to look on the knickers of another. Even to wear knickers was not entirely unproblematic: it was only OK as long you didn't *acknowledge* your own knickers, didn't look at your own knickers, acted as if the knickers had come to be on your body through divine intervention, completely outside of your knowledge and control, although of course, to *refrain* from wearing knickers was even worse, the gravest sin of all.

Rosaleen shudders at her years in Dublin.

Her mother's ten children, the three who died in infancy.

Steve returns with two bowls of chocolate ice cream.

'What time are you meeting Phil tomorrow?' he says.

'Two p.m. It was meant to be midday, but now it's two p.m.'

'Where?'

'At his house.'

'Where's that?'

'Why don't you text him yourself and find out?'

'Do you not already know?'

'Of course I know. But you never make any effort with him. Or with Callum.'

'They don't want to hear from me. They've other things to be doing.'

'I want you to stay in touch with them. I won't be around forever.'

He's quiet for a moment. He scratches his head and spoons some ice cream into his mouth. He picks up the remote, then puts it down. Then he mumbles, 'Don't say that.'

Rosaleen looks at Steve.

He looks at the TV.

He's annoyed, she thinks, although there are no signs of it. He thinks he keeps his feelings to himself, but he doesn't really; he just expresses them indirectly, so that everyone has to jump through hoops to interpret whatever he means in his one-word answers, his silent staring at the TV, his getting up from the dinner table without saying a word to anybody.

'I love you,' he says, putting his hand on Rosaleen's hand, on the crevasse between the cushions of the cream leather couch.

'I love you too,' she says, quietly, in a sing-song voice, like she's speaking in the tune of a nursery rhyme you'd sing to a child to put them to sleep.

Then, her phone pings with a text.

She glances at it, then says to Steve, 'It's Holly.'

'What's she saying?'

She looks at him, sighs a familiar sigh.

'It's Callum,' she says. 'Missing again.'

. . .

ED SEYMOUR CAN'T STOP CHECKING HIS PHONE. HE grabs it after emerging from the shower without drying his hands. He checks it again in the hallway, and again when he gets to his bedroom. Still no messages. He has cycled home, peeled off his clothes, and tried to scrub the day's crusted sweat from his skin, almost as if to scrub off the encounter with Phil.

Now, he stands naked in front of his bedroom mirror.

Phone in hand, he looks at his body.

He used to have a high metabolism. He would boast about all the food he could eat as if it were a measure of manhood to stumble into takeaways each Friday night to order meal deals called things like 'The Hungry Man' or 'The Heart Attack' and still remain skinny as a stick insect. Looking at the swell of his belly now, he accepts that those days are behind him.

His chest, he shaves. His pubes, he trims. His cock varies wildly in size; tiny when soft, thick when hard, but he has a distant relationship with it either way. His relationship with his entire body is distant. He doesn't exactly hate it, but he doesn't relate to it either. He looks in the mirror and can't be sure that this body is his. There's nothing wrong with it; there are even parts of it he can admire. It just seems as if it belongs to somebody else.

He unlocks his phone to take a photo. He tries to get hard and zooms in for a close-up, but refracted through the screen of his phone, he recognises his body even less.

He remembers seeing his dad's body as a child. Even then, it was worn and creaky from manual labour. His dad carried his body from place to place as if carrying a rubbish bag on the verge of exploding on the pavement, dripping onto his slippers, and at fifty years old, lungs crowded with tumours, the bag finally burst a metre from the bin and now look: eggshells, vegetable peel, plastic wrapping, and if Ed doesn't clean it up, then who will?

His dad, unlike Ed's extroverted mother, was shy, but despite his shyness, he was nearly always naked on weekend mornings. Ed remembers the abject spectacle of an adult penis, like a malignant skin growth, like an overgrown and hairy cold sore, and all that terrible scraggly armpit hair, longer than the hair on Ed's head. Ed looks at his own body in the mirror and is repulsed in the same way he was repulsed by his dad's body as a child.

He has pushed so many memories to the back of his mind. Seventeen, eighteen, he hadn't yet started dating Maggie and he'd get the train to London to hang around in the station toilets. Before today, it had been more than ten years. He's shocked, in some ways. Maggie's pregnancy should have been even more reason not to do it, but somehow it was the impetus. He had seen a future hurtling towards him, and he had wanted to dive out of its way.

His phone pings with a message. He flinches.

He expects a text from Maggie.

He pictures something like: *Phil told me what happened. It's over.*

He wheezes, coughs, looks at the screen.

It's from his mum. She wants him to call. He tries to inhale.

He throws on a polo shirt and jeans, makes his way to the kitchen. He takes another breath and calls, hoping she won't answer. He puts it on speaker and starts cooking.

'Sorry,' Joan answers eventually. 'I'm spending time with the magpie.'

'Oh yeah?' he calls, digging around for a chopping board. 'What you doing that for?'

'They have thirty-six colours on their wings.'

'How do you know that?'

'I counted.'

'Wow. That must have taken ages.'

While the chat turns to Maggie's pregnancy, Ed cuts potatoes into chips. He chops carrots, turnips, beetroot, tosses them in olive oil, rosemary, sea salt, and chucks them in the oven. He lights candles; he sets the table; he peels the blood-soaked steaks from their plastic sheets and slaps them on top of a sizzling pan. He shoves a bottle of alcohol-free prosecco in the freezer. He puts handfuls of fancy crisps into dishes and opens a tub of hummus so that the crisps and hummus basically function as a sort of starter and/or savoury dessert.

Joan says, 'Have you found a school for the wee one yet?'

'No, Mum. The baby's not been born.'

'You need to be thinking about these things. You and this baby are all I've got now.'

'I know, Mum.'

'You need to look out for each other. I don't want you to be like your dad.'

'I'm not like Dad.'

'You're like him in more ways than you think.'

'Please stop telling me that.'

'Am I annoying you?'

'It's fine, hang on—'

She hangs up. She always does. Since Maggie got pregnant, his mother has messaged all day, every day, and her messages can be loosely grouped into two categories. The first category is to do with Ed's soon-to-be born baby and recently deceased dad – only ever mentioned in relation to each other – and the second category is random facts about magpies. There are thirty-six colours on their wings. In Australia, they are large and deadly and sometimes kill children. In England, they're friendly, and Joan likes to talk to them, which is more of an anecdote than a fact, but you get the picture. These are her three areas of interest: dead dad, unborn baby, friendly conversations with magpies. Ed googles things like *psychotic break* and *delusional fantasies* and *dementia* but the information is too terrifying to consider.

It's a few minutes to 10 p.m. He takes the pan from the heat, turns off the oven; the plates clatter as he digs them from the cupboard. The whole time, he thinks about Maggie and prepares his response, just in case Phil tells her what happened today. It's not easy. The voices in his body are very loud. There's a mob in his mind, and another mob just below his ribcage. One demands that he cheats and steals to get out of this situation. The other wants revenge, not on Phil, but on Ed, who is responsible for ruining his own life. Someone needs to hurt him for what he's done to himself: if no one else will do it, then he should hurt himself.

He puts on music. He starts to sing along. Initially, he keeps time with the song, but too anxious to focus, he veers wildly off into countless other melodies. Frank Sinatra melts into Madonna and Madonna takes a sharp left turn into Pavarotti, who self-combusts into a tuneless chorus of *la la la la la* more discordant than the most experimental noise shows that Maggie ever dragged him to. It's about volume, rather than tune. Every time Ed thinks of himself in Liverpool Street station earlier today, he finds a new song and sings even louder.

Over the din, he hears his phone beep with two texts at once; his chest tightens – is this the last time Maggie will ever text him? – and he lunges across the room to grab it, dropping a plate in the process; it shatters while he glimpses the lit-up screen: one message from Rosaleen, one from Holly. *Jesus*, he thinks. This can only mean one thing.

Have you seen Callum? they both say.

He immediately tries to call: it goes to voicemail.

He tries again, and again the voicemail robot answers, just like it did the last time Callum disappeared and they were about to report him as a missing person, when he turned up, walked into his flat as if nothing had happened. Callum downplayed it but Ed knew his friend got depressed. He took risks. A voice in his head said *You don't really have to live, do you? You could just decide to not live.*

There's a knock on the door. Not even a knock, but rather, a *pounding*.

Ed hurries to answer it. He opens it to see a bleary-eyed Callum, drunk, in a half-tucked shirt stained with brown patches, and chewing on a stale baguette.

Ed can't suppress a groan.

'Mate, what are you doing here?'

'Been at a party, haven't I?'

'Your mum's been texting me. So has Holly.'

'My mum? Why's she texting you?'

'She's worried. She doesn't know where you are.'

'I only spoke to her yesterday.'

'Well, you could do with giving her a call now.'

'My phone's dead. Can I use your charger?'

Ed looks at his watch.

'It's date night, Cal. Maggie's going to be back in a second. I'm cooking.'

Callum stands there, defiant, as if to say, 'What more do you want from me?'

Ed can't resist. He invites him in.

Callum makes his way into the living room and sits down on the couch next to the huge pile of junk in the middle of the floor. 'It's a tip in here,' he says.

'We're moving in a few days.'

'Smells a bit mouldy.'

'We've got a problem with damp.'

Ed goes to the kitchen to clean up the smashed plate and make Callum a cup of tea while Callum plugs in his phone to charge. Back in the living room, he hands Callum the tea.

'Any plans for the evening?' he says.

Callum squeezes his nose and rubs his twitching legs.

'Not much. Getting some rest. Big business night tomorrow. Parties all over. There's a rave at my little brother's place. Another in Elephant. Holly's got her hen party in the daytime. She's staying at her mum's tonight, and I'm meeting my dad tomorrow afternoon.'

Ed feels an anxious stab at the mention of Phil. He moves the conversation away.

'Your dad?' he says. 'What you seeing him for?'

'Watching the football.'

'I didn't think you got on.'

'He's having a rough time. I want to be there for him.'

'Oh, mate. I'm sorry. I hope he's alright.'

'He's fine.'

Ed nods and looks at his watch again and says, 'Look, Callum, Maggie is going to be back any minute, and as I said, it's date night, and I'd invite you to join, only there's not really enough food, and I want to be able to celebrate her last day at work with her, and—'

'Relax, I'm not going to spoil your night.'

Ed hears his phone ping with a text. He stands up with a jolt, panicked that Maggie might nearly be home. He goes to the kitchen to find it, while Callum calls out, a casual ambivalence in his voice, 'There's actually something I wanted to talk to you about.'

'Oh yeah?'

Ed unlocks his phone.

'It's my mum. She's not well.'

'Not well?'

There's a message from Maggie; she says she loves him, she's staying over at Ali's, and she'll be back in the morning. Ed groans, feeling a small flare of disappointment as he looks from his phone towards the feast he's prepared, half-served and getting cold.

'She's got cancer. They don't know how long she's got left.'

He snaps back to his senses. He returns to the living room.

'Oh my God. Mate. I'm sorry.'

He sits down on the couch so he's within reach of Callum. He puts his hand on his back, pats once, twice, three times.

'It's alright,' says Callum. 'Not your fault, is it?'

'No. It's tough though, mate. It's really tough.'

'Yeah.'

'I'm here for you. Anything you need. I'm always on the other end of a phone call.'

Ed says this, knowing it's useless. Callum will never ask him for anything. When Ed's dad was dying, he had no shortage of people who said to let them know if he needed anything, but at that time, he had no idea what he needed, let alone how to ask for it.

He offers a hug, and Callum accepts. It's one of those man hugs. It begins as a handshake, and then using the handshake as a sort of launch pad, they yank themselves towards each other. They pat their friend's back three times, with real force, more of a wallop than a pat, and never clutch or caress. It's as if to touch the back of another man without beating it at the same time would be a depth of intimacy that neither can stomach.

'I better go,' says Callum eventually. 'Don't want to alarm Maggie by my presence.'

'It's fine. She's not coming any more.'

'After you've gone to all this effort?'

'She's at karaoke with Ali.'

'Jesus. She must be really trying to avoid something.'

'Fuck off, mate,' says Ed affectionately.

He excuses himself to go to the toilet.

He locks the door, looks in the mirror, splashes his face with water. He texts Maggie, says that he loves her. He pauses, and texts again: *did you know that Phil's mum has cancer?*

. . .

MAGGIE AND ALI STAND SIDE BY SIDE ON STAGE. THEY position themselves at the mic, stare out at the overcrowded pub, while Ali requests 'Summertime Sadness' by Lana Del Rey. The man in the booth presses play on the song's dance remix; Ali shouts, 'No, the original!' and looks immediately embarrassed (Ali believes that both karaoke and Lana are phenomena to be enjoyed through a strictly ironic lens and is probably afraid that she has taken things too seriously by favouring one version of the song over the other). In the moment of Ali's embarrassment – her smile bashful – Maggie swells with love for her friend and wonders why she loves people best when they are at their most vulnerable.

In any case, it's too late to switch to the original: the song has begun. They sing in unison, dancing around, directing the chorus at each other. Maggie is impressed by her ability to do all of this without alcohol, although admittedly, she does feel drunk on the knowledge that next week, she'll leave this city for good, and it no longer matters what people here think of her. It's true, too, that Maggie used to go to nightclubs sober nearly every week, because – as she said at the time – she wanted to really *feel* the music. Looking back now, she had no interest in 'feeling' anything; rather, she was young and insecure and grasping frantically for the makings of a personality (Maggie: a woman with an appreciation of techno).

The second chorus has just ended, and they're singing the bridge. There's a lyric which goes like 'Think I'll miss you forever, like the stars miss the sun in the morning sky' and Maggie and Ali look each other in the eye while trying to croon. The words catch in Maggie's throat; she almost cries. She *will* miss Ali forever, just as she'll miss London, and all of this. Ali, her lovely friend, who is loyal and kind and who everyone is afraid of, not because she's scary, but because she's blunt and has a healthy disregard for what people think of her. Maggie wants to reach out and hold her. She wants to be recklessly affectionate, to grasp her hand and say, 'I love you,' but is worried that this would change things. If Maggie held Ali now, they would cease to be women who are doing an ironic impersonation of a karaoke performance. Rather, they would metamorphose into women who are *actually doing a karaoke performance*, and this would pose all sorts of challenging questions for how they perceive themselves, and each other, and Lana, too.

On Lana: she is a bone of contention. Maggie adores her, and is embarrassed about it, and to justify her adoration, contextualises it within a tiring academic framework. Maggie knows that an intellectual engagement with Lana's music can only go so far in explaining its magic, and eventually one has to resort to the realm of emotion, which is to risk being seen as earnest and sentimental, but suffice to say, sometimes she looks at Ed – his big arms, his sleepy morning face – and casts him in the role of a classic Lana anti-hero. She pictures him as tough and troubled – which is somewhat true – and fantasises about how her gentle charms could coax him out of his macho truculence. Ali would argue that this is problematic, maybe self-destructive, certainly anti-feminist, but Maggie would retort that the tenets of feminism are shifting, and it is now seen as anti-feminist to exclude formerly anti-feminist practices from your conception of feminism. So basically, she would say, it's fine, and besides, it's possible to support a political cause without your every emotional, sexual and psychological drive aligning precisely with the principles of that cause. Perhaps it's more than possible; perhaps it's typical – universal! – and although it leads one to being accused of the same moral failings that Lana is accused of – chiefly of not acting in accordance with an *authentic self* – Maggie and Ali both know that political infallibility is an impossible goal to begin with.

Ali is known for her cynicism. She's been Maggie's friend for years, and still maintains the charade of pretending not to know who Kim Kardashian is. She's prone to mining every situation for analysis, so much so that she can't go to Sainsbury's to buy, for example, hummus, bananas, washing-up liquid, without asking: what broader cultural forces are at play here? How can I describe them – all in lower case – with irony and insight to my 2,000 and climbing Twitter followers? Admittedly, Maggie finds this difficult, although she understands critical distance is a pragmatic position for any Londoner to take. Norms of what's cool, beautiful, useful or revolutionary shift from day to day, from group to group, from borough to borough, and an interesting cultural trend in Hackney might be seen as naff and embarrassing in Lewisham. Cynicism is a safety valve: if you accidentally place too many eggs in an unfashionable basket, you need to be able to pretend that the relationship between eggs and basket is, and always has been, part of an ironic metanarrative.

Besides all this, Ali is a great friend. They met at art school. Maggie was nineteen and new to London. They used to sleep in the same bed after parties, and get up the next day so Ali could drive them to McDonald's where they'd sit in her car eating boxes of chicken nuggets. Ali was amazing to Maggie. She was articulate, political, knowledgeable. She knew how to intervene when police harassed young men on the street and went to parties wearing sheer bodysuits and sunglasses. Best of all, she's a source of gossip. The first thing she said to Maggie when they met earlier this evening was *Babe, listen, I have something important to tell you.* She'd heard through the lesbian grapevine that the marine biologist, Diana, Princess of Whales, has been having an affair with a much-loved celebrity chef, who had previously been thought of as the epitome of conservative English heterosexuality.

She makes Maggie feel like an important person. Before Ali, nearly all of Maggie's best friends had been terminally unreliable gay men. First Phil, then Kyle, then the group of boys who adopted her when she first moved to London, who cackled at everything she said, unable to resist her vulgar jokes and fluent command of pop culture trivia. She began to style herself as a sort of Pat Butcher meets Paris Hilton figure, a fully fledged gay icon. Like Lana before her, she had fabricated a fabulous persona after moving to a big city, and she too had done so, at least partially, for the gratification of overly excitable gays in their twenties.

It was hard-won, this public persona. She certainly didn't feel so confident at the start.

She remembers her first critical theory tutorial at art school. She was in the throes of a bad cold, but unsure of the etiquette of blowing her nose. She let the snot harden to a scabby crust around the rim of her nostril that she would later painfully prise from her skin. Everyone was hungover. Students rubbed their eyes beneath fluorescent lights and picked old bits of Sellotape off the desks. There were no windows, and it was hot: the bone-dry heat of old electric radiators. Every bad smell to have ever occurred in that room had lingered stagnant in the air. Coffee breath, fag breath, corn beef, tuna salad, curdled milk spilled on the scratchy green carpet, and farts. She could smell it through her stuffy nose. The topic was historical materialism. The tutor read from various scholars – Marxist, feminist, postcolonial – and from Marx himself. He gave his own analysis, and then threw questions out to the class. Two students spoke at length, using superfluous rhetorical flourishes in the hope of winning the tutor's approval. Like the tutor, they spoke with North London accents, tinged by South London twangs. Their names were Ireland and Oslo – people with this accent were often named after European cities or former British colonies – and Maggie, who never spoke in class, envied them. She tried to gather her thoughts, plucking quotes from memory, putting one word after another, but class finished before her sentence had time to leave her mouth.

She's leaving London next week, and still, it's as if the words are stuck in her throat.

Now, the song ends. Maggie bursts with love. She thinks; fuck it, and scoops Ali into a hug while they begin to cry. They tumble outside and lean against the beer garden wall.

'I can't believe I'm moving back to Basildon,' she says, expressing out loud for the first time what she'd been dwelling on for weeks: that she's a city girl. Ambivalent about the countryside and hostile towards the suburbs. *It feels so good to get out of London* – that's a thing that people say. They go on Sunday strolls on the South Downs: on the train back sink into their seats and say *Ahhhhhhh. Restored.* Maggie can't relate. Ed takes her on drives to green fields beyond the A12. They watch birds; they search for snakes. She puts on a smile and hates it. She's anxious in the countryside. She's never sure what she's meant to be looking at. Yes, it's true that there are gurgling streams and baby sheep and cows of different colours. It's true that the clouds roll across the sky in a peaceful fashion and certain clouds resemble nation states or common household objects. Maggie understands these things to be beautiful in an abstract sense but is left untouched. She watches Ed watch the countryside; she listens to him describe the plumage of lesser-known English birds. She smiles, says *wow*.

When she was a teenager, she wanted nothing more than to move to New York, specifically New York in the seventies, which was ridiculous, having only been born in 1991.

The problem, probably, had been Patti Smith.

Patti, with her poetry, her snarl, her relationship with Robert Mapplethorpe, who was gay, so it wasn't properly sexual, but it wasn't just a friendship either.

Patti, who sang the words *Jesus died for somebody's sins but not mine* and when Maggie heard these words for the first time, twelve years old and in the throes of an early adolescent devotion to God, her heart thumped so hard that she needed to take a walk around the estate and inhale gulps of cool summer air and her cheeks felt hot but they also felt cold.

The problem had been that she longed to go to a place she couldn't go. Even if she could have afforded to go to New York, it wouldn't have been the New York of Patti Smith or Kathy Acker; it wouldn't even have been the New York of Ross and Rachel. Those New Yorks didn't exist any more, if they had ever existed at all. Instead, what Maggie had was London.

Ali gulps from a fresh pint.

'I know, babe. I know it's hard, and you don't feel like you're finished with London, but look at it this way: leaving now is like leaving an afterparty at a sensible hour. The party is still fun, everyone's having a great time, sharing their drugs, dancing and what not, but soon, the sun will rise, and everyone will be zombified, and we'll all be licking the corners of our little bags of K, even though those bags are completely and utterly empty and we've not been properly high for hours and hours at this stage. Meanwhile, you, clever girl, will be tucked up in bed, watching a cute little David Attenborough doc with Ed.'

Maggie laughs.

'That's a good allegory,' she says.

'And I'm jealous of you, babe. I wouldn't mind getting out of London.'

'Don't you love it here?'

'I just feel like I'm always waiting for something to happen, like one of these eight million lives is going to collide with mine and knock me off course towards something else.

But they never do! Nothing ever happens. People keep their heads down. They mind their own business. People in London are too tired to be colliding with each other all the time.'

'We're all too busy trying to pay rent.'

'Well, yes, exactly. We're all too busy trying to survive. I feel like living in London is like being on the constant verge of an orgasm but never being able to cum. Do you know what I mean? It's not that you're not turned on. It's not that you aren't having a lovely time. But something deep down inside your body won't allow for it no matter how hard you try. And you, babe, are doing the right thing. You're not waiting for the city to transform you any more. You're getting out while you can. You're transforming yourself.'

Maggie laughs. 'That's one way to say it.'

'Come on,' murmurs Ali while struggling to light her fag and then attempting to smoke it even though it remains unlit. 'You're excited to have the baby as well, right?'

Maggie smiles, takes in a gulp of air.

'I am,' she concedes. 'I've been talking to it, you know.'

'Stop! What you been saying?'

'Just introducing it to the world. Hello, Kingsland High Street. Hello, Tesco. Hello, reduce-to-clear aisle and four pack of mini-cheesecakes for only 50p. I am going to eat you now, and baby will eat you too. Or like, sometimes I take concepts, big and small – the House of Lords, feminism, sticky toffee pudding – and break them down into child-friendly language. You know, like, magazines, falafel, marriage. And I tell it jokes as well.'

Talking to Ali now, Maggie hopes for the baby to be a girl, and for any babies after that to be girls too, or gay boys, or at least vaguely non-binary. She's already responsible for the emotional well-being of Ed and Phil and she doesn't want to be responsible for yet another man. She grew up in a house of women, and it stood her well. She loved her mother, who was tired and funny, cynical from her bygone days as a radical, having seen too many political projects fail, and admired her big sister, from whom she had inherited her cultural sensibilities. Her sister is only two years older, but as a teenager Maggie had regarded her as a sort of surviving Warhol superstar, as if she were Patti Smith herself, as if she had lived through a golden age of art and culture, and Maggie, by comparison, had been born after the gold rush.

To say she grew up in a house full of women is to discount her father, but he was only around until she was twelve, and before that just occasionally, basically invisible except for the times that he was suddenly, horrifyingly *there*, like a repetitive strain injury you don't notice for years until one day you rearrange your weight the wrong way and then: excruciating pain for the rest of your life. She was certainly influenced by him, his dreams of grandeur, how he told his children they could be anything they wanted to be, not meaning that if they worked hard, they could get a job and a mortgage, but meaning they could be president of the world, go to space, become gazillionaires, the richest women on earth.

Like her father before her, Maggie is a schemer, but unlike her father, she is also a grafter. Her first big heist had been getting out of Basildon at seventeen and making it all the way to art school. At art school, her gritty backstory was the envy of her classmates, but it didn't matter in the end: they were the ones with enough family wealth to launch their art careers.

Maggie was the one who had to take a full-time job in a café.

She'd gone through art school with ambition and naivety. Working to pay for materials and rent, it had taken almost a year to realise that most of the other students didn't have to work, even though they lived in spacious central London flats. She hadn't even heard of that kind of wealth before she'd moved to London. It was another world. Before, she had thought that her peers were glamorous by their own merits, and by extension, that she was plain by her own deficiencies. Back then, she'd described her art as *tracing emotional and political cartographies of London*, literally calling herself an *experimental archivist of the city*, which now makes her shiver with dread to think she'd uttered such a phrase in public.

Ali lights another fag. They talk about Theresa May.

They watched her resign on TV a few weeks ago. At Downing Street, her face crunched into a mask of Greek tragedy. Her voice broke as she burst into tears on the words *to serve the country that I love*, the word *love* deep and tremoring. 'People go on about her as if she were a sweet old lady,' says Ali. 'As if she's not got blood on her hands.'

'Yeah, exactly,' agrees Maggie. It's one year since the Windrush scandal broke, two since Grenfell, six since Theresa May, as Home Secretary, sent vans to the London boroughs of Brent, Hounslow, Barking and Dagenham – areas where high numbers of migrants lived – with the words GO HOME printed on the side. 'People act as if this had nothing to do with her. As if she's a sort of saint, just because she's a fraction less heinous than Boris Johnson.'

A man overhears. He leans too close and says sorry too many times. Slurring, he says he couldn't help but overhear.

'I just feel sorry for her,' he says. 'At the end of the day, she's still a person.'

Maggie and Ali ignore him. One of his friends pulls at his sleeve. He keeps talking.

'Imagine, right, that she was your mum.'

He stretches his arms wide as if to say *you can't argue with that.*

Ali rolls her eyes.

'She's not my mum.'

'But imagine.'

'My mum was born in Trinidad.'

'Why you telling me that though?'

Ali laughs in disbelief and mumbles, 'Fuck's sake.'

Maggie can tell that she's weighing up her options, considering whether to explain Windrush, Grenfell, the Hostile Environment. Not worth it, she decides. 'Fuck off,' she says.

The man backs off. He slinks towards his friends.

'At the end of the day, she's still a person,' he says a final time, sinking his pint.

'So were the people she deported,' says Ali, but the man doesn't hear.

Shortly after, they leave the pub and walk arm-in-arm to Ali's flat.

They talk quickly, a little too loud, trying to brush off the encounter with the man.

'Phil's brother texted today,' Ali says. 'Special offer: free K with every three items.'

'Enterprising bastard.'

Ali nods, chews her lip. 'You going to Phil's party tomorrow?'

Maggie stops.

'What party?'

'Do you not know? In the warehouse off Long Lane.'

'He didn't invite me.'

Ali squeezes her arm. 'Everyone's invited. You should go.'

Even as Maggie speaks, she pictures Ed on the dance floor. Always been a good dancer. More expressive with his limbs than he is with his words; he sweats profusely, then takes off his shirt. She wants her arms around the wet skin of his waist, her tongue in his mouth; she wants techno, disco, jungle, house. She can't accept that her last Saturday in London should be spent in front of his laptop, crowded on all sides by their life in boxes.

She takes out her phone to text him, but he's already messaged.

She reads his text three times, then says, 'Oh my God.'

'What's up?' says Ali.

Maggie looks at her.

'Phil's mum has cancer. Had you heard?'

'Fuck. Is he OK?'

'I don't know. He hasn't told me. Ed did.'

She texts Phil now: she says she loves him so much. She says she can't wait to see him tomorrow and asks what he'd like to do. They could go to the Heath, or she could come to his place, or Soho, or Hyde Park, or they could swim in the River Lea (polluted but beautiful when the sun dapples through the trees). They can do anything he wants.

5

THE NEXT DAY, PHIL WAKES AT 7 A.M. KEITH IS SNORING next to him.

The sopping paper-thin bedsheet that covered them during the night was flung to the floor in a fit of 4 a.m. sweats. They lie naked, with damp pillows and glistening foreheads.

He can hear pigeons flirtatiously coo on the roof and a bin truck stretch its muscles outside. It makes a noise like a dinosaur's mating call, feeding on plastic, blackened banana skins, and things that should have gone in the recycling bin. He looks to his phone for information on how the dinosaurs became extinct. He skims a few sentences here and there, without taking them in.

Keith, half-asleep, nuzzles his face against Phil. Phil looks again to his phone, first to the news (a headline on the Tory leadership race), then to Instagram (someone's garden, someone's abs, a page which memorialises people who died during the AIDS crisis; lives cut short, lovers left behind, eyes that went blind, skin eaten by cancer), then back to Keith, who has not quite woken up, and he thinks: as soon as you're awake enough to be kissed, I should kiss you on your chest, your eye, your back, your armpit, your chin, your elbow, your hand, your belly – its trail of wiry black hair – ten kisses in quick succession on your cheek, your neck, your forehead, your ear. Then, he feels the terrible pang of a hangover headache, a throat singed raw by fag smoke, and reminds himself to keep his emotions in check.

Last night, Callum responded to Phil's texts at 11 p.m.: he said he was at Ed's place and was fine, and Phil collapsed in relief onto his bed. How many times had he imagined the phone call from his father? Middle of the night, Mum too upset to speak. When Callum was nineteen, he took an overdose and ended up in hospital. When he was twenty-two, he nearly drowned in the sea at Southend. He was drunk, out with his friends, and there was a buoy half a mile out that he wanted to prove he could swim to. Callum insisted that these events were accidental. His parents believed him, but Phil knew better. For years, Callum would text Phil late at night, *it's too much I can't cope I'm sorry*, and Phil would call, talk him down from whatever metaphorical or literal ledge he was teetering on the edge of. The calls stopped when Callum met Holly, and now Phil's relationship to Callum is trapped inside an old web of in-jokes and memes and impersonations of things Auntie Sue said twenty-five years ago.

He replied to Callum, *you're a dickhead xx*

Callum responded, *love you too little bro xx*

By that time, Phil's mind had been straddling two crises all evening: one, his missing older brother, and two, his best friend's gay boyfriend. *Too much!* he thought. He wanted it to be over: he would tell Maggie the truth. She was his best friend. Her partner was cheating.

Or at least, *probably*. What had Phil really seen?

Basically, he had seen nothing. Just a man in a public toilet. Normal.

Come on now, said one side of his mind. You of all people know that Ed Seymour wasn't in there to trade Pokémon cards. You know from first-hand experience, do you not?

Well, I don't want to dwell on that first-hand experience, he thought in response. It's traumatic. I've suppressed it. As is my right! And even if I *did* see something, is it really my business? Am I not bound by a gay code of honour to refrain from snitching on guys who are cruising? What's more: do I not have the compassion, the emotional intelligence, to understand that even now, the year 2019, our homophobic world forces men like Ed to fuck on the downlow, and therefore should we not refrain from branding him a villain, but rather an unwitting product of structural forces beyond his control?

Yes, but is she not your best friend?

Yes, but has she not said – more than once – that she wants an open relationship?

Hypothetical. He was cheating on her!

Cheating is an archaic term. Maggie would never use it.

She may not say *cheating*, but she'd feel betrayed all the same.

He paused. He felt a pang of guilt.

It was true. *She'd feel betrayed all the same.*

He didn't want to be the one to betray her.

He dwelled on it, then drafted more lines about London clay.

'Keith,' he wrote in the final version of the book's inscription, 'before I met you, I never knew that all the earth beneath London was made of clay – one of many deep things I learned through you.' He examined it then and was dissatisfied. It had seemed like a sweet thing to say when it was on the notes app of his phone, but now it felt corny. He scratched out the word 'all', because of course not *all* the earth beneath London was made of clay, only some of it was, and Phil didn't want his romantic sentiment to be undermined by its geological inaccuracy. He regretted this too; his inscription would be forever marred by his indecision. His handwriting was indecisive too, veering between cursive and block capitals.

His phone vibrated with a text from Maggie, a bizarrely detailed menu of activities for things they could do tomorrow. Instantly, he wondered if she knew about Ed. She only ever sent texts this long when stressed or upset. He calculated the journey times and estimated that he could meet her in Hampstead at 11 a.m. and still make it back to Bermondsey in time to meet his mum at 2 p.m. He replied and told her he'd love to go to the Heath with her.

Then, he got drunk by himself and chain-smoked while waiting for Keith, who didn't get home until after 2 a.m., when he finally put his drunken arms around Phil and said that he had been at the Barbican with Louis and one thing led to another thing, and he was sorry to be late. Phil was hurt, but his hurt feelings didn't last. His performance of ease and affection melted to reveal his actual affection (if not his ease), and they stayed awake talking until late.

And now here he is. 7.30 a.m.

Keith wakes.

He scrunches his eyes.

His mouth opens so wide you can see the yellow-green fuzz at the back of his tongue.

He sleepily scoops Phil into his arms and rolls him around so that Phil is lying on top.

He slaps Phil's ass with one hand and rubs the back of his head with the other, half-asleep, dazed, horny, and grinning.

'Morning, babe,' says Phil. 'How are you feeling?'

'Well, I just woke up, so I'm not sure yet. But it's nice to be back in your bed.'

'It's nice to have you here.'

'I don't know why we don't do it more often.'

'Our hectic cosmopolitan lifestyles probably.'

They laugh; they kiss; their skin smacks against each other, unpeeling each time they pull back. After a while, Keith smiles. He looks Phil in the eye and says, 'Can I fuck you?'

Without missing a beat, Phil replies, 'I don't think now's a good time,' thinking as he does so, *Why am I like this?* He is always wanting things, then saying that he doesn't. He is always hungry and claiming to be full. When he goes to someone's house, he has to be offered food three times before accepting. The words *No, thanks, I'm fine* dribble from his mouth with automated ease. His mother would argue that his knack for self-punishment is part of his birthright as the son of an Irish woman. Maggie would argue that his internalised homophobia has left him with a deficit of respect for his own desires. Although Phil accepts that the imagined interjections from both Rosaleen and Maggie to be good points well made, he also accepts that when it comes down to it, he has been flinching incessantly at the touch of other people – even when gentle, even when tender – for more than nine years now, ever since he was nineteen and went out to Burgess Park at night looking for something to happen.

Now, sex is too much or not enough. Phil can rarely form an opinion on whether the touch of another hand is pleasing. To most partners, he usually says, *I've been having a hard time with sex lately. I had a weird-sort-of-non-consensual-encounter and have been getting in my head a lot.* That's OK, the other person would say, and they'd kiss him, but even the kissing would be too much, and kissing noises in films were too much too, and sex scenes were certainly too much, and a lover's head on Phil's shoulder felt like someone scaling the walls of a city to set it alight and Phil needed to pour boiling tar on them to prevent them from reaching the top. His body has screamed at even the brush of a hand: *Get the fuck off me.*

Keith pauses for a second. He nods his head and looks slightly hurt.

Then he smiles. 'No worries,' he says, and they kiss on the mouth.

Phil allows himself to be scooped into Keith's arms and tries to forget the blossoms from the Burgess Park cherry trees turning to wet sludge around his knees.

He chews on Keith's neck for a few sweet seconds, leaving behind the faint trace of a hickey, then leans back to admire his work – a purple and brown splodge – and admits, with some pleasure, that he hopes Keith's main boyfriend sees it and knows Phil has been there.

Here's what Phil knows of Keith's relationship with Louis: they've been together for five years, open for three. They can date who they want, fuck who they want. Louis's idea initially; before that, Keith had only been monogamous. Hard at first, Keith said, but he's been getting the hang of it. Beyond that, Phil knows little of their private dynamic – it feels taboo to ask, and Keith never says – but he's observed them at length in public: Louis is part of their extended group of friends, and Phil often finds himself across from them at dinners.

Louis is nice to Phil. *Competitively* so.

Yet Phil can't help but like him. He shares good stories and interesting bits of trivia, and never speaks over anyone or for longer than he should. He's curious about the world, knowledgeable, and always does more than his fair share of the washing-up after a big meal. It's true that he can be tactless and rude without meaning to be – in conversation with strangers, he name-drops the famous artists he knows, referring to them by first names alone, assuming that everyone knows (and cares) who these people are – but aside from that, yes, he's a charmer, and Phil resents him for it. He's jealous, ashamed to resent someone so generally nice. It suggests a pettiness, a small mind, a far cry from the comradely goodwill and easy affection with which a truly radical queer would treat their partner's other partners.

Louis is a rising star academic, whose father was a celebrated sculptor in the nineties and whose mother is a property developer. His childhood was speckled with summers in the south of France and Central European camping trips during which he learned about cooperation, kindness, and skinning wild boars. Phil sees him as someone who had the world handed to him on a silver plate and now spends all his time rehashing anecdotes about minor celebrities he went to Oxford with. Sometimes, Keith tells jokes about escaping the drudgery of wage labour by marrying rich and Phil wonders if these are intended entirely in jest.

Still, Phil remembers how in the two weeks after Keith's father died, Louis didn't go to work at all, but instead stayed by Keith's side the whole time, cooking his meals, doing his laundry, holding his hand while they silently watched mind-numbing reality TV shows. Phil wanted so badly to care for Keith then, but Louis had already looked after everything.

He speculated that Louis had only been able to take time off at short notice because he was rich enough to make spontaneous decisions about his working life and for there to be no major risk associated with those choices, which was probably true, but it was also true that Louis took the time off simply because he was a good partner and was in love with Keith.

Recently, Phil has asked his friends for advice.

Maggie said she's worried that Phil is being taken advantage of.

Debs said she's jealous that Phil has anyone to hook up with at all.

Frank said 'the open relationship' is a scourge on the happiness of gay men everywhere. Frank, a few years older than Phil, has taken his fair share of walks around the polyamorous block and is now retired into relative monogamy at the age of thirty-six. His assessment was this: everyone's in an open relationship. Everyone's fucking everyone else. Fine. No big deal. But what happens when these boys in open relationships start staying over with their casual hook-ups? What happens when they have coffee the next day and go for a little walk and share anecdotes about each other's troubled siblings and grandmother's demented quirks? When happens when they say *Oh my God, that's my favourite album too*, or, *Oh my God, my dad was the exact same kind of asshole as your dad?* What happens when the words *I love you* get bandied about? Inevitable: the casual fuckbuddy wants to be treated as a boyfriend in his own right, and someone, somewhere down the line, is going to get hurt.

In any case, Frank said that Phil is in the best position of all. All that yearning! *Sumptuous.* The decadence of always being left, lolling about in bed afterwards with just too many feelings to put into words. He said you should only ever get what you want *for the most extraordinarily brief window of time.* The rest of your life, you should spend in the pining.

It's called inflation, honey, he'd said, luxuriating on a long drag of his fag. If the object of your desire were within perpetual reach, it would be worthless. You must only ever *graze* it. A whiff of perfume on a busy street: gone before you knew it was there, and then, you look around in dismay, *in ecstasy,* thinking: *Wait, did something just happen here?* You'll spend the rest of your days wanting that feeling back.

Phil wasn't having any of it.

'You can't be suggesting I spend my life in a state of permanent emotional edging!'

'I'm suggesting,' said Frank, '*that desire is about lack.* You're not in love with Keith: you're in love with the distance between what you *want* and what you can *have.* That's why boys like you go after boys with boyfriends. Make no mistake, chica, the reason he's so unbearably sexy is *precisely* because of his unavailability; as soon as he decides to commit, you'll wonder what you ever saw in him. The best thing is to stay exactly where you are.'

As Frank saw it, there were only three other options, all as terrible as each other:

1. Keith dumps Phil and stays with Louis. Phil is upset for months.
2. Keith dumps Louis and commits to Phil. Both are disappointed, realising that too much of their chemistry was necessarily predicated on their mutual unavailability.
3. Worst of all, Keith attempts to amend the terms of his relationship so that it's fully *polyamorous*, rather than simply *open*. All three of them are miserable for the duration of this agreement. They each become jealous, paranoid, conceal shocking acts of cruelty beneath politically palatable terminology – social conditioning, homonormativity, relationship anarchy – and, finally, they experience precisely ten months of severe mental illness before deciding that polyamory isn't right for them.

'Enjoy it while you can,' said Frank. 'Thank your lucky stars you're not Louis: *he's* got the least power. What's in it for him? At least you and Keith *get* something out of it.'

'Excuse me,' Phil clarified, 'Louis was the one who opened up their relationship in the first place, *not* Keith.' And besides, the idea that Phil had more power than Louis was ludicrous, not least because of Louis's wealth, but also because of his claim on Keith's time. Louis can see Keith whenever he wants: Phil is stuck with early morning scraps, like now.

. . .

NOW, PHIL TURNS TO KEITH IN BED AND SAYS, 'YOU hungry? I could get breakfast stuff.'

Keith smiles.

'That's very sweet of you. Let me give you some money for it.'

'Don't worry about it. My treat.'

Phil kisses Keith twice on the lips and starts to get up.

He puts his clothes on and climbs down the rickety steps that lead to his bed. He skips down the hall, his housemates already lugging a sound system up the stairs and planning their party outfits with the seriousness of those who are planning a war. The other topics of conversation are a giant porcelain statue of a penguin, and several smaller statues of the same penguin: should these be thrown out or incorporated into the party's overall aesthetic? Also on the agenda: the hotel trolley, the pottery wheel, the broken lawn mower. Where do these things come from? Nobody knows. Large items simply appear. Debs and Janet and Frank have gathered to clear space for the party but already are disagreeing over which items can or can't be dumped and whether these penguin statues are too precious to disregard.

Phil, Keith and Debs live in a warehouse with nine other people, but technically there shouldn't be anyone living there at all. It's registered as a commercial address and although the landlord leases it for residential use, the tenants have no rights, no legal contract, and they could be evicted at a moment's notice. If the council ever finds out they're there, the warehouse – all the deadly fire hazards within – could be shut down without warning or notice.

But still, the rent is cheap, the building huge and beautiful, nestled among the alleyways and Victorian blocks between Bermondsey, Borough and Elephant & Castle. Most industrial buildings in the area have been turned into luxury lofts, *industrial-chic living solutions with original maritime features*, but against all odds, this warehouse has teetered on the edge of semi-dereliction for years, with its home-made plumbing, home-made electrical wiring, and home-made fire alert systems. Sometimes, when older friends come to visit, they get a wistful look in their eyes and say they haven't seen a place like this since the eighties.

Phil loves the labyrinth of corridors, the mezzanines, the huge piles of junk that people drag in off the street. He loves the twelve bedrooms, three toilets, and four fridges each with its own stench, so that you have to hold your nose when you go to get milk.

He loves the freezer that's frozen completely shut. He loves the Sainsbury's *Taste the Difference* haggis that's buried within. He loves the people in the house who harbour dreams of retrieving it one day, even though he himself believes it to be impossible.

There have been many failed attempts at devising an effective cleaning rota; some are punitive, some emphasise individual responsibility, and some focus on collective care. The evidence of these failed projects can be found scrawled on sheets of A1 paper Blu-Tacked to the walls. There are three couches, thickly blanketed in cat hair, and further cat hair hangs suspended in the air, illuminated beautifully by the golden summer light. The couches are arranged around the TV, which is a big TV, bought off eBay several months ago. At the time, many people in the house had worried that the TV would dominate the room, that it would result in less conversation and the remaining conversation would be of a lower quality, but after a few days everyone realised that the

TV enhanced their life rather than making it worse and it gave more prompts for conversation than it took away.

When Phil left Basildon at eighteen, he lived in a series of overpriced shitholes, sinks invariably filled with unwashed dishes and stagnant water, bits of mouldy bread and raw chicken floating on top, damp hovels on London's outskirts, where people stashed their own toilet roll in their bedroom, labelled their milk in the fridge, and left passive aggressive messages in the house WhatsApp when they suspected someone of using their Worcester sauce or stain removal spray or barista-style instant coffee, signing the message 'Regards, Samuel' but never saying two words when they were in the kitchen together, microwaving a tinned lentil soup in nail-biting silence. He lived in places that looked like office canteens or Airbnbs; a bowl of plastic fruit on a white plastic table, a canvas print of a New York yellow taxi, a London Underground logo painted on every door, except instead of saying the names of Tube stations, they said things like *Bathroom*, *Kitchen* and *Bedroom*; a tea towel hung from the oven, imploring you to 'Keep Calm and Drink Tea' while black mould laid its claim to the windowsills. The idea of living in a place which felt like an actual home was such an abstract concept that he didn't even consider it to be possible within his lifetime.

Now, Phil often goes into the kitchen to get a glass of water and ends up staying to talk for hours. He doesn't get anything done on those days, but his life is all the better for it. During those marathon conversations, Phil feels as if he is living his actual life, and everything that came before was a dry run. He moved in three years ago and for the first time became properly conscious of his own happiness. He'd been happy before, but only became aware of it after the happiness was already gone. Finally, his happiness is vivid and big. He can't help but notice it.

. . .

TODAY, HE BREEZES PAST THE PARTY-PLANNERS IN THE corridor ('Have you had a gentleman caller?' shouts Frank) and swings through the front door ('A lady never tells,' he calls back).

He steps outside and blinks. On the pavement below, four mangy pigeons bicker over discarded fried chicken bones. Crushed glass and beer cans glimmer in the sunshine. The air is hot, heavy, completely still. The smell is soupy and pungent, like gone off meat left to languish in the depths of the fridge. Still, it's sort of pleasant: intense and heady and rich.

Phil gulps. He stretches his limbs. He hasn't showered, brushed his teeth, shaved, or had a shit. There's a yellow crust in the corners of his eyes and his face feels clammy and dry at the same time. His mouth tastes like an ashtray and there's a prickly sensation in his armpits where today's fresh sweat fraternises with yesterday's fermented sweat.

And yet, he can't help it.

He feels better than ever.

The flyover at Bricklayers Arms swerves towards the sky; a 453 hurtles over it, seeming to rock from side to side, and Phil passes under, feeling compulsively, unavoidably, as if there is nothing he can do but smile a smile so wide that people on the street will probably see it as antisocial. He floats down the Old Kent Road, where old men smoke around stainless-steel tables and old women amble towards the bus stop. To his right is Burgess Park: he barely even shivers in panic at the sight of its gate. To his left is big Tesco, and walking through its glass doors he feels as if today things are possible, which yesterday, were unimaginable. Yesterday, he had thumped computer keys to send emails to apologise for the other emails he hadn't sent yet. This seems like a world away. It's hard to even remember. It took place during an era of history so ancient that its fossils have decomposed beyond the understanding of archaeologists, back when Phil was a person who wrote emails, and worried about rent, and cooked a large batch of soup to freeze and ration for each day of the week.

It's always this way after being with Keith. It makes the city feel bigger, the future feel wider, and even though it only happens every so often, he thinks it could be different.

Slipping through the crowds, he begins to think that sex with Keith might not always be so *entirely* casual, and standing in the queue for the self-service checkouts he thinks how strange it is that coffee and eggs on a sunny morning should be such a thrill (such an ordinary thing!). Back out in the sun, the Shard looming like a mirage of science fiction in the distance, he thinks that they are clearly compatible (sexually, emotionally, culturally), and maybe, after breakfast, they will smoke a cigarette on the street below; one might play Nina Simone from the speakers on their phone; and they might feel dizzy from smoking so early on so hot a day, but they will brush their teeth, drink some water, and then, probably, feel OK. He is thinking this until he walks into the kitchen to find Keith leaning against the counter, and Phil finds himself, as he often does in the first moments of meeting, a little bit lost for words.

He scrambles the eggs and feels nervous that something in the way he cooks his eggs will give Keith a reason to like him less.

'So, what you doing today then?' says Keith after breakfast.

Phil takes a moment to remember his schedule.

'Maggie at the Heath, then meeting my mum, then the party later on.'

'You got a bit of spare time now?'

'About an hour. Why?'

'Thought we could go on a romantic date.'

Phil grins.

'What do you have in mind?'

'Well, it would involve three of us.'

The grin plummets.

'What? Louis?'

Keith laughs. 'Sorry, bad joke. I meant we should go and see the whale.'

Phil smiles in relief. 'OK. Sure. Sounds good.'

They gather their things, slather sunscreen, re-fill their water bottles, and search for lost sunglasses. They leave the house and walk towards Bermondsey Beach, the whole way holding hands, and Phil thinks it's the longest time he's publicly held hands with a man.

'What's your mum like?' says Keith on the way. 'Does she have an Irish accent?'

'She lost it. I never remember her having one. She barely ever mentions Ireland. I ask her about it and she just says *Ah well, none of it will matter in the grand scheme of things.*'

It's true. None of it will matter in the grand scheme of things. Rosaleen says it in response to events large and small. She used to say it when teachers sent home notes detailing how Callum had been disruptive in class, and she said it when both of her parents passed away within six months of each other. Sometimes she says it with a lackadaisical giddiness, as if to say: it's not that big a deal so let's just have fun. Sometimes she says it with a solemn look in her eyes, as if to say: nothing means anything and we're all going to die.

Phil loves to talk about her. He describes her as hard-working, hilarious, a giantess of working-class camp. He speaks like her and cooks the same old Delia recipes that she used to, albeit with an affected sense of kitsch which for her may have been automatic. He never thought much about class when he lived at home, but since moving to London it's become a sort of currency. He can make statements like *Speaking as a gay man from a working class background I think that what you're saying is quite problematic, actually*, and although he hates himself for it, his arguments instantly, wrongly, become more credible. Plus if he ever decides to apply for some sort of Arts Council funding, he could probably describe his project as *unabashedly queer, unapologetically working class* and presumably whoever is in charge of the diversity and inclusion strategy would look on his application more favourably.

Besides all this, class has helped to bond him to Keith. They're from similar backgrounds, similar towns, and it seems to Phil that they experience the world in a remarkably similar way. This, partially, is why he likes him so much. He feels an affinity.

'Are you looking forward to seeing her?' he asks.

'In some ways, but I'm nervous too. She always thinks that I'm judging her. Going to university, London, being gay, liking art: she thinks that by virtue of having a different life from her, I'm necessarily saying that her life is shit. To be honest, I do think Basildon is pretty grim and I'm glad not to live there, but I mean that subjectively: just because it's grim for me, doesn't mean it's grim for everyone. Anyway, the only thing she ever talks about these days is my brother's wedding, and the conversation always ends up with her implying that I'm some sort of feckless weirdo for not getting married or having a mortgage or both.'

Keith pauses.

He says, 'Do you have a plus one to the wedding?'

They stop at the traffic lights on Jamaica Road. Phil looks at Keith, handsome and gregarious, a big beard and soft body, cartoonishly butch but with flashes of high camp, his gravelly voice cloaked in the swish and pomp of a 1960s northern drag queen, flirting outrageously with heavy drinking husbands at working men's clubs, sleeves rolled up, arms tattooed, charming the socks off all within earshot.

'Yeah,' says Phil. 'Why do you ask?'

Another pause.

'Just thought you could bring Maggie or whatever. Might make it easier.'

Phil deflates.

'She's going anyway,' he says. 'Ed is Callum's best friend.'

'Fair enough,' says Keith, and drops it.

Before they know it, they're at the river. They weave through the thickening crowds and news cameras to get to the railings – Tower Bridge and converted warehouses to the left, Canary Wharf menacing the river bend – and there it is: the half-beached whale. Beautiful, smooth, in pain. Its forehead: bulbous and square. Its fin: shaped like half a waxing moon.

Rich chocolate, olive brown, dark grey. Half its body is in the water, half lodged on the shore, thrashing, frantic, somewhere between stuck and unstuck. Hundreds of people line the river to catch a glimpse, and lifeboats position themselves near the river's edge.

'Oh my God, there she is,' says Keith.

'The whale?'

'The Princess of Whales,' he says, pointing towards a woman perched on a lifeboat, talking rapidly into a walkie-talkie, and gesturing to five people at once. She's taller in real life than Phil imagined, but beyond that, looks exactly like she does on camera, which is to say, the spitting image of Diana, right down to the perfectly blow-dried quiff.

'Wow,' says Phil, meaning that it's surreal to see an internet celebrity in person, also meaning *I didn't know you could still get hair like that*, but Keith seems to think he meant it as an expression of wonder at the whale.

'It's amazing,' Keith agrees, letting out a noise that can only be described as a gasp. He beams like a child on a TV show whose dad, a soldier, has been away for a long time and returns to surprise the child at Christmas. Phil loves Keith for this. He is always ready to be awed. He takes the world as it comes, luxuriating in the uncomplicated pleasures of glorious weather and witnessing a rare animal in the flesh.

Phil, on the other hand, isn't sure what to say. What should a person feel when in front of a whale? The whale, certainly, is big – this is undeniable – and according to the news, rare. He stands in front of the whale – imagining himself standing in front of the whale – and notes down details that he can recount or embellish in service of a future anecdote.

'Do you see the way its skin turns from brown to grey?' says Keith. 'So beautiful!'

Phil hums with forced enthusiasm.

'What do you reckon she's thinking?' he says.

Keith considers it. 'Well, she's probably panicked. She's missing home.'

'I'm not sure. Maybe she likes it here.'

'Why would she like it here?'

'She likes the hustle and bustle.'

'Much like ourselves.'

'Exactly.'

'Young and single and trying to make it in the city.'

Phil pauses, grins.

'Although you're not really single, are you?'

'Well, neither are you.'

'I'm more single than you.'

Keith laughs and says, 'I suppose,' and they don't talk about it any more.

Phil looks at the crowds. He overhears a dad tell his kids that whales eat squid and can dive as deep as seven hundred metres into the sea. An activist from the Socialist Workers Party tries to give them a paper, explaining that the crisis of climate is a crisis of capital and the whale is living proof. They decline, and the man goes on his way. Phil struggles to relax. Whenever he looks at art or nature with friends, he feels obliged to express feelings on it even when he has none, and this discrepancy between feelings spoken and feelings felt gives him the sensation of not existing at all.

Eventually, it's time for Keith to go.

'Sorry,' he says. 'I've got plans with Louis.'

Phil looks at the whale while speaking; he squints as if trying to make out the most intricate details of its skin, the thousand tiny injuries from which blood seeps into the river.

'Sure. Fair enough. Tell him I said hi.'

Keith kisses him, leaves, and Phil immediately messages Maggie to tell her about it. Thirty seconds later, his phone vibrates with a response: *sorry babe – he's a nightmare boy!!*

She's right. Keith *is* a nightmare boy. It's not that he isn't kind or caring or a good lover, but he's unreliable. Phil tries to reason that their relationship is a casual one and he can't expect the same commitment from Keith as he might expect from an actual boyfriend, and it's possible, too, that Phil gives mixed signals. He tries to act as if he were fashionably uninterested in monogamy, but it's possible he overdoes things, acting not only as if his feelings on monogamy were ambivalent, but as if his feelings on Keith were ambivalent too.

He takes a last look at the whale and walks back from the river. The roadworks on the corner of Jamaica Road and Abbey Street have blown dust clouds into the air and Bermondsey feels like a desert. Men glug pints outside the far-right pub and fag smoke wafts towards the tattered Union Jack bunting. The whites of the flags have been stained cigarette-brown and piss-yellow, and the red crosses have been bleached a sunburnt shade of pink.

Phil remembers the sunburn on Ed's neck the summer they were seventeen. He remembers the silver chain cutting across it, Ed without a shirt on, the paleness of his back.

He descends into the cool shade of Bermondsey station, thinking of the first time that Ed sent him a text, and knowing, with unease, that it's probably time to tell Maggie about it.

6

ROSALEEN LIES IN BED. SHE'S BEEN AWAKE SINCE IT GOT bright, a long time ago now, watching the sunlight peek cheekily beneath the curtains. She barely slept, biting her nails until Callum finally messaged at midnight to say he was fine. At an earlier point in life, she would have been furious. She would have said, *You don't think of anyone but yourself.* Not any more.

She stares at the wardrobe, bulging with all the old clothes she never wears, and thinks, wearily, that something's gotta give. When she tries to explain it to herself, the best she can come up with is that just once, she wants to be at the *centre* of things. No longer an afterthought. No longer a peripheral figure in her own life.

Thirty years, she's looked after her sons. Thirty years, she's arranged her life to make theirs possible. Now, they're grown, and she's practically incidental. She knows it's normal. She's hardly the first mother to have gone through it. But that doesn't make it easier.

'Callum,' she'll say. 'Before I had you, I never knew just

how many creatures could live beneath the earth of one tiny back garden. You've taught me so many things.'

When she says that at the wedding, she won't just be describing the diverse ecosystems that Callum discovered in their little garden as a child, she'll be describing the things that she learned about herself through being his mother; a wonder at the world that she hadn't felt since she was little. He helped her to see the world as a place where even the oldest, dreariest things could become new again if you only looked at them sideways.

Beside her, Steve snores. She can't deny that she's central to his story too, and she loves him after all these years, as convinced of his goodness as ever. It's undeniable that he treats her well, although she can't help but feel that she's invisible to him, not because he doesn't pay attention to her but because when the moment comes to express some deeper part of herself – say, a memory from childhood or an opinion on a book – she seizes up and finds herself unable to speak, which is to say, she's sort of invisible to herself as well.

She used to be certain that she was going to hell.

She had spent every waking second of childhood trying to be good so that she might at least get into limbo. It was never enough. She thought too often of knickers. She sang when she shouldn't have been singing. She was slow at arithmetic and got distracted in class, and according to the nuns who taught her at school, not only did this mean she was stupid, it also meant she was bad. She remembers how they'd smack the back of her hands and legs for that.

Rosaleen had *bad insides*. That's the term she'd used as a six-year-old child, as if it were a diagnosable disease, like cancer or tuberculosis. But there was no cure for bad insides. You had to carry them around with you. You couldn't put them down and say *That's enough of you, I need to get on with my life now.* Sometimes she tried to work up the courage to confess to the priest. She rehearsed the speech – *I've got bad insides* – but she could never bring herself to do it, and she had taken this as even further evidence of her own badness.

But at that time, nearly every person in Ireland believed they had bad insides. They were all walking around, in a constant state of emotional flinching, trying to hide their bad insides from each other. Everyone was suspicious of everyone else in case it turned out that the bad insides of another were even worse than your own and you'd be infected by them.

She has often worried that she passed her bad insides down to her children. Phil certainly has a touch of it. When he was six, he became obsessed with the idea that he was fat, and therefore, as he told her at the time, *bad*, and he pleaded to be put on a diet, even though there wasn't a pick on him.

It was only when Rosaleen saw Pauline do a cartwheel and the nun said she was going to hell for it that Rosaleen began to think: *Something's not quite right here.* How could a cartwheel be a mortal sin? What kind of charade *is* this? Pauline wasn't trying to flash her knickers on purpose (and so what if she was?). She just liked the rush of blood to her head.

Rosaleen moved to England to get the kind of life Pauline never could have had.

And what's she done with it?

She's got a cream leather couch. It reclines. She's got a big TV.

Today, she'll meet Phil, who has opted for a different sort of life than hers. She'll visit his house, and then they'll go shopping. He's the only one who doesn't know about the cancer, so she'll tell him about that, also about the bargains she got in the reduced-to-clear aisle, and how she'd love to get a new toilet seat for the bathroom, a wood-effect one, not unlike Auntie Sue's, and Steve, meanwhile, will meet Callum so they can watch the football.

She misses Phil. She never knows what's going on for him. It was different at one time, when she was closer to him than anyone else in the family. She used to buy him books. She remembers *The Lion, the Witch and the Wardrobe*, the first one he loved. He was six. Every morning of the Christmas holidays, he stood at her bed while *Gone with the Wind* or *Casablanca* played on the TV and the room smelled of the bashed remnants of a boiled egg.

He would give her a breathless and painstakingly detailed account of the events he'd read in the novel since the last time he spoke to her – Edmund was evil, no, actually, Edmund was good, Aslan was dead, no, actually Aslan was alive – and Rosaleen listened patiently, thrilled that Phil had taken up an interest in reading, because this meant he was like her.

He looks down on her now. He sees her as provincial, her cream leather couch, her big TV, him being the only one in the family to go to university. Now, he's got London, maybe a love life, certainly literature: she wouldn't have a clue what books to buy for him any more. She can't give him a gift at all without immediately blurting out: *I can take it back if you don't like it!* and reminding him for weeks that she still has the gift receipt.

Steve wakes up. He yawns. His yawn transitions into a sort of bellow, which transforms into a yodel, which lasts nearly a full minute. She can't help but laugh.

'What are you laughing at?' he says, his bushy eyebrows dancing.

'I'm laughing at you,' she replies, laughing still.

'Laughing at me? You better watch out or there'll be no breakfast in bed.'

'Breakfast in bed? What's the occasion?'

'Do I need an occasion to make breakfast for my beautiful wife?'

'Well, at least let me help you.'

'Absolutely not. You stay there and I'll look after everything.'

He kisses her lightly on the hand. Off he goes down the stairs to make the breakfast. Within a few minutes, the smell of sizzling vegetable oil, rashers, and hot coffee sneaks through the crack of her bedroom door. Of course, she knows what the occasion is. The occasion is that her birthday was several weeks ago, and as always she had insisted that they didn't celebrate. She hates her birthday and banned it years ago – like a radical new government bans the feast days of the old regime – but Steve, resisting such an embargo, always picks a day weeks later to spoil her, as if it occurred to him for no reason in particular.

It's not that she's self-conscious about ageing; she just doesn't like the fuss, that's all. She's the same with Christmas and New Year and Easter and St Patrick's Day. She's struggles with anything that involves a gathering of people, a voicing of feeling. It's not that she doesn't have feelings of her own, but as soon as they're spoken aloud, they sound false, and she's afraid of revealing something bad about herself. If someone made a birthday cake and lit candles and sang happy birthday, she wouldn't be able to enjoy it, because her mind would be so busy commenting on the various implications of the act of blowing out candles, that she might as well not blow them out at all.

When she pictures the cancer, she pictures a blockage. She thinks of the purple lumps as if they were fatty feelings that wanted out. She believes that every time the words gathered in her throat and got ready to explode, they left behind a physical residue and that's what made her sick. It's absurd to think such a thing, and no doctor would agree with her, but ever since she got her diagnosis, her mind has been spinning its own private folklore of disease.

She thinks of Joan Seymour sometimes, who is, without a shadow of a doubt, alive. Joan is big. She moves through the world as if the world is meant for her. She sits on her armchair out on the pavement as if the only important thing is satisfying her own pleasures.

Rosaleen makes herself smaller and smaller to the point of barely existing at all.

Pauline, she thinks. Now *she* had been big, and when Rosaleen was with her, she had felt big as well. She had felt as if she were expanding, stretching the outer walls of her life.

Yes: that's what it was like.

The pleasure of knowing Pauline had been the simple pleasure of a stretch in the morning, reaching towards the sun, getting longer, blood rushing to dormant bits of muscle.

Steve brings up the breakfast. It's buttery, oily, hot, and delicious. He's a great cook, like his mother before him, and they both gobble their food with the bedroom telly playing softly in the background and Steve absentmindedly singing along to the jingles from the ads.

She feels a bit sick. She always feels a bit sick when she eats these days.

After they've finished, she turns and says, 'Do you ever feel like you're not alive?'

He checks his pulse. He says, 'I think I'm alive.'

'I don't mean physically. I mean emotionally, I suppose. Alive on the inside.'

He considers this for a moment.

He puts on a Hollywood accent as if he were Clint Eastwood or John Wayne.

'You make me feel alive,' he says, and she almost cries, feeling almost certain that the accent means that he's embarrassed, not that he's insincere. She squeezes his hand and tries to clear up the breakfast things despite his insistence that she sit down and relax.

. . .

MEANWHILE, IN LONDON, ED AND CALLUM TRAVEL north up Kingsland High Street, which heaves, a catwalk: fashion queers strut past the station, dressed like early-2000s pop stars and characters from *The Matrix*. On the corner of Ridley Road, old communists distribute leaflets and berate the working class of Hackney for failing to grasp their revolutionary potential. Kind-faced women sing hymns and pass flyers. They want to explain that Jesus loves even you. Outside the Curve Garden, the patriarchs settle on benches and repeat what they have repeated every day of the past seven years, which is that since the Olympics, this place has gone to the dogs. A tired drag queen smokes a hurried fag. She's hosting her second of five brunches at Superstore this weekend and fantasising about a normal job. Up and down the street, people dart in front of traffic, no time to wait for a safe moment to cross. Up and down the street, people beg for money, for food, for fags, for energy drinks. Up and down the street, people buy hair extensions, phone chargers, SIM cards, baklawa, cheap houseplants from the Chinese supermarket, diamante mirrors, fibre-optic Big Bens, and sparkling silver tigers from the glistening homeware emporiums. Everywhere Ed looks, someone is having the best day of their life. Everywhere he looks, there's someone in terrible agony. A bunch of teenage boys lose control of their football on the corner of Ball's Pond Road and a passing man heads it back with spectacular finesse. The boys cheer, the man beams, and Ed thinks: *Go on, my son!* A bus lets out a prolonged beep at a woman who stumbles in front of it. 'Suck your mum,' retorts the woman, defiant. It is hot. Fabulously hot. The air is parched, dusty, dry like cracked desert earth that rain hasn't touched for years. The ground around every tree in Hackney Downs and London Fields is marshy with the piss of yesterday's post-work boozers. Ed trips over a stray copy of *The Sun*; its headline screams of *THERESA MAY'S BREXIT SHAMBLES*. A man outside Tesco asks for someone to buy him food.

Callum, getting on the bus. Callum, pissed already. These are the images that Ed records in his mind as they make their way to Tottenham to have a drink before meeting Steve. Last night, they picked at the cold meal that Ed had made for Maggie before Callum fell asleep at the table and couldn't be roused. They didn't say anything further about Callum's mum's cancer. When Callum finally woke this morning, hungover, desolate, he asked Ed to come to watch the football, and Ed didn't have the heart to say no.

The 149 is standing room only, and they cram together with Saturday shoppers on all sides. Ed thinks that this is a higher quality of intimacy than their hug last night. Their chests are pressed together. He can smell the reek of a two-day bender on Callum's breath. Everyone here can. An old woman holds her nose and mutters aloud, 'For Jesus's sake.'

Outside is Dalston: Turkish barbers, Turkish restaurants, the best falafel outside of Istanbul, the best skin fade in Hackney, two Irish pubs, one worse than the other, Ridley Road Market, smell of barbecue, jerk chicken, drifting across the road to Dalston Kingsland station.

As Dalston melts into Stoke Newington, Ed can see the wealthy weekend moochers trail between the hand-crafted cookware shops and sip flat whites from little paper cups. As Stoke Newington melts into Stamford Hill, he can see old Haredi men pace around in pairs, locked in conversation, their brows furrowed, and their hands clasped behind their backs.

While they wait for their stop, Callum talks business.

'I'm doing a special offer this weekend,' he says.

'Oh yeah?'

'Free bag of K with every three items. Do you think it's a good idea?'

'I don't know. You're the entrepreneur.'

'I think it is. Everyone loves ketamine.'

'Might want to keep your voice down.'

'Everyone. They go to the office and they get on the bus and they meet their mum and they're all on ketamine. Including the mums, might I add. They watch TV on ketamine. They eat their lunch on ketamine. They snort ketamine in the canned goods aisle in Sainsbury's.'

They get off the bus south of Seven Sisters. The weight of midday heat. Callum stumbles, confused and squinting for the first few steps, before continuing to walk after Ed. 'Wait,' he calls out. 'I need to take a piss.'

He trails off. Dashes down a lane and undoes his fly. Ed sighs, checks his watch. While Callum's piss splashes against a wall, Ed paces around and takes in the scene.

They're at the corner of a derelict site. Rubble, baked earth, little yellow flowers. A pile of rubbish bags that someone chucked over the iron fence. Wooden hoardings on one side, a row of sun-bleached posters for a drum 'n' bass festival that happened three summers ago and never happened again. Ed and Maggie went to a festival like that once. Ed took ecstasy and danced non-stop for ten hours. It wasn't about the music: he would have danced to the sound of a dripping tap when he was with her. Behind the hoardings: a demolished building, plasterboard wall, graffitied urban slander: *Nat has herpes*. Ancient East End proverb. Scrawled on the door of every cubicle in Hackney. Who *is* Nat? Are they OK? We'll never know, Ed thinks, thinking too of his own cold sores, and the time he had chlamydia at eighteen, the burning pains, how he thought he'd die. He laughs, relieved to be clear of adolescence, and looks towards Callum, still pissing. Ed sighs and smiles at once, knowing there won't be another moment like this again. He's leaving London next week, and even if he wasn't, he'll die eventually, and so will Callum, and the world might end soon either way, and there's a last time for everything. Lately, each time Ed has said goodbye to a friend, he's taken to wondering *How many hours together do we have left?* Callum finishes, walks back towards Ed. Knowing that this is a special moment, and knowing that Callum knows it too, but not sure how to acknowledge it, or if it needs to be acknowledged at all, he claps Callum on the back three times, and Callum does the same. Seeing their own awkwardness – caricatures of their dads and their dads' dads – they laugh, say nothing, and keeping walking.

Unannounced, Ed's guilt begins to clamber for attention. It feels ignored. It froths at the corners of its lips.

Then, a text from Maggie.

About to meet Phil at the heath, will let you know how I get on xx

Ed breathes sharply through his nostrils. He closes his eyes and pleads with himself to calm down. *I'm here*, he promises. *I'm on top of things. I'm going to come up with a plan.*

'Hang on,' he says to Callum. 'Need to do something.'

He takes out his phone. He calls her. He doesn't even think about it and is not sure what he's going to say. All he knows is that he needs to stop her from meeting Phil today.

It goes straight to voicemail: she must have gone underground.

Shit. He closes his eyes and rubs his temple. He's short of breath already.

'You OK?' says Callum.

'Fine. I just – just need to text Maggie.'

He bashes out a message and presses send within two seconds.

Think I left the back door unlocked. Any chance you could go home and check?

He puts his phone back in his pocket and smiles as if nothing happened.

'All good?' says Callum.

'All good,' confirms Ed, wheezing slightly.

They continue towards Tottenham, Ed's mind falling off the edge of countless cliffs.

'How's your brother doing?' he asks after a few steps.

'Phil? Why do you ask?'

'I just wondered how he's coping with your mum's news.'

'I don't know. We don't talk about that kind of thing.'

'Probably would if you asked.'

'Yeah. I don't know. I'm not saying we don't get on, because we do, but when we're together, all we manage to do is crack joke after joke. Don't get me wrong: I like the jokes. We're both funny fuckers if you ask me, but, yeah, I don't know, it's just, sort of . . . I don't know . . .' He trails off here. He looks around, digs his hands in his pocket, quickens his pace.

He strains the muscles in his face as he speaks, and in a hammy attempt to change the subject, he practically shouts, 'So tell me: when are you and Mags going to tie the knot?'

Ed laughs.

'I don't know if she wants to.'

Callum says nothing at first, but when he speaks next, he sounds sweet.

'Do you want to though?' he says.

Ed pauses, taken aback by Callum's softness. He mulls it over, remembering how Callum and Holly had been so determined to marry each other from the moment they met. He stares at the sky through the canopy of trees that line this street and almost zones out while a seagull glides above. Did seagulls always live in London? Is this a climate change thing?

Does Ed want marriage? Who knows! They hadn't even spoken about children before she got pregnant, too broke to even consider it. It hadn't even occurred to them to want kids.

He can't speak for Maggie, but Ed had had an unnamed, unnameable desire for something – what? Domesticity? Adulthood? To look after something smaller than him? – but you couldn't articulate a desire for something you didn't have the right language for.

At times, it's seemed like every decision Ed ever made was simply because it was a hot day and he was horny or angry or both. He never knows what he wants. It changes completely from minute to minute, and he has no decisive inner voice that says *This is the real you, this is what you desire.* Ed is blurry, to even himself. His outlines are vague. This is fine except that you need to be solid for other people. To have relationships, to be trusted, you have to say 'This is me, this is what I want' and act as if that were true at all times.

At school, he had liked Phil and Maggie for the same reason: he had thought they'd lead to a life beyond Basildon. Everyone knew they'd leave; Maggie was always going to go to art school, and being her boyfriend was like bolting through the door of a train about to depart.

'I don't know,' he says. 'I just want to be with her either way. And to be a dad.'

Callum is quiet for a moment, and when he finally speaks, it's with his signature blend of affection and derision. 'Always so emotional,' he says, rapping Ed on the head, as if a head full of emotion makes a certain sound, like a wall full of pipes or asbestos.

Ed sighs. 'That's me,' he says.

'You're like my little brother.'

Ed laughs a lone *ha!*

A little too loud.

'Oh yeah?' he says.

Callum grins.

'Did you pick it up from him then?'

'Mate, we never even see each other.'

'You used to see each other.'

'When we were in school.'

'When you were down the laneway with him.'

Ed stops still.

What is this lurch in his stomach? What is this sensation? It's a sensation of the world ending.

There was one time, about six years ago, when Ed was extremely broke, and no matter how many interviews he did, he couldn't get a job. He remembers the feeling of doom after his sixth rejection and fifteen pounds left in the bank. He remembers the queasy repetition of *my life is over, my life is over.* He feels the same now: as if his life is ending.

He mumbles, quieter than intended, 'What are you talking about?'

Callum gestures to his earlobe. 'Didn't catch that, mate.'

Ed is sweating everywhere. Suddenly, he stinks. He has pins and needles in his face and hands and chest, and his voice quivers. He repeats, 'What are you talking about?'

Callum grins, looks around – is he sheepish? Is he vindictive? – and looks back.

'I think you know what I'm talking about.'

Then, a reply from Maggie.

Sorry, can't right now. I'm w Phil xx

7

MAGGIE SPOTS PHIL OUTSIDE HAMPSTEAD HEATH station. A split-second passes.

She pauses, watches him.

Then, their eyes meet, and they both let out a sort of squeal, and launch into their usual routine, talking over each other, not watching where they're going, bumping into pedestrians.

There are kisses, hugs. They compliment each other's hairstyle, their skimpy summer outfits. They describe what they got up to last night. Phil reports an item of gossip regarding two prominent East London drag queens he recently spied getting hot and heavy at Bethnal Green Working Men's Club. He tells the story well, and they are both suitably scandalised.

She scans for gaps in the conversation to ask about Rosaleen. Should she be direct? Should she be gentle? She can't focus: too many distractions. It seems like at least half the city's population is surging towards the ponds. Music plays from five different phone speakers at once and the air is thick with pollen. A backfiring sports car belches its way around the park's perimeter, while rich local families complain to each other in hushed tones outside the organic skincare boutiques. It gets busier and busier every year, they tut, fingering their vitamin shots, their activated-charcoal exfoliants. This is a family park, but now look: hordes of who-knows-who from who-knows-where. Surely the council will have to step in, they agree. Surely something must be done. But summer in London stops for no one, retort the half-naked boozers, stoners and cruisers, the South London lesbians itching to get topless by the ladies' pond, the East End boys diving into the pond-not-meant-for-swimming-in, upsetting the ducklings, provoking the swans. It matters not what the families of Hampstead say or do, agrees Phil, sipping a beer he just bought from the corner shop, conceding, of course, that it is a little too early to drink, but reasoning that being alive on the Heath on the hottest day of the year is a cause for celebration. Chiselled gays in speedos parade in pairs by the men's pond, looking around to see who is looking at them. Drops of water cling to freshly shaved chests. Rihanna drawls from a phone speaker and the pong of weed is general.

They make a beeline by the mixed pond and find a spot.

They lay out their towels, sit down, survey the scene.

There's a pause in the conversation. This is her chance.

First, she'll get her pregnancy news out of the way, then she'll ask about Rosaleen.

She braces herself, she shuts her eyes, she says, 'I've got—'

'Do you—'

They laugh.

'Sorry,' she says. 'You go.'

'I was just going to ask if you wanted a beer.'

'A beer?' she says, wanting to tell him that she can't drink at the moment.

It is unimaginably hard. She can't get the words out.

Why is it so difficult? What is she afraid of?

OK. It's this: Maggie's world is queer. She goes to queer parties, queer cafés, queer festivals, queer performance art events, queer bike repair workshops, queer learn-how-to-DJ workshops, queer stick-and-poke tattoo workshops, queer reading groups, queer hairdressers, queer astrologers, queer yoga, queer screenings of classic 1990s rom-coms so that the classic 1990s rom-coms can be analysed through a contemporary queer lens. Her friends are queer. The writers she reads are queer. Ed is practically the only other straight person she knows.

And yet: here she is, having a baby with a cis man in the suburbs.

Well, why shouldn't she?

The problem is this: for Phil, a binary exists, which places reproduction, normativity and family on one side, and queerness, virility and childlessness on the other. Babygros, breast milk, pregnancy yoga: suburban, normie, boring. Ketamine, harnesses, being in a polycule: vanguard of the revolution.

For years, she's felt embarrassed for her relationship with Ed. Every time she's told Phil about her weekend plans with him, he's been disparaging, dismissive, as if her relationship were so pedestrian and dull that he couldn't lower himself to discuss it.

Look: he doesn't even invite her to his parties any more.

She suspects that Phil sees it like this: he and his friends are always fucking in toilets, fucking in parks, fucking *wherever* in this vast playground of gay pleasure, while she and Ed are in the cinema watching a superhero film, convening later in Pizza Hut to share a plate of mozzarella sticks and debate which of the Spiderman reboots was the superior of the two.

And beyond that, it's not entirely true that Ed is the only straight person she knows.

There is her extended family, and her old schoolfriends, and Renée.

Nearly all of them have babies. Her cousins have babies, the girls she went to school with have babies, Renée has Jackson, who only last week was the tiniest baby in the world, and now, without warning, has become a fully fledged child and amateur marine biologist.

Happy babies, angry babies, she has known them all. She has known babies who have just learned the word *chair. Chair!* they have announced, pointing to the nearest chair, looking seriously at whichever adult is to hand, as if to make sure that they, too, understand that they are in the presence of a new object and that new object is called *chair. Car!* they have proclaimed, and *dog dog*, too, pointing at dogs, also at ornamental front garden statues of dogs, also at cats, being too young to understand the difference. *Kiss for mama?* their mothers have solicited. *Eskimo kiss for mama? Twenty Eskimo kisses for mama?* and the baby, withholding, giggles as the mama leans in to kiss their forehead anyway. *I stole one!*

Maggie admits that she has envied it. The depth of feeling on stealing a kiss.

She has felt that nothing in her life could ever measure up to it.

She has played with babies. *Where's baby's arm?* she's said, *Where's baby's leg? Isn't that lovely?* she has gasped when the baby has ambled around the room, considered various items, eventually picking up their shoe, and passing it to her as if it were a makeshift gift, as if they were an adult who says *I wish I knew you were coming, then I could have prepared!*

She has laughed at babies, and with them, too.

She has waved goodbye to babies.

She has caught air kisses blown by pudgy fingers. She has placed the air kisses so delicately in her pocket for safekeeping, and then, boarding the bus back towards her life, thought *Why do I feel like crying?*

There was nothing like a baby to make you doubt every decision you'd ever made.

What if she reached forty, fifty, surveyed her life and said, *No, this isn't mine. This life has nothing to do with me. My life is over there, with a baby, but now it's too late to get to it.*

All of a sudden, to be over the hill. Only last year, she had looked towards the horizon, and the hill was nowhere to be seen. Now, scrambling down the descent, she realised that she'd been at the summit and not even noticed! She hadn't even paused for lunch or to admire the view or to congratulate herself for making it to the top.

And it felt good to be seen as a mother. Mothers were important. When Maggie spent time with a mother, the conversation exclusively focused on what words the baby had learned, the baby's normal or abnormal relationship to pooing. They asked few questions of Maggie's life, because why would they? What was there to say? It was only a half-life to them, and it was a half-life, too, to the relatives at family get-togethers who always prodded *You won't be young forever!* It was a half-life to the doctors who had mentioned, unsolicited, that her eggs were deteriorating in quality, declining in number, and biologically speaking, she was already past her prime.

It was a half-life to Maggie, in some ways, at certain times.

She was so used to the grief of encountering other people's children that when she actually got pregnant, she felt almost as if she could collapse in relief. It was happening now. She would make it work. The conditions weren't perfect, but they were workable, just about.

One word from Phil could puncture her optimism.

By the mixed pond, he looks at her, expectant, and passes a beer.

'Yes, please,' she says, and then, 'actually, no,' and then, 'Let's take a swim.'

They strip to their pants and hurl themselves into the blue-green water, truly freezing despite the heatwave, cold enough to make you take ten sharp intakes of breath and yelp in shock and then laugh at your own response, every muscle tense and alert with sensation.

They swim out to the nearest buoy and cling on. She stays in the pond for longer than he does, emerging almost half an hour later, shaking and breathless, her legs pale purple.

Phil looks up and smiles as she approaches. She collapses next to him and props herself up on her elbow. The heat from the sun warms their bones in tiny increments.

She takes a breath, smiles, and thinks, *Yes, OK, it's time.*

. . .

PHIL'S STOMACH LURCHES. HE THINKS OF ED'S STAR-tled face in the train station toilets, and his mind repeats the same words: *She'd feel betrayed all the same.*

'How are things going between you and Ed?' he says.

'Really great, thanks. But how about you? I'm sorry things aren't good with Keith.'

He sits up and shades his eyes from the sun.

'Well, I mean, it's not that big a deal,' he explains while another boy plops into the pond. 'I'm not sure where it's going, but we're having a nice time. It's casual. It's fun.'

She nods. 'I'm glad.'

She hugs her legs and rests her head on her knees and stares at him for a second.

'You know you can always talk to me about anything.'

'Of course.'

'Whatever you need, babe. I'm always here for you.'

Phil chafes at her tone, briefly forgetting about Ed. He has just admitted to her that things with Keith are casual and fun and she responds as if something terrible is happening.

Maggie has a history of looking at Phil's sex life as scandalous and trivial. She often gasps and says, 'You did *what*?' as Phil recounts tales of blowjobs in surprising locations and men with exotic body piercings. Even though he tells these stories as if he were a closeted stand-up comic from the sixties and she, a housewife, drunk and easily scandalised, the experiences on which the stories are based are nearly never funny in real life, often leading Phil to feel numb at best, or suicidal at worst. Since they were teenagers, Maggie has seen Phil's sex life as a form of light entertainment, not something with the potential to hurt, enrich, or transform, but something small. Phil suspects that a conservatism lurks beneath.

When they were aged twenty-one or so, and Phil was making his way through Soho's blandest gay bars, wasted on discounted shots of brightly coloured alcohol and going home with a new man every night, Maggie turned one day and said, 'If you were one of my girlfriends, I'd ask why you hate yourself so much, but you're gay, so I guess it's OK.' Phil laughed; what else could he do? He didn't know how to talk about his sex life apart from as a joke and, either way, she was right. He found himself to be repulsive, deeply so, and he used sex as a way of feeling desirable. He would lie there and try to see himself through the eyes of men who wanted him so that he might want himself as well. Even though Maggie talks as if she were a kindly missionary, and he, a wayward heretic struggling toward repentance, he never told her what happened in Burgess Park because he was afraid of what she'd say: that it was his fault for being alone in the park at night, that he was explicitly looking for sex, so what did he expect to happen, that it was funny, ridiculous, that he was young and gay and male and therefore *always* horny, *always* consenting to sex, someone who *can't* be assaulted.

Even if she didn't say any of this, he was afraid that she'd think it. He thought it too.

Sitting beside her at the ponds, he says, 'Things with Keith are great. The sex is hot. He's still with Louis, and I see other people too, and neither of us care about monogamy.'

Maggie looks away.

'Sounds nice,' she says.

Phil continues, 'We're having a party tonight actually. A solstice thing. The same one we do every year. Sorry I haven't mentioned it to you. Wasn't sure if you'd be into it.'

'Why wouldn't I be into it?'

'I never see you at parties any more.'

'I literally went to a party last night.'

'Well, come along if you're free.'

She pauses, then smiles from one side of her mouth.

'Alright. I will.'

They lie back on the grass and let the conversation lapse. Phil already feels guilty for responding defensively. For the most part, he loves being with Maggie. He wishes he saw her more often, but friendship in London means bumping into each other once or twice a year, saying you need to hang out more, and never doing anything about it.

'What else has been going on?' he says. 'Done any painting lately?'

She looks at the pond.

'I haven't, actually.'

'I was thinking recently about the last film you made. It was so good, that.'

'It wasn't really.'

'Come on, what are you talking about? It was beautiful. You've gotta make another.'

She rips a clump of grass and shreds it into tiny portions.

'I threw out my art stuff.'

'What? When?'

'Yesterday.'

He looks at her. She looks around.

'Maybe we could go for a walk?' she says.

He speaks softly. 'Sure. Where?'

'I don't know. Primrose Hill? St John's Wood?'

'Yeah, great.' He pauses, then cracks a smile. 'You know, I read that Rihanna lives around there now.'

'What? That can't be true. Why would Rihanna live in London?'

'I don't know, but she does.'

He shows her a picture on his phone from a tabloid newspaper.

'Should we try to find it?' he says, half-joking, half-not.

He laughs, and she laughs too.

'OK,' she says. 'Let's go.'

. . .

WHY HAS PHIL SUGGESTED THAT THEY LOOK FOR Rihanna's house? Why has Maggie agreed? It's hard to explain. Neither are particularly big fans, though of course they have enjoyed her hits over the years. Of course, they have screamed the lyrics to 'Only Girl In the World' after discounted shots of sambuca at student parties in the early 2010s, and of course they have choked back tears to 'We Found Love' while watching their crush kiss someone else on the dance floor, on more than one occasion. Of course, they have remarked upon how good her voice has become since she leaned into the rich Bajan inflections of her accent, the raspy grit of her lower register. Of course, they know she is beautiful, and talented, of course, too.

It doesn't matter that they're looking for Rihanna's house, specifically. What matters is that they're looking together. Too often, the city is no more than a grim backdrop for morning and evening commutes, the work hours sandwiched between, but this quest has turned it into a playground for exploration, as if finding it were a mission to complete in a video game. What will they do when they find it? Perhaps pose for a photo; perhaps not. Phil often feels awkward in front of a camera, but

Maggie has a great knack for physical comedy. She will think of something funny to do. The end goal is beside the point, the house itself unimportant. In this moment, strolling down Finchley Road – bare arms swinging, chatting excitedly, everything easy – what matters is that it's summer. What matters is that they're best friends. Neither has ever felt so comfortable around another person.

'So, my news,' she says.

'Yes, your news!'

She speaks faster than he's ever heard her speak.

'It's quite big, actually, and I'm sorry I haven't told you yet, but everything's moved very quickly, and we haven't had long to make up our minds on things. It's sort of a ticking time bomb really, and we have to do one thing or another, so we've made a choice.'

'Babe, what are you on about? This sounds like the plot of *Die Hard*.'

'It's as different from *Die Hard* as you could possibly imagine.'

'Are you going to tell me or not?'

'Yes. Well. The thing is that I'm pregnant.'

Phil stops in his tracks.

Tell her! he thinks. She's building a life with him. An irreversible life. If Ed conceals this from her, what else might he conceal? What if, years from now, Ed is still cruising train station toilets for sex? What if, years from now, Ed finally gets it together and leaves her, and she finds out that Phil had known all along and kept it from her?

He hesitates.

What if she thinks I'm a snake? he thinks.

He closes his eyes.

What if I *am* a snake?

He gulps.

He turns to face her and puts his hand on her shoulder and says the next thing that comes to mind, which, regrettably, are the words, 'Oh my God, Maggie, I'm so sorry.'

She shrugs his hand away and keeps walking.

'No, Phil, it's a good thing. We're keeping the baby.'

'Oh, right. Sure. Congratulations. Maggie, it's just that—'

'Hang on. Do you mind if we pop in here? I just want to get a Coke.'

They're standing beneath the shadow of the Finchley Road Waitrose, much cooler here than it was at the Heath, and Maggie goes inside without waiting for a response.

Phil follows.

'Maggie, that's huge,' he calls after her. 'I mean, congrats. I'm thrilled for you.'

'Yeah, thanks. I'm quite thirsty actually. Just need a Coke.'

'Are you OK? Should we not stop and talk?'

'In a sec, Phil, I'm just – I'm just fucking thirsty, to be honest.'

He trails behind while she speeds up, fingering the fancy snacks and juices, products which describe themselves as having extra protein, reduced salt, zero sugar.

She grabs a Coke from the fridge and hovers there for a few more seconds. She looks completely dazed. With her eyes still fixed on the supermarket's meagre selection of canned fizzy drinks, she mumbles vaguely as if to no one, 'And we're moving back to Basildon.'

She speeds towards the checkout, and he hurries after her.

'What?' he says. 'Why are you moving to Basildon?'

'Why wouldn't we move to Basildon?'

'Sorry, no, I don't mean to dismiss it. It's just that you hate it there.'

'I don't hate it there.'

'Well, you used to hate it.'

'Not everyone can afford to hate their hometown.'

'So you're moving because it's cheaper?'

She turns around to face him. They're in the pasta aisle.

'Phil, I'm thirty now, and I want some security, you know? That's why I'm going. I've never been able to plan any more than a few months into the future, so many shit work contracts and dodgy landlords, and I'm more risk averse than I used to be, and the baby, and Basildon, are futures that I can count on. No matter what happens, me and Ed will be parents. We'll have our child, and we'll have each other, and we'll be a family. Not everyone can afford to fuck around in London forever. Some people need a serious life eventually.'

Phil, taken aback, frowns and smiles at the same time.

He says, 'I have a serious life.'

'I'm not saying you don't.'

'You're implying it.'

'Can you not be happy for me?'

'I am. It's just that Ed—'

'It's just that he's what?'

'I'm not sure if he's right for you.'

Maggie pauses.

She has wondered before if Ed is right for her too.

It is, at times, baffling to her that she is still dating her teenage boyfriend.

Every week of art school she thought of breaking up with him, but she always backed out at the last minute. Out of concern for his feelings, yes, and concern for her own feelings, and the comfort of having someone to come home to. Her early years in London hurt. She felt inadequate, bumbling, she didn't know how to order at restaurants, she was always mispronouncing the names of fashion brands. She had never been to Rome or Prague. In compensation, she'd softened the hard edges of her Essex accent, regretted it, hardened again.

With Ed, she could simply unfurl. She still can. In all other parts of her life, she's a performer. With him, she can be quiet. A silence comes over her, and everything is still, and she sinks into a love beyond analysis. Usually, she looks at the world and tries to explain it. She places her feelings within a broader political and social context. With Ed, nothing has a broader context. There is no history or politics or economics or art. Nothing is to do with anything. It's just love lodged in her belly, too big and too old and too deep to be described.

Phil has no idea what is or isn't right for her.

She says, 'OK. Fine. Thanks for the input,' and hurries towards the checkout.

Phil slows down then and lets the moment sink in.

It wasn't such a long time ago that their lives were remarkably similar. From their birth until their late twenties, they shared nearly all the same formative experiences. If something happened to one of them, it could be almost guaranteed to happen to the other.

All of a sudden, her life is different, and his is the same, which is to say, his life is small, while hers is big. *She's having a baby.* No matter how much queer theory he reads, he can't help but think that anything he ever does, feels, or says will be trivial by comparison.

Of course, he loves his home, his friends, his lovers, and although he's always had a sense that one day he'd have to get a move on and make plans for the future, the future was too far away to be worth considering. With Maggie's announcement, she's ushered the future into the present, and Phil feels like he's fallen behind. He is fucking around with someone else's boyfriend, living in a filthy semi-derelict building with eleven other people and one horny cat, and working in a pointless, underpaid job that he doesn't care about. Before, he'd seen himself as a vivacious young queer, the entire city spread before him, not held down by the trappings of a normal life. Now, he feels like a lonely old gay, like the old men who stand for hours beneath the communal showers at the gym, stroking their semi-flaccid dicks and trying to attract the attention of hot disinterested twinks. When he was seven, his mother broke down in tears at the kitchen table and told him and his brother that she knew they weren't gay – *Of course my sons aren't gay!* – but still, they should never be unkind to gay people, because they lived a lonely life, grew old alone, got shunned by entire towns, lost control of their bowels, died destitute, got skin lesions, had no one to care for them in their hour of need. Phil feels like the tragic figures of his mother's paranoid fantasies.

In the sharp chill of the supermarket, he feels suddenly underdressed, a little vulnerable, his leg hair standing to attention. There are families everywhere, expensively dressed Belsize Park children – the musical quality of their bespoke first names – demanding upmarket desserts from their parents and au pairs. The hot rush of the Heath feels like a lifetime ago. The bright day seems grey. He takes out his phone and writes a message to Keith. He wants to say exactly how he feels. Nothing seems more important. Instead, he just writes *you missed a great swim* and adds a winky-face. Keith writes back, *I'm sorry!! I'll be back in the house soon. Can we talk?* just as Maggie finishes paying.

It's nearly 1 p.m. and Phil hums with anxiety.

'I'm going to head off,' he says.

Her face drops.

'Come on, mate. What are you talking about? I bought you a KitKat Chunky.'

'I know. I'm sorry. It's just that my mum is coming around and I want to have time to talk to Keith beforehand. He's on his way now.' He takes the KitKat Chunky and adds, 'But let's talk more later, yeah?'

Maggie sighs, and then smiles widely. It's a smile that floods her whole face. Maggie has endless reserves of kindness for any situation. She's always ready to smooth things over. 'Don't worry about it, my love. You should go catch up with Keith. And send my love to your mum and dad too, yeah? I'd love to see them soon.'

'I will. Thanks, babe. See you at the party then?'

'Of course. I'll bring Ed.'

Phil tenses at Ed's name. He remembers that he still hasn't told her about yesterday.

Still, he leaves Waitrose and walks to the station. He gets a Jubilee Line to London Bridge, and almost sprints to his house, hundreds of things he could say to Keith forming and reforming in his head, none of which, he knows, will sound as eloquent as he imagines.

. . .

THE SUMMER OF THE SHOPPING TROLLEY WAS THE ONE time that Kyle Connolly played a leading role in Phil and Maggie's story; after that, he became a bit part. Kyle Connolly, who had smoked a cigarette, Kyle Connolly, who was unspeakably glamorous; he went to a different school, moved to a new estate, was wrenched from their world on the brink of adolescence.

The day after Maggie found them in bed, Phil walked up to Kyle on the pavement, rehearsing a pre-scripted joke about last night's episode of *Buffy the Vampire Slayer*. Kyle walked in the opposite direction and didn't acknowledge that Phil had been there at all.

He called at Kyle's house twice more that summer, and on both occasions his mother said he wasn't at home, even though Phil could see Kyle's trainers behind the sliding doors of the porch extension, white and red and a little dusty, their sides bisected by a Nike logo, that great swooping tick, and Phil couldn't understand why Kyle didn't want to see him.

Soon, Kyle became a myth. They would spend long hours sketching bizarre fictional biographies for him. When they told a joke about Kyle, they weren't really telling a joke about Kyle. Maggie and Phil were projecting an image of their own friendship. When they said the word 'Kyle' they were reminding each other that they had been friends since they were little, that they had history, that their lives were populated by the same characters.

Since then, Kyle Connolly has, in fact, become moderately famous. He writes opinion pieces for fashion websites about how gay men need to embrace body positivity and treat each other with kindness. Every few days he posts pictures of his ass to Instagram, captioned with re-contextualised Audre Lorde quotes and cryptic yet vaguely poetic messages about taking risks, seizing the day, and rejecting toxic energy from your life. Last year, his wedding to his long-term partner was featured in a reality TV show about 'bridezillas' and Maggie bought a subscription to the Wedding Channel so that she and Phil could watch it. They've seen him on the streets of East London on more than one occasion, and although they've both been too shy to approach, Maggie and Phil have daydreamed about a reunion.

8

DEBS CYCLES TO ALI'S FLAT AT I P.M. TO COLLECT AN amp for the party, a cart fixed to the back of her bike. It's a short trip, one she's made before, but this time, it's not short enough.

She hasn't been there since they broke up a year ago, but she's often cycled past it. She's not sure what she hopes will happen. That she will see Ali at the door and their eyes will meet, and Ali will think: Debs looks great. Her hair is better like that, and her backpack looks expensive. *Debs! It's so good to see you!* she'll say and they'll talk, and Ali will think: I never should have left her. Is that what Debs expects to happen? Is that what she dreamed of in the house meeting today when tasks were being assigned for the party? As soon as someone was asked to go to Ali's place to collect the amp, Debs shouted *I'll do it!* more enthusiastically than necessary and everyone looked around awkwardly.

She approaches now. What will she say at the door? *I'm here to see Ali.*

No, of course not. She can't say that. What are the right words?

She's sweating. She shouldn't have cycled. When is this heatwave finally going to break? Every day of the past week has promised to be the day it would finally rain, and still no rain. Everything, everywhere, is parched, the air so heavy it could crush you.

She knocks: the door swings open: Ali, her T-shirt stained with clay from the pottery wheel, her hands brick-red and wet. Once they had sex while Ali was in the middle of making a vase, and her hands, still slimy with unset clay, clawed at Deb's back, her neck, her ass; they left handprints; the handprints dried, then cracked, and Debs never wanted to wash them off.

Ali looks at her. No one says anything.

What is Debs here to do? She can't even remember.

She stammers, stutters, smiles.

'Hi,' she says. 'I'm here to collect Ali.'

Ali laughs, says, 'Nice to see you too, babe,' and Debs, realising her mistake, mumbles towards an explanation. She's cut off: her phone vibrates in her pocket. It's Keith.

'Hang on,' she says. 'Hello?'

Keith's voice on the other end.

'Did you see the letter from the landlord?' he says.

'What are you talking about?'

'Can you get back here now? It's quite urgent.'

. . .

ROSALEEN IS TAKING A LOAF OF BREAD FROM THE OVEN while a scientist speaks on the television.

'Within the next few hours, the crane will lift the whale aboard the barge. The barge, in turn, will race down the

Thames, through the estuary, and back out to sea. From there, and we must be honest here, we just don't know what's going to happen. We have no real idea. We want to get her as close to her North Atlantic home as we possibly can, but without the appropriate infrastructure, we may have to release her at Margate, much closer to the coast than we would like. Although blood samples have been promising, and she may not be as ill as we had feared, her injuries are undeniable and serious. Her survival is far from assured.'

Steve passes through the room, ferrying laundry from the washing line to the bedroom, and pausing to observe the television he remarks, 'She looks like Lady Gaga.'

Rosaleen scoffs. 'And how would you know what Lady Gaga looks like?'

'I don't live under a rock. I'm a man of culture.'

He laughs, but she isn't in the mood.

'Where are you taking that laundry? It won't be dry yet.'

'It's going to rain later.'

'What?' she says, craning her neck to glimpse a pale blue sky beyond the kitchen window. 'I'll believe it when I see it,' she huffs, and then, 'we need to get a move on. I still have to shower and find something to wear and do my hair and pack a bag, and knowing you, you'll end up on the toilet for ten minutes just as we're about to leave.'

Steve ignores the toilet comment.

She continues, 'And the bread! Does Phil even eat bread any more? So many people go gluten-intolerant now – whether their intolerance is real or imagined, I've yet to decide – but either way, I'm not sure if bread is the done thing. What do you think?'

He puts the laundry basket down so that he can put his arms around her.

'He'll love the bread. Don't worry so much about it.'

'It's too late at this stage anyway: the bread is baked.'

'Your bread is lovely. Anyone would be thrilled.'

With that, he kisses her on the head and continues towards the bedroom.

That's when Rosaleen pauses, as if she had the time to pause, and stands, open-mouthed, in front of the TV, watching the scientist gesture towards the crane.

It's a proper crane, like you might see on a building site.

The news camera pans from the scientist towards the bustling crowd, and it brings to mind the wedding of Diana and Charles, the sense of occasion, the feeling of being alive during an important moment in history, even though Rosaleen privately thought at the time that people in this country were nutjobs for caring about the royals so much. That feeling was irresistible though, of being part of something. She wonders if Phil would come to see the whale with her, so that he can look back and say, 'Me and my mum were there on the day when the whale was saved from the Thames.' The news footage will be featured in nostalgic TV shows that are broadcast over Christmas, the bloated evening hours when you've eaten too much to move, trapped in the glow of the fairy lights, and if she and Phil were together for such an event, an event that people will always recall, then she'd be a major event in his own life too, a major memory in his mind, a person who looms large.

'We need to leave soon!' she shouts, although she's not even sure if Steve's within earshot at all. 'We need to leave!' she shouts once more, panicked they'll miss their train.

She leaves the bread to cool and rushes upstairs to get dressed.

They make their train just in time. They arrive in London a little before 2 p.m., and part ways at Fenchurch Street, wishing each other luck. Steve travels north on a 149 to meet Callum and Ed, and Rosaleen crosses London Bridge by foot, on her way to Phil.

. . .

SOON AFTER, STEVE STANDS IN THE CROWDED PUB IN Tottenham with Callum and Ed, trying to get served. He notices a tension between them. He has no intention of remarking upon it.

Callum is quiet, tetchy, insists on being the one to order and pay for the drinks. He leans over the bar with a fifty-pound note tucked between his thumb and index finger while Steve asks Ed about Joan. 'You know my mum,' Ed says. 'She has her days.'

Steve nods conspiratorially as if he, a married man, knows all about the 'days' of middle-aged women. He says, 'Rosaleen is the same. It's always one thing or the other.'

Ed laughs.

'Don't I know it!' he says, every inch of him aware of every inch of Callum.

They find a table, they sit down with their pints, Steve rises again to go to the toilet, and Ed rises too, afraid of being left alone with his friend. 'I need to go as well,' he declares, childlike, too loud. He stands, knocks over his chair, scrambles to pick it up – excruciating – and everyone looks at him like this was a weird thing to do, which is fair, because it was.

Back at the table, he is shy. He can't stop watching Callum.

Maybe it would be fine for Callum to know. Would it not? Callum is coarse, sure, and lashes out at people because of his own insecurities, but he has a kind streak too, has he not? He wants to love and be loved, and he's not homophobic in spite of appearances, not in the true sense. At school, whenever anyone insulted Phil behind his back, Callum would punch them square in the jaw and make sure that Phil never found out, not wanting Phil to feel like a burden or an imposition. Callum would get into fights a few times a week in Phil's defence, and Callum, at the time, was not a strong fighter; in the end, he got beaten up even more than Phil did. He even bloodied Ed's nose and blackened his two eyes after what Ed did to Phil during their last week at school. Ed didn't try to defend himself; he knew he deserved it.

Callum orders more drinks. He returns with three pints sloshing over his wrists and onto his shoes and jeans. Ed places his phone face up on the table. Callum takes a long sip and asks if Steve remembers the matches he took him to as a child, but Steve can't recall.

'You have to remember. You used to have me up on your shoulders and we'd be all going mad. Ed was there too. And Mum and Phil, the odd time. I'd be up on your shoulders.'

Steve's face creases in concentration.

'I don't think I remember that. Are you sure it was me? It could have been your uncle. Or Ed's dad. Did your dad ever take the two of you to the football, Ed?'

'Dad, it was definitely you. It was. You took us to the football all the time.'

'Are you sure it wasn't the playground? Or the cinema. We took you to the cinema.'

'It was the football, Dad.'

'Yeah.'

'You'd have me on your shoulders. It was like a tradition.'

Ed remembers how Rosaleen, Callum's mum, used to always say that things were a family tradition, even if they'd only done them on one occasion, or never done them at all.

'It was a long time ago,' says Steve. 'You should ask your mum.'

Ed's phone pings with a text. From the corner of his eye, he can see Maggie's name.

Downing his pint in one go, he excuses himself to go outside.

He leans on the wall of the pub, holds the phone in front of his face.

His eyes are clamped shut. He tries to coax them open.

On the count of ten, I'll open my eyes, he says.

Instead, he counts to thirty. He struggles to breathe.

He prizes his eyelids apart and reads.

. . .

AFTER PHIL LEAVES MAGGIE AT WAITROSE, SHE WRITES a text to Ed: *told phil about the baby. Had a weird argument in the supermarket. Scandalised the local yummy mummies I think lol.*

She quietly groans. Why does she always make a joke?

He responds within moments: *Do you want to talk?*

He calls without waiting for a response. She tells him about her morning with Phil, the argument in Waitrose, and soon her humour gives way to anger.

'It was just so weird, Ed. The first thing he did when I told him was offer his commiserations. It was like I had a month to live. Literally. Like my life was over.'

Ed pauses for a second and then says, 'I'm sorry, babe. Maybe he's jealous.'

'I really don't think so. He looked at me as if he thought the baby was a tumour.'

'His mum's not well. He's probably out of sorts.'

She remembers with a jolt Rosaleen's cancer and feels guilty for forgetting it.

'He didn't even mention that,' she admits.

'It takes time. My dad was sick for a year before I told Callum.'

'You don't tell each other anything though.'

'You'd be surprised.'

She paces around for a second, and then slumps against the wall.

'Phil told me that I should make another film.'

'He's right.'

'It's hard to imagine.'

'Why is it hard to imagine?'

She pauses.

'It just feels that up until now, our lives could have turned out lots of different ways. We could have got different jobs. Lived in different places. It's going to be harder now. And I don't want to be working in these jobs forever. I don't want to be dependent on these people so that I can put food on the table, and it's not just for me and you any more. It's for another person. A baby. I don't want to be doing this when I'm eighty.'

'Babe,' he says with softness and tiredness. 'I'm sorry that you had a rough morning. But you will not be doing this when you're eighty. There's not a chance of it.'

'You don't know that though.'

'I do know it. I know it because I won't let it happen.'

There's a pause during which neither of them speaks.

She thinks that Ed, like her own dad, is a little too reckless in his optimism. He says he won't let it happen, as if any of this were even within his power.

Then he says, 'Why don't you ditch the hen party? Let's go for a walk instead.'

'What? I thought you wanted me to go to the hen.'

'This is more important. I want to see you.'

'I'm not going to pull out last minute. It took weeks to convince Ali to come.'

'Well, let me pick you up in the car afterwards. I'm sure you'll be tired.'

'OK. Yeah, that would be good actually.'

Silence again.

'What are you thinking about?' she says.

'I've been thinking of the places I want to show our kid someday.'

'What would you show them, then?'

'Well, so many things!' says Ed, setting out the scene. He says he'll show them the riverbank. He'll teach them the names of seabirds and little wildflowers and he'll invent new names too. He'll tell them about a monster who lives in the water, and the monster will be a river monster, and although people will think of the monster as very scary, it will simply be misunderstood. Literally misunderstood, he says, because it won't be an English speaker and will have a language of its own, understood by no one but itself. Ed, the little one, and Maggie if she'd like to get involved, will teach themselves the river monster's language, and they'll go to the river on Saturdays and they'll all make a hilarious and indescribable noise and Ed will pretend he sees the river monster come out from the river and the little one will say, 'Where where where!' and Ed will say, 'Over there! Over there! Do you not hear?' and then Ed will listen for some noise, a boat in the water, and he will pretend that this noise is the monster's wailing, and he himself will translate. The monster will say something along the lines of, 'Finally my people are here! I've been waiting so long and I've been so alone and so misunderstood!' and they'll all have a laugh together, basically.

'OK,' she says, 'but tell me again, what's the noise to make the monster appear?'

'Babe, let me remind you that I'm in Tottenham with 100,000 screaming blokes, all bolloxed, and let's just say I got a few funny looks when I made the noise a second ago.'

'Don't worry. They'll think it's a chant and you're just an enthusiastic fan.'

'The things I do for you,' he groans, and then, '*Ah ah ah ah ah ah ooooieieiei ygraum.*'

Maggie falls about the place laughing, and says, 'OK. OK. Great, thank you, that was really helpful. But just so I'm clear, can you tell me one more time? Just want to be certain.'

'You're pushing your luck.'

'I know. I'm sorry. It's just a very amusing noise.'

'Well, I'm glad to be of amusement,' he says, and then makes the noise once more.

They both laugh uncontrollably, and then, in the silent gap after the laughter ends but before new words begin, she wants badly to hold him. She doesn't want to be separated even by a mere few hours. She tells him how she wants to kiss him right now, and he tells her how the shape of her body in his arms makes him feel entirely whole. He tells her that it feels as if his body were a custom-made, bespoke container, specifically designed for holding this one rare, very precious substance, which is her. That's how it feels. Like this is what he was made for.

9

WHEN PHIL GETS HOME, KEITH ASKS TO MEET HIM ON the fire escape that leads from the first floor of the warehouse to the courtyard below and Phil promises to join him in a second.

He doesn't know what Keith wants to talk about. A tentative part of him wonders if something has happened with Louis. He tries not to let the thought get ahead of itself.

Someone, somehow has built a seven-foot-tall sculpture in the hallway, made of Perspex and LED, and someone else is hanging battered old theatre lamps from the rafters. Old disco tracks waft from an unidentified source as the warehouse transforms into a club.

Phil rushes to his room and grabs the book on London clay. He opens it and scans the inscription. 'Keith,' he has written. 'Before I met you, I never knew that the earth beneath London was made out of clay – one of many deep things I learned from you.'

It's not so bad really. And either way, he means it.

He clutches the book and closes his eyes and breathes through his nostrils.

Oh God, he thinks.

'Oh God,' he says out loud.

He practically skips the few steps back to the fire escape, and finds Keith there, already smoking. Three unwieldy tomato plants grow from pots on the stairs – scorched half to death, Phil says they won't survive another dry day; Keith says it's going to rain later anyway – and Phil feels, as he always does when alone with Keith, a little shiver of pleasure. He is smiling already, almost giggling. With Keith, everything is funny. Mundane activities are laden with surprising new meanings. Phil, absent-mindedly, runs his index finger along the front of Keith's T-shirt. With his other hand, he clings to the book like the edge of a cliff.

'I've got something for you,' he says.

He passes Keith the book. Keith takes it, smiles slightly, and says, 'Wow.'

'It's a book,' says Phil. 'I mean, obviously it's a book. It's a book I thought you'd like. It's about the geology of London. I saw it in the charity shop and picked it up for you.'

This last sentence is not strictly true. Phil didn't see the book in a charity shop; he bought it online after hours of research. He watched YouTube reviews and read academic papers and followed geology influencers on Instagram. The book sat in his shopping basket for four days before he clicked 'Pay Now'. He almost backed out on four separate occasions. He feared that it would be too dramatic a gesture, that it would make him look ridiculous, pathetic, desperate to love and to be loved in return, which of course, he was.

'That's so kind of you,' says Keith, but to Phil's alarm, he has a pained look.

He hasn't seen the inscription. Phil wants to point it out.
Keith takes a deep breath.

He says, 'I take it you've seen the letter.'

'What letter? Is that what you want to talk about?'

'You don't know? Sorry, I thought Debs told you.'

'What are you talking about?'

'The letter from the landlord. We're getting evicted.'

Phil involuntarily touches Keith's shoulder.

'We've been given a month's notice. The landlord is sell-
ing.' Keith looks down at the courtyard, quizzical, puzzled by
his own words. 'I'm sorry I ran off this morning.'

Phil doesn't know what to say. He says, 'It's OK.'

'Part of the reason I left was to see Louis.'

'I know.'

'We'd been planning to have a conversation about something. Well, the conversation has been going on for a few
months to be honest, but it's starting to become more real.'

'What are you talking about?'

'Well' – he looks at Phil – 'we've been thinking of leaving
London.'

Phil realises that his hand has been on Keith's shoulder the
entire time, which now seems like an inappropriate gesture. He
pulls back, puts his hand in his pocket, takes it out again, then
grips the railing. 'Oh. Right. Of course. Cool. Erm, where?'

'Folkestone. Louis's aunt owned a house, and she died,
and now no one's living in it. He wants to go until the academic year starts again. Maybe longer. His mum says she'll sell
it eventually, but she's got so much money that I suspect she's
in no rush.'

Alarm spreads through every part of Phil's body.

Still, all he says is, 'OK, well, cool. Fair enough. Best of luck with it.'

'We haven't decided for sure. I mean, I haven't decided for sure.'

How should a person speak? What words do people say? He asks, 'Well, what are the pros and cons?' but it sounds like a dumb question before he's even finished asking it.

'Well, there are things that could keep me in London.'

'Like what?'

'Well, there's my friends, and we've got our thing . . .'

'Yeah.' Phil raises his head. He holds his breath.

'And sometimes I wonder where that's going.'

Phil hesitates. He can tell that it's his turn to speak, to share his own thoughts and feelings. His thoughts and feelings are that he doesn't want Keith to leave, or get evicted, or move out, or move on, or for things to ever be any different from how they were this morning when he was on his way to big Tesco, thinking the future was big and full of possibilities.

He says, 'I mean, our thing isn't really a thing, strictly speaking.'

'What do you mean?' says Keith, a little on edge now.

'It's just, you know, casual. Isn't it? You shouldn't make decisions based on me.'

His voice trembles. He feels as if he might fall over. He rapidly analyses but can't grasp his thoughts. It's happening too quickly. He's hurt that Keith's leaving. Is that it? He's hurt and wants to hurt Keith in turn. Or not hurt Keith, exactly, but rather prove himself as someone above hurt, to save himself from the degradation of being a person with capacity for pain.

Keith says, 'Yeah?'

'Just do what's right for you.'

'OK. Alright. Fair enough.'

'You're going to have a great time.'

'Hopefully.'

'You'll swim in the sea.'

'Yeah. Feels a bit surreal.'

'Anyway, I better go get ready. Me and mum are going to Westfield.'

'Phil.'

'Sorry. I gotta go. See you later, man.'

Phil rushes down the corridor.

Man. Why did Phil say *man*? He spoke to Keith like a bloke, not a lover.

He makes his way back to his bedroom. He can hear news of the eviction filter through the warehouse as people down tools to discuss it in upset voices. He hears someone say that they should cancel the party tonight. He hears someone else say they should have a bigger party than ever. He doesn't stop to talk. He no longer has any opinion on the party.

He goes to his bedroom to take a breather before preparing to meet his mum. He closes the door and bends down to retrieve a stale sliver of toast from the floor but instead of picking it up, lowers his entire body and lies on the dusty rug, which is meant to look antique, as if it belongs to a Victorian gentlemen's club, but really is from IKEA, dark red and richly patterned. You don't notice the dirt if you're standing up, but from down on the floor, Phil can see that it's filthy, flecked with severed toenails, cat hair, dust and dead flies.

He admits to himself that this rug has not been hoovered in quite some time.

He used to fantasise about moving to the countryside with Keith, or to a smaller city like Glasgow or Sheffield, or even just going on holiday to one of these places. They always said that they'd go to Derek Jarman's house in Dungeness, to look at the gardens, the nuclear power plant from *Modern Nature*. Folkestone isn't too far from Dungeness. Maybe that's why they're going: to turn their lives into a Derek Jarman role-playing exercise, to imagine themselves as bohemian, gentle, close to the earth. Phil, for his part, had fantasised about comfort. He had wanted to wake up hungover and have someone to watch YouTube with. He had wanted them to go to Barcelona together, do the Spanish Civil War Walking Tour, see the old hotels that the anarchist unions briefly, spectacularly collectivised, history invisible to the naked eye unless you knew where to look. He had wanted to take in the sights of a new city together, drink beers in an ornate old square overrun with tourists, get drunk on the nude beach, dicks quite shrivelled by the cool sea and Mediterranean breeze, among the seedy middle-aged gays and elderly straight swingers, sunburnt thighs and brilliant blue skies. He had wanted the guarantee of love, someone to protect and feel protected by.

These are now desperately humiliating things to have wanted.

He is desperately humiliated.

Well, Frank was right. This is the problem with polyamory, relationship anarchy, ethical non-monogamy, whatever other terms. You've got no security. Nobody stays.

He thinks of Maggie and Ed, the family they'll have, the home. He envies them, their legitimacy, how everyone would look on their relationship as a real and serious thing. On paper,

Phil's relationship with Keith never existed at all. Just like their tenancy of this warehouse, Phil and Keith's relationship was under the table, implicit, unofficial.

He lies on that floor and quietly cries. Embarrassing. The melodrama. He tries to lighten the mood. Pop songs about this very activity are common enough for it to be considered a cliché. He thinks of karaoke. He can hardly listen to a song without imagining himself on stage. As a child, he used to picture himself as a pop star, but is now content with the humble dream of a modestly well-received karaoke performance. The problem is that when he sings, he becomes so self-conscious that it's hard to enjoy himself. Not like Keith, who is excellent at karaoke; funny and self-deprecating without being annoying, and a decent singer too. Another problem is that Phil looks to karaoke to be a profound tool of communication, a sacred exchange, when really, it's no more than casual fun on a night out. Phil is always demanding that mundane activities take on a significance above their station.

The doorbell rings. His mother is here.

. . .

ROSALEEN SITS ON THE CAT-HAIR-CARPETED COUCH IN Phil's kitchen. Phil arranges biscuits on a plate, and she can think of nothing to do but ask for the WiFi password, interrupting Phil mid-sentence, who has been babbling ceaselessly, nervously, and somewhat incoherently about the massive improvements Tesco has made to their own-brand range of biscuits over the past few years. He calls out the password, and although it doesn't work when she types it into her phone, she continues to frantically enter it over and over again, until eventually, she types a lower-case 'c' instead of an upper-case 'C' and Phil, still in the midst of a monologue about big Tesco, places the plate of biscuits on front of her.

She tries to think of things to talk about.

She tries to keep the conversation going.

But there is too much happening; too many people coming in and out, building things, cooking things, singing songs, exchanging gossip. Someone is always making a pot of coffee. One girl walks in, talking as she enters, addressing the room at large and no one in particular, complaining about the *suburban mums* she works with.

She stays for nearly twenty minutes without asking Rosaleen her name.

Rosaleen looks around, but there is too much to look at. There are too many people coming in and out, too many dirty dishes, too many stains, too many broken toys and books and fake plants and real plants and cushions piled around the place, too much grease caked into the cooker, too much black mould growing from the corners of every windowsill.

There is too much to say and no way to say it. It's impossible for anyone to describe the detail of their life, the minute-to-minute transition from one thought to the next, and unless you speak to a person on a regular basis, how can you know what their life is like? You can't. She wants to know everything: his love life, whether he's still with Keith, and if so, what's Keith like, is he kind, does he treat him alright? She wants to know about his job, his manager, if he's doing OK for money, does he get the bus to work, does he read a book on the bus, and if so, what book is he reading, and what does he do to unwind when he gets home in the evening, does he watch films, does he watch the telly, and if he does watch the telly, does he pay for Sky or Virgin or Netflix, or does he download it illegally and is he ever afraid of getting caught? All the while, the bread sits in her handbag. What words should a person use when giving a loaf of bread to another? I've made this bread, or you might enjoy this bread, or here: it's a loaf, it's yours. It should be simple, but it's not.

'So how are things?' says Phil.

She thinks, '*I've got cancer.*'

She says, 'We've no news.'

'Do you want another biscuit?'

'Thanks. These are lovely biscuits.'

'I'm glad you like them.'

She pulls at her sleeves. She thinks, '*I've got something to tell you.*'

She says, 'It must be lovely having breakfast in here.'

'It is.'

'What do you have for breakfast yourself?'

'Usually porridge. Sometimes I stir peanut butter into it.'

'Peanut butter in porridge? I've never heard that one before.'

'It's nice.'

'Porridge is great for energy, isn't it?'

'It is.'

'It is.'

The conversation continues like this until the biscuits are gone and the loose thread on Rosaleen's sleeve has unravelled to such an extent that a gaping hole emerges, even though she only bought it in the Boxing Day sales, and it had seemed like good quality at the time.

She remembers: the whale.

'Have you heard of this whale?' she says, ready to suggest they go and see it right now.

'Me and Keith went to see it earlier.'

Oh, she thinks, pausing for a second before realising it's her turn to speak.

'Oh,' she says aloud, pausing again, and embarrassed by the pause, she says in a louder voice than intended, 'I was hoping to see it myself.'

He nods, says something about how it'll probably be there for a few more days.

'Will I get to meet Keith?' she goes on.

'Maybe. I'm not sure where he's gone. He might be in his room.'

The doorbell rings. A man crashes through the kitchen on his way to answer. From what Rosaleen can gather, the only way to the front door is through the kitchen. He pauses briefly to say 'Hello! Nice to meet you. My name's Keith. I'll be back in a second' before disappearing again, and returning a moment later with another man, who warmly bends down to shake her hands, maintaining alarming eye contact the whole time, as if he were a politician dependent on her vote. 'Hi, hi, hi, so pleased to meet you. Louis.'

'Nice to meet you,' she says. 'I'm Rosaleen. Are you Phil's housemate?'

Louis clears his throat, smiles, and says, 'Keith is, yes, but I'm just an occasional lodger. I'm not stopping long, I just need to collect some tools. Are you having a nice day?'

'We are. We'll go to Westfield in a bit, won't we, Phil?'

'It's such a beautiful day,' says Louis. 'You're Irish, aren't you? There's actually an interesting bit of Irish history around here that you might like to see. There's a graveyard in Southwark, where these nineteenth-century Irish labourers are buried. They must have come here around the time of the Famine, but some of the headstones are very beautiful.'

Rosaleen nods, thinking that this was a strange thing to say.

'Have you Irish family yourself?' she says.

'Me? No, no. My great-grandfather was Greek, but apart from that, all English. I've never actually been to Ireland – that's terrible, isn't it? – but I must go sometime.'

People in England are always apologising for having never been to Ireland, as if what they do with their annual leave is a matter of grave importance to Rosaleen. They speak as if they're royals, with a God-given duty to travel to all corners of the Empire.

'I'll be back in two seconds,' says Phil abruptly.

He leaves the room, followed by Keith.

'There's been such beautiful *big* poetry to emerge from that island,' continues Louis, unperturbed and possibly even oblivious to the interruption of his monologue. 'It's always punched above its weight, hasn't it? In the realm of literature certainly.'

'I was friends with a poet once,' says Rosaleen without really thinking.

Louis gives a look of enthusiasm. 'Oh really? What was their name?'

'Oh, it's no one you would have heard of. Her name was Pauline.'

'Does she have any work online? I'd love to hear some.'

'You can't. It was a long time ago. It's not that kind of thing.' She rearranges the cushion behind her back. 'It's lovely to be out. I normally work on Saturdays.'

Louis nods vigorously. He strokes his face.

'Where do you work?'

'I work in a call centre.'

'Really? That's so fascinating. Really interesting stuff. You know, I read this great book recently about labour conditions for call centre workers. I can't remember the writer's name' – he pressed his fist to his forehead – 'it'll come to me in a minute, but he did this really sophisticated, really nuanced, sort of historical materialist analysis which drew comparisons between the development of call centre working conditions in the twenty-first century and the development of factory working conditions in the nineteenth century. Do you know it?'

'I haven't heard of it.'

She tries to laugh a little, but isn't sure if this is a part of the conversation during which laughter is appropriate. She smiles, feels stupid for smiling, tugs at one of her earrings.

'Ah well,' he goes on. 'When I remember, I'll tell Phil so he can tell you. Anyway, I don't want to interrupt too long, but lovely to meet you. Hopefully see you again soon.'

Louis leaves the room, and Rosaleen waits quietly for Phil.

When he gets back, Rosaleen tells him that Keith and Louis seem like nice lads.

'Yeah,' he says. 'They're a couple.'

'I thought you and Keith were a couple?'

'Not really. Only a bit.'

She takes a big gulp of her cup of tea and cracks a smile.

'What does that mean? When me and your dad were young, you were either with someone or you weren't.'

Phil laughs.

He throws up his hands like a saint about to martyr himself in a Renaissance painting.

'If only it were still like that!' he says.

. . .

AN HOUR LATER, ROSALEEN TRIES TO TAKE A SELFIE outside Westfield Stratford. She can't get it right. How can the photo look so different from her face in the mirror? The proportions are off. One eye is bigger than the other. Even her hair is the wrong colour. She experiments with a few angles, facing the sun, then away from the sun, taking twelve photos before eventually giving up and posting the best of a bad bunch. She captions it: 'Lovely day to go shopping x x' and tags Westfield Stratford and Phil. Within a few seconds, the likes come rolling in.

She puts her phone away, and they make their way inside. They plonk themselves down on the brick-red seats of Costa, each with a cappuccino in front of them.

She thinks that this is where she'll tell him about the cancer. She gathers her words.

She smiles and says that this is just like old times.

'It's nice to be able to catch up,' he agrees. 'I've been looking forward to it.'

'I have too. Remember when we used to go to that place in the shopping centre at home? Me and you always went there. I remember when you were about twelve and unhappy at school, and you'd pretend to be sick. I knew you weren't sick, but I never said anything. I always took you there on those days. We'd have great chats, you and me.'

'I remember. I used to love that.'

'We must go back. See if it's changed.'

'That's a good idea. I wonder what it's like now.'

'Not that you come home very often, mind you! We're lucky to see you twice a year.'

'I know, I know. I'm sorry. I've meant to visit more. I've just had a lot on.'

He speaks differently than he used to, but it's hard to describe how.

'Ah, I know you have,' she says. 'We'd love to see more of you, but it's not the end of the world, not in the grand scheme of things. What have you been up to anyway?'

'Just work really. I'm very boring these days. How have you been?'

She takes a second to answer. She looks at something in the distance, and then looks back. There are so many people here. The air conditioning is too cold.

She thought she'd say, '*I've a bit of news*' and '*It's cancer*' and '*It'll be fine*' but instead, what she says is, 'Same as ever. We've got a new team lead at work, who's much better than Julian, thank God. And I spoke to Joan Seymour last night as well. The poor woman's not doing great, but she tells me that Ed and Maggie are moving back to Basildon, a baby on the way! Do you ever think you might settle down?'

Phil takes a sip from his coffee.

'What do you mean?' he says.

'Well, you don't have much stability. Everyone needs a home to call their own.'

'Yeah,' he says, bristling. 'I know what you mean.'

'I know you like your housemates, but they're not the same as family.'

'Hmm.'

'One thing I've learned is that you can't trust people. People are crap. You meet someone and you think you can rely on them but they let you down. I trust you, your brother, and your dad, and that's it. Your brother, he's saving for a mortgage. Ed Seymour, he'll almost certainly buy a house as well. Ed's a good lad, Phil, and Basildon's not a bad place. It's changed since you were there. There's a new gastro pub. New cinema.'

'Mum.'

'The Tesco has a great vegetarian selection.'

'So does every Tesco.'

'I just think you need a home, Phil. Somewhere to call your own.'

'I suppose,' he says, 'where I live now *is* my home.'

He looks into his coffee.

'My friends are my family.'

Rosaleen pauses.

She thinks of the girl in Phil's house who hadn't even asked her name, and all that junk piled up, and the wet bathroom floor. She thinks of the dirty dishes and the cat hair and the grease caked into the corners of the cooker, mucky grease hardened to a crusty shell.

'Do you think gay men settle down later?' she says.

Phil speaks with his old guilt, trying to apologise for something he never did.

'Yes, maybe,' he says, 'but I'm telling you that I'm already settled down. I'm happier than I've ever been. There's no way I'll ever live like Ed or Callum.'

She thinks about Pauline. She wants to laugh and cry at the same time.

Pauline wouldn't have wanted to move to Basildon either.

Pauline wouldn't have touched Basildon with a ten-foot pole.

Music plays from the shopping centre speakers. It had blended with the background before, but it suddenly seems loud. It captures her mood so well that it's embarrassing. Excruciating. She wishes badly for the song to end. It's a piano ballad. It could be Adele.

'Well, if you're happy, then I'm happy,' she says. 'That's all anyone can ask for.'

. . .

THEY FINISH THEIR COFFEES AND WANDER TOWARDS THE fancy supermarket in the basement of the shopping centre. She navigates them to the meat aisle, and she tries to buy him a ham.

'Would you eat this?' she asks.

He checks his phone. He wants to return home.

'I'm not eating much meat at the moment, but thanks.'

'Are you sure? It might be nice for you and your housemates.'

'OK then, thanks, Mum.'

'You don't have to if you don't want to. I don't want it to go to waste either.'

'No, I do want it. You're right – we'll enjoy it. Thanks, Mum.'

She places the ham in the basket. They stroll past the fancy cheeses, and she tells a story about a ham that Steve once cooked. 'Your dad does the cooking a few nights a week now,' she says, 'and it makes a big difference to me. Would you eat this cranberry sauce?'

'OK, thanks, Mum.'

'No problem. It's nice to have a treat every now and then.'

'Thanks, Mum,' he says again.

'You'll need some cabbage to go with it.'

She leads them to the veg section to find that there's no cabbage.

'That's ridiculous,' she says. 'They've got every other vegetable under the sun.'

She looks around, slightly manic, and says, 'I'll ask this man over here.'

'Mum, please don't.'

'It's no hassle, I don't mind.'

'They obviously don't have any cabbage. Don't bother them.'

'I'm not bothering anyone,' she says, but still pulls back from approaching the man.

In the queue for the self-service checkouts, another thought occurs to her.

'Is Tesco still on Stratford High Street?' she says. 'There used to be one when your dad lived around here. We could go there to look for cabbage. I've always thought that Tesco is better than Waitrose. You pay a fortune at Waitrose, but the quality is the exact same, if not worse. It's a money racket if you ask me. Will we have a look over at Tesco?'

'I'd prefer not to, if that's OK.'

'It's only around the corner.'

'Mum, I don't even like cabbage.'

'You used to love cabbage. It was your favourite.'

'I don't any more.'

'Since when?'

'I don't remember ever liking it. It stinks up the whole house.'

'It never stank up our house.'

'Well, it stinks up mine.'

He can feel it now: the boiled Sunday afternoon pong, the speechless decades in front of the telly (the silence interrupted only by eating sounds and the murmur of soap operas), the casual homophobia of the neighbours in the supermarket. None of it. Phil wants none of it.

He says, 'I need to go soon, Mum.'

'But we only just got here.'

'We've been here for hours. I've got things to do.'

'You've always got things to do.'

'I mean, yeah, I do. So what? I've got a life of my own.'

'Your brother has a life of his own and he still makes time for us.'

'Am I not making time for you now? Have we not been together all afternoon? I don't believe that Callum spends any more time with you than I do.'

'He's working all the time. He's saving for a mortgage.'

Phil tries to resist the urge to shout, 'Callum is a drug dealer, Mum!'

Still, he shouts, 'Callum is a drug dealer, Mum!'

She flinches.

'Don't say that,' she says. 'That's not true. He's with your dad at the football today.'

'That doesn't mean he's not a drug dealer.'

'You've never gone to the football with your dad.'

'Dad has literally never asked a single question about my life.'

'That's only because you don't take an interest in him. He worked very hard for you.'

'I'm not saying he didn't.'

She thinks about the cancer. What if she tells him about it, and he doesn't even care? What if she tells him about it, and he's still too busy to visit her in the hospital with flowers?

'When Peter Seymour was sick,' she says, 'Ed came to see his parents every night. He still goes to see his mam a few times every week. He's a good lad, Ed. He's decent.'

How many times has Phil had to listen to tales of Ed Seymour's decency? How many times has he had to sit there and hear about what a good lad he is and know the truth of it?

He says, 'Ed Seymour isn't a good lad, Mum. He's never been one. Why are you so obsessed with Ed Seymour being a good lad? Do you have any idea what he gets up to?'

Rosaleen's nostrils flare. She chews her lower lip.

She says, 'Are you going to accuse him of being a drug dealer too then?'

'I'm not accusing anyone of anything.'

'I think you've put a distance between us.'

'I haven't. I just have a life of my own.'

'We came to London today. We're the ones who came to you.'

'For the first time since I moved here. For the first time in ten years!'

'Well, don't let us burden you then. If coming to see us is so horrible, you needn't bother. If you think I'm such a horrible mother, then I don't want to see you.'

Rosaleen's voice cracks: she's on the verge of tears and is trying to hold them back.

'Look, Mum,' he says, 'it's not a horrible experience. I love spending time with you, and with Dad as well. I just feel, sometimes, that you don't take my life seriously. I feel like whenever I'm happy about something, it makes you unhappy. It's tiring, that's all.'

She looks at him and purses her lips. She seems unsure what to do with herself. Eventually, she says in a quiet voice, 'We've always been happy for you.'

They reach the front of the queue; she pays for the ham; they leave.

They say goodbye on the concourse of Stratford station.

Phil mentions that it will rain later. Rosaleen says we could do with a bit of rain.

He asks her if she's taken her laundry in, which she has.

Phil says, 'That's good,' and Rosaleen agrees.

There's a silence. They're both waiting for something to happen.

They hug. He ascends the escalator, lump in throat.

Halfway up, he looks back and sees her dawdling alone on the concourse, a little flustered, rubbing her face. She tries to open her handbag, but drops it, and clambers to pick it up. She walks in one direction, then walks in another, then back again.

She doesn't know where to go.

He wants to go back and help her. He wants to shout, *Where are you trying to get to, Mum?* Well, what's he waiting for then! He'll go to her now and he'll help her find whatever it is she needs. He sprints up the escalator, two steps at a time, so that he can descend again on the other side, but – *shit!* – the downward escalator is broken and sealed off, and Stratford station is such a maze that it takes five minutes to find another way through.

He gets back to the concourse. He scans the crowd. He's frantic. It's like being a small child and waiting for her at the school gate, and with even a split second's delay, he'd be afraid she was never coming at all, even though she always came, was always there for him, and they'd walk home from school and he'd yap yap yap about whatever happened that day and show her the drawing he'd made and she'd say he was very creative, just like her.

Now, she's nowhere to be seen.

It's fine, he says. Get a grip. What are you getting so upset over? She's a grown woman. She can navigate London perfectly well without you.

Back on the escalator, he thinks of his mother's words. *Ed Seymour is a nice lad.*

He's angry with Ed. He's angry that Ed gets to be seen as nice.

He drafts a text message to Maggie. His hands shake as he types and sweat buckets from his brow. He's flustered from the heat. *Babe, thanks for telling me your news earlier. I'm so excited for you. Can we talk though? There's something I need to tell you about Ed.*

. . .

ROSALEEN SCRUBS HER SKIN BENEATH THE HOT TAP.
She's in the public toilets of Stratford station and there's no
soap in any of the soap dispensers. Since she left the house, she
must have touched a million and one different surfaces, and
now she can't even wash her hands.

They spent the day together, she and Phil, but when they
said goodbye she was struck by a feeling of having not had
enough time. She was with him for hours, but it passed in five
minutes. They were in the station together only a second ago;
he, on the escalator, she, on the concourse. He was on his way
to the Jubilee Line, glued to his phone, already sucked back
into the drama of his life. She watched him go, without giving
him the loaf of bread.

She has always imagined that if she had five minutes left
on earth, she'd call the person she loved most and tell them all
the things she needed them to know. But most goodbyes are
small. They take place in the middle of stations and shopping
centres, where there's too much going on to really focus on the
goodbye at all, distracted by the counter-terrorism alerts blar-
ing from the station loudspeakers, and the queue for Greggs
that snakes through the concourse. Instead of saying the things
she was burning to say, she ended up saying something completely inconsequential about how it's no wonder that Greggs
is so popular now, given their great value and expanded vegan
range, and even though she spoke in an offhand, casual sort of
way, inside she trembled, inside she pulsated, inside she was
dying to explain her feelings, her thoughts, why she was the
way she was. But when push came to shove, she hadn't mentioned the cancer at all. She babbled about how she preferred a
cheese and onion bake to a steak bake, but surely a sausage roll

is the greatest Greggs product of all, and before she knew it the afternoon was gone. It was time to go their separate ways. Phil was on the escalator, on his way towards the train, and after that, the rest of his life.

She remembers how school was hard for him. She remembers his bruises, the day he came home with egg all over his head and face and school uniform. It was her day off, a hot day. Phil had walked past her in the hall, gone to the kitchen, then to his room, a smattering of instant coffee granules left on the counter in his wake. She had wiped them into her hand, then looked in the fridge to check if he had eaten anything, which he hadn't, even though there was a tub of the cheesy coleslaw, which she had bought especially because he made cheesy coleslaw sandwiches to take to school, or eat during his break at work, which was fifteen minutes in a six hour shift, and he was always tired when he got home and smelled of grease.

She remembers thinking that she'd ask if he was OK.

She remembers thinking that she'd talk to him, be there for him, get to the bottom of it. She'd ask if he wanted to do a bit of shopping and go for a coffee and cake, and she remembers how she left the kitchen, went through the hall and up the stairs, but by the time she reached his room, she felt silly for thinking he'd go to town with his mother – at his age! – and instead, knocked on his door and said, 'Have you eaten? There's cheesy coleslaw in the fridge.'

Now, she moves through the gates of the Olympic Park. Steve used to live with his parents in a terrace not far from here. She had lived in a bedsit in Canning Town. Every day, she got the bus to work in an Oxford Street department store, sprayed herself with free samples of perfume after her shift – taking care to be covert about this – and then she got the bus back east to meet Steve. His father would make jokes. He'd say: *I hope you're not leading my son astray. I know what you people are like. A devious people, your people.* Everyone would laugh, even Rosaleen. She had wanted it to be easy. The only one who didn't laugh was Steve. Mild-mannered as he was, he stood up to his father every time. *If you don't stop that,* he said, *we're not coming around any more, not even on Christmas.* But Steve wasn't always around. One time, there'd been an assassination. Airey Neave, a Tory MP, blown to bits outside Westminster. It was 1979, and when Steve and his mother left the room to set the table for dinner, Steve's father had said, 'I hope you don't have a bomb under your shirt! I'd inspect you myself, only I don't want Stephen to be jealous!' He laughed breathlessly. He clutched his belly and wiped tears of joy from his eye, amazed at his own wit, and Rosaleen was struck by a churning feeling in her gut: she was glad the Tory had been killed. It didn't matter if the pundits on the news said he was a national hero or he'd escaped German prisoner-of-war camps. People in this country saw the Irish back then as drunken simpletons with red faces, who made fools of themselves with their superstitions and mispronunciations of the Queen's English. Her managers at work used to patronise her in exaggerated baby talk, sounding words phonetically as if she didn't speak the same language as them. In 1979 a man threw a can of beer at her head, half-full, and said she was a terrorist.

She remembers being a migrant. When did she become something else? Was there an exact moment? She remembers thinking, after the man threw the beer at her, that everything good about this country was good because of migration.

Everything. London wouldn't be half the city it was without
the people who had dragged themselves there from all over
the world.

She used to long to sit at her mother's table and half-listen
to her monologue on the events of the day; the things she'd
bought at the market, which vegetables had been a bargain,
the gossip she'd elicited from the market women about whose
daughters had emigrated and whose sons had died. People's
sons were always dying. They were always dying of suicide
and car crashes and alcoholism and heroin overdoses and no
one ever mentioned it out loud.

People's daughters died too, to be fair. No one ever mentioned that aloud either.

No one mentioned how they'd died from having too many
children or children they didn't want or pregnancies they'd
have to keep hidden because they hadn't been married.

She clamps her eyes shut and tries to stay still. If she moves
her face the tears will come, and she knows they won't stop.
She thinks about Pauline. She starts walking again.

It was ridiculous, what Phil said about Callum being a
drug dealer. How could a son of hers be a drug dealer? How
many of the men she once knew in Dublin had their lives
ruined by drugs? It must be at least half of them. At least
twelve or thirteen of them died.

She wouldn't even know how to find Steve's parents' old
house at this stage anyway. It might have been demolished for
all she knows. She surveys the scene and imagines describing
it to Pauline. The new station and the Olympic Park. The
tower blocks and the cranes and the weird public art. *Stunning
developments, iconic locations, Manhattan living in the heart of*

East London. She might as well be on a different planet to that little house, where she had politely laughed at an old man's jokes and felt glad to the marrow of her bones that a politician had been blown to bits in his car.

She's got two hours to kill before she meets Steve.

What'll she do? Who cares what she'll do.

When her husband is done at the match, she'll get a DLR, a train, a bus. At home, she'll ask him about his day. She'll remind him to pick up bin bags and dishwasher tablets in the morning. They'll have a takeaway, which they'll enjoy, and that will be the end of that.

10

PHIL, ON THE PLATFORM OF STRATFORD STATION, HIS thumb hovering over the message to Maggie. He thinks of the first text he ever received from Ed, how his thumb had hovered then too.

Ed Seymour is a nice lad.

He looks left down the platform, he looks right, his heart beats harder. Sweaty palms, hot face. It's as if he might have to break into a run at any moment.

He looks back at the text he's drafted.

There's something I need to tell you about Ed.

What to even say to her? Where to begin?

. . .

IT WAS TEN YEARS AGO NOW. TEN YEARS AND ONE month, give or take a few days.

A hot evening in Basildon. A Friday. An orange sun was setting, just about visible in the top right corner of the window. Spring had tiptoed on tenterhooks for months, but the warm weather had barged in. It was at the stage of May when the seasons accelerate without warning, and everything, everywhere was brutally lurching towards the summer.

Phil was seventeen and this text was the biggest thing to have ever happened to him.

He was watching TV in his family living room. His mother, father, and big brother were there.

Ed's text read: *hey hw u.*

Phil reread it more than thirty times. He turned it over in his mind, examining from all angles, searching for hidden meaning or allusion or innuendo. Ed lived across the road, and Phil had known him for years. These three words, despite their smallness, felt enormous.

It took a long time for Phil to reply. He switched from sentence-case to lower-case, from abbreviated text speak to full sentences and back again. After his thumb had hovered a millimetre above the 'send' button and ounces of prickly sweat had dribbled from his armpits, he eventually wrote *yeh gd u??* and immediately regretted the second question mark.

This was before Maggie and Ed got together.

. . .

PHIL CAN REMEMBER THE EXACT CONFIGURATION OF his family living room that evening. He closes his eyes in Stratford station and arranges it before him. Mugs dotted around, hidden behind the curtain, on the coffee table next to women's magazines and wasted AAA batteries. Tea bags left in a few of the mugs, half-dried out, lurking beneath orange peels and crumpled Mini-KitKat wrappers. A photo on the

wall of his mother and father on their wedding day: Rosaleen
wore a dress that looked like the one from the Kate Bush video for 'Wuthering Heights', Steve had a full head of hair. The
big couch, the small couch, the armchair, all arranged around
the TV, which was a big TV. When they bought the TV, Phil
had made a comment about how the old TV worked just fine
and he didn't know why they had to spend so much on a new
one; his mother had replied that watching TV on evenings
and weekends was the most relaxing time in her stressful life,
and it was well within her rights to make that experience as
enjoyable as it possibly could be. Admittedly, Phil had come
to enjoy the big TV just as much as everyone else did and he
regretted ever saying a bad word against it.

Who Wants to Be a Millionaire? was on, nearly over.

One contestant remained, stumbling on a question about
Spanish poetry.

The contestant scratched his chin, rubbed his temples:
Rosaleen said 'Come on! You're well able!' and this was the
moment Phil's phone vibrated with a response from Ed.

He remembers it well: how he'd held his breath.

A split second passed before he opened the text.

This split second felt like years. It felt like an era of human
history had been and gone. He closed his eyes and clenched
his teeth and plunged his thumb towards the keypad.

The text read: *yeh gud mate. what u doin tomo? wanna
meet up?*

Something exploded in Phil's chest.

It was like random phenomena of chemistry and phys-
ics had spontaneously erupted inside him, like a black hole,
like the Big Bang, like in the beginning there was nothing,

but now, there were constellations, asteroids, microorganisms evolving into life as we know it.

He thought: *Yes!*

He messaged: *yeh cool. where when?*

He said (with a vigour that surprised even himself): 'Lorca! The answer is Lorca!'

Rosaleen said, 'Know it all. I never would have got that one,' and then, 'There's a stain on that carpet,' speaking as if these were sequential parts of the same thought.

. . .

IN STRATFORD STATION, HE THINKS OF ROSALEEN. Always entering competitions on Facebook. *Share this post to win a holiday or a hamper or a bespoke spa treatment.* She is older, and Steve is older; the retirement age will be increased before long, and the state pension will be reduced, and he doesn't want them to have to open a Government Gateway account to manage their Universal Credit claim. He doesn't want them to have become *digitally literate.* A time will come when his parents are old, and he is old, and if the state won't look after them, and if he can't look after them either, then who? He grinds his teeth. He should have let her buy him the cabbage. When his mother asks questions on 'settling down' – questions that come from a place of care – why does he patronise her with opinions on how today's queers have moved beyond the confines of the nuclear unit to imagine new and better models of kinship? Not for the first time today, he asks: why am I like this?

. . .

THERE'S SOMETHING I NEED TO TELL YOU ABOUT ED.

What exactly does Phil mean by that?

On the night Ed sent that first text, Rosaleen and Steve fell asleep on the couch, then woke up, then went to bed. Callum went out to meet friends, and Phil didn't go to bed at all.

What did he do? He made a cup of coffee; two spoons of freeze-dried Nescafé, three spoons of granulated sugar, a splash of milk, a splash of hot water. He stirred it with a little silver teaspoon, wincing each time the spoon chimed against the wall of the mug, and took it to the living room. He perched in front of the TV, volume on the lowest setting, index finger hovering above the on/off button of the remote. With one ear tuned to the murmur of the TV, and one ear tuned to the stirrings of his parents upstairs, he turned to Channel 4.

This had been his Friday routine every week of the previous four years, ever since he caught his first glimpse of a penis on film, a mental image of which he had gone on to masturbate over for several years subsequent to the event. Since then, Phil had been a scavenger. He had nibbled weekly on the remains of Channel 4's experimental late-night programming, sniffing about for nourishment, learning more about the world beyond his town than he ever learned at school. Channel 4 had dangled life in front of him, so that he could observe and comment, but never quite participate. That was until he received a text message from Ed Seymour in May 2009, with an orange sunset loitering in the top right corner of the living-room window, and only a week until he would finish school forever.

It had been five hours since Ed sent that text. The sun had set, and Phil sat as he had always sat, his coffee half drunk, across from the photo of his mother and father, the Kate Bush dress, the full head of hair, waiting for Channel 4 to serve more glimpses of life.

. . .

THERE ARE FOUR MINUTES UNTIL THE NEXT JUBILEE Line from Stratford.

Phil sees a woman wiping spit off the mouth of a small baby.

What should he tell Maggie? It's hard to remember the exact chain of events. Should he tell her that in February 2006 there had been a school trip to Kent, a hike and an overnight stay in a cheap youth hostel and fifty of Phil's classmates shivering in the cold air, indifferent to the team-bonding activities and pleasant green scenery? Before they'd got off the bus, the teacher had made an announcement; there had been a mistake with the booking, and some of the boys would have to share beds. It was random allocation and Phil was paired up with Ed.

Then, it was 2 a.m. The five other boys in the room were asleep, but Phil couldn't relax, irked by the shape of an unfamiliar body in an unfamiliar bed, and if he opened his eyes and glanced to the left, he could see the chilled condensation in Ed's slow breath.

Ed turned onto his back. Their baby fingers grazed. It happened so slowly that it was imperceptible at first, but after several hours had elapsed, Ed's entire hand was on top of Phil's entire hand, grasping it, and then guiding it towards Ed's crotch, and arranging Phil's fingers around Ed's cock, whispering, eventually, 'Will you wank me off?'

Phil felt tense and thrilled and short of breath. Without thinking, he moved his hand up and down like he had done before on his own. Ed's breath was fast. His eyes were closed. Phil couldn't believe how different it felt to do this to someone who wasn't himself. Thrilled, he thought: I am a person who gives illicit handjobs to straight boys on school trips. He spent the rest of that night fantasising about how he'd describe this turn of events to Maggie.

So, why didn't he tell her then? He didn't think she'd believe him.

He and Ed didn't speak again until September 2008, when their English classes merged, and they ended up sitting together. It was the first day of their last year at school. By this time, Ed had had many girlfriends, and even by conservative estimates, was the most well-liked boy at school. He was good-looking and friendly, he played football and did well in exams. He was confident, almost arrogant, famously funny, but shy at the same time; he often seemed startled, embarrassed, as if by simply being a person in public he had been caught in a shameful act, and most people took this as a sign of his sensitivity and decency.

There was rarely a moment when one part of Phil's brain wasn't hypothesising scenarios in which he and Ed might get together; at the town fair, after assembly, in the rain on the dual carriageway overpass from which, at an angle, you could see the edge of London.

A long, wet kiss.

The weight of each other's frames pressed up against each other.

The swell of each other's bellies.

Phil understood that these were ridiculous fantasies.

He understood that there were rules and etiquette; implication and convention; the done thing, the wrong thing, men, women. He knew that Callum, for example, was a man; there was his temper, the holidays he had spoiled, the vivid and passionate hatred he felt towards his dad. Steve was also a man. There was his bald head, his fat belly, the ridicule he received from his family and the fact he never gave any indication as to whether or not it hurt him. Phil's father and brother ate ravenously, and so, Phil, like his mother, became interested in weight. There were calories. There was sugar. There were treats and there were sins. There was the terrible, crippling guilt of eating a chocolate caramel digestive, a Mini-KitKat, a Chicken Dipper, or any kind of crisp. Phil experienced this guilt from about the age of six.

Rosaleen was a woman. There was her competence. There was her knowledge of the precise location of an array of household items. There was her perpetual annoyance at men, the various things she said they were not able to do, for example: multitasking, childcare, listening to a single word that anyone else was saying, hoovering the hall, stairs and landing without someone else having to do it again, cooking food that wasn't burnt, getting home on time from work, or shitting without stinking up the whole house.

Also: there were the clothes she would wear; there were her skirts; there was her longish hair that she would dye a reddish-brown, which five-year-old Phil compared favourably to the L'Oréal ads starring Andie MacDowell. There was one time, after much pestering, and no one else was at home, when she let five-year-old Phil put on her dressing gown and a pair of high heels. There was the chapstick he smeared on his mouth to pretend it was lipstick and the yellow towel he wrapped around his head to pretend it was long blonde hair. There was Rosaleen's memorably panicked tone when she impressed upon him that it was very important that no one else was ever allowed to know.

At school, there were rumours that Phil was gay and the lengths that he went to counteract these rumours. There were the conversations he avoided. There was the exaggeration of his low gruff voice. Still, the items thrown in the corridor. The implications that he was a rapist or a paedophile. The threats of physical violence (for example: 'I'll smash your head open with a brick, you faggot') and the physical violence itself (for example: held down after PE, face mashed into the floor, a knee in his back, a carton of milk dumped over his head, boys saying things like 'Careful! He'll try bum you any minute now.').

During these incidents, Phil tried to focus his attention on the smallest details of what was happening, as if by narrating the banal minutiae of his experience, he could detach from it. Calmly, from a position outside himself, he observed the scratchy municipal carpet of the sports hall corridor; the sweet metallic scent of men's antiperspirant and sweat; the cold splash of milk on the back of his neck; the spongy quality of his milk-logged school jumper.

Ed had been there on all of these occasions – he was a close friend of many of the boys who would attack Phil – but although he never asked the other boys to stop, he never joined in either. Instead, Ed would laugh very slightly and throw his eyes up to heaven, like a person does when their friend does something foolish but ultimately quite endearing, like a person does when a puppy shits in the hall, unable to get properly angry because the puppy doesn't know any better and is otherwise extremely lovable. For this, Phil had always liked him.

. . .

PHIL'S FAMILY HOME WAS LIKE THIS: BLUE LINO KITCHEN and sink forever blocked with miscellaneous gunk. Beyond the kitchen there was the hallway, its green carpet, cream walls, its small wooden table and disconnected landline. The green carpet continued to the top of the stairs, halting at the toilet door, behind which was a peach floor, pink bath, and blue see-through toilet seat with decorative seashells entombed within. It was considered suspect for a man to spend a long amount of time in the toilet, unless he was pooing, poo being perceived as the preserve of the masculine, and Phil, reluctant to be associated with such a masculine activity, would become deeply defensive when anyone commented on how much time he spent in there (putting varying amounts of gel in his hair, brushing his fringe in different directions, trimming his pubic hair with the family nail scissors, and once dry-shaving his pubic hair with the same rusty razor he used on his face, which was an itchy red mistake).

Next door to the toilet was Phil's room – a box room, decorated with precision and pride – and beside that, Callum's room: crunchy crushed-up toilet tissue and empty packets of popcorn, the smell of a Lynx Africa gift set that Aunt Sue bought each nephew every Christmas. Beside that was Rosaleen and Steve's room, clean and comfortable, the TV broadcasting a reassuring babble throughout the night. Steve, generally a quiet man, could often be heard through the walls on weekends, belting out misremembered lyrics, quoting lines from ancient yoghurt adverts in strange approximations of American accents, or reciting vulgar riddles with the reverence of sacred scripture while Rosaleen laughed in escalating fits. His parents loved their house, had worked for it, and Phil couldn't wait until he was old enough to leave.

Beyond the house, there was the estate. There were the browning hydrangeas and the squat stone pillars by the gate. There were the porches, kitchen extensions and utility rooms which distinguished the privately owned from the council homes. There was the green, which had recently conceded territory to a block of energy-efficient new-builds, that Angie Michaels, chair of the residents' association, had petitioned fruitlessly against for two years.

The estate was bordered by a dual carriageway: everything Phil knew about his dad, he had learned sitting in the passenger seat driving up and down it. It was so much easier for Phil and Steve to talk when they could look straight ahead instead of facing each other. He had learned that when Steve was young, he had saved up to buy a camera and taken photos of the potted plants in his mother's kitchen and known the names of the plants and what kind of soil they'd thrive in. He learned how Steve had tried to start a vegetable patch in his mother's tiny garden where nothing would ever grow but would still speak of becoming self-sufficient one day, of one day living off the land. Whenever Phil was in the car with his dad, they nearly always stopped for food. He would tell Phil not to let his mother know, not wanting her to worry any more than she already did about the heart attack that had killed his own dad, his family history of type 2 diabetes, the broccoli stir fry she'd made because she didn't want him to die decades before she did. They would get their food and park the car to eat it.

It was here that Steve asked Phil, aged seventeen, if he knew what a condom was, and Phil was too embarrassed to say the word 'penis' in front of his dad. The only time his parents had spoken about sex was when he was seven years old. It had been a Sunday; he and Callum had sat at the foot of their parents' bed while Rosaleen and Steve ate their boiled eggs and explained that sex is when a man and a woman love each other, and a man puts his penis in a woman's vagina, and a baby is made, as if sex were only physiologically possible between a man and a woman, and only when they are in love. By the time he was thirteen, Phil was terrified of AIDS and skin lesions and being ostracised by entire towns and losing control over his bowels and sex always being something that was painful or shameful. After his initial encounter with Ed, he had two more sexual encounters between the ages of fifteen and seventeen, and on both occasions he was acutely aware of the need to use a condom; he spent the entire experience feeling tense, in pain, imagining ways his life might change if the condom were to break, how his body could be turned into something abject by the hands of the man who was caressing his back, who was kissing his neck, who was trying to hold him.

Beyond the dual carriageway, there was the town; high street speckled with shuttered shop fronts and hoardings of abandoned building sites, rendered graphics of future shoppers: *Building Basildon a Brighter Future*. On one end of

the high street, there was Brooke House, an enormous tower block made of glass and brick that balanced on stilts. For
years, it had a crumbling interior, broken lifts, asbestos, windows that let draughts in, mould on the windowsills, rubbish
in the stairwells, and lights in the hallways that cut out at unpredictable times, but by 2009 there were coffee-table books
about Brutalism and Architectural Modernism with its image
on the cover, flats sold to private developers whose marketing
materials described a once in a lifetime opportunity to live in
a national treasure.

At the far end of the high street, there was the conglom-
eration of recently opened cash-4-gold shops, and across from
that there was the cathedral, with its nightmarish modernist
Jesus suffering in perpetual agony above the square. Across
from that was the Eastgate Shopping Centre, which used to be
the biggest indoor shopping centre in Europe, and its younger
cousin, the Westgate Shopping Park, which opened when Phil
was eight years old. Before Ed's text, walking through the glass
doors of the new shopping centre for the first time had been
the most exciting moment in his life. It was like in a film when
someone catches their first glimpse of the Manhattan skyline
on their way to the city from JFK Airport. Dumbstruck, they
stare from the backseat of a yellow taxi, mouth agape, lights
reflected on their face. He had always dreamed of living in
a city, and when the shopping centre opened, with its high
street brands and cinema and food court, it felt like he didn't
have to wait until he was old enough to leave home: the city
had come to him.

. . .

BEYOND THE TOWN, THERE WAS THE RETAIL PARK, AND the American-themed fast-food restaurant where Phil worked. The day after Ed sent the text was quiet, with nothing to do but clean spotless surfaces and listen to Elvis sing over the loudspeakers. After his shift, he walked through the empty arcade, the dance machines whirring and bleeping for attention. It was 7 p.m. It had started raining, even though there had been a blazing sun at the start of his shift. At home, Phil ran to his room, shouting 'Hi Mum!' on the way, before rapidly examining his three nice shirts, trying each one on four times, and dousing himself in aftershave courtesy of Auntie Sue. He ran out the door again, shouting 'Bye Mum!' without waiting for an answer.

The rain had now stopped, but the ground was wet, and the lane where Phil had agreed to meet Ed had turned into a waterlogged marsh. Crushed beer cans and plastic tubes for cigarette filters floated on top of the water. The lane had spiked fences on either side, and Phil found a patch of concrete by an electricity box to stand on, the only place not flooded.

The sun was setting, and the clouds were dyed a urine-shade of yellow; everything there, from the rusty fence to sunset-dyed clouds, was copper, yellow, or brown.

Phil was the only person around. When it wasn't flooded, the place would be packed with young people on Saturday nights; there would be secrets shared, stories told, and great and minor cruelties inflicted; there would be private desires to kiss and there would be kissing itself; there would be sexually experimenting there in the lane and there would be brokering agreements to sexually experiment at other, more private locations (for example, behind the tall metal shelves in Rick

Lewis's parents' shed which smelled of white spirit and rotting cut grass, where at least eight different couples had stared at the rusted metal of a pair of huge garden shears during sloppy first attempts at mutual masturbation or oral sex).

But on that night, the lane was dead.

His white trainers were caked in mud. The ends of his jeans were damp and cold around his ankles. He wasn't wearing a jacket, because his shirt looked better without one, and he was shivering alone by the electricity box when Ed appeared, wearing a white shirt, blue jeans, and white trainers, just like Phil.

'Alright, mate!' shouted Ed. He did an awkward dance through the mud, like an actor in a silent film slipping on a stray banana skin.

Ed looked around. 'Should we find somewhere to sit down?'

They peered out from the concrete island.

'I'm not sure there is anywhere,' said Phil.

'Good point. Well, here's alright, isn't it?'

Ed retrieved a beer from the plastic bag in his hand. He passed it to Phil, and then cracked one open for himself. They both looked at each other, then looked away, and then laughed as if to acknowledge the strangeness of them being there together.

Ed asked, 'So what have you been up to, man?'

'Nothing, to be honest. Just work and school. What about you?'

'Same, man. Can't wait to finish.'

'Do you not like school?'

'Nobody likes school.'

Everything Ed said, he said with a smile, like each syllable contributed to a wider joke. 'It's a shithole, this town,' Ed continued. 'I'm getting out. You should too.'

Phil didn't know what to say. To delay, he simply said, 'Should I?'

'You're too good for this place. They don't deserve you around here.'

Phil blushed: Ed saw him as someone to be *deserved*. A thing worth having.

He said nothing. He took a long drag from his fag and readjusted his feet. He became aware that he was smiling, while staring at Ed. Minutes could have passed and he wouldn't have known. The concrete island was very small; they were standing very close.

Ed continued, 'You and your mate – what's her name – Maggie – you two are on a different planet. I hear you two speak and I think: those two aren't meant for this place.'

Ed shifted his weight so that they were standing closer. He narrowed his eyes, grinned, and licked his lips. Phil thought: *Is this what happens before a kiss?*

He moved a further two inches towards Phil. He leaned in, smiled, looked away. It became clear in one bright, brutal moment that Ed was making a move. Phil grinned ear to ear and thought *yes*. This *is* it! This is exactly what happens in advance of a kiss.

He could smell Ed's aftershave, and his own aftershave, and the fag smoke and beer on Ed's hot breath. He could see the places on Ed's face where the stubble hadn't grown yet.

At seventeen, on the concrete island by the electricity box, Phil would have done whatever it took to make Ed happy. He would have done whatever he said.

He said, 'Man, your mate Maggie, I don't know how she's so smart.'

Phil made an indeterminate noise.

He said, 'Yeah. She's great. She's my best friend.'

'I've tried it on with her before, to be honest.'

He could hear the traffic, a bird flapping its wings. There was a discarded fag packet on the concrete by his foot; it had a warning picture of what smoking does to your lungs.

'Did you?' he said.

'She said my mates are pricks. She's right. They are pricks.'

Phil laughed. He said nothing.

'She said they bully you.'

He tore at a cigarette filter in one pocket. He fingered a 20p coin in the other.

'You don't think I'm like that, do you?'

'I'd never think that.'

'Because I really like you, man. I always thought you were cool.'

'I always thought you were cool too.'

He could see the trail of hair on Ed's chest sticking out over the top of his shirt, the border between the pink and white of his cheeks, the jagged tips of his chipped front teeth. Phil hadn't been there when those teeth got chipped, but he had heard later how Ed got punched in PE. If anyone tried to punch Ed again, he wanted to be the one who'd protect him.

Ed paused. He flicked his fag into the mud.

He said, 'I wondered if you might put in a good word with Maggie?'

A bird flapped its wings. Phil took a second to answer.

He stammered and then said, 'What do you mean?'

'You know. Tell her I'm sound. That I don't bully you.'

Everything, right then, came to a halt. Phil could feel tears pool in the corner of his eyes. He could see Ed notice the tears and pretend not to notice and smile as if nothing had happened. Then, he remembered how cold it was. It was like his skin had suspended its sensitivity to temperature the moment Ed arrived but had now resumed its business as usual.

He said, 'Oh. OK. I suppose.'

Ed said, 'Seriously? Man, you're a legend. I really appreciate it. You're a top lad.'

Phil said, 'Thanks.'

Ed said, 'Any time, man.'

. . .

THE TRAIN PULLS INTO STRATFORD STATION. PHIL STEPS on. He rides it all the way to London Bridge where he gets off and ascends the station's early-2000s aspirational spaceship motif. Outside, it's bright. It's even hotter than it was before. He leans against a wall and reads the message.

Can we talk though? There's something I need to tell you about Ed.

What's to be gained from revealing all this now? He doesn't even like telling the story to himself: to recount it to another person would be excruciating. What's he supposed to say?

That to be pelted with eggs is uniquely humiliating? That Phil had this thought during his last week at school, a Tuesday, still blisteringly hot, three days after he met up with Ed?

There had been a tradition in Phil's school. Maggie will remember it just as much as anyone. It was a tradition which existed in most schools: during the last week of term, the sixth

form students did various pranks. Rotten fish behind the radiators. Alarm clocks placed in the cavities above the ceiling
tiles. Various foodstuffs brought in to throw at each other;
flour, milk, baking powder, eggs.

Phil had been pelted with many foodstuffs over the years,
cooked and raw, digested and undigested, pasteurised and
otherwise, Coca-Cola, Lucozade, apple cider vinegar.

But eggs: there was something special about eggs.

Maybe it was because they were hard and soft all at once.
The impact of the shell as it cracked against the face was genuinely painful, almost like a punch, and then he was covered in
gloopy liquid, full of salmonella and bad smells and so hard
to get out of your hair.

Phil was at the gates of the school. It was the end of the
day.

Two boys held him with his arms behind his back.

Another three boys took turns pelting him with eggs.

He was almost happy about it. Should he tell her that?

Should he tell her that part of him felt almost pleased to
be included in the tradition, as if he, too, were one of the lads?
He tried to tell himself that they weren't really attacking him –
it was just a bit of fun, and they were kind enough to involve
him in it.

He laughed when they laughed as if they were in on the
same joke. Is that an important detail to share?

'What are you laughing at?' one boy said while throwing
the next egg.

So many people walked by. Classmates, the parents of
classmates, teachers, the old woman who walked her dog there
at the same time every day. So many people walked by and

averted their gaze or looked right at him or laughed and maybe thought, 'Boys will be boys.'

One of the people who walked by was Ed.

Ed was a friend of these boys. They were all part of the same gang.

They called out to him. They said, 'Ed! Come on and throw an egg at him!'

Ed pretended at first not to hear. They said, 'Awwww he doesn't want to hurt his boyfriend.' Then they made kissy noises, and then they said, 'Getting bummed down in the laneway on Saturday night. We all saw you, mate! We all know you were there with him.'

The boys kept making kissy noises and telling jokes about bumming until Ed turned back. He walked right up and stared them down. He glared at their laughing faces. This is it, Phil thought. This is the moment where Ed is going to say, 'Phil's alright. Leave him alone,' and they will all listen because Ed has authority, and is beautiful, and everyone adores him. Ed walked right up to them and stared in their faces, and then he took an egg from the box, and he walked up to Phil, and he didn't just throw the egg at him, he mashed it into the top of his head with a thump. He thumped Phil's head so hard, the egg enclosed in his fist, so hard that Phil felt dizzy and sick almost right away. He mashed the egg into Phil's head so that the egg ran down his hair and onto his face and it got in his eye, and Phil's arms were still held behind his back so he even couldn't wipe it away and it stung. Ed mashed the egg into Phil's head so that Ed's hand was covered in egg as well, and Phil thought in a brief moment of lucidity that Ed is fucking himself over too; now he's got raw egg all over himself.

Apart from that, Phil had no other feelings or thoughts or opinions on what was happening to him. His body was in Basildon, but in every other way, he was far away. Beyond Basildon, there was the dual carriageway, and beyond that, there was London. In London, there was the Tate Modern, Covent Garden and Kingsland High Street. There was dancing at a party, holding hands on the street, getting the Tube with a boyfriend and putting an arm around him. There was sleeping together, and learning each other's favourite dinners, and cooking those dinners as a surprise on special occasions – maybe it would be lasagne or burgers or something to do with noodles – and actually, it wouldn't be just on special occasions, but on mundane occasions too, on days on which nothing in particular was happening, on days when they just wanted to do something small and simple to say they were in love.

· · ·

OUTSIDE LONDON BRIDGE STATION, HE LOOKS UP FROM his phone. The paramedics smoke around the corner from Guy's Hospital, sweating through their uniforms, and sharply dressed straight couples take pictures of themselves, holding flutes of pink prosecco beneath the Shard.

He looks back to the text. *There's something I need to tell you about Ed.*

Fuck it, he thinks. He presses send.

Then, his phone vibrates with a message from Keith.

I just read your inscription. Please can we meet?

11

THE THING ABOUT VALERIE IS THAT SHE RELATES TO the whale. She looks at the whale and sees herself in it. We don't know how the whale got here. Frightened by NATO war drills? Her environment destroyed by the melting of Arctic ice? Either way, Valerie knows how it feels to move through life's motions, responding to events as they happen, and then, one day, without intention, you've found yourself miles from where you started, with no way to return.

It's been a surprising week.

She was asked to speak to the news cameras on the whale's rescue operation, and the public response has been this: she resembles a dead princess. Or what's more, that she *is* a dead princess. Now, Diana truthers find photos of her from twenty years ago to post on internet forums. Bored teens and gays on Twitter say she is a *cult figure*, an *iconique queen*; *slay mama* they write in response to her posts about rising pH levels in the world's oceans. It makes her feel on edge, afraid, also thrilled, to have had her phone ping all morning with the messages of friends, news articles and her face photoshopped onto images from *Mean Girls*, *Spiderman*, *Titanic*, an opinion piece comparing her to Greta Thunberg, Alexandria Ocasio-Cortez, and other 'kickass women at the forefront of progressive global change'. She doesn't recognise the woman who appears in those articles and images, even though the woman, technically, is her.

This morning, she sent a text to Tamsin: *I'm more famous than you now.*

She allowed herself a minute of fantasy: she pictured no longer having to meet in budget hotels off Essex dual carriageways but being together in public.

She is tired of public relations, tired of optics.

Valerie stands on the barge, clutching a red watering can and biting her nails. The whale's eyes have been covered for fear that if she saw what was happening to her, she wouldn't survive the shock of her own distress. The barge is positioned; a crane will lift her on board. It heaves, screeches, and the whale is suspended above the river. She seems bigger this way, helpless and monstrous all at once. Water and blood flood from her back.

The whale briefly hangs high in the sky, blocking the sun as if she's a freshly discovered moon on her first solar eclipse. The descent happens slowly. It's almost imperceptible. She's gripped by the claws of the crane, held so tenderly while the onlookers hold their breath. Finally, she is lowered onto the deck, and the engine of the barge revs into life. This barge can be fast when it needs to be and there's no time to kill.

. . .

AND WE'RE OFF. STEVE SCREAMS AT THE TOP OF HIS lungs. Callum stands beside him. He's screaming too. He clenches his fists so tight that his knuckles have turned pale grey. Eric Dier has scored a goal during a free kick with seventeen minutes to go. England have taken the lead in the nick of time. This moment is euphoria. It is ecstasy, joy, the happiest moment in both of their lives. Pints smash. The lager soaks into the pub carpet.

Ed stands next to them, now sober as a judge. Every breath is shallower than the last. Everything in this pub is loud, bright, and wet. Everyone's palms are sticky with sloshed lager, T-shirts marshy with gone-off sweat.

Callum claps Ed on the back and tousles his hair.

'Mate!' he says, slurring.

'It's lovely watching football with your son,' says Steve. 'It's all ahead of you.'

He gives a warm and conspiratorial wink, as if to suggest that he and Ed are part of a private club and one day soon Ed will be just like him. Steve gets up to go to the toilet, and Callum lays his face on the table, half passed out, a damp beer mat sticking to his forehead.

Ed clenches his body. He tries to stay still as if to move would draw Callum's attention. Callum rolls his face around so he's staring up at Ed.

'Why don't you just tell her?' he says.

Ed rubs his face.

'What are you talking about?'

'You know what I'm talking about.'

He raps his knuckles on the table. He tilts an ice cube from his empty Coke glass into his mouth and crunches it until it can slide down his throat like gravel.

'Come on. I know. Holly knows. Everyone knows.'

Holly knows? He picks up his phone to see if he's heard from Maggie.

He says, 'Don't know what you're talking about.'

'You do, though.'

Ed lowers his eyes. He says, 'Stop.'

'The only thing she'll care about is how you treated my brother.'

'Stop,' he says, this time with firmness.

He closes his eyes and replays the whole thing. He had been so young. He had liked Maggie because he had seen that she was different, and he had felt himself to be different too, and he had believed that by getting close to her, he'd find a way out of Basildon. He'd seen how hard things had been for Phil, and he didn't want that for himself, so he used Phil as a stepping stone towards a future with Maggie, and lashed out when that future was threatened.

Callum goes on, 'It was a shit thing to do.'

'Do you think I don't know that?'

'It's a miracle he still talks to you.'

'Count my lucky stars, should I?'

'I'm not trying to upset you.'

He looks at the TV screen. He looks at the bar.

'You are upsetting me.'

His eyes stay on the bar; his whole body is shaking.

Callum says, 'You're about to make a big change, mate.'

Ed wonders does Callum notice the shaking. He wonders if he should try to stop.

Callum smiles slightly, speaks softly. He raises his head. He says, 'All I'm saying is that I don't want you to make a mistake.'

Ed says nothing. He looks towards the door.

'Alright,' says Callum. 'No need to talk about it now.'

Steve gets back and announces that he'd love a Big Mac. They leave the pub. After its dim fluorescence, the sunlight outside glares like a nuclear bomb. Tottenham is radioactive. They're just off the main road, traffic roars, and Ed guides their group towards McDonald's.

'These used to be my ends,' says Steve. 'Did you know that? My auntie's house was near here. Gone now. McDonald's is still here though. That's where I'd go when I took a girl out. Did you know that? Back then, two pounds was enough. Two cinema tickets, two burgers, two strawberry milkshakes. If she wanted chips, she'd get them herself.'

'You're a real Romeo, aren't you?' says Callum.

'It was different back then. McDonald's and the cinema was a big treat. Not that I should eat too many Big Macs myself. Your mother is never happy when I do. Hey, Ed, you have all that to look forward to with your missus as well, don't you?'

Ed laughs, not sure what the joke is, and says, 'Don't I know it!'

Steve pauses.

'My own wife's not well,' he says from nowhere.

Ed says nothing, and then, 'I know. I'm sorry to hear.'

'She's not well at all,' continues Steve, keeping his eyes on the sky the whole time. Callum places his hand on his dad's shoulder. Steve seems as if he is addressing the world at large, or no one at all. 'I'd like to see more of you,' he says to Callum.

Callum says nothing.

Steve says again, 'I don't see you enough. Or your brother.'

Callum nods, and says he'd like that, and then they continue towards McDonald's.

. . .

TWO WORDS: BOOZE CRUISE. THIS IS HOW CHRISTINE, Holly's maid of honour, explains what's going to happen today when they all gather in Greenwich for the hen party.

Everyone claps. They all say, 'Oooooooooh.'

Then Christine clarifies, 'Actually, no. Three words: 1980s booze cruise.'

They're standing on a jetty that juts out from the bend in the Thames. It's just after 5 p.m. There are twenty people here, mostly women of Maggie's age, but a few older ones too. The air vibrates with the buzzing of insects. A mosquito lands on Maggie's forearm and bites before she can swat it away.

She takes a moment to consider her choices. She is twelve weeks pregnant and hasn't been home since yesterday morning. Is this a strange state of affairs? Does it reveal something worrying about her emotional life? Her main concern is that she's worked a full shift, slept on a flea-bitten couch, and hurled herself into the murky waters of the mixed pond and still hasn't showered or changed her clothes in more than a day. Holly is resplendent in a white summer dress. Ali wears a tight vest, vintage tracksuit bottoms, and Matrix-style shades. Maggie's clothes are creased, her hair is greasy, and she wishes she could smoke, so that at least she could maintain her tenuous claim on glamour. At least she has a get-out clause. *Sorry, Pregnant!* she'll announce after two hours. Ed will pick her up at 7 p.m.

Ali calls out, 'You'll have to elaborate, babe.'

'OK,' says Christine. 'Picture it. We're sailing down the Thames. Think exclusivity. Think luxury. But it's not, like, just drinking on a boat. It's immersive. It's a curated experience. There's a theme. As we all know, if there's one thing that Holly loves, it's the eighties, and that's why we're doing a fully immersive, fully catered, 1980s booze cruise!'

Everyone claps. They all say, 'Ooooooooooh.'

'Oh my God. I can't believe it,' says Holly.

Christine continues, 'There'll be classic eighties hits, and there's a projector screen which will be showing, you know, *The Breakfast Club* or whatever, and cocktails will be eighties-themed too. And as I said, it's really immersive. It's an experience. They say it's like a time machine, like actually *being* in the eighties, but also, like, being on a boat.'

With that, the group is ushered on board. The staff on the boat are all dressed like Michael Jackson, red military blazers and one white glove, and 'Thriller' is playing from a loudspeaker. There's a bar and a dance floor and a little seating area, and everyone is handed a glass of prosecco. Ali drinks hers in one gulp and then starts to dance. Maggie sits down to gaze at the shore as the boat pulls away and sails west towards Tower Bridge.

Ali seems to be having a great time already. She and an old woman, presumably Holly's grandmother, are dancing in sync, doing the werewolf thing from the 'Thriller' video, and suddenly everyone is wearing a wig. When did that happen? It reminds Maggie of a story Phil told her about a Christmas party at work. The theme of the party was 'silly wigs' but because the theme had been controversial and not everyone agreed that there should be a theme at all, HR was forced to concede that while adherence to the theme was encouraged, ultimately it was optional. In the end, the only person to wear a wig was Phil's manager Alan, until Phil, feeling bad, put one on too. That night, he sent Maggie a picture of himself in a neon-pink bob, grinning in the bathroom mirror. She wants to send him a picture of herself in a wig now too, but is afraid that maybe she and Phil are on bad terms since their meeting earlier on, and in any case she doesn't know where everyone got the wigs from.

Then, a text from Phil. He says he has something to say about Ed.

She shakes her head in disbelief.

Not this again. Phil sees Ed, like he sees all straight men, as big, dumb, an inanimate lump, and Maggie as a sort of shallow suburban housewife for ever being with him.

She takes a moment to calm down, then replies, *can't talk.*

The heat. It's too much. She wants to lie down on the ground and be entirely still.

He texts again, *ok well, can we talk at the party?*

Then, Holly sits down beside her and places a curly blonde wig on her head.

'Oh thanks,' says Maggie. 'I was looking for one of these.'

Holly pauses and then says, 'I suppose you've heard the news?'

News? Maggie shuffles through her mind for recent gossip.

'What are you talking about?'

'Rosaleen. She's not well. Couldn't be here today, bless her.'

'Oh right, of course. Ed told me. It's awful.'

'Have you heard from Phil?'

'Sort of. I'm not sure how he's doing. How's Callum?'

'Well, I was hoping you could tell me! He's been a bit distant, to be honest. Drinking a bit too much. Staying out late and not texting. I wondered if you had any info via Ed?'

Holly fidgets while she speaks and smiles all the time. Maggie takes a breath and wants to hold her. 'I'm sorry,' she says. 'That sounds tough. Ed hasn't told me, but I'll ask.'

Holly grins, puts a hand on Maggie's forearm and says, 'Not to worry. Tell me, how's it all going?' She nods meaningfully towards Maggie's tummy.

'Oh, things are going fine. I'm twelve weeks now. Can't believe it, really.'

'Only six months left! You must be excited.'

Something in the way Holly speaks makes Maggie want to cry. She says, 'I am excited. I really am. But scared too. Literally terrified. I'm kind of just assuming that when the baby comes, I'll automatically know how to be a mum, but that might not be true at all.'

'Oh hun. My sister was the exact same when she had her first little one. Petrified. But she was OK in the end, and you will be too. I'm not saying it'll be easy. Of course there'll be moments when you're scared and insecure and think you're doing everything wrong. But you'll have people around you who love you and want the best for you, people like Ed and Phil and your mum and me and Callum, and we'll all be there to figure it out together. Bringing this baby into the world is a group project. Everyone's right here with you.'

There's a commotion on the other end of the boat. A stripper has appeared. He's dressed like the Terminator and is speaking in a bad Russian accent. He searches for the bride-to-be while the hen party screams in delight.

'Oh God,' says Holly. 'Catch you later, babe. Looks like I'm wanted over here.'

Holly sits on a chair in the middle of the dance floor to receive her lap dance and Maggie leans back to watch the show. The Terminator swings his leather jacket above his head, whips off his jeans to reveal a thong underneath and all the guests scream and laugh. Holly covers her eyes, and Ali jokes, 'You'd think they'd never seen an ass before!'

Just then, a barge sails up beside them, moving at speed towards the east.

It seems impossible, ridiculous, completely surreal.

But it can't be denied. The whale is lying on top of the barge, and the scientist from the news is pouring water over it using a little red watering can, looking very tired.

It can't be denied that the sun is shining beautifully too, and there is noise and colour and tourists clambering for a view over the railings of Tower Bridge. The sky is pure pink.

Today has been one of those rare days – only one or two each year – where time works differently, where the day is so long that it can house each of your desires. You can wake in South London, go to bed in North London and travel between East, West and everywhere between, and still have time to stop for McDonald's. On days like this one, you don't have to choose between one thing and another thing; there is time for everything.

The whale is only a few metres from the booze cruise. It's huge. Its eyes open and close and its skin is dyed golden by the sun. Helicopters swarm ahead.

She stops her thinking to stand. Maggie and Ali and all the women and the Michael Jacksons and even the Terminator, now nude, stop what they are doing to cheer the whale on.

'Go on, my son!' shouts Holly from her seat on the dance floor. 'Good lass!'

. . .

ALREADY, PHIL IS ON A BUS TO SOHO: HE HOPPED ON one as soon as Keith messaged.

He sits in the front seat of the top deck. His leg twitches.

The bus ambles across Waterloo Bridge – to the left, the sun hangs beyond a scaffolded Big Ben – and Phil feels like hot blood. Sticky. Pumped through the city by a hard-beating heart, and the city itself like a body under stress, drenched in sweat and panting.

Phil has no more capacity for conscious thought. Pulsing towards Keith is beyond bad or good: it's an automatic bodily function.

From the top deck, Phil can hear a man trying to fight the driver. Fists bash against the perspex. *Don't fucking start because you don't know me.* Outside, it's hot and windy. Plastic bags fly in small cyclones before flopping towards the pavement. Surely it will rain soon.

He thinks about Maggie.

He cares enormously about her happiness. Her happiness is bound to his own. He wants the best for her, and Ed is not it.

Soho approaches. He gets off the bus. He knows it's not what it once was, but he loves it still; jaded socialites, retired rent boys, once-magnificent drag queens who tell anyone who'll listen in the smoking area of Trisha's that this place has gone to the dogs. He and Keith went there on the first day they met, and since then he's seen Soho as a place of magic, where chance encounters flourish, despite its transformation into a tourist-trap theme park.

He meets Keith outside the Admiral Duncan. He's leaning against the wall and smoking and Soho surges all around. Just this minute, the temperature has become bearable.

Phil remembers that it's not the first time they planned to meet at this pub.

He remembers a vigil on Old Compton Street for people killed in the Orlando massacre. That morning, Keith had lain on his side while Phil held him from behind. He kissed his back softly and said 'It's OK' quietly, without a response. He remembers deciding that the next time he kissed Keith's armpits, his eyelids, his thighs, he would do so as if he were at the end of an arduous pilgrimage to a sacred site, as if Keith's body were the holiest thing he knew, because it was. They agreed to meet at the vigil, and when Keith didn't arrive, Phil muttered 'Where are you?' under his breath and checked his phone to see if the ticks beneath his message had turned blue, which they didn't, and a choir sang 'Somewhere Over the Rainbow' beneath a plaque for victims of the Admiral Duncan bombing.

He remembers how there were walks, and there were weekends, and there was eating crisps in bed. There was a train to Sussex, and a trek across the South Downs, and there was a stroll along the river where Virginia Woolf had drowned. Keith could recite word for word the scene from *The Hours* in which Leonard and Virginia argued at the train station; in his impression of Nicole Kidman's Oscar-winning performance, Keith would sometimes say through curdled lips: *If it is a choice between Richmond and death, I choose death.*

He remembers a renewed appreciation for nature. He remembers living things; the brightness, the green-ness, the
pink-ness of spring. He remembers a bus to Hampstead Heath,
a stroll down The Bishop's Avenue, and stories Keith made up
about the cartoon super-villains who lived in the empty mansions. He remembers Camden, discussing where they'd been
when Amy Winehouse had died. Phil remembered being at
work in the American-themed fast-food restaurant, the stench
of grease clogging his nose, shocked at the scale of his own sadness for someone he didn't know. Keith remembered the Brixton
squat where he lived with twenty anarchists, each believing that
the revolution was only around the corner and listening to *Back
to Black* three times a day for the rest of that summer.

Now, they lean against the front of the pub.

Keith hands him a pint of lager and a cigarette and gives
him a kiss on the cheek.

'I've just come from home,' he says. 'Looks like the party
is back on.'

Phil nods, while Keith squeezes his arm and asks about
his day.

'Well, it was a mixed bag. But I think my mum enjoyed
Westfield.'

'I don't blame her. It's a glamorous place.'

'Have you ever taken your mum there?'

'God, no. My mum doesn't come to London.'

They're quiet for a moment, and Phil looks out across the
street while puffing on his fag. Old Compton Street is chaos,
rammed with hen parties and old gays who have been coming
here since the nineties. Phil looks back and says, 'Why did you
want to meet?'

Keith considers it for a second.

'I wasn't happy with how things went earlier on. I wanted to explain things.'

Phil nods. 'I wasn't going to come. I was going to say I had other plans.'

'Why would you do that?'

Phil slumps back on the wall and takes a moment to answer. 'You stand me up all the time. You only respond to half of my messages. I feel so incidental to your life, but you're so central to mine. It doesn't feel good. I can't do it forever.'

Keith says nothing. Then he nods and says, 'Yeah.'

Phil pictures himself walking away towards nothing in particular.

'I wish that you treated me better.'

Keith looks at his feet.

'I think I'm afraid of commitment.'

'Are you not committed to Louis?'

'I'm afraid of commitment to you. Specifically.'

Phil laughs and the noise that comes out of his own mouth shocks him. He says, 'There's nothing to be afraid of! Have you met me? Do you know how passive I am? I'd roll over and let you rub my belly if you wanted. I'd sit on command. You act like I'm demanding some unpayable dowry. All I want is for you to fuck me and hold me and . . .'

'What?'

'Nothing. It doesn't matter. You're moving. You're with Louis.'

'This is the problem though. I want you to ask me for things. I want you to act like you want me. I didn't even know until today you were really that interested at all.'

Phil doesn't know what to say, so he just says, 'What do you mean?'

Keith chews his lip for a second. He says, 'I don't know if you know this, but you're quite aloof. I suggest places we could go, things we could eat, films we could watch, and you barely seem to notice I'm talking. Sometimes, I don't know if you're in the room at all.'

'You're with Louis. What do you expect?'

'You're with other people too, aren't you?'

'Not in the same way. You're moving to a new town with him.'

'I thought that didn't bother you.'

'Of course it bothers me.'

'Well, why didn't you say so then? I never know how you feel because you never tell me. I need to feel wanted.' Keith pauses, takes a breath, looks exasperated. He continues, 'Can I tell you something? I just want to explain where I'm coming from. I grew up in an Irish Catholic family, right? They treated their Catholicism and their Irishness with that weird sort of fanaticism of third generation migrants who fetishise their ancestral customs without understanding the first thing about them. My parents were pious, my teachers were pious, and I was full of shame. I knew I was gay from the age of eight, and to know I was gay was to know I was going to hell. I knew because all the adults never shut up about it. It was hell this, hell that, sodomy this, sodomy that, and I thought, aged eight, that if I was still gay by the age of twelve, I'd be left with no choice but to kill myself. I moved away as soon as I could, but it left me with a sense of my own wrongness. Do you know what I mean? Whenever anyone loved me, even just wanted to fuck me, I couldn't help thinking of them as a sick freak – not in a hot way – because how could anyone other than a sick freak want such an abomination?'

Phil reaches out to touch him.

Keith bats his hand away.

'It's fine. I mean, really, it's actually fine. It took ages but I managed to shake that feeling to a point where I straight-forwardly adore sex and all the guys I do it with, but that was until I met you. When I try to show you that I want you and you act like you're not in the room at all, I feel so unlovable, Phil, I feel like a weird little pervert. Like I'm hounding you.'

Phil looks at him, puts an arm around his shoulder and kisses his cheek.

He thinks about the night in Burgess Park, how it ruined his relationship to his own body and everyone who wanted to love it, including Keith. He doesn't want this any more.

He wants more than anything to make Keith's adult life indescribably good, never not pleasurable, rich and bright, so great that any pain will become a vague and distant memory.

He says, 'I want you so much, Keith.'

Keith pulls back, and says softly, 'Well, why can't you act like it?'

Phil closes his eyes, tries to breathe slowly, almost laughs.

What's he got to lose? Why try to keep it in any longer?

'OK,' he says, uncertain. 'Maybe I can try to explain.'

He takes a few more breaths. Clenches his fists.

'There's something that happened to me in Burgess Park.'

12

JOAN, ON HER ARMCHAIR, IS SURE THAT THE WORLD can be withstood. That's what she's believed for her whole life, and even in her sixth decade, she finds her mantra has gone unchallenged. Her husband: dead. Her bank account: on its last legs. She's sixty-two, staring down the barrel of two to three more decades of life, poor and alone and in pain, and still she finds that everything, more or less, is fine. Her daily experience of the world: fine. Her TV shows: fine. The porridge she eats every morning: fine, and nourishing too, and good for her digestive health, which also is fine, even though she gets a little heartburn every now and then.

She learned as a child that things can be tolerated. All you have to do is focus on the details of each second, which are nearly always easier to take than the bigger picture. The bigger picture, of course, is hard to stomach. Her husband is dead, and he shouldn't be.

She sits in her armchair and counts the shades of blue on a loitering magpie, then the shades of green, then purple, then tallies these three subtotals to calculate the total number of colours: thirty-six, she believes. Also: she salutes the magpie. How's your wife? she says. She only learned in her forties that the reason people enquire after a magpie's wife is because it implies the existence of a second magpie, two magpies being a good omen, while a single magpie is a bad omen. She'd always thought it was for the sake of common courtesy!

Either way, she likes the magpies. Since Peter died, people have treated her as a single magpie: to be respected, yes, but also to be avoided. She does karaoke in the local pub every Saturday night, and they applaud her performances, but no one asks to buy her a drink.

There was a time when she thought her husband's death would be the end of her. When she was eighteen, for example, she saw a public information film on what to do in the event of a nuclear attack. It said to crouch under the table, in the bathtub, get shelter, pray to God, but all Joan could think was that there was no way in hell she'd hide from the bomb.

She'd sprint across the city to find him. That's what she'd do. She'd be an action hero. James Bond, Jean Grey, Joan of Arc. Leaping over every burnt-out bus in her way, all for the chance to cling to her boyfriend's lovely back: she'd have her last street corner kiss.

She can see now that she stood to lose more than Peter in the event of a nuclear war, but surely that's what a global catastrophe means for anyone: it's not the loss of the world at large you mourn, it's the loss of *your* world, your life, your boyfriend's gorgeous little smile in the morning, the way he says *mwah mwah mwah mwah* while planting big slobbery kisses all over your forearm. That's when she knew that she loved him: when she started thinking of his death. She knew she'd found something good when she knew she couldn't stand to lose it.

Anyway, now that he's finally gone, she finds that she can survive after all. Each second, taken on its own, is nearly always tolerable. All she needs to do is put one foot after the other, tally the colours on the back of a magpie, consider each piece of chewing gum stuck to the pavement ahead of her and estimate which year the chewing gum originally dropped to the ground based on how grey and weather-beaten it is compared to its peers.

When she was six years old, Joan's class was taken on a school trip to witness the opening of the new dual carriage-way. It was a big deal: even the Queen was there. Joan and her classmates stood on the overpass and were instructed to cheer for the vehicles. Children were always being instruct-ed to cheer back then. A big round of applause, her teacher would demand at the drop of a hat.

The Queen was the first to use the dual carriageway: she was driven down it by the Duke of Edinburgh himself. A careful driver, the papers said the next day, and also, that the asphalt cracked under the weight of the lorries that came after her. The asphalt, it turned out, was of a poor quality and required replacement. Joan's father turned to her while read-ing the paper that morning and said, 'Did you hear that? Your dual carriageway's not fit for purpose.'

Your dual carriageway. As if she, a child, had any stake in the dual carriageway at all! She had felt entirely ambivalent about it, and outright annoyed at her teacher's insistence that she find it impressive and joyful, although to be fair, she did sing its praises when she went home to her family that day, and also sang the praises of the Duke of Edinburgh's driving skills, and also claimed that the Queen waved, not at the children in a general sense, but at her specifically. She was six years old: she wanted to be part of a bigger story. She would never forget the pleasure her father took in taking her down a peg. There are adults who thrive off the puncturing of children's fantasies. *Who did those children think they were?* said the adults. *What right had a child to their own happiness?* Joan swore she would never puncture the fantasies of her own son: she would let him believe in anything. He wanted to spend his weekends counting the blues and greens and purples on the wings of passing magpies, so she bought a pair of pound shop binoculars and took him to the Thames estuary. She showed him that there were more birds than magpies alone. Dozens of colours on each one. Even the ones that from a distance seem drab and beige are shocking on closer inspection. If you squint, focus, stay very still, you'll see. Electric blue, bottle green, magenta.

She inhales, exhales, looks across the street at Rosaleen's house.

She wonders when she's coming home.

. . .

ROSALEEN MEETS STEVE AT STRATFORD STATION AT 6 p.m. to return to Basildon. She has spent the past two hours wandering in and out of shops, buying nothing, looking at nothing, trying as hard as she could to think of nothing either, and even the air conditioning couldn't cool her down.

Steve's skin is red and shiny with sweat. He's got a smile on his face which suggests he's been drinking.

They sit down on the train and he asks did she tell Phil the news.

'I didn't,' she says.

He nods.

'We just didn't have enough time,' she clarifies.

He nods again and gives her leg a squeeze.

She wipes sweat from her brow and asks how Callum is.

'Alright,' says Steve.

She thinks of Phil's expression in the supermarket when he said that Callum was a drug dealer. She squirms in her seat.

'He didn't have too much to drink, did he?'

'No,' says Steve, his arms folded across his chest.

She wants Steve to reveal more information, but she can't figure out what she wants to ask, or if she even wants to know at all.

Then, out of nowhere, he says, 'I gave him a hug.'

'Did you?'

'I did.'

'I'm sure he appreciated it.'

'I don't know.'

She squeezes his hand. She says, 'You're a lovely dad.'

He nods and says, 'I'll give Phil a text.'

They're both quiet then. He wipes sweat from his forehead and gives her a packet of crisps from his backpack.

They sit silently for most of the journey, both looking out of the window, making occasional observations. She says at one point, 'Oh look at those big pylons.' Steve nods: there's nothing further to say about the pylons beyond that they're big and they're there.

A woman gets off the train carrying twelve bags of shopping and wearing a coat that many people would think of as too warm for the heat. Steve says, 'She had a lot of shopping bags,' and Rosaleen says, 'Big coat too.' This is not a value judgement on whether it is good or it is bad to be a woman with a lot of shopping bags and a big coat; it is simply remarking that such a thing exists and Rosaleen and Steve had been there to witness it together.

Their wordlessness is a symptom of their intimacy, so attuned to each other that they are beyond verbal language altogether. Barely saying a word, these two are understood. They will go home; they will watch telly; they will go to bed. She will turn over onto her side and he will hold her from behind, the same position they have slept in for nearly forty years.

They will be like that when they doze off and they will be like that when they wake up and he will bring her a cup of tea and say, 'I love you,' and she will say, 'I love you too.'

There is no need to waste time saying 'I will miss you when you're gone' and 'I don't want to go to a place where I can't hold you any more' because all of this is understood. She knows that she'll die and her mornings with Steve are numbered, as are her train trips with him, and the glasses of wine on Friday nights, and the walks around the estate when the two of them are trying to lose weight, and asking strangers to take pictures of them on the beach, or on holidays, or in restaurants in town when they go out for a bite to eat and he gets tomato sauce all over his shirt even though she's only just washed it.

Even if the doctor gives good news on Monday, she's only got so much time left. They both know this, so there's no need to say anything; all they need to do is live out their time as best as they can and be together. She puts her head on his shoulder. He squeezes her leg. He says it won't be long until the days are shorter. She says that it's the summer solstice tonight and that Phil is having a party in his house, and there'll be singing and dancing. Steve says it sounds very pagan. Rosaleen says, 'That's our Phil, isn't it?' and Steve agrees.

Rosaleen drives them home from Basildon station. On the radio, there's news of the whale, a dramatic rescue operation and people lining the Thames to catch a glimpse. The latest reports say that the whale is alive, but in a critical condition, and is due to pass under the Dartford Crossing in thirty minutes' time. Rosaleen lets out a quiet chuckle. Only a few hours ago, she thought she'd go to see the whale with Phil. It seems like a silly idea now.

She pulls in to the driveway and notices Joan Seymour sitting across the road as usual. Rosaleen wonders if she goes into the house at all at this stage. The nights are probably warm enough to sleep outside, although of course it's not safe, especially for a woman.

'Hiya, Joan,' she calls out, as Steve stumbles into the house.

'Hello!' shouts Joan, louder than necessary.

Rosaleen walks up to her. Joan is wearing the same clothes as yesterday, and there's rubbish strewn around her feet.

Rosaleen doesn't like what she sees. She doesn't like that Joan sits there all day and barely speaks to anyone, except for Ed when he visits, and Rosaleen every now and then, and she worries about what will happen to Steve after she dies. Who's he going to talk to? The men at work, and his sons when they can be bothered to text, but that's not enough.

She sits on Peter's chair, and says, 'What do you make of the whale business then?'

'The whale business?'

'The whale in the Thames. She's being rescued on a barge. The news said that people are lining the river to catch a glimpse. She'll be going under the Dartford Crossing soon.'

Joan nods, nonplussed. Rosaleen feels ridiculous, but still presses on.

'I'm thinking of going. Will you come?'

Joan says nothing for a long time.

Then, she says, 'Aye.'

'You'll come?'

'Aye. My son was telling me about it.'

'Was he?'

'He saw it and thought he'd gone mad. I gave him a good slagging off.'

Joan stands and starts dragging her furniture back inside.

'Don't just stand there,' she says. 'Help me with these.'

Ten minutes later, they're speeding down the dual carriageway in Rosaleen's car. There's only fifteen minutes until the whale is due to pass under the Dartford Crossing and it takes half an hour to get there. Joan turns up the volume on the radio without asking permission, but Rosaleen doesn't mind. They lower the windows and a pop song blares from the speakers, and Joan says, 'Go on, Rosaleen! We don't have all the time in the world.'

The Thelma and Louise comparison is unavoidable. It's so obvious that it's a miracle that neither of them has said it aloud. Rosaleen adores that film and watches it alone whenever she has the house to herself. She can't stop crying at the bit where Thelma says, 'Just keep going,' the two women parked right at the edge of the cliff and the police all lined up behind them. Then, Louise grabs Thelma's face and they kiss full on the lips.

Rosaleen wants to turn to Joan and say, 'We're just like Thelma and Louise.' She wants for Joan to laugh and say, 'We're a right pair,' but she's afraid that the lesbian subtext would make Joan feel uncomfortable, even though Thelma and Louise only kissed when seconds from grisly death and lived a heterosexual life when they weren't under such pressure.

Then, Joan throws her head back, shouts, 'Thelma and Louise, eat your heart out!'

Rosaleen laughs. She sees the Dartford Crossing rise before them.

She drives them onto the centre of the bridge and pulls into the hard shoulder. It's a motorway, and no one's meant to stop, but she does it anyway. Cars beep their horns. She undoes her seatbelt, grabs her handbag, clambers out of the car. Joan is ahead, rushing towards the two-dozen people who lean over the railings with binoculars. Joan left the car door open behind her, and Rosaleen, checking the time, decides to leave her car door open too. There's only a minute until the whale is due to pass. The wind whips her hair about her face and the traffic clogs her ears. 'Pauline,' she whispers once, twice, three times, as if asking Pauline to be here beside her, remembering the precise shape of Pauline's waist.

Standing by the barrier, she feels foolish. She feels surveilled. Even though the people here are directing their attention towards the barge in the distance, she still feels self-conscious, as if to be a lone woman staring at a whale is an inappropriate thing to be in public, a transgression for which she will be silently judged, if not violently harassed.

She remembers herself as a six-year-old child.

Going to hell for her bad insides.

'Oh God,' she mutters, her voice vibrating with a barely suppressed sob.

She breathes short, shallow breaths.

She closes her eyes. She opens them again.

The barge approaches. The whale lies atop. It's incredible and unlikely and moving at speed. Everyone cheers and whoops and says 'Yes!' and Rosaleen, overwhelmed, yelps 'Pauline!' at volume into the wind. She gasps at her own voice; she covers her mouth.

'You what?' says Joan, turning to look at her.

Rosaleen stammers, looks around.

'Nothing,' she blurts out.

'Why did you say Pauline?'

'I didn't.'

'I heard you.'

'It must have been someone else.'

Joan looks at her for a second and puts a hand on her shoulder.

'Are you alright?'

'Me? Yes, fine.'

'Are you sure?'

'It's getting cold.'

Joan takes another pause, and then says, 'Who is Pauline?'

Rosaleen thinks about the question. Who was Pauline? Impossible to answer.

She was a poet. Good at cartwheels. Everyone was always seeing her knickers.

She was scandalous. Never not mortally sinning. A glint in her eye, she said *dare me.*

And you know what? Maybe Pauline *did* mean to show her knickers. Maybe Rosaleen *did* mean to look at them. Maybe she enjoyed it and thought about it again, more than once.

The barge passes under the bridge. It continues east towards the sea.

And another thing that happened more than once? *Rosaleen and Pauline wrestled.* So what? It was the only excuse they had to touch each other. And Rosaleen, oh God, she wanted to touch. She was dying to see what the soft bits of flesh around Pauline's sides felt like – *gorgeous*, is how they felt, *sublime*, is how they felt – and it's not even that wrestling was *particularly* acceptable behaviour for a girl in Dublin at that time, but at least wrestling was a story to tell. It made their craving to touch and be touched halfway legible to themselves.

What they told themselves was this: Dublin wasn't safe for a young woman. Drugs: *everywhere*. Perverts and winos stalking the streets. A brutal mugging: all but inevitable.

As such, they agreed: one must always be ready to wrestle.

In fact, Dublin was so perilous, they said, that they needed to practise wrestling every day without fail. They began the moment they finished their homework and wrestled non-stop until Rosaleen had to go home for her tea. They held each other in all imaginable positions. Rosaleen hadn't known that bodies could move like that. She hadn't known that a bicep could clench around your thigh, or a chin could massage the groove of your lower back. They yanked at each other. They squeezed. They became breathless and still went on. All that sweat! Their school uniforms reeked of *body*. The other girls teased them for the foul smell, but Rosaleen didn't care: better to be bullied for being a stinker than bullied for loving a girl.

It changed her very sensation of having a body.

Before that, she'd barely had a body at all.

She turns to Joan, sheepish.

'Someone I knew in Ireland,' she says. 'We were friends before I left.'

Joan stares, expectant, wanting more.

Rosaleen goes on, 'Would you like a bit of bread? It's not very good.'

She reaches into her handbag and unwraps the bread from its clingfilm.

'I'd love some, thanks, Rosaleen,' says Joan, tearing off a chunk and chewing it.

They both look east towards the sea.

'This is delicious, Rosaleen. You sell yourself short when you say it's not good.'

Rosaleen blushes, says, 'Thanks,' and unprompted Joan mentions there's karaoke on in the local pub tonight. 'Would you like to go?' she ventures, and Rosaleen says she would.

13

ED AND MAGGIE STAND BY THE RIVER AT DEPTFORD. He drove to Greenwich to collect her after the match and picked her up when she disembarked from the boat. She was tired. He was happy to see her. Ten minutes into the journey, they noticed the sun was setting, and stopped by the river to watch. They stand on the wall. He points out birds and tells her their names. He doesn't know the name of each one, but he tries to exude a confidence. There's a red-necked grebe. There's a heron and a curlew. There's a floppy-beaked tufty, he shouts, even though a floppy-beaked tufty is not the name of a real bird at all. Maggie says, 'That sounds fake.'

'Well, I suppose that's because I made it up.'

'Why did you make it up?'

'I was testing you.'

Laughing, she says, 'What are you like,' then she gives him a kiss on the cheek.

Finally, next to Maggie, his breathing gets deeper and longer. He relaxes.

She's always had this effect. She's the only one who can calm him down.

. . .

MAGGIE NEXT TO ED, ON THE A12 BACK TO HACKNEY. Old romantic garage tracks play from the car speakers and he puts his hand on her leg whenever they stop at a red light. Ed's car smells like cheese and onion crisps. There is mud all over the floor and the dashboard, and the back seat is stuffed with junk that he one day plans on taking to the landfill. Maggie is calmer than she's been all day. Phil's text gets lost beneath the familiar comfort of sitting next to Ed in the car. She thinks of her mum. A recent argument, the topic, as usual: Jeremy Corbyn.

A one-time radical, her mum was let down too often. Revolutions came and went, and things only ever got worse. The GLC, the poll-tax riots, the road protests.

It all ends the same, she said: *the road gets built.*

Maggie thinks of her mother's fatalism as a choice: thousands of others lived through the same historic defeats, and they didn't come to those conclusions. She knows that these people exist because she's met them in their droves at Hackney Labour meetings. She knows, too, that her mum speaks from a place of love. She sees Maggie's dreams: how she knocks on doors in marginal seats to talk to strangers about the Labour manifesto, how she genuinely, *ecstatically*, believes that a Corbyn government is not only possible, but inevitable, imminent, just around the corner, and it's going to change *everything for everyone*. She sees her daughter's dreams, and she shudders. *No*, she says. *Please don't do this to yourself.*

Maggie looks up.

'Did you know that part of the A12 only opened in ninety-seven?' she says. 'Seems eternal now but this was all residential. Near where we're driving. My mum and her friends squatted a house here. Declared independence from the UK. Even had their own flag: called it the *Union Jill*. Left us with my dad, and he left us with my gran, the prick.'

'I'm sorry,' Ed says quietly.

'It's fine. Gran's house was jokes. The road got built though. Obviously. That's my mum's catchphrase: *It ends the same. The road gets built.*'

'Is that where that's from?'

'It's funny. When she started saying it, she meant it as a statement of political fatigue. Like, the road's always going to get built so why bother trying to stop it? But then she started saying it about anything. Like once, after my dad left and we had no money for Christmas dinner, my aunt dropped around a frozen turkey and Yorkshire puds, and my mum, in sheer jubilation, announces to the room *The road gets built!* as if she were clinking glasses with someone at the pub. When I told her I was pregnant, I half expected her to say it then. Can you imagine? *Mum, I'm pregnant*, and her, sighing, resigned: *Well, the road gets built.*'

Maggie thinks about what her mother really said.

I've always been unsure about Ed.

She pauses, changes the subject.

'Hey, I bought acid off this druid once. Do you remember? At the rave beneath the flyover at Canning Town. Beginning of summer. Six years ago. Seven? Anyway, this druid, I'm trying to buy the acid off him, and he literally will not stop talking about how the A12 is an ancient road that the Celts used for transporting energy from one sacred site to the next.'

Ed bursts into laughter.

'Mate,' he says, 'you're always chatting shit to druids at raves.'

'What are you on about? Only happened once.'

'Swear to God, it happens every time we go out. If you lose Maggie at a party, look no further than the smoking area: there she is, chatting to a druid about magical yew trees.'

'Excuse me, that wasn't a druid. It was just a man with a long beard.'

'Looked like a druid to me.'

'*Looking* like a druid doesn't *make* you one. They've got a whole set of customs.'

'You know a lot about druids for someone who's only met one once.'

'Funny boy.' She smiles, and he smiles back.

A missed exit, a wrong turn: they end up being diverted all the way to Shoreditch. Neither of them mind. Maggie's often thought that they're at their best in the car. She breathes in deep, turns up the radio, feels calmer than she's felt in months. *I love him more than ever*, she thinks to herself, also thinking of Phil's message and how there's nothing Phil could say that would turn her against Ed. *I love you more than ever*, she almost says out loud, almost thinking, too, of telling Ed about the message, but holding back each time she goes to speak.

'Callum's not taking the news about his mum well,' he says.

She hesitates for a moment. 'God, I can imagine.'

'Do you think Phil's OK?'

She blows air through her lips. 'I honestly don't know, babe.'
She looks at him, pauses.

Then, she goes on, 'Today was quite weird. I'm not sure what's up with him.'

Ed drums on the steering wheel. 'What do you mean?'

'I don't know. Why hasn't he told me? He's close to his mum.'

Ed puts his hand on her leg and says, 'You're a good friend.'
She places both hands on top of his.

'There's a party at his tonight,' she says.

Ed, eyes on the road, responds absent-mindedly, 'Oh yeah, I think he mentioned.'

He swerves into the slow lane.

'You spoke to him?' she says.

Ed pauses. He stares hard at passing road signs as if he doesn't know where to go, and answers five seconds later, as if it's an afterthought, 'Yeah. Ran into him. Was it yesterday? I can't remember now. Days blending into each other. But yeah, he mentioned the party then.'

'You didn't mention that.'

'Wasn't worth mentioning.'

'He didn't mention it either.'

'Well, he's got a lot on his plate.'

'Where did you see him?'

'Euston? Or maybe Liverpool Street? I worked so much this week, it's all a blur.'

She hums. 'That's strange,' she says, thinking again of Phil's text.

They drive up Shoreditch High Street. Maggie read an article at sixteen about how Shoreditch was the *avant-garde heart of East London* – Tracey Emin had lived there! Alexander McQueen! – and driving up the high street now she compares the actual Shoreditch to the Shoreditch of her teenage dreams. They pass a billboard for a sportswear brand, the slogan 'We Are Londoners' printed on it, and she thinks: every ad in the city is about being a Londoner now. We are Londoners, says the window display of Pret A Manger, to the bleary-eyed office workers with indigestion and a veggie brioche bap. We are Londoners, say the ads on the Tube for banks and co-working spaces and multivitamins and magnesium supplements and apps for finding a dentist or a partner or a marriage or a house-plant or someone to wax your eyebrows. We are Londoners, said an estate agent who led a couple past Maggie's front door last week, claiming the totality of urban life was churning in every square metre of this street. It's got it all, he told them as he showed them around an ex-council flat with a south-facing balcony from which you could gaze at the skyscrap-ers of the City and contemplate London's enormity, its sheer volume and variety of life. It's a dynamic area, said the estate agent. Vibrant. Diverse. Lots of local colour.

When they get home, she goes upstairs to change her clothes.

When she and Ed moved in at first, they were so used to dodgy landlords and letting agents that they expected to be evicted within six months, but as time went on they did the place up. They painted over the smudges on the walls, bought frames for their posters and nailed hooks to the walls so that Blu Tack didn't pockmark the fresh paint job. The mould was fine if they didn't smell it. Furniture could be positioned in front of it, fabric draped over it, windows opened and candles lit. There was only so much you could do to make these places feel clean: they had been unloved and neglected too long. Generations of tenants, seeing the flat was unloved, withheld their love in turn. They made baked beans and the beans splashed across the floor. They stayed there, hardened, ceased to be beans and became part of the lino.

Now, Ed comes in and lies down on the bed.

She can see his belly hair as he sticks his hand down his pants. She can't resist it, the dumb boyishness of the gesture, and she lays down beside him, tucking herself under his arm.

Hello, she says. Hello, he says.

She kisses him and snuggles her face against the side of his chest. She can't remember the last time they had sex. She is always so tired, and he is always so tired, and neither of them is ever home at the same time. But now, she is undeniably horny, yes, and the firmness of his chest feels so nice against the side of her head, and yes, it is undeniable that she wants to have sex. 'I love you,' she says. 'Thanks for doing the driving.'

She climbs on top and plants a firm kiss on his lips. *This*, she thinks, is always the best bit. Long bouts of kissing preceding long bouts of fucking. She loves to plunge into his mouth, and bite down on his lower lip. She runs her tongue along the backs of his teeth as if to say, 'I have a stake in these teeth. These teeth are my teeth too.' She loves kissing with her eyes open. She loves that he licks his lips. She loves that he smiles as he goes down on her, and smiles when he comes back up, childlike delight, as if her body were strange and new each time. They both have favourite bits of each other; she loves the soft thickness of his thighs, how the black hairs grow thicker until they merge with his pubes, neatly trimmed; he loves the wide expanse of her hips; he kisses them often and says *Fuck, I love this bit.*

. . .

YES, HE THINKS. THE SOFT SKIN OF A WOMAN. IT'S THE year 2019 and you're able to love. Love that's appropriate for a man like you (good man, normal man, man with a pregnant girlfriend). A nice guy, a good dad. You want her. She wants you. She doesn't know that you cracked an egg on the head of her best friend and that yesterday you followed a man into a toilet and you would have done whatever he said.

Intrusive thought: the pissy floors of Liverpool Street station.

No, he thinks. You are here with Maggie. Think about her soft lower back, the curve towards her ass. Here she is, giving you a blowjob, fine, good, we're both having fun, but *why oh why* did you mention the party at Phil's place; surely she will suspect you now, and surely she will leave you, and surely her leaving you will constitute a doom beyond words. Images of downfall flash through his mind, just briefly, too terrifying to look at for more than a second: he is sleeping on the streets, he has nowhere to live, no one to love or be loved by, and someone will crack eggs over *his* head and someone will dump milk over *his* back, and his lungs, dank and mouldy as the mattress beneath them, will crust over with tumours.

Needless to say, he has lost his erection.

His throat closes, his eyes water, he suppresses a coughing fit.

Maggie looks up and says, 'You OK, babe?'

'Yeah. Sorry. Just got in my head a bit.'

'It's OK,' she says, taking his dick in her hand and stroking it to try to get it hard again.

He tries to focus on the feel of her hand. Useless. He panics. He can't get a grasp of the situation. It's like being on the shore of a choppy sea: every time he tries to stand up a new wave knocks him down. 'It's OK,' he says. 'Hang on, just a second.'

He removes her hand. He tries to do it himself.

He looks at her while stroking his dick. He puts one hand on her breast.

The pressure. Too much. Doom beyond words.

Why did he tell her about Phil's party?

What is she going to think of him now?

He slows his hand to a full stop, then drops his dick as if by accident.

'Sorry,' he says. 'Don't think it's going to work.'

. . .

'IT'S FINE,' SHE SAYS. SHE LIES DOWN BESIDE HIM. 'WE can do it another time.'

It *is* fine. Honestly. She accepts that erections are unpredictable. She accepts that being turned on or turned off is delicate alchemy, mysterious and necessarily beyond our understanding, and not only determined by what's happening here in the room – by the shape of her body, for example, or whether or not he wants to fuck a pregnant woman – but determined by things that happened last week, or twenty years ago, or things that haven't happened yet at all but which have tunnelled like time-travellers into the present moment and come into your bedroom and messed up your bed and said *No sex for you today!* In any case, she knows that erections aren't always a barometer of being turned on or off: there are guys with soft dicks who are horny as fuck, and guys with hard dicks who just want to go to sleep. It's an automatic bodily impulse. It doesn't have to mean anything.

However: she wants him immensely, she *loves* him immensely, and they haven't fucked in twelve weeks. Will they ever fuck again? Years from now, will they come to categorise their lives into two discreet eras, not only defined by before and after parenthood, but before and after sex? And *why* can't they have sex now? What's changed? Yes, they are stressed about money, and yes, they are moving to Basildon, and yes, her relationship to London has always been an erotic one – never has she been so horny as when passing through London on a hot day, the city smelling of sex, sounding of sex, everyone, always, only ever having sex – but still, they used to fuck all the time. Why is it so difficult now?

She lies next to Ed. They are on their backs, both naked.

Their fingers are touching, but in an incidental way.

It's grazing, more than touching. It's like sitting beside a stranger on public transport. Your knees are in contact, but the contact doesn't mean anything. You're only sharing the same space by pure coincidence.

She could grab his hand.

She could squeeze his thigh.

It's within her power to put her head on his chest.

The touching doesn't have to be incidental. It could be deliberate, passionate, full of love. There are millimetres between them. If nothing else, to touch would be convenient.

And imagine how good it would feel. She could turn onto her side and kiss him. I love you, she could say, I'm happy to be here, or I love you, she could say, I can't wait to spend the rest of my life with you. By saying these things, these things could come true.

Remember a minute ago, how her tongue had licked the backs of his teeth?

All of this is still within reach. She has control over her own body. She's not paralysed. Her brain can easily say to her fingers *Fingers, touch Ed*, and her fingers, naturally, will always say yes.

Then, an idea. The party, she thinks with a rush of blood. We've always been happiest together at parties. Maybe the problem is that we haven't danced together in too long, and so our bodies aren't used to each other any more, and maybe tonight we could change that.

She thinks again of Phil's message. *There's something I need to tell you about Ed.*

She pushes the thought away.

'I thought we could go to Phil's party,' she says.

A door slams somewhere in the building. It makes an alarmingly loud crash.

Ed hesitates. 'Sure. Yeah. Maybe,' he eventually says.

'Do you not want to?'

He mumbles as if he were reading from a complicated instruction manual.

'Don't know if tonight's good for me.'

'We wouldn't have to go for long. It might be nice.'

'You know we need to save money.'

'What are you talking about? It'll hardly cost us anything.'

'It's just that I'm working so much at the moment.'

'Well, I work all the time too. I need to feel like I have things happening in my life beyond being pregnant and waitressing and packing up our flat.'

'You've got more than that. You've got me.'

'It's just that we don't *do* much any more.'

'Did we ever "do" much?'

'More than we do now.'

'I don't remember that.'

'What do you mean you don't remember *doing* stuff? That doesn't make sense. Do you not remember that we used to go to raves all the time? Do you not want that back? I do.'

He is quiet then. He says, 'I'm sorry, babe. Of course I'll come.'

He kisses her shoulder twice.

. . .

TO SUMMARISE AS QUICKLY AS POSSIBLE, WITHOUT dwelling unnecessarily, Phil's particularly regrettable night in Burgess Park went like this. It was midnight. He took the 21 bus, got off on the Old Kent Road, and walked towards the cherry trees. He could hear traffic coming from the street. Leaves rustling in the breeze. A fox darted out from behind a bush.

He thought of the films in which men were murdered while trying to cruise. He thought of the gay news websites who published stories of eyes lost and ribs crushed in brutal homophobic assaults. But still, he pushed on. He was nineteen. He had just moved to London but was still working in Basildon on the weekends. He had made new friends, who seemed to move through the world with such glamour and ease, spending all night at parties, sleeping with multiple people every week. Phil wanted to try moving with ease as well.

A man emerged from the trees. He was about fifty, big, wearing a suit and tie. Phil wondered if he was a local dad who had stayed late at the office. He wondered if he was a principal at a school. The man had his dick out, held as if taking a piss. The man saw Phil. Phil said, 'Hi.'

The man said nothing, but nodded towards his cock, which was hard now. Phil assumed that the man meant for him to suck it, so he did. He had learned a few tricks over the years, but the man didn't give much time to try them out; he thrust erratically into Phil's mouth, and all he could do was crouch on the ground and resist the urge to gag.

It wasn't entirely unpleasant. He was excited by the idea of sucking a strange man's dick in the park, even if it was less enjoyable in practice.

The man pulled him up, spun him around and shoved him against a tree. He yanked Phil's jeans down to his ankles and shoved some fingers into his ass.

'Woah, woah, woah. I'm not up for that,' said Phil, and then, worrying that he'd led the man on, added the word, 'Sorry.'

The man held firm. He said, 'Go on.'

Phil wondered if this man was originally from North

London, maybe West London, and had moved to Camberwell in an early wave of gentrification. Maybe he was an architect.

'No, I don't think so.'

'Come on.'

'No, I don't want to.'

'Come on, you little slut.'

Then, without further discussion, the man, laughing, manoeuvred himself inside Phil and started thrusting. Phil – tired, resigned – didn't offer more resistance. He was very easily coerced. Older men often assumed that because he was young and shy and smooth-bodied, he was always available. There had been times when he'd been glad to be coerced – he didn't always know what he wanted until he had it – but this wasn't one of those times. The way the man said 'slut' made Phil feel sick. The man acted like he'd seen all of this in porn and was now doing a sloppy imitation of moves that were already corny and lame.

The man said, 'Look at me.'

Phil didn't move.

The man slapped the back of Phil's head and said 'Look at me' again.

Phil craned his neck and the man spat a glob of phlegm on the side of his face.

That was the thing with dom tops: they thought you wanted to be treated like dirt. In many ways, Phil did want to feel owned. He wanted to feel like an object, but a cherished one, a priceless heirloom, something that you could do whatever you wanted to, but what you wanted to do was to treat it with care. He wanted to be a hole to get fucked, yes, but also, he wanted to be loved. He didn't want these two desires to be mutually exclusive.

He wiped the glob from his eye, and felt it clump in his eyelashes.

Even in the dark, the phlegm glowed neon yellow.

While the man thrusted and said *Yeah, take it slut, bet you like Daddy's cock*, Phil thought: too many men conceive of Daddy too narrowly. They act with dominance, but never with softness. Of course, Daddy is an authority figure, but Daddy is also loving. Daddy has your best interests at heart. Daddy only punishes you because he cares. Daddy may turn you over and fuck you raw at a moment's notice, yes, but he does so with tenderness. He makes it known that he's in charge, but also, that you're in safe hands.

He thought about the events of the day, the mould in his bathroom, the curry sauce he'd have to make at work tomorrow, how he'd like to go to Glasgow one day. Phil was only getting fucked – or raped, he wondered – by the man in Burgess Park in the physical sense. Emotionally, mentally, psychologically, even spiritually, he was somewhere else. From then on, this would happen to Phil nearly every time he had sex: during sex, he would cease to have a body at all. All he had was abstract trains of thought.

Of course, it was still painful, in the physical sense.

In the physical sense, it had been painful before he was even touched.

In any case, the man didn't take that long to come.

He finished, zipped up his pants, and hurried off without speaking.

Phil was cold now, and also, bleeding, and he had to get up in the morning to have breakfast, to shower, to brush his teeth, and get the train to Basildon.

He would open the restaurant at 8 a.m.; he would defrost the burgers, turn on the fryers, and mix the powdered curry sauce with a vat of hot water.

It was strange to think that it was only a week since the last time he'd been in Basildon. That felt like a long time ago now.

He put one foot after the other. He shivered. He ached.

. . .

PHIL EXPLAINS ALL OF THIS TO KEITH WHILE THEY chain-smoke fags outside the Admiral Duncan. Any moment now the evening twilight will bow out and give way to full-on night-time.

Keith is quiet while Phil speaks. His serious eyes don't move.

When Phil has finished telling the story, Keith puts his empty pint glass down on the ground and scoops Phil into a tight hug and kisses him again and again on the cheek.

Keith has a great physical intelligence. Phil admires it. His body is articulate, eloquent, verbose; it makes it known that Phil is loved, will be looked after, that Keith cares.

Phil's body is an illiterate body. It's a body that doesn't speak the language. His mind is never not describing the world, an over-articulate mind, a mind that is hyperactive in its desire to narrate, but his body is dumbstruck, bumbling, upset with itself like a child who hasn't yet learned to speak and becomes enraged when no one understands what is meant by their babbling, their little face scrunched into a small and wounded tantrum.

'I hate that that happened to you,' says Keith, still holding Phil close.

'It's OK. Happens to most people, doesn't it?'

'It doesn't happen to most people.'

Keith hugs Phil tighter and kisses his forehead.

They pull back. Phil says, 'So, yeah. Sorry. That's probably a lot to land on you.'

'Don't apologise.'

'Just wanted to explain why I'm weird about sex.'

Phil draws a breath, looks down at the ground, and goes on, 'But the reason I'm saying this now is because sex with you is easier and better than any sex I've had in my life.'

Keith smiles. 'That's good to know,' he says. 'I like it too.'

'Good. And thanks for your patience.'

Keith's face is serious. 'You don't need to thank me. We never need to do anything you don't want. I don't care if we fuck. I just want to know that you're having a good time.'

Phil exhales, smiles.

'OK. Good.'

They hug again, Keith's body warm and soft. Phil, with his face buried into Keith's chest, laughs for a few seconds and then says, 'Just to clarify, I do still want to fuck though.'

Keith laughs too and his belly heaves against Phil's.

'OK,' he says. 'I'm glad to hear it.'

They stay in the hug, until eventually it's time to leave.

'I better make tracks,' Keith says. 'Gotta pick up an extra amp for the party.'

'Do you want a hand?'

'Nah, it's OK. I have to go all the way to Homerton for it, it's going to take ages.'

'Alright. Well, see you at the party then?'

'See you there.'

With that, Keith kisses him on the lips, squeezes his hand and leaves.

Phil starts making his way to the party alone. He buys a beer to drink on the Tube. He descends the escalator, bolts through the closing doors and listens to music on headphones. It's packed. Heaving. Nearly everyone is drinking, apart from a few people commuting to or from work, cleaners, probably annoyed by the noise. The revellers mingle. People from different groups get chatting with each other. 'I love talking to drunk strangers on the Tube,' is something that many of Phil's colleagues have said over the years. Even while they're talking, they're probably narrating the experience in their head. 'It was a mad night,' they imagine telling their housemates the next day. 'We got chatting to a stranger on the Tube.'

Phil can see their mouths move, their smiles, and with techno pulsing in his ears, everything looks like a music video in which people are having a good time on a night out.

His mind turns again to Maggie. He thinks about what he'll tell her.

. . .

THE FOYER OF THE BRITISH LIBRARY NORMALLY VI-brates with life – students submerged in permanent crisis, the clash and clang of cutlery dumped in the overpriced café, everyone darting about for a single spare socket – but now, late in the day, there is only Louis.

He sits charging his phone, sipping on the last dregs of an iced coffee. He sucks hard on the paper straw as if taking the first drag from a much longed-for fag. He watches again and again the viral clip of Princess Diana. *Well, there were three of us in this marriage.*

He has watched it six times in a row.

He grips his phone. He thinks of the hickey Phil left on Keith's neck. Such deep red.

His knee is twitching.

It's ridiculous. He tells his knee to go still. He takes another long drag on the straw, even though the cup is mostly filled with melting ice, faintly perfumed of formerly strong coffee and oat milk. His slurping tongue and the clacking of ice echo around the empty foyer.

Another thing about Diana is that there used to be a bronze statue of her in Harrods and Keith took Louis there on a date. A classic Keith outing. He's a walking map of London kitsch. Drop him in any of the city's postcodes and he'll know exactly which actress threw a glass of wine over which playwright in the local café and her precise turn of phrase as she sashayed out the door. He speaks effortlessly and beautifully on London's local histories.

Drop Louis on any street in London and he'll tell you exactly what was on his mind as he waited there for Keith, and which of Keith's knees were mud-stained when he arrived, and the general back and forth of conversation as they rounded the corner onto Long Lane on the first hot day of April 2016. There's not even anything to say about that day, or the chips they bought from the place beside the laundrette, beyond that the day was hot enough to be out without a jacket, and they had returned from West London on the C10 and it was Louis's first time on that bus route. They had gone to Hyde Park, and discussed the eternal mourning of Queen Victoria, and then they took a detour to Harrods. Two weeks before, Keith had taken Louis to the house on Dean Street where Marx had lived: *a tour of London's revolutionary heroes,* he'd said. *Comrade Marx and Comrade Spencer.*

As for the chips that day: a little too much vinegar, but better too much than too little, they agreed, sitting on the kerb, sharing a beer too, then a cigarette, and Louis thought about paying attention as an act of love: he noted all the details of the day because he loved it, and loved Keith too, and that was all there was to it. It was entirely trivial. Truly, nothing had happened, and yet, it was the biggest thing in his life. It was gigantic, the love. The love was like this: it was like every text message was grammatically incorrect if it didn't include the words 'I love you' at the end. It was as if each loveless text were written by an inexperienced speaker of English. He wanted to say it constantly. What was an appropriate amount of time to wait between declarations of love? Was it possible to simply say *I love you I love you I love you* with no intermission? He would have to pause to kiss, he supposed then. It was important to kiss. It was important to kiss Keith's neck and chest and of course, his lips.

In the British Library, he asks: are there places Keith's taken Phil but not taken him?

He grinds his teeth, looks again to his phone, opens Instagram. A familiar scene. An endless ocean of pastel graphics: eight early signs you've met The One, three ways to tell if he's micro-flirting, how someone who's been mentally abused may behave in a relationship.

Lately, he has become amenable to emotional and spiritual guidance in whichever form it may come, including these pastel graphics. He is desperate, and therefore optimistic. He recently downloaded an astrology app, then downloaded another. In May, he spent a full day inconsolably distressed when the second app told him that the following month would bring about a painful reckoning in his love life. He deleted both apps and revised his opinion on astrology. No longer harmless fun, he said, no longer the inherited wisdom of our genderqueer ancestors. Rather, a sinister exploitation of heartbrokenness, he said, and it didn't matter that he was a Sagittarius, Keith a Taurus, and Phil a Cancer, meaning that he and Keith were an incompatible match, while Keith and Phil were a match made in heaven.

Enough. He stands. He leaves the library. He needs to clear his head.

He emerges onto Euston Road claggy with traffic and walks east. He passes the hotel where the famous Spice Girls video was filmed, and remembers a recent conversation between him, Keith, and Phil about which Spice Girl they each would be. Keith: a sort of Scary-Sporty hybrid, Phil: aspirational Ginger, actual Baby, and Louis, unavoidably, yet reluctantly Posh. Nothing to be done about it. Phil then posed the bigger question: which Spice Girl would you be if you didn't have to subscribe to the existing five categories of Spice and could, in fact, be a Spice Girl of your own invention, tailored to the precise contours of your personality? Well, that set them off for hours. There were an infinite number of Spice Girls, and Keith and Phil could imagine dozens. See: this is why those two got along so well! A mutual sense of humour, a cultural sensibility. When the question was posed to Louis, he had nothing to offer. He is overly serious, austere, dull. He is, quite literally, Posh Spice: he never smiles and never sings lead. He didn't even join the band for the reunion tour.

For Louis, there is never enough time. Every day is packed with activities and none of these activities accomplish anything. He ends each day as he begins, tired, resigned – somewhat happy – with a sense that he should be trying to embrace the conditions of his life.

The conditions of his life are this: his boyfriend is falling for somebody else.

He breathes deeply through his nostrils. He walks a little faster.

Complicated. Not catastrophic. Keith's happiness is important to Louis, and Phil is clearly bound up in it. Sure, he wasn't *thrilled* on the day Keith finally began to embrace the phrases *ethical non-monogamy* and *relationship anarchy* and *I've met someone else* and *I think you'd like him* but he had to admit that he, too, had nursed fantasies about alternative models of kinship. It was Louis, after all, who had introduced these phrases to their relationship in the first place. Besides, Keith was right: Louis *does* like Phil.

In fact, he more than likes him. This is hard to admit and harder to describe.

When Louis is in the room with Phil, he talks incessantly, has no idea what he's saying, and leaves no gaps for anyone else to speak. This is entirely beyond his control. It's like sweating or breathing or sneezing. What are these feelings? Where did they come from? Certainly, he's preoccupied with Phil because he wants to find out what Keith sees in him. Sometimes, he manages to grab on to the faintest wisp of his more-than-liking and corral it into rough verbal language. He grasps at words like jealously, or obsession, or infatuation.

But these words don't cut it. They are dwarfed by the scale of the task at hand.

Fine. So be it.

The present conditions are this: Louis, probably, is a little in love with Phil.

He rolls the word around in his mind, pausing briefly to catch his breath at the traffic lights. He had been walking so fast that it was almost a sprint, and the air is damp with early evening heat. It will rain later, he thinks. It is almost undeniable, the love, the rain. He had not necessarily sought out either of these things. He had not put a plan in place. Surely, he thinks, there are arrangements to be made before falling in love. Who will water the plants, for example, and who will feed the dog, and what will happen if it all goes wrong?

And yet, here he is, in love, or at least, probably.

The way Phil articulates his thoughts: Louis loves it. The way he thinks out loud, ambling towards a conclusion, clarifying and re-clarifying himself. Louis loves it.

So what is he saying then? That he wants some sort of *throuple*? No. What he's saying is this: he wants somebody, *anybody*, to look at him the way Keith looks at Phil.

He doesn't care which: he'll take it from either of them. He wants a little romance, adventure. Keith looks on Louis as a *companion*, not a lover. When is the last time Louis sucked hard enough on Keith's neck to leave a bruise as purple as the one Phil left behind? It's not that he begrudges Keith the hot physicality of new romance, but he wants it for himself too. He wants the thrill of those first months together, those big words balanced precariously on teeth, never sure if they'll tumble into the world or back beneath your tongue.

It is not unusual for Louis to plunge his existence into the realm of soap opera. He loves life and knows that it's on its way out. He wants to embrace it while it's still around. He wants, in fact, *a lot* of it, and ideally all at once. He wants food: the crumbling of pastry, the picking-off of crumbs from his jumper to dissolve on his tongue. He wants the mouldiest cheese. Cheese that smells like a corpse. Cheese so mouldy it could turn you *into* a corpse. He wants a whole bulb of garlic in every meal, even at breakfast, even for pudding: he wants garlic in his chocolate ice cream. He wants gossip – to hear it, spread it, be the subject of it – and he wants risk. He wants to dive off every pier, rocks or no rocks.

Louis knows that something is in the air. Anyone can see there has been a pattern of events. These events might be described as *the last days of Rome* or *the decline of the West* or *the creeping rise of fascism.* Most of us know in our hearts but don't say aloud: we are living through a period of history during which certain kinds of queers have been granted certain kinds of freedoms, but those freedoms are precarious. They may not last our lifetimes.

This makes it urgent for Louis to kiss as many parts of Keith's body as he can while it's still around to be kissed.

It also makes it urgent for him to accept the tools he has to hand, and use these tools to fashion the semblance of a happy or happy-ish life.

He turns left, remembers there's an old gay bar in the backstreets beyond King's Cross station. At ground level: a karaoke machine and discount pints of lager. The basement: a fetish club famous among those who love getting pissed on. Louis has only ever attended for the former of these amenities but has heard glowing reports of the latter. He charts a course for it, hoping it's still there, and is pleased to find that it is. He pushes through the door to the dimly lit bar. It feels like a small-town gay pub transplanted to the centre of London. Only three customers, all older men on their own, a drag queen on stage, dressed in pound-shop pearls and a blonde perm, and Louis laughs in realisation: she is lip syncing to the news clip of the marine biologist *Diana, Princess of Whales*.

He orders a beer, watches the performance. It's decent. Classics from *The Little Mermaid*, 'In the Navy'. He is glad to be in a gay bar. He glugs half his beer in one go, delicious, and thinks these are the tools available.

He finishes his pint, leaves the pub, and starts to make his way towards the party.

14

ROSALEEN AND STEVE JOIN JOAN AT KARAOKE. THE PUB
is lit by fluorescent lights. There's a dartboard which no one
uses, a carpet which there's nothing to say about, an old couple in a booth by the wall.

Joan has just got up to sing a song by Donna Summer,
and it makes Rosaleen think of London when she first arrived,
the early shimmers of disco breaking through on the radio.
She closes her eyes, remembers Soho in spring, night-time,
and wanting the city to transform her into a mythical bird.
Enormous, gorgeous, blue and pink plumage. She had wanted
for the city to change her so profoundly that she may as well
have grown wings.

Joan finishes the song. She makes a lewd joke directed at
the men in the bar but the microphone is dodgy and makes
a screeching noise so Rosaleen can't catch every detail. Still,
everyone else seems to find it funny, so Rosaleen decides to
find it funny too.

Joan returns to her seat. She says that she loves to sing. She
says she loves to have a laugh and loves to have a drink as well.

She misses her husband more than anything in the world, she says, and he loved to have a drink too. She only wants to have him in her arms and to put her head on his chest and to curl up on a Saturday night. Is that too much to ask? she says. Is that not a fair thing to want? Rosaleen tells her it is a fair thing to want. Rosaleen tells her she's sorry, and she puts her hand on top of Joan's hand, and Joan tells her she's a good friend. She goes to the toilet then, Steve goes to the bar, and Rosaleen wonders how people will speak of her after she dies. She wants to note down everything, all the details of her life. She finds a receipt and pen in her purse; a small part of her wonders if years from now this old receipt will fossilise and be retrieved by an archaeologist. They would dust off the clay with their delicate little brush, and they would gesture to their colleagues to come see, come look, come bear witness to the past. Look, they would say. Look. There once was a woman and she sat in the pub and these are the things she wrote of her life.

She turns the receipt over. It's for a dressing gown she bought in Marks & Spencer. More money than she'd spent on herself in a decade. When she bought it, she imagined the ways her life would change. She imagined being leisurely, easy, content by herself. A hefty ask from a flimsy bit of fabric. She'd been the same way with London, and Pauline before that: always seeking to be transformed by things that were indifferent to her. Once at sixteen, Rosaleen had held Pauline from behind in bed, and after an hour of puckering and un-puckering her lips, she placed the smallest kiss on Pauline's upper back, bare skin, the space after her nightgown ended but before her neck began. She remembers the freckles and veins, pale green like a coppery penny, pale blue as if stained by jewellery. She remembers how Pauline's hand squeezed her own, and then, that was that. They went to sleep. Barely a kiss at all. But still; one story of Rosaleen's life is this: she is a woman, she sits in the pub, and forty years ago, in a cold bed in Dublin, she held a girl from behind.

Joan and Steve resume their seats.

Joan says that she had a fabulous time singing, and suggests Rosaleen does the same.

'Oh no, not for me, thank you,' says Rosaleen, a sense of loss even as she speaks.

Even when she wants something, her first instinct is to say that she doesn't.

Even when hungry, her first instinct is to say that she's full.

When she goes to someone's house, she has to be offered food five times before accepting. The words 'Ah no, I'm fine' spill from her mouth with automatic ease.

Joan is still telling her to go for it; Steve is still silent; the stage, still empty.

She takes a bigger gulp from her cider than she normally would and wipes her mouth coarsely with the back of her hand. A message migrates from her brain to her legs. It says that in a fraction of a second, it will be time to walk towards the stage. Her heart rate bolts like a horse flinging a rider from its back. The muscles in her legs begin the task of standing up –

And someone else gets there first.

Her heart rate comes to a full stop, then resumes its unsteady trot.

A man is on stage now. He sings 'Purple Rain' and Rosaleen looks around nervously to see if anyone had noticed that she wanted to get up. Oh but how would they have noticed? She had barely moved an inch.

Again, she feels it: she's a six-year-old child.

Going to hell for her bad insides.

Now, here she is: a sixty-year-old woman, admitting to herself that she's in a pit.

She's been in this pit for decades. This pit is where she lives. Sometimes she tries to claw her way out of it. Sometimes she bashes her body off its walls in fury at her inability to climb them. Sometimes she simply accepts the pit and tries to decorate it as best she can.

Sometimes, she has stood at the base of the pit and shouted for help. Sometimes, she has stood at the base of the pit and whispered for help, too, and felt hurt and abandoned when no one responded because her whispers were too soft to be audible to anyone but herself.

On the times when people have offered to help, she has been envious of the fact that they weren't in the pit with her and responded bitterly. Then, sensing she didn't want their help and feeling their own egos bruised, they have left her, and she has missed them, and she has wished that she could have climbed up to be near them, and to say she was sorry.

She teetered on the pit's edge for longer than she cared to admit. She used to wish that friends or family would come, and friends or family, being sensitive and perceptive, would point out there's a hole in the ground. Holes are notoriously easy to fall into, they would advise, but Rosaleen, having fallen into more than a few holes in her day, would believe she had trained her balance well enough to never fall again. And falling isn't even the right word for it. Her journey into the pit was a motion so incremental that it was barely legible as motion at all. Rather, it was like clouds moving across the sky on a placid day; the clouds themselves don't seem to budge an inch, but if you fall asleep on the grass, you might find when you wake that the clouds have rearranged themselves. Before you dozed off, they were shaped like giraffes, France, the Battersea Power Station. Now, they're gone, and the new clouds don't look at all like France. Rosaleen's journey into the pit was something like that.

She takes a gulp of her cider. The man finishes 'Purple Rain'. What are you so worried about? she thinks to herself What's anyone going to say? It's true that once, Rosaleen wanted to be a singer. It's true that when she and Pauline were younger they would pretend their hairbrushes were microphones and that Rosaleen was the redhead from ABBA, and Pauline: the blonde. It's true that once, when her sons were small, she booked a singing lesson without telling anyone. She left the boys at the creche and walked up to the building where the lesson was due to take place. She slowed down her pace as she approached, and then she walked past. She thought: it's not for me. She thought: they'll think I'm a fool. Even then, she was nervous. Even then, she thought: what'll the people on this street think of me, doddering around with nothing to do? In a panic, she walked into the nearest shop and bought the first item to hand: a cabbage, a loose and lonely cabbage, which she did not need, which did not fit with her dinner plans for that week, which she would then have to boil and salt and serve on a plate, and she'd have to wash those plates afterwards because this was in the days before they had a dishwasher, and her hands were raw-red and cracked with the washing-up.

Enough. She stands. She walks towards the stage. She asks for 'Believe' by Cher please, and the chords flare into life. She grips the mic. A television screen counts down to the beginning of the lyrics. A droplet of sweat dangles from her temples; it plummets towards the floor. She hesitates. She comes in a little too late. Steve smiles; Joan whoops; the disco lamp casts a flurry of pinks and blues on her blouse. And Rosaleen? With the mic, alone on the stage. Rosaleen, long gone the days when she longed for the city to make her into a bird. She sings. For the first time in close to forty years, she sings. For the first time since she stopped going to Mass with her poor dead mam, she sings. She sings as if Cher herself was wailing from deep down inside of her belly. She sings and sings and nobody cares. The men at the bar who were staring into the dregs of their pints before she began are still staring into the dregs of their pints now. The teenagers at the back, dressed all in black and so much like her second son, continue looking at their phones and taking small conspiratorial sips from their vodka Red Bulls. The floor is still sticky; the room still smells of booze; people still stumble in and out and the sound of dual carriageway traffic still revs around the room. The dual carriageway itself remains unchanged too. There are still the cars full of people; there are still the places they could go; there is London, Europe, anywhere.

The music peters out; everything returns to how it was before.

There's the noise of the pub; the hacking of a smoker's cough, the fruit machine bleeping and blooping, the screech of a chair dragged on the floor.

But for Rosaleen, to sing: it was nothing short of the world.

. . .

VALERIE STANDS ON THE BARGE OFF THE COAST OF Margate and pronounces the whale dead.

Exhausted, she crouches and puts her head in her hands. She wonders what she'll have for dinner and what shops will be open by the time she gets home. She walks over to the whale, rubs it, gawks at the blood that pools around it. A rare steak that bleeds onto a plate. Crushed by the weight of her own body. That's what killed her – the weight of her own body.

The barge docks at Margate. She disembarks and stands on the pier. There's a big crowd, people who had gathered in the hopes of catching a glimpse of the whale as it was released into the sea. A few people point and stare. Out of awkwardness, she checks her phone once, twice, three times. The battery is almost dead. She has a text from her friend.

A woman taps on her shoulder. She holds the hand of a little boy.

'Excuse me,' she says. 'I'm sorry to interrupt. My name is Renée and this is my son Jackson. I know you must be very busy, but we've been watching you on the news. We drove all the way here from London today to try to see the whale. Jackson wants to be a marine biologist, you see. He's obsessed with whales and sharks and dolphins and even crabs—'

'Not just crabs,' interrupts Jackson. '*All* crustaceans.'

'Yes, baby,' says Renée. 'All crustaceans. Anyway, I know you must be exhausted after the day you've had, but Jackson's a big fan, and he's never met a proper marine biologist in person before, so I told him we'd come over and say hello. I hope that's OK.'

Valerie looks down at the boy. He looks back at her, expectant, his eyes big and blank and unflinching, and she wonders what he wants from her. She's always struggled with children. Adults too. She's got no intuition when it comes to social interaction, and if she does have any, it's buried beneath layers of awkwardness and self-consciousness.

She looks at the boy. The boy looks at her. They wait for something to happen.

She realises that she's still clutching the red watering can. She hands it to him, feeling embarrassed and truly ridiculous, not sure what words a person should say in this situation.

'This is what I used on the barge to keep the whale hydrated,' she says.

Jackson takes it, examines it, lets it hang loosely by his side, and then looks back up.

'Oh, isn't that lovely?' says Renée. 'What do you say, Jackson?'

Jackson says nothing.

'It helped keep the whale alive,' she says.

'The whale died though,' says Jackson.

'Jackson!' says Renée. 'Don't be rude.'

'It did though.'

'He's right,' says Valerie, laughing awkwardly.

'How did it die?' says Jackson.

Valerie considers mincing her words, but suspects that Jackson will get more enjoyment from the whole truth. She says, 'She was crushed by the weight of her own body.'

Jackson's eyes bulge, thrilled and huge. Valerie feels the most competent she's felt all day. She leaves Renée and Jackson with the red watering can and tries to find some food.

Later, another hotel. Perched on the edge of an empty dual carriageway roundabout. Miscellaneous Essex. Fifth exit off the A12. Broken lights in reception. Fluorescent twinkle, a strobe effect. The walls: pale blue. The vending machine contains a single Mars Bar.

Tamsin, half-asleep on an armchair next to a dying parlour palm. Valerie meets her there. Too exhausted to care who sees, she hugs her, and to her surprise Tamsin hugs back.

They pull away to look at each other: Valerie puts her hand on Tamsin's face.

Who are they fooling? Valerie leans in to kiss her. It's their first kiss outside of a private bedroom. A proper kiss, mouths wide open. Tamsin softens: she kisses back.

The receptionist watches, munches on biscuits, thinks *Do I know them?*

Tamsin asks if Valerie is hungry, and Valerie laughs, says that she's indescribably starving. Tamsin looks around, almost asks the receptionist for one of her biscuits, instead buys the single vending machine Mars Bar, and won't accept any when Valerie tries to share.

15

CALLUM DRIVES SOUTH IN A HIRED CAR. A LITTLE TIPSY but not so drunk that he can't keep his eyes on the road. The A10: Bishopsgate and Liverpool Street, deserted, the City bankers gone home for the weekend. Callum's work week is just about to begin.

He wishes in some ways that he were going to the party tonight, but he needs to earn money. He had a fine day still. Nice to see his dad, nice to see Ed, nice to watch the football.

Nice. He's always saying things are nice. How's your food: it's nice. How was your holiday: it was nice. I'm going to see the girls tonight: that's nice. It means nothing, nice.

Callum isn't like Holly. She never lets things slide. She's not a person whose kettle breaks and instead of buying a new kettle, simply resigns themselves to a life without tea. She goes out, buys replacement parts, watches a ten-minute YouTube video about how to repair it. Callum, on the other hand, lets things deteriorate.

Further south now, nearly at London Bridge. The roads empty apart from a few 149s. The 149: the bus of kings. Goes all night, comes every two minutes, takes you anywhere worth going. Ridley Road Market, White Hart Lane, Liverpool Street station if you fancy hopping on a train to Southend for a little sojourn to the seaside. Union Jack bunting. Tins of lager on the beach. The longest pleasure pier in the world: hotter than it should be at any time of year. Seagulls – vicious, swift, and bold – menacing your tray of soggy lukewarm chips, ruined by too much ketchup anyway. Topless old men. All that red flesh. Tufts of wispy hair sprouting from their shoulders. Imagine yourself: hobbling down the pier, white hairs on a red back, moles and freckles, big belly and bad breath. A minor but pointed argument over whether it's too early to start drinking yet. A cigarette, rolled. The smoke: it singes the back of your throat. You've already smoked much too much for the day and the cigarette is deeply unpleasurable. You smoke it down to the filter anyway. The seagull: it makes its final bid for the chips. And you, recognising you're no match for your opponent, let it.

Stop. He screeches to a halt by Monument station. Something on the road. He squints, then groans: it's only a common toad crossing the street at about a quarter of a mile per hour.

'Come on, mate,' shouts Callum to the toad. 'What the hell do you think you're doing?' He beeps his horn in impatience. The toad, unperturbed, continues its glacial pace.

Callum knows about toads. Up to 40 per cent are killed every year by hurtling cars. They're too slow, not like frogs who leap across in seconds. Toads crawl. They *might* manage the odd hop. He knows about it because a few summers ago he volunteered with something called the Toad Patrol, who went to popular toad spots during the busy season and helped the poor little fuckers cross safely. He loved the toads but couldn't stand the other patrollers. They were convinced that there was something *specifically English* about what they were doing. *Quintessentially British!* they said, as if there was anything unique to this country about wanting to save animals from passing cars. He was sure that people in Estonia or Guatemala cared about toads too, and it wasn't just the toads that the patrollers claimed for queen and country. It was everything. Queuing, tea, saying 'thank you' to bus drivers. *Common decency.* But there's nothing 'British' about any of these things: people queue in all countries.

The toad has barely budged. Callum groans again, gets out of the car, scoops it into his hand, and says, 'Alright, mate. You're coming with me tonight.' He plops the toad on the passenger seat, who sits there without moving. Seems happy enough. Callum takes a selfie with the toad to send to Ed, who sends back a heart-eyes emoji. Callum smiles and continues.

He drives over London Bridge. The sky is navy and dark pink. He looks left to Tower Bridge and beyond, three tower blocks in the distance framed by its turrets.

Eyes off the road, he swerves.

A split-second passes: he ends up in the wrong lane and a rogue 149 thrusts itself in his path like a punch: it hurtles towards him and he hurtles towards it, and for a moment, he thinks he's dead. It's a sort of relief. He laughs.

But his hands take over.

He spins the wheel to the left. He just about avoids the bus, breathless, and speeds down Borough High Street. He eventually pulls in near the library. He looks at the toad.

'You OK, mate?' he says.

The toad says nothing.

He parks near Borough station and waits for his first customer.

. . .

THREE MINUTES LATER, DEBS OPENS THE CAR DOOR and begins to climb in.

'Wait, the toad!' Callum shouts.

'Sorry, what?'

He gestures to the small, stout toad on the passenger seat. He scoops it up, puts it in his lap, and Debs shrugs: she is unshockable. She has lived in the warehouse for almost ten years: the only other person who's been there so long is the cat. Everyone knew the eviction would happen eventually, but it still seems impossible. Earlier in the kitchen, she said: *We don't have to leave, do we really have to leave?* We do, came the reply. Everyone wishes that this early bit of the party would last forever, that *every* bit of the party would last forever.

She climbs in, and Callum says, 'Aren't you going to ask me about the toad?'

She sighs. 'Alright. Why've you got a toad?'

'My right-hand man, innit.'

She laughs, says, 'Fair enough,' thinks it's true what everyone says: he *is* a hot drug dealer. He hands over two bags of MDMA, two bags of ketamine – enough for herself, enough for Keith, enough to share with Ali if she shows up and they get to talking – and she hands him a wad of cash. 'I hope you're not sharing these with my baby brother,' he says, and she replies that Phil's an angel: never touches the stuff. They both laugh, she climbs out of the car, and he speeds off. So strange, the intimacy of the gesture: they hardly know each other, but she's met him for these brief exchanges dozens of times over the years. She knows, too, that he's getting married, is obsessed with nature. Phil, in confidence, told her that Callum tried to drown himself at Southend a few years ago and Phil was helping to pay for his counselling. She likes him, this stranger, and wishes him well for the night. She almost invites him to the party but thinks to herself that Phil probably has enough on his plate.

. . .

BACK INSIDE, DEBS SAYS TO PHIL, 'YOUR BROTHER'S GOT a pet toad now.'

'Not surprised,' says Phil.

Frank, hanging a strobe light off a rafter, chimes in, 'He just gets hotter and hotter.'

Phil laughs, then sighs. 'Fuck off,' he says.

Meanwhile, walls are knocked through. Bedrooms become bars. Debs posits a theory: the house must be destroyed in order for everyone to feel OK about leaving it. She takes a sledgehammer and knocks through from her bedroom to the next; it's thrilling and unsettling to see passages open up between previously private rooms, dust crumbling on the floor.

The party starts. There were only a few people here an hour ago, smoking one cigarette after the next, trying to stave off the awkwardness of having arrived early. Now, the place is so crowded that you can't move. People push past each other in the cavernous hall, some dressed in extravagant home-made outfits – floppy hats in the style of Virginia Woolf transplanted to the early nineties – and some dressed in tattered bits of old sportswear.

The house was surging when Phil arrived back, everyone cleaning and making food and setting up a sound system, cycling between various South London squats to pick up things for the party: a hot plate, a cardboard box full of confetti, an IKEA bag stuffed with mesh sports bras which someone has used to complete their outfit and someone else has used for a sort of contemporary art installation. This is a significant event, he tells himself.

Now there are hundreds of people here, complex knots of lovers and ex-lovers and friends and ex-friends. Many have slept together in various combinations. Many have hurt each other.

He thinks again: this is a significant event. He is so busy reminding himself of the event's significance that the significance becomes abstract. He doesn't feel much. A little tired. Keen to take some drugs so that he doesn't fall asleep, and anxious, too, at the thought that the drugs will eventually wear off. Should I have some ketamine? he thinks. Should I have some cocaine? Is this what life is? Events come, then go. You're still tired. You think of something inane. *What should I have for dinner?* you might ask yourself at your husband's funeral. *Should I stop at this supermarket or the next?* Phil's tiredness always distracts from having a good time. He is always at parties and thinking of getting a kebab. Is this because of his vegetarianism? as his mother would surely argue. Does he have a vitamin B12 deficiency, as she likes to suggest in her late-night text messages, at random, without impetus or context?

Then: he spots Ed and Maggie across the room. She detaches herself from him and starts making her way towards the toilet, leaving Ed to lean awkwardly against the wall.

Phil takes a deep breath. OK, he thinks. This is my chance.

He pushes through the crowd towards her.

. . .

ED, ALONE IN THE HALLWAY, HE PANICS. WHERE IS PHIL? Where is Maggie? She left to go to the toilets twenty minutes ago. What if they're together now? What might they be talking about?

He can't stay still any longer. He moves through the party to find them.

Someone pushes past and Ed's beer spills down his top. There are too many people in here. The floor is shaking and the air is boiling. It definitely wouldn't pass fire regulations. In his head, he does an impersonation of himself, bent over, wearing oversized glasses Sellotaped at the bridge and speaking in a nasal American accent: 'Excuse me, this building does not pass health and safety regulations as stipulated by the law in this jurisdiction.'

He stalls. He tries to be strategic. Would they be in Phil's room? In the toilets?

He then begins to think: what is the correct way to stand? How should a person at a party arrange their limbs? These become pressing questions. He has one hand in his pocket, using his house keys to rip skin from his fingertips. One hand clutches a beer, denting the tin.

He thinks of his dad: another awkward man. He never said, 'I love you,' but instead, he'd come round to make sure your boiler was working so it didn't explode and maim everyone in the building like it did at cousin Sandra's ex-boyfriend's brother's house. He never said, 'I'm proud of you,' but instead, he would send strangely punctuated Facebook messages with links to local news articles about a man wielding a large knife on Oxford Street and advise you not to travel to Central London until it was all blown over.

An idea: why not ask someone else where Phil and Maggie are?

He could turn to this man and say, *You haven't seen Phil, have you?*

He eavesdrops. He hears someone say there are too many cis men here. Ed wonders if the comment is directed at him. Fair enough, he thinks, I don't think I should be here either.

Ed is never sure if he is a man anyway. Sometimes, he's certain he's a woman. Other times, he feels like nothing at all. When it comes down to it, Ed isn't sure if he wants to belong, not to gay clubs, or queer spaces, or straight bars. He doesn't want to decide on his pronouns with confidence and clarity, and he doesn't want to announce them to the world via his Twitter bio or email signature or when introducing himself at parties. He doesn't want his identity to be valid. He doesn't want his feelings to matter. He doesn't want to change his name, or his life, and to say, 'I feel so seen,' because Ed doesn't want to be seen at all. He doesn't want to be seen as a man, or a woman, or a non-binary person. What Ed wants is to be invisible. What Ed wants is to disappear entirely. He wants to be nothing, by which he means not only that he wants to die, but that he wants to have not ever existed at all, for his body and every person's memory of his body to be instantly and utterly erased from the world.

He can feel himself start to wheeze again. He struggles to catch his breath.

When he was a teenager, Ed hung around in fields, beneath billboards for estates that were never built, the building sites left derelict, like decomposed versions of the computer-generated graphics that advertised them. He and his friends drank as much as they could before inevitably blacking out or passing out or throwing up, and in the short window between feeling giddy and becoming catatonic, the normal rules became slippery. During these windows, the boys would become physical with each other, they would throw their arms around each other, they would hug, they would kiss, on the cheek, on the mouth, smack each other on the ass, end up getting naked, and laugh the whole time to make sure everyone knew it was just a laugh, nothing more. Then, in Kent, Phil made Ed cum.

He put his arm around Phil's shoulder for five minutes, once.

There's a tightness in his chest. When he thinks about Kent, he feels a panic, a tension and panic. His lungs empty, his armpits prickle, he has an almost irresistible urge to bash his head off the nearest hard surface (a pebble-dash wall, the corner of the bar) partially so that the panic will end, partially so that he can punish himself for the things that he did.

It's hard to remember the exact chain of events. Ed had been horny, stupid and horny, and he had known that hand-jobs existed because he'd seen it in porn and he knew that Janet Ford gave Rick Lewis one, and he liked Phil, he thought

Phil was cool, he wanted to be around him, and so during the school trip to Kent, he had thought to himself: tonight Phil is going to give me a handjob. Does this mean he was gay? Had he assaulted Phil? Was he a sex offender? Was Phil going to tell Maggie and would Maggie leave him forever? These questions are so loud in Ed's mind, babbling and screeching and clamouring to be heard, hollering for attention at all times of day and night. He can't sleep with the noise. It's hard to eat with the noise. The noise has affected his relationship. He's always trying to distract himself by shouting and joking and singing, and it annoys her. It drives her crazy, but he can't help it, and he pushes her away. He's unkind. He complains of her friends and finds it particularly hard to be around Phil. Ed is a bad person, of this he is sure, and he can't go on like this. Everyone needs to see themselves as basically good, as the hero of their own life.

The only other option is, quite literally, to die. Of course, he thinks about it. Of course, he wonders if he'd be better off that way. What then? He just ends his life because he can't come to terms with something he did at fourteen? No! He shakes himself. He slaps himself in the face. He has a partner. A baby on the way.

He opens another can and wades through the thick crowds to find Phil.

Finally, he spots him: in the packed courtyard next to a long-haired man.

Ed's already out of breath. He wheezes through his words.

He says, 'Hey. How's it going, man?'

'Oh hey, Ed. This is my friend Frank. Do you know each other?'

'How's it going, man?' says Ed again.

'Frank's a teacher,' says Phil.

'Oh yeah? What's that like?'

'Well, I've just been chewing Phil's ear off,' says Frank – Phil makes a gesture to suggest he hadn't minded his ear being chewed off – 'but I'm struggling a bit. Classrooms are overcrowded, targets are rudimentary, and it's like the system is built to stunt these kids' development. I feel like I'm there to *hinder* their lives. Do you know we teach *happiness classes* now? Like these kids are meant to be fucking *happy* despite everything.'

Phil touches Frank's shoulder. He says, 'That sounds hard, babe.'

'I don't know, mate. Everything feels pointless. I wake up in the morning and have to convince myself to get out of bed.' Frank takes a gulp of his beer. He doesn't say anything for a second, and then, seeming to notice how morbid he's become, adds, 'It's like how Mariah won't get up for less than a hundred thousand dollars a day.'

'You and Mariah have always had a lot in common,' concedes Phil.

'I'm glad you noticed.'

Frank excuses himself, spotting someone he knows in the crowd, and Ed turns to Phil.

He takes a deep breath, and then dives in.

'I hope this is OK to say,' he says, 'but I've been thinking about the time with the egg.'

Phil looks around. He checks his phone and tries and fails to catch the eye of someone he knows. He mumbles furtively, 'Maybe this isn't the best place to talk about it?'

'I shouldn't have done that to you, man.'

'It's a long time ago.'

Ed wants to apologise; he wants for Phil to accept it.

'I didn't treat you right,' he says.

'Don't worry about it.'

Once Ed has started speaking, he finds it very hard to stop. 'I am so ashamed of myself for what happened. So ashamed. So embarrassed and guilty. You were always a nice lad, always sound to me, and I took advantage. When I asked you to put in a good word with Maggie – it was a way of pretending that nothing happened between us. Acting as if things were normal. I know this sounds stupid but I *was* stupid. I *am* stupid. I'm sorry to bring this up now. I know you don't want to talk about this. I know you're trying to enjoy your fag.'

Ed stops to catch his breath. He's panting.

'Don't worry about it. It's fine.'

He laughs, embarrassed, and claps Phil on the back.

Then, Ed sees Maggie across the courtyard. She's walking towards them, and the slight bump in her belly and Ed's knowledge of the baby growing inside her reminds him of motherhood. It reminds him of Phil's mother, who's not very well, and urgently wanting to change the subject before Maggie arrives, he puts a hand on Phil's arm.

'Phil, I'm so sorry. I forgot to mention. I heard about your mum.'

. . .

MAGGIE IS ALARMED TO SEE THEM TALKING. IN FACT, more than alarmed. She's furious. She had been searching for

Ed for fifteen minutes, only wanting to dance with him, and now, what's Phil trying to do? Is he trying to tell Ed that he's not right for her? She notices a tension on their faces. Phil is saying, '. . . What are you on about? I don't know what you mean.'

Ed is drunk and struggling to explain.

'Your mum, Phil. I saw Callum today. He told me about your mum.'

She sees the lost look on Phil's face and realises he doesn't know.

She feels herself clench.

'There are my two boys!' she says. 'Where have you two been all night?'

'Hey babe,' says Phil. 'Ed was just telling me something about my mum.'

'Your mum? God, I haven't seen her in ages. She's a formidable woman, your mum.'

Phil ignores her.

'Ed,' he says. 'Tell me what you heard about my mum.'

Ed looks from Phil to Maggie, his eyes wide and alarmed, as if he needs further instructions on how to speak. In the split second when Phil is looking away from her, Maggie tries to gesture to Ed, but still he says, 'I saw Callum today. He told me the news.'

She widens her eyes, shakes her head, makes a subtle attempt at a grimace.

'What news did he tell you?' says Phil.

Maggie's cheeks are inflamed. She says the first thing that comes into her mind.

'Did you not hear, Phil? Your mum entered a competition on Facebook. It was a competition to win a new patio. A new patio and lovely new garden furniture and one of those big outdoor umbrellas. And she was announced as the winner of the competition, but when she tried to claim her prize, she got no response! Looks like it was some sort of scam.'

Phil is obviously distressed, his big eyes welling with tears.

'Really? Maggie, are you serious? Did she lose any money?'

'No, no, don't worry, babe, it wasn't, like, a *scam* scam. It was totally benign, just a stupid Facebook thing, although I'm sure it was disappointing for her. I'm sure it was sad.'

Ed looks at her, confused.

Phil goes on, 'She's always entering those competitions. Every single day.'

'I know, babe. You've told me about it.'

'I always want to ask her to stop but I'm afraid of patronising her.'

Maggie puts her hand gently on Phil's back and strokes it.

'It's not your fault, my love. You couldn't have stopped it.'

'Yeah,' says Ed, the truth dawning. 'My mum's the same. It's a generational thing.'

Then, she says, 'Come here,' and scoops Phil up into a hug, and because Ed is standing there too, she scoops him into the hug as well.

The hug ends, and Maggie says, 'Come on then. Let's have a dance,' and the three of them shove their way to the centre of the dance floor. There has been a shift in the room since they went outside. People have settled into the party and various drugs have begun to work. More guests arrive and everyone yelps their hellos. The music transitions from techno to disco. One second, every conversation is being drowned by brutal thumping, then: horns! Strings! Melody!

The shock of sudden disco blows open every window. People become physical. They throw arms around each spare shoulder and waist. Phil checks his phone.

Maggie is often fast and loose with affection when at parties. She turns to Phil and says, 'I love you. You're my best friend.' He gives a thumbs-up. He hasn't heard and thinks it's too loud to ask her to repeat herself. She makes a love heart shape with her hands instead.

She looks towards Ed: he casts his glance around as if on guard. Barely dancing at all, he sways from left to right and taps his fingers against his beer can. She grabs his hands, pulls herself towards him, flings her arms around his waist and kisses him hard on the mouth.

She realises she's looking for something to happen.

She's staring at Ed, a knot in her chest, badly wanting him to stare back. She presses her body against his and tries to dance. She grinds on his waist. She smiles, tries to catch his eye. He's stiff. Tense. She kisses his neck. He glances around the room as if she's not in it.

She starts to feel as if her dancing is making him uncomfortable. Is she being too sexual? Is it OK to touch like this? She remembers a drunk older woman in Stoke Newington Wetherspoons, trying to dance with the teenage barman. The woman put her arms around the boy's waist, she even grabbed his ass, and the boy – smiling, sweating, humiliated – remained utterly still, except to shake his head. Maggie feels like she's doing the same to Ed.

'You OK?' she says.

'Yeah,' he says.

She pulls away and looks around.

Phil is still here. He'd witnessed the whole thing.

He makes a gesture to suggest he wants to go for a smoke.

She looks towards Ed, his eyes glazed with alcohol, and feels a pang of guilt.

Then, she cups her hands over Ed's ear and says, 'Can you get me some water, babe?'

Ed, dutiful, makes his way towards the kitchen, and Maggie leads Phil by the hand outside. The music becomes a background hum and is replaced by the chatter of conversation.

Phil starts to roll a cig, struggles with the paper. Then, he says, 'Ed seems a bit off.'

She bristles. 'No, he doesn't.'

'Sorry, no, I don't mean to be flippant, it's just that . . .'

'It's just that what?'

'It's just that I don't want you to make a mistake.'

'I'm not.'

'I'm not sure if you know him.'

'And you do?'

'Well, yeah. I do.'

But before Phil can go on, a man approaches. It takes Maggie a second to register who this man is – shorter than he seems at a distance – but then she clocks his white teeth, his smile, the same smile that had charmed Phil and Maggie the summer of the shopping trolley.

She almost gasps. It's Kyle Connolly.

'Hello, you two,' says Kyle in a low, conspiratorial drawl. 'Long time, no see.'

Maggie can't quite compute that Kyle is standing in front of her. It's almost like a mirage. With Phil's words still in her ears, Kyle couldn't have chosen a more inconvenient moment.

'How are you doing?' she says, wanting to talk to him, also wanting him to leave.

'Well, darling, a lot has changed for me since we last spoke.'

Kyle launches into a detailed account of his life since he left the estate all those years ago. He speaks without asking Maggie or Phil any questions about their own lives, while the two of them maintain their best serious expressions and try to act as if they haven't discussed him at length and followed his life online for two decades. His story is convoluted. She can't follow. He pauses often to laugh, lightly tapping her on the arm as if to encourage her to laugh as well, but she can never identify the punch line. She tunes out, still thinking of Phil's words. Kyle is describing the ins and outs of his working life, the websites he writes for, and his most recent article.

'It was sort of inspired by the whale in the Thames,' he says. 'You know that woman Valerie, the whale woman? We wanted to write an article to promote the amazing work she does, and then we thought, why not shine a spotlight on other inspiring women around the globe? So it ended up being called Twenty Kickass Women Driving Global Change.'

This is too much.

She can't help it: she bursts out laughing.

Kyle's face drops.

'What are you laughing at?' he says.

She tries to stop, but she can't.

'Nothing, no,' she says through giddy tears. 'I was just thinking of something else.'

Phil laughs then too, and it makes her laugh even more, bent over and wheezing.

Kyle purses his lips and takes a sip from his drink.

'You two have always been like this,' he says.

'Been like what?'

'You think you're above everybody.'

'Sorry, Kyle,' says Maggie, still laughing. 'I'm pregnant. I get a bit light-headed.'

'You've always been a nasty piece of work,' he says.

Maggie's laughter falters. 'What are you talking about?' she says.

He sucks his lips.

'When you saw me and Phil. When you threatened to tell everyone.'

Maggie and Phil look at each other through the corners of their eyes.

Kyle pauses, looks away, then smirks.

'Still with Ed then?' he goes on.

'Yeah. He's here somewhere.'

'I'm surprised he got you pregnant.'

'Why do you say that?'

Kyle licks his teeth, still smiling.

'Phil wasn't the only boy on the estate who liked playing games in my bedroom.'

Maggie looks at Phil; Phil looks at Kyle; Kyle smiles, winks, and then walks away.

. . .

EVERYWHERE, THEN, IT STARTS TO RAIN. BIG BIBLICAL droplets, thick, juicy, voluptuous; literally bursting on the metal roof of the warehouse. They clatter, too, on the windscreen of Callum's car, parked outside with the toad, still content, waiting for more customers, and on the window of Valerie and Tamsin's dual carriageway hotel room, still awake. Lodged in a difficult discussion, they veer between *I can't do this any more* and *Let's not be so hasty.* They pause, go to the window, watch the rain fall in great sheets. The rain pounds the roof over Rosaleen's head. She lies awake still, mind too wired for sleep. It falls, too, on the body of the whale; it dribbles down her skin and blends with the pool of blood that still seeps from her thousand tiny cuts, and it falls on the ravers outside the warehouse, who love it. too hot anyway, too sweaty, it cools them down instantly, ready now for a fresh round on the dance floor. Maggie and Phil dash under an awning, lean against damp brick, think *What now?*

Phil turns to her. He tries to catch her eye.

'Are you OK?' he says.

She looks back. 'Yeah. I mean, that was surreal.'

'Yeah.'

She looks at him and says, 'Did you know?'

She speaks like her words are trying to find their footing.

'Not about Kyle,' he says. 'But I know other stuff about Ed.'

'Is this what you're trying to tell me?'

'Sort of.'

She nods. 'Why are you only telling me now?'

He thinks about it. He's drunk and inclined towards honesty.

He says, 'I was afraid of what you'd think of me.'

She nods and says nothing.

'Are you upset?' Phil ventures.

She thinks about it.

'I don't know,' she says.

He puts an arm around her; she leans into it. They watch the rain in silence.

. . .

LATER, PHIL STAYS SMOKING ALONE UNDER THE AWNING while Maggie looks for Ali.

Across from Phil, Louis stands in the doorway that leads to the courtyard. Behind Louis is the blare of the party, the smell of the smoke machine and spilled spirits. In front of him, torrents of rain. He is trying to work up the courage to approach. He is telling his legs that now is the time to run – not away, but across the courtyard towards Phil – and his legs, finally, relent. He dashes. He's pelted with rain. It falls with such force on his head.

He reaches Phil, dripping wet: the awning beneath which Phil stands doesn't have much space, and Louis has to shuffle so close that it feels a little inappropriate.

'Oh, hi,' says Phil, annoyed at the disturbance. 'What's up?'

Phil is agitated, still thinking of Maggie, and he keeps checking his phone for a message from Keith, who's still not here even though it's 2 a.m.

Louis speaks tentatively.

'I'm sorry I was weird with your mum,' he says. 'I get nervous when I meet new people. It's extremely embarrassing.'

'I didn't notice anything embarrassing.'

'You're kind. I always feel like I'm making a fool of myself around you.'

'I didn't notice.'

'No, sure, you had other things on your mind.'

'What do you mean?'

'The eviction. What a nightmare. No one should be treated that way.'

Phil laughs and rubs his face. Louis, son of a property developer won't ever know what it's like to have nowhere to live. He's trying to be kind, but his kindness is hard to take.

'Thanks,' says Phil. 'I'm going to go dance.'

Phil drifts inside and Louis follows.

The party has spilled into the complex of adjoining warehouses and sheds. Phil pushes through various dance floors that seem to have sprung from nowhere and Louis pushes after. There must be a thousand people in here, smushed against each other, crammed inside almost pitch-black rooms, with glimmers of pink and green and red lights bursting through. The air drips with moisture. The wet skin of dozens of people rubs up against them on the dance floor.

The rain crashes on the roof.

Louis shouts in Phil's ear, 'Please, can we just talk for a second?'

Phil stops. He looks at Louis, then looks away.

'What about?' he says, nonchalant, focusing his eyes on the dancers.

Louis laughs and shakes his head.

'I mean,' he says, rubbing the back of his neck, rubbing his face, and grimacing, 'I'm trying to talk to you. Can you just listen?'

Phil looks at him, impatient.

'I am listening.'

Louis rubs his face. He exhales, speaks carefully. 'I know you don't want to know me. But you *do* know me. Unavoidably, you do know me.'

Phil says nothing. Louis closes his eyes.

'What I'm trying to say is that I'm a part of your life whether you like it or not, and I think we should try to make the most of that.'

Louis waits, sheepish, then opens his eyes.

Looking at Phil, he continues, 'I'm trying to say that I like you.'

Phil isn't sure what's happening.

Louis goes on, 'I'm not sure what I mean by that.'

Phil stops fidgeting. He's taken aback.

His irritation softens into something else. Instinctively, he reaches out his hand to touch Louis's shoulder. His palm presses against it.

After a moment, he says, 'I'm not sure what you mean either.'

Louis laughs.

'No, of course not. It's a vague word. *Like.* Doesn't mean much.'

He says the word *like* as if to sample its taste and texture.

'Thanks for saying it though,' says Phil, before venturing, 'I like you too.'

Louis closes his eyes, breathes in, smiles in a sad way.

'You don't though,' he says. 'That's the point. You don't like me.'

Phil keeps his hand on Louis's shoulder. He says nothing.

'I saw the hickey on Keith's neck,' says Louis.

It takes a moment to understand what Louis is saying.

Phil shuffles from side to side as if he's bursting to pee.

Louis goes on, 'It's pretty big. Must have taken – what – a few minutes? More?'

Phil, dumbstruck, says, 'I can't really remember.'

'Did you not think that I'd see it? Did you not think that it might be weird for me?'

Phil hesitates.

'I don't know,' he says. 'I suppose I wasn't really thinking of you.'

Louis laughs. He raises his eyebrows and shakes his head.

'I mean, yeah,' he sighs. 'Exactly.'

They're quiet then. Phil wants to say more.

They stand next to each other on the dance floor. Occasionally their elbows brush.

Then, they part. They're separated by the currents of the party – Phil needs a drink, Louis needs to pee – and they move towards the rest of the night without saying goodbye.

. . .

ED, AGAIN, IS ALONE. HE TRIES TO GLUG FROM HIS BEER but looks down at his hands to learn that he no longer has one. What happened to it? He can't say for sure. He should probably sit down.

There's a man to his right. Ed smiles at him. Why shouldn't he? He tries to wink too but finds that he's no longer able to isolate the muscles in one eyelid alone. He blinks instead.

He stumbles around. Where is Maggie? How long since he's seen her?

There she is: with Ali and Debs.

He sits down beside her.

'Where have you been all night?' he says.

'I've been here.'

'Well, I'm going.'

'I'll come with you.'

'You don't have to.'

'I'll come. It's late.'

Ed hovers while Maggie says goodbye to Ali and Debs.

They leave the party and walk to the bus stop. There's a misty rain and they're both wet from condensation and sweat. The footpath is closed for building works, so they have to walk on the side of the road, sometimes stepping into single file to avoid a hurtling night bus.

'Did you have a good time?' says Maggie.

'Yeah, it was fine.'

Ed is walking very fast and Maggie is trying to slow down.

'Are you OK?' she says.

'Yeah, I'm fine.'

She pauses, and then says, 'I saw Kyle Connolly tonight.'

'I don't know who that is.'

'He says he knows you.'

'Well, he doesn't.'

'He knows you from the estate. Says you two used to play together.'

Ed says nothing and walks even faster.

She calls after him, 'Would have been nice to dance earlier.'

He turns to face her.

'How were we supposed to dance when I didn't see you all night?'

'I was with Ali.'

'Why did you want me to come if you weren't going to spend any time with me?'

'It didn't seem like you wanted to spend time with me either.'

They're quiet for a moment.

They're standing on the side of the road and cars dangerously swerve around. Maggie and Ed have to keep breaking eye contact to make sure they're not going to get run over.

A car beeps its horn. They keep walking.

She continues, 'It would have been nice to have sex earlier too.'

He shakes his head and scoffs.

'How am I supposed to have sex in a room that's so damp?'

'I don't think that's the reason we don't have sex.'

'Are you serious? Do you realise how fucked up my lungs are?'

'Of course I do. I'm just saying you can't blame this on the damp.'

'We wouldn't have lived there if it wasn't for you.'

She scrunches her face in disbelief.

'*What?*' she says. 'You're blaming this on me? It's not my fault that flats in London are so chronically fucking hazardous. I've been calling the letting agent every day for a month to sort it out. When's the last time you called? Besides, you wanted to live there too.'

'Only because I thought it would make you happy.'

They catch a bus and are silent until they disembark at Dalston Junction station. On Kingsland High Street, people with tired faces clutch their kebabs and avoid eye contact.

Ed slows his pace and reaches out to touch her before pulling back.

She finally speaks.

'I'm not always sure if we're right for each other.'

'What do you mean?' he says, facing her, eyes huge.

She pauses. She pulls back.

The sun is starting to rise.

Ed retrieves a receipt from his pocket. He un-crumbles it. He crumbles it again.

The leaves are so green on this street. Someone across the road is moving out and has left a box of Disney VHS tapes and a yellow-stained plastic hand blender on the pavement.

'I love you,' she mumbles, eyes half-closed and tired. 'I'm sorry I left you tonight.'

They let themselves into their flat, turn on the lights, and try to fall asleep.

16

THE NEXT MORNING, ED WAKES ON A MISSION. IT'S 11 a.m., anxiety courses through his veins and before he has time to think, he suggests they go to Lidl. He'll buy food and cook breakfast and they can spend the day doing whatever she likes. She says she's too tired and doesn't really want to do anything, and he says, sure, that's OK, he'll go alone. But ten minutes later, after he's brushed his teeth and put shoes on, she's there waiting at the door.

They haven't mentioned what happened last night. He's determined to make it better.

When they get to Lidl, the supermarket is rammed.

They can't find a shopping basket so he picks up an empty crate that had previously been full of cabbages and he loads it up with bacon and sausages and cheese and eggs and bread and butter and orange juice and pineapple juice and alcohol-free prosecco so that they can have alcohol-free mimosas and then he navigates towards the shop's middle aisle, the one that's chocked full of miscellaneous bargains, gazebos and micro-waves and child-sized karate costumes. 'Hey, shall we get one of these?' he says. 'Might come in handy when the little one is old enough. It's only a fiver. Saves us the hassle of buying one when they're six and obsessed with Jackie Chan. It's a tale as old as time, isn't it? I went through a karate phase, and my dad went through a karate phase, and well, my dad's dad probably didn't, but that's only because he died in a factory accident when he was thirty years old and presumably that was before they had karate in England.' She seems so tired. He knows he should shut up. He places the karate outfit in the crate on top of the breakfast stuff, and then he finds the bright red highchair she'd wanted. He tries to pick up it. He can't. He's holding the crate with both hands and he can't manage. Some of the stuff falls out. 'It's fine,' she says. 'I'll carry it,' but he refuses: he tells her he can do it, and he does do it, even though he has to walk to the checkout in an awfully lopsided manner. They queue. He whistles a tuneless tune. When they get to the front he smiles at the cashier and asks her how she is. When she doesn't answer, Ed tells her it's a beautiful day. 'Forty pounds, thirty pence,' she eventually says, and Ed takes out his bankcard and enters his PIN and the screen displays a message: *Payment Declined.*

. . .

MAGGIE CAN'T BEAR IT. SHE WATCHES HER BOYFRIEND at the top of the queue while the cashier asks him to step aside and a security guard approaches to ask what's wrong, and Ed, unbelievably, tries to say there must be a problem with the card machine. She puts a hand on his shoulder.

'Babe,' she says pointlessly.

'It's OK. Just a problem with the machine.'

A split-second passes. She's silent, stammering. She doesn't know what to do.

A word in her head. It's been on the periphery of her thoughts for weeks but now it muscles its way to the front. *Unsalvageable.* It's the only way to describe what's happening here. She thinks of her mum and almost cries. *It all ends the same: the road gets built.* She tries to reason. *What do you mean?* she asks herself. *Do you mean that this attempt to buy breakfast is unsalvageable, or the entire relationship? The years? The love?* The answer is obvious: if they can't reliably buy food for themselves, how can they buy food for a baby?

She swallows a lump. *The road gets built.*

'Babe,' she says again.

He turns to her, 'I'm sorry. I'm so sorry, and I thought I had money to pay for this stuff, but actually I don't, and I'm sorry, I'm sorry, I'll buy the stuff next week.'

On these last few words, he starts to wheeze. He can't catch his breath.

'Babe, it's fine. We don't need any of it.'

'I mean, we do need a highchair. We absolutely do.'

'But your cousin can get us one. Remember?'

'I just want things to be right.'

'Things are right.'

'They're not though.'

She tries to pull him away from the checkout; they're holding up the queue and the security guard is looming above them and the cashier covers her eyes. She manages to pull him away, but he stops by the exit and all the shoppers have to step out around them.

He says, 'What did you mean when you said you're not sure if we're right for each other?'

She considers it. She speaks tentatively.

'I feel like we're forcing each other to act out these pre-scripted roles, which have very little to do with what we actually feel or want or think. We're on autopilot, Ed. We don't even have sex any more. I tried to dance with you last night and you didn't even notice.'

He is becoming upset.

'I know, I'm sorry, I just – I'm sorry.'

She pauses for a second, then continues.

'I don't think I want to go to Basildon,' she says.

'Well, what then? What other options do we have?'

He's still wheezing. He's bent over with his hands on his knees.

His face turns from red to purple and he's sweating like he's just finished a marathon.

She thinks of the asthma attacks he's had a few times a week since he took on more work at the beginning of the pregnancy, how Ed's dad became sick from working as well.

He won't survive this, she thinks. He's not built to survive this.

She closes her eyes. She breathes slowly so that she might not cry in the supermarket.

She puts her hand on his back and speaks softly.

'I mean, look,' she says, eyes still closed, voice high. 'You're struggling to breathe.'

'That's because of the damp in our flat. It's not because of you.'

She opens her eyes. She tries to put her hand around his.

'I don't think this is good for you.'

He stands upright. He tries to gulp down more air.

'I mean, of course it's not,' he says, almost laughing, but not.

He rubs his face. He looks at her.

He almost laughs again, then says, 'Do you know what happened with me and Phil?'

'What do you mean?'

'You don't know?'

He looks straight in her eye.

She looks around. Everyone is staring. She says, 'Can we get out of the shop?'

He turns around then and walks through the double doors and into the car park, pacing frantically away from her, so that she has to run to keep up, and raise her voice to be heard.

She calls after him, 'Stop. What do you mean?'

He's on the street now. He keeps pacing for a few more seconds and then pauses outside the kebab shop on Well Street. He waits to catch his breath and then keeps walking.

'We did stuff. When we were younger. Before I knew you.'

'By "stuff" do you mean sex?'

'No. Well, yes. Well, a handjob. He gave me a handjob. I asked him to.'

The entire time Ed speaks, he keeps his eyes down.

'Why are you telling me this?' she says.

He takes a receipt out of his pocket and starts ripping little bits off the corner.

'I can't keep this up,' he says. His voice shakes. 'I'm not able.'

They are walking more slowly now, and she realises they're going in the opposite direction to home. They've moved deeper into Hackney and are nearly at the Marshes.

'It's normal, Ed. Lots of teenagers experiment.'

'I smashed an egg on his head.'

'You what?'

'I took an egg out of a box of eggs and I walked up to him and I mashed it into his head. There were lads holding him from behind. He couldn't even wipe it out of his eye.'

'Jesus, Ed. When?'

'A few days after my first date with you.'

Nobody says anything for a moment; they can hear their own breath.

He continues, 'It wasn't just Phil. There've been loads of men.'

She pauses to take this in.

'When we were together?'

'No. It was only before then.'

He pauses, then goes on.

'I almost hooked up with a guy on Friday.'

'What do you mean *almost*?'

He pulls at the silver chain around his neck.

'I thought I would, but then I didn't,' he says.

She senses that this isn't the whole story. She thinks she doesn't want to know.

Still, they keep going. They walk side by side, until they reach the Marshes. They walk across the football pitch, past the teams of five-a-side and the people reading books and the birthday parties with balloons and the group of teenagers passing around a joint. The smell of weed is everywhere.

They reach the River Lea. Dozens of people splash around in it. On the first hot day of every May Maggie used to make a point of wading into it and doing a few strokes of front crawl before collapsing onto the bank and drinking beers or getting stoned with Ali or Phil or both. She didn't do it this year, afraid of the pollution and the rumours that someone got shigella from swallowing the water, and she didn't want to do damage to the baby.

They sit down on the riverbank. The light dapples through the canopy.

She says again, 'Why are you telling me this?'

He covers his face and groans deeply. 'I'm trying to tell you that you're not the only one who compromised. You're not the only one who wanted more. I've got desires too.'

'I never wanted to stop you from acting on your desires.'

'But that's what it means to love someone. It means to lose things. It means to have deep needs that go unfulfilled, because the person you love is most important. That's love.'

'Are you saying you never wanted a family?'

'I'm saying I wanted lots of things, but I wanted you more than any of them.'

She considers this.

She wants to disagree. She wants to say that love doesn't mean denying yourself.

She says, 'I wanted you too.'

He looks up and scrunches his eyes. He opens and closes his mouth a few times, like a sentence is getting ready to go out, but keeps forgetting something and has to go back inside.

She says, 'I don't think we can do this, Ed.'

He says nothing, and then whispers, 'I know,' and she puts her arm around him.

She wonders why Ed hadn't told her, and why Phil hadn't told her, and she feels upset at the idea that either of them thought it would bother her. She remembers with a pang that Phil had stopped talking to her for a while after she got with Ed, which in retrospect makes sense. She remembers the time she called him a slut.

She thinks now that maybe she does feel hurt.

Maybe she feels terrible and bereft and angry.

She can't explain her feelings. But Ed is very upset, so she puts her feelings aside. He falls asleep with his head on her lap, there on the banks of the River Lea with all the kids splashing about before them. She falls asleep as well, but wakes every now and then with pins and needles from the pressure of his head on her leg.

. . .

THE AIR THIS MORNING IS THICK AND FRAGRANT. THE rain has fallen for hours on the tarmac streets and now the city is perfumed with its steam. The leaves on the trees have grown greener and the pigeons clamber for shelter and the river bulges beneath the bridges.

It's Sunday morning, and Phil lies next to Keith. He listens to the patter of rain on the warehouse roof and tries to put together the pieces of what happened last night.

He'd been trying to find Maggie, wandering through the corridors of the building for what felt like hours, certain that something had gone wrong and desperate to make it right.

Her phone went straight to voicemail; the ticks beneath his messages would not turn blue.

She must have found Ed, he thought. He'd try to call again tomorrow.

At 4 a.m., he made his way to the front door to be alone.

That's when Keith tapped on his shoulder.

'You're not leaving, are you?' he said.

Phil laughed. 'It's been a long night. I was just on my way to get a veggie kebab.'

'Oh really? Well, don't let me interrupt.'

He checked his phone one last time for messages from Maggie.

'I suppose I could rearrange my appointment with Lebanese Grill,' he said.

'I'll buy you a kebab tomorrow, and chips if you're good.'

'You really know how to make a lady feel special.'

They kissed, and Keith led Phil by the hand towards the storage room at the back of the house that had been transformed into a makeshift darkroom. The effects of the drugs that Phil took earlier had worn off, but when Keith took his hand, he had a second wind. His skin tingled, his belly fizzed. They moved through the party with the blissful ease of the blissfully high, squeezing each other's fingers intermittently, and smiling often. Once, while they walked across the dance floor, Phil said 'Wait' and Keith turned to face him. He thought he was going to say, 'Don't go to Folkestone.' He thought he was going to say this with a cheeky grin – a grin so casual and cute that no one would possibly speculate on the hurt feelings it concealed – but in an instant, he realised he was too high to carry off such a feat with the requisite delicacy, so instead he said nothing and kissed Keith on the mouth.

Occasionally, he thought about Louis, and something stirred in him that he wasn't ready to name.

They continued into the darkroom. Shapes moved around, silhouettes kissing, sucking, fucking. Keith pushed Phil against the wall. He sunk his tongue deep into his mouth, licked the backs of his teeth, and undid Phil's belt. He yanked Phil's pants down and spun him around. Men gathered to watch, moaning little moans, stroking their cocks. The bass from the dance floor pulsed through the walls and Phil thought: Monday is many years from now. Keith's breath was hot, wet. His spit dripped down the back of Phil's neck while his fingers slipped between Phil's thighs. Exhaling deeply, he said, 'Can I fuck you tonight?'

And here was Phil's body and mind: shy of intense experiences. Seizing up and shutting down on the precipice of deep, vivid feeling. When faced with something hot, unknown, frightening, or desirable, every part of Phil's body and mind would usually implore him to reject it, no matter how much he wanted it, no matter how much he missed it, no matter how much it would have improved his life and love and experience of the world to have it. But last night when he felt Keith's breath in his ear, his hands on his waist, he thought: soon Keith is going to leave, and a door will close for good. Phil wanted to bolt through the closing door while he could. He wanted to be yearned for, malleable, vulnerable like a needy dog who lolls on its back each time its owner tries to leave the room, belly and genitals exposed, and then, picturing himself as a sort of human-dog hybrid – sweet, stupid,

owned – he became irrepressibly turned on. He became
pliable, soft. His body relented in a way that never felt remote-
ly possible before, revealing a cavernous capacity for pleasure
he hadn't known was there. He said 'Yes' when Keith asked the
question, and yes, he said, repeatedly throughout. For years,
Phil had narrated without pause. He had looked at the world
and catalogued what he saw. But in the darkroom with Keith,
there were no words but yes. For the first time in his life,
he was a person with a body.

Afterwards, he only wanted to draw Keith closer. He
wanted to bury his face in Keith's armpit and sleep with that
sweet and sour smell squatting in his nostrils. He didn't care
what parts of his body or bedsheets the cum dried to a hardened crust on and he had no interest in hastily wiping bodily
fluid off a single thing in that room. He only wanted to stay
in the pose that his body and Keith's body would create when
they collapsed on top of each other, and remain in that pose
when they both dozed off, and make a whole new pose when
they both woke up, and do the same thing again and again
on as many evenings, weekends, and mornings as possible,
without either of them having to neglect other important
commitments, like earning money, having friends, or speaking to their parents on the phone.

. . .

KEITH ROLLS OVER.

'I'm so hungover,' he groans.

Phil sits up. He smiles.

'Same. Have you been awake for long?'

'I'm not sure I slept at all.'

'Did you have a good time?'

'It was great.'

'It was hot.'

'It was,' agrees Keith, digging out a piece of toilet paper from around the side of the mattress to blow his nose.

'I really like you,' says Phil.

'I like you too.'

Phil takes Keith's hand and kisses it.

'I'll be back in a second,' says Keith. 'Just need to pee.'

Keith climbs down the stairs, and Phil lays back. He's hungover, and his thoughts are scattered. The rain on the roof is thunderous, his skin is tingling. Everything feels very vivid.

Keith comes back and collapses into the bed. He lies on the far side of the mattress and faces away from Phil. Phil lightly touches his shoulder with the tips of his fingers and Keith's upper back moves with his breath. He has moles that Phil never noticed before.

He says, 'I really like the way you make me feel.'

'That's sweet,' says Keith.

'Maybe we can do something today?'

'Yeah, maybe.'

Keith is still facing away from Phil. The rain pounds on the roof.

'Are you OK?' says Phil.

He wants to sound gentle, easy, but it comes out accusatory. Keith turns around.

'I'm sorry,' he says. 'I just had a lot of drugs last night.'

Phil says nothing, and then Keith says, 'Let's definitely do something today.'

They climb down the stairs together. The place looks like it was hit by a bomb fifty years ago and never rebuilt. Still, someone in the kitchen is cooking eggs and someone else is plunging their fist down on the cafetiere. The radio is on and the DJ has a warm voice. She's playing a Billie Holiday song, everyone sings along while they gather cutlery for breakfast. There are eight other people here, all stayed over last night, and are now swapping stories. Keith is wearing someone's baggy lavender boxer shorts and a white T-shirt. Debs is wearing a silky emerald dressing gown, and Ali is here too, wrapped around Debs from behind.

The crowd dissipates. People need to work, open emails and respond. They have bedclothes they need to put in the washing machine and hang up to dry. They have parents and lovers to meet up with or call, the cramped aisles of Lidl to navigate, cats and dogs to feed. They need to be by themselves, coming down off last night's drugs and longing for their duvets. They need to hydrate. The house is all the more quiet for having been so loud only an hour ago. It's almost ghostly. The radio plays a reggae song, and Phil and Keith go outside.

The rain has stopped, but the streets are still soaked. They walk down the Old Kent Road, packed with people doing their weekly food shop, the zips of their overstuffed backpacks straining against sacks of frozen veg and instant coffee. They do a lap of the park. They pass a few solitary joggers and the bustling barbecue area. A heron stands on the bridge in the middle of the artificial lake, refusing to move out of the joggers' way.

They walk south through the industrial estate and end up at South Bermondsey McDonald's. They sit on a picnic bench outside, shovel chips into their mouths, and slurp from a big Diet Coke. Phil can smell the traffic of the Old Kent Road. He can smell Keith, fag breath, and the tree that smells like cum, and he can feel the skin on his face glow red in the evening sun. Reggaeton wafts from one car radio; a Yorkshire accent wafts from another.

Keith happily wolfs down the soft lukewarm chips.

It's no longer deniable that Phil is in love with him.

He's in love in that way which is simple and enormous. He's in love in a way that soars, swells and bowls him over. It's like there's a spongy substance expanding in his chest. It causes a painful, forceful, pleasurable ache. It is lovely, and also, it is too much to take.

And also: there is doubt.

And also: there is shame.

And still, there are moments of fear and pain and alienation from his own body and from Keith's body and from all bodies, as if he doesn't belong in the realm of bodies at all.

But also, he thinks, life is short.

Why not just try to see what happens? Why not try to push things forward?

He says, 'I think you're gorgeous. I think you're so nice. And also, the other thing . . .'

He looks out at the street. He exhales. He smiles.

'The other thing is that I love you.'

He strains to get these clunky words through his mouth and places the emphasis on strange-sounding syllables. But even though he sounds like an artificially intelligent robot mispronouncing a name it hasn't been programmed to recognise, the message gets through.

Keith says, quietly, beaming, 'I love you too.'

Phil says, 'Do you really?'

Keith says, 'Of course I fucking do.'

Then they kiss with their mouths wide open, globs of mashed-up chips lodged in their molars, premolars, and underneath their tongues. Both men taste of salt. There are flecks of curry sauce from the plastic tub drying around their chapped lips. They smile wide smiles while they kiss, feeling the outer muscles of their mouths stretch against each other.

17

ROSALEEN WAKES ON MONDAY MORNING AT THE USUAL time. She has the usual breakfast and listens to the usual thing on the radio. There is a controversy over what happens to the body of the whale. Some say it should be incinerated. Some say it should be donated to the Natural History Museum. Yesterday's rain has cleared up and the heatwave roars back into the kitchen. She's not at work today. She's tired. It's her first Monday off in a long time.

She gets into the car at 9 a.m. Already, it's boiling. It's the sort of car a dog would die in. It smells only of crisps; the ancient air freshener lost its lemon scent years ago.

She's in the passenger seat. Steve's in the driving seat. Joan busies herself across the street, arranging her living room on the pavement, and when she sees Rosaleen she stops to lean against the palm tree. Rosaleen smiles. She thinks she'll pop in to see her later today, she'll do the same tomorrow, and every day after that. Joan's grass is scorched yellow.

They arrive at the hospital at 9.30 a.m. It looks terribly grim. It's like a coffin in the sky, all grey and boxed in, and the paint on the sign is peeling and stained by rust.

They tell the receptionist they're here and then take a seat.

'It's very quiet,' says Rosaleen.

She's anxious, observing the quietness as if it means something.

She says again, 'It's very quiet. Do you know that? It's very quiet.'

Steve nods and hums in agreement.

The doctor comes. He takes them to a room. There's not much to say about the room; it's just the sort of room where doctors see patients; a reclining grey bed, scales, and a poster of an illustrated human body flayed so that its muscles are exposed for educational purposes.

The doctor is a young man, good-looking, a little fat.

The sky through the window is brilliantly blue. A brilliant yellow crane fills the whole frame. It's almost like a painting, like a piece of pop art, not unlike the Andy Warhol print that used to hang on Phil's wardrobe door. What happened to it? She doesn't know.

Six weeks of chemotherapy, six weeks of radiotherapy.

Emergency surgery as soon as this Wednesday.

Even at that, she might have no more than six months.

All going well, she'll have as many as three years.

They leave the same way they came in. They walk through the waiting room, still quiet, and wave goodbye to the receptionist, who looks up from her phone to say, 'Take care.'

They climb into the car. They turn the radio on. They drive down the dual carriageway with the windows open.

They pull into the driveway.

Steve opens the front door, they go inside, and he sits down at the computer.

She thinks this is unusual. She asks what he's doing.

He says in six weeks' time, they're going to Ireland. When she's finished her treatment, they're going to Dublin, and she'll show him all the places she loved. They'll do it no matter what happens. He'll take her wherever she wants to go and he won't hear a single word against it. He gets up from the computer and goes straight to the kitchen. He rummages through the drawer where their passports are kept and he calls out, 'That's good news. They're both still in date,' and then he goes to the bathroom. He shouts down the stairs, 'We still have the travel-size deodorants from Portugal.' He comes back down, digs through the medicine drawer and happily announces that they still have a full pack of paracetamol in case she feels sick on the plane. He goes to the bookshelf and stares at it and says, 'Have you read all of these? We better get you some new ones to read in the airport,' and then he goes back to the computer and he says, 'Now tell me. Where in the city would you like to stay?' and she comes up behind him, crouches down and puts her forehead against his shoulder and kisses him and tells him she doesn't mind as long as she's with him.

. . .

LATER, SHE THINKS ABOUT PAULINE.

Ireland changed when Pauline died. It stopped meaning home.

No one ever told her how it happened. She never

asked. Everyone said it was 'all of a sudden' and the family were silent on the state she was in when they found her after Mass.

Normal at the time. These mysterious ends.

She never learned the full details of Pauline's death, but she knew she was pregnant, and afraid to tell her family, and the man she'd got pregnant by was nowhere to be seen.

She knew about Ireland.

She knew about the church: how they said that the people of Ireland couldn't be trusted with cartwheels, nor could they be trusted with knickers, nor could they be trusted with condoms (illegal until the eighties). They couldn't be trusted with speaking the word *condom*, understanding that a condom fitted over a penis, or *hearing* the word penis when muttered in passing by a doctor (let alone the word *vagina*.) They couldn't be trusted with homosexuality (illegal until the nineties), or heterosexuality, if your definition of it allowed for the experience of pleasure at another person's body, or your own. The people of Ireland weren't to be trusted with bodies. They weren't to acknowledge bodies. The existence of bodies was to be flat-out denied. As for bisexuality, that was unheard of at the time, but if it had been heard of, surely the people of Ireland could not have been trusted with that either. Crucially, the people of Ireland could not be trusted with pregnancy, with safe childbirth or safe childhood, and above all, they couldn't be trusted with abortion (illegal until this year).

If cartwheels were allowed, condoms would be next, but if Pauline had been allowed the use of a condom (let alone an abortion) she might not have ended up where she did.

Rosaleen's most vivid memory of Pauline is this: her, doing cartwheel after cartwheel around the school yard, and in Rosaleen's memory it's a slapstick scene: Pauline cartwheeling all over the tarmac and the nun helplessly chasing with clenched fists like she was in a silent movie. That, and the smell of dust on her mother's living-room carpet after they'd wrestled, Rosaleen's head on Pauline's soft belly, which expanded and contracted in search of lost breath, pretending their bodies had landed in that position by pure coincidence.

When Pauline died, Ireland became a place she never wanted to return to.

And now, here she is: soon to be on her way back.

. . .

ED WAKES ON THE COUCH. HE TRIES TO GO BACK TO sleep. He's not working today, and he lies there for as long as possible, wanting to prolong the moment before the day must begin. He remembers all the other mornings they've had in this flat. He remembers the future. They used to talk of Basildon and babies and how to raise a child. They used to go on property websites and imagine buying a house. They spent hours describing how they'd decorate it and the interior design choices that their parents made in the nineties; the fibre-optic lampshades, sequins on every bit of fabric, the deep but unfulfilled dreams of a back garden water feature. Every day since Maggie found out she was pregnant, she has come home after work and spoken softly as they arranged themselves on the couch, their limbs finding routes around each other, like plants that grow through cracks in concrete towards sunlight.

They've made their decision. He wishes they hadn't.

. . .

MAGGIE HEARS A PATTER ON THE DOOR, PROBABLY THE neighbour come to pass on gossip about the drug dealers in the flat across the way. She gets out of bed, dazed, and goes down to answer.

There's no one there.

She cranes her neck, looks left, looks right. There's a cardboard box on the ground.

She hauls it into the flat and opens it, confused by its contents.

It contains a whole new paint set, sheets of folded up fabric, yellows and pinks and pale greens, a big roll of black latex, a sewing kit, glue, and a good pair of scissors.

There's a note scrawled on A4 paper, and she instantly recognises Phil's handwriting, how it sways indecisively between five different styles, each 'f' and 's' completely different from the last. It says, 'Hope to see some work of yours soon. I'm a massive fan.'

She feels full up with love for her friend Phil. She misses him. She wants to be back with him in the shopping centre at sixteen, seeing the future as enormous and free.

Ed rouses on the couch.

He asks what time it is.

'It's morning. Nearly 10 a.m.'

'I think I overslept on purpose.'

'Why?'

'I knew that if I woke up I'd have to remember what happened this weekend.'

'That's sad, Ed.'

He yawns comically as he stretches his arms.

'We don't have to break up,' he says.

'You know we do.'

He turns to face her. He's bathed in sunlight.

'You can change your mind,' he says.

'Ed.'

'I could go back to education. Get a better job.'

'It's not just about the money.'

'Remember Phil's mate who grew up in a commune?'

'Phil's mate grew up in the eighties. Things are different now.'

'What about Louis? Didn't he say he was planning to have a kid with his lesbian friends and they were all going to raise it together in the countryside? We don't have to be a normal straight couple in the suburbs. There are loads of different things we could be.'

'Louis can do stuff like that because he never has to think about money.'

'Yes, but if I work ten or twelve more hours every week, and if we move into a place where rent is about four hundred pounds cheaper – and it doesn't have to be Basildon, it could be anywhere – and if we went out a bit less, maybe like once a month, then I don't think money would be so much of an issue for us. We could make it work.'

She says nothing. She puts her head in her hands.

He continues, 'Even if we didn't go out at all, we'd still have each other.'

She looks at him. When she speaks, her voice is tired.

'We can't make it work, Ed.'

She says this, wanting to cry. Just this week, a break-up had been unthinkable. She'd been giving the baby a tour of Kingsland High Street.

But she knew yesterday in Lidl what she needed to do.

Ed, bent over, asked her what options they had, and instantly, she knew the answer.

He didn't recover his breath until night-time. Even then, he kept on wheezing.

She doesn't see it as an act of selflessness on her part. She's not martyring her happiness for the sake of Ed's survival. She *has* no happiness without his survival, and not just his survival, but his giddiness, the dimples on each side of his lips, his Sinatra crooning.

She doesn't accept that he should give up his own happiness for her either. His martyrdom is no use to anyone.

Sure, she had wanted to hold a baby to her face and kiss it for approximately sixteen hours without intermission. She had wanted the baby to giggle non-stop at the non-stop kisses, for non-stop kissing to be the funniest thing there ever has been or ever will be.

And sure, she is thinking about half-lives again. How will people see her now? Someone who was almost a mother, but not. Someone who could have, but didn't. Will the people who saw her as a half-life before see her as a three-quarter life now? One third? She had started telling people. All her cousins know, the girls from school. What will they think? At forty, fifty, will she look back and wish she'd grabbed this chance while she could?

She could do it on her own. Couldn't she? She and Ed could break up, and still she could have the baby. All of this is still in reach. If she sits here, does nothing, in six months' time the baby will come whether she likes it or not, and then she'll just find a way to make it work.

She looks at Ed. She does a half-smile. She sighs.

She doesn't want to make it work.

Her life, as it stands, can't fit a baby, Ed, and herself inside of it. It would be too cramped. There's only so much air. She needs to save it for herself. She wishes that air were more abundant than this. She doesn't want to ration so carefully, but she needs to breathe too.

He nods and says, 'OK.'

He moves slowly through the flat, full of half-packed boxes and a bag full of baby clothes he got from his mum. Their life together is a mess in every way. They've called the landlord in Basildon and told him they won't be moving in. Ed will go with her to the clinic.

On Friday morning, he brings her scrambled eggs and coffee.

They get in the car and drive to Homerton Hospital for her second appointment.

She watches this as if from above.

Maggie, on her way to an abortion.

Maggie, silent and tired beside Ed.

She remembers how Tracey Emin made an art film about her abortion. Maggie narrates what she sees as if one day she'll make an art film too, as if one day all of this will be useful and meaningful and profitable to her art career, rather than tiring and sad.

She is early enough in her pregnancy to take the abortion pill, but too late to be able to take the pill at home. She had her first appointment on Wednesday, the second is today.

They find a parking space. They sit quietly in the car before going in.

He says, 'You're my best friend.'

She says, 'You're my best friend too.'

He squeezes her hand. She continues to narrate.

Maggie, walking through the door.

Maggie, giving her name to the receptionist.

Maggie, listening to the nurse who explains the procedure.

The nurse has a soothing manner. Maggie feels very safe.

She loves the NHS. She has choked back tears of gratitude during or after every medical appointment she's been to for the past decade, and today is no different. She cries, thinking of the dream that every person deserves to be treated with care. She cries at the beauty of that dream and feels lucky to have lived a part of her life before the dream dies.

Oh sure. She is being nostalgic. But she's entitled to her nostalgia, and to her free NHS abortion too. She'll walk out of here today and she won't pay a penny. She will be cared for and treated kindly, and no one will make her feel ashamed for being pregnant and poor at the same time.

The nurse gives her a sympathetic look. She squeezes her hand. She thinks that Maggie is crying for the baby. She thinks these are tears of grief or regret or sorrow.

She's right, to be fair. They are tears of grief as well.

She thinks of a statistic she recently read.

Since 2010, Tory austerity has resulted in 130,000 preventable deaths.

She thinks of social housing. Her mother bought their terrace from the council when Maggie was four years old, and since Maggie moved to London nearly a decade ago, she's only ever lived in ex-council flats. She thinks of the fifties and sixties, all those people who were finally given a secure place to live, somewhere to care for their families forever and the promise that they would be treated with dignity when sick, or poor, or hungry, or dying.

How excited the people must have felt back then, to feel as if there were a place for them. How thrilling it must have been, to look towards the future and to see yourself in it.

She remembers the 2017 general election. She knocked on hundreds of doors across Wimbledon, Putney and Kensington, in huge estates built in the fifties, sixties and seventies, relics from bygone eras. Some were shoddy, freezing cold and damp, but some were beautiful too, like the Alton Estate in Roehampton, concrete blocks spread on stilts over a rolling green field. An Eritrean man who'd lived there since 1975 remembered voting for Callaghan in 1979, the election Labour lost to Thatcher. He said the world changed on that day. *When we get a Corbyn government, we'll build one million of these every year*, said the man who was leading the canvas. *We'll all be living in one of these in a few years' time.* She believed him. She looked towards the future and saw herself in it.

She remembers the Irish abortion referendum. She remembers how she and Phil cried with happiness on the day of results, piggybacking on Phil's Irish heritage to think of it as their own victory too, a struggle of their own. It was a great day. She thinks of all the protests she went to over the years in solidarity with the Irish, the Chileans, the Polish, and all the protests that have happened throughout human history so that she can sit where she sits now.

At a certain point, she realises that she is no longer narrating to the abstract audience in her mind, but rather, she is narrating to her hypothetical child, this formerly possible baby, this baby that could have been hers.

Maggie, your hypothetical mother.

Maggie, who would have loved you as best she could, if she could.

Maggie, who can't. Maggie, who's sorry. Maggie, who was not able to make you feel real, even though she badly wanted to guide you by the hand to your first day at school and be nervous for you, restless, so afraid you wouldn't make friends. She wanted to bite her nails at the school gate until she saw you run towards her, delighted. She wanted to scoop you into a hug and kiss you and feed you sugary foods that made you squeal in joy even though the nutritionists would call this bad parenting. She wanted to take your happiness so seriously.

She thinks again of the 130,000 preventable deaths since 2010.

She didn't just want the choice to have an abortion.

She wanted the choice to have a baby as well.

She takes the pill and waits for the cramps. Ed drives her home and runs her a bath and illegally downloads Seasons 3, 4 and 5 of *The Simpsons*. He makes her a lasagne.

It's also fine.

Isn't it?

It's also the best thing to do.

It's terrible too.

He tells her he loves her, and she loves him too.

. . .

PHIL STANDS ON THE PLATFORM OF FENCHURCH STREET
station. Bankers surge from trains. The clip clop of formal
shoes and the beep of Oyster cards combine at the turnstiles
to create a sense of rhythm. It sounds like the intro of a pop
song played on loop, the chorus always deferred.

Travelling against the tide of commuters, the train carriage
is nearly empty. The only people here are Phil and a handful of
cleaners who have finished their morning shift.

He rubs his face; he didn't have time to grab a coffee be
fore the train departed. His body feels dry, and his eyelids
feel stiff. The 'See It, Say It, Sort It' counter-terrorism alert
malfunctions on loop for the first ten minutes, but then melts
into a blissful quiet.

He woke earlier, manic. Keith had gone back to his own
room, and Phil tossed and turned all night with the impression
that today would be a big day, a day on which his life might
change, and he should make himself available for it. Faced
with the sanctity of this knowledge, he did the one thing he
saw fit to do: he called in sick to work. He hung up the phone,
high on the sudden injection of free time. He could spend the
day as he pleased.

He decided to go to his parents' house.

Now, the train pulls into Basildon station. He's amazed
at how little time it took. London and his hometown used
to feel like light years apart, but really, there's only forty minutes between them. He walks into the heat, through the town
centre and towards the retail park, to spend an hour slouch-
ing through the homeware section of TK Maxx, wondering

whether his mother would prefer a floral mug, a non-stick wok, a Nando's gift set, or a bottle of chilli-infused olive oil with Jamie Oliver's face on it. He goes with the floral mug.

He gets the bus past his old school, which now has a bill-board advertising its Ofsted rating – 'Officially Good And On The Way To Outstanding' – and hears his footsteps echo on the ground of the estate. The hum of traffic ricochets off the dual carriageway.

With the floral mug hidden behind his back and an un-placeable anxiety humming in his belly, he turns the key to the door of the house he grew up in. He walks through the hall-way, the living room, the kitchen, and the ceilings feel much lower than they used to.

Nobody's home because everyone's at work. Phil had been so distracted by his general sense of looming epiphany that he hadn't even thought to call ahead.

He makes a cup of coffee – two spoons of freeze-dried Nescafé, three spoons of granulated sugar, a splash of milk, a splash of hot water – stirs it with a little silver teaspoon and settles down in front of the TV to wait. Re-runs of *Who Wants to Be a Millionaire?* are on.

Rosaleen and Steve arrive back home. They're alarmed.

They say, 'Why aren't you at work? Has something happened?'

Phil assures them that it's fine, that he has annual leave, and he just happened to be in the area anyway. He hands over the floral mug, and they both agree that it's a lovely mug.

They go to the Chinese restaurant.

They order their food and discuss previous times they've been here – Callum's sixteenth birthday, Phil being offered a place at university, the first of his family to attend. They talk about which is nicer: the satay skewers or the spring rolls, while in between their starter and main course Rosaleen puts down her glass of water and says, 'I need to tell you. I've got cancer.' No one says anything at first, so she continues, 'I'm going to get better.'

Steve looks at her. 'Love,' he says.

'What? I'm serious. I'm going to get better.'

'But the doctor, love. You know what he said.'

'Don't mind the doctor.'

Phil looks around. There are black lacquer walls. There's gentle harp music and a little gurgling water feature. Bowls of hot lemon water stained by sauce from the barbecue spare ribs litter the table. He thinks of himself as a good communicator. He thinks of himself as having transcended the stereotype of men as being unable to describe their feelings. But around his family he becomes the most repressed of all, like the sad old patriarchs who were brought up to believe that the strength of society relies on their continued silence.

She hardly tells him anything. She doesn't say when she was diagnosed, or what the doctor's name was, whether the doctor was a man or a woman, kind or mean, whether they made Rosaleen feel big or small or cared for or not. She doesn't say which hospital it was, and what the hospital smelled like, and whether Steve went to get her a sandwich while she waited, and if so, was the sandwich overpriced or reasonable. She doesn't say which of them drove, and how long it took, and if they had any trouble finding parking. She doesn't say what type of cancer it is, or how it will be treated. She doesn't tell him if it's the same cancer that killed her mother, and what it was like to know her mother was dying across the Irish Sea.

She doesn't say how she feels about death.

She doesn't say that she's afraid.

She doesn't explain when she says 'I'm going to get better' if she says that because of her bravado, her optimism, her denial of reality, or whether it's based on an actual prognosis.

She doesn't say any of this, and he doesn't ask.

It's not that he doesn't want to know. There are a thousand questions in his head clamouring for attention all at once. It's just that he doesn't know which words to use.

He doesn't know what you're meant to say to someone with a cancer diagnosis, and not just anyone, but specifically his mother. He doesn't know what words might help her feel loved and cared for and comforted. If she can't believe she's not going to die, he doesn't know what words might help her believe everything will be fine anyway. She'll still be loved and looked after and incomparably adored, and everyone will be with her until the very end, and they'll hold her hand, and they'll never forget her, and they'll all be together again someday.

Does a dying person need to be convinced that they might not die, or do they need to be helped to accept that they will? He doesn't know what words his mother might need, because he doesn't know his mother very well at all; why else had she taken so long to tell him? Why hadn't she told him on Saturday while they were in Westfield? Surely she hadn't been diagnosed overnight. Surely she had known while they sat on the brick-red seats and sipped on cappuccinos. It dawns on him; she had wanted to tell him on Saturday, but for some reason she hadn't. He's not the only one who can't talk; neither of them can.

He notices her glass of water is empty; he takes the jug and refills it for her.

He thanks her for letting him know. She says again, 'It's going to be fine,' and he can tell that the conversation is set up so that she can comfort him, not the other way around.

Feeling the weight of this, the guilt, a lump inflates in the back of his throat. Tears expand to fill up his lower eyelids, ready to burst. He doesn't want her to have to comfort him any more than she is already trying to do, so he excuses himself to go to the bathroom.

He quietly cries between the mahogany-effect walls of the men's toilet cubicles, which smell of citrus-scented cleaning products and stale chewing gum.

He gets himself together. He goes back to the table.

The conversation moves on and the main courses come. Phil's parents eye his tofu curry with polite suspicion, while he explains, frantically, that tofu's not bland at all; you've just got to season it carefully, cook it at the right temperature and serve it with a nice sauce, maybe something peanut-based. He recommends several vegetarian sausage brands, available at most major supermarkets, which, as far as he's concerned, are as good as the real thing. His parents concede that there have been impressive improvements in the quality of fake meats over recent years, and the ecological and health benefits have become hard to ignore.

18

THEN, EVERYTHING MOVES VERY FAST. IN SIX WEEKS, Callum and Holly will get married, and the week after Rosaleen will fly to Ireland with Steve and her two sons. On Wednesday, she has her operation. On Friday, she begins chemo. On Sunday, she goes shopping for a fascinator.

The fascinator has become a major event. Everyone has something to say about it. Since she's gone public with her cancer diagnosis, her family, her neighbours, even her team lead at work, all compete for her time. It's nice to feel wanted, but it's tiring too.

That's how she ended up here, in the bridal wear shop, looking at herself in the mirror with a huge magenta feather sticking out of her head, and Phil, Callum, Holly and Joan all stating various opinions on the merits of bold colours versus neutrals.

They're a motley crew. She can understand Phil's presence at least. He's been a pernickety aesthete ever since he came out of the womb, and she values his opinion on both clothes and interiors. Callum's eagerness to join them surprised her – she never knew her eldest son had so much to say about women's fashion – but she can understand why Holly came along; she wanted to bond with her future mother-in-law. Joan, famously, doesn't give a toss about fashion, and says so all the time. Rosaleen can't deny that Joan has been an unhelpful addition to proceedings. Every time Rosaleen tries on a new fascinator, Joan makes a whole song and dance of saying how this one looks exactly the same as the last one.

Still, despite their differences, everyone agrees that magenta is not her colour.

Phil says it's tacky.

Callum says it hurts his eyes.

Holly says that neutrals are more suited to Rosaleen's skin tone.

Joan says she looks like Long John Silver.

But what can Rosaleen say? She completely adores it.

Why does she adore it? Well, at least partially because everyone else hates it, and what an utter joy it is to finally do something against the wishes of other people.

She wishes that Pauline could be here to see it.

'I'm going to go with this one,' she says.

Everyone looks at each other, as if to discern whether she's joking or not.

'Are you really?' says Phil.

'Yes. I like it the best.'

They exchange glances again, and realising she's serious, revise their opinions.

Phil says it's camp.

Callum says it's quirky.

Holly says it makes her eyes pop.

Joan says she looks like David Bowie.

Rosaleen understands that these are all intended as compliments, muddled as they are.

She thanks them, and pays for the fascinator.

. . .

HOLLY, ON HER WEDDING DAY, BEGS HER BRAIN TO TAKE a break. All morning, it has been narrating non-stop, mentally describing things as if they had already happened, and every time someone takes her picture, she imagines posting it online and wondering what distant cousins and ex-friends will think. She imagines people looking at the picture three decades from now. Will they wonder what was happening behind her eyes? What was happening behind her eyes was this: a practice session for how she'd describe the day to the girls at work. *Pink prosecco in the morning and there were strawberries in the glasses, and the bridesmaids' dresses were peach and puffy, that eighties opulence, that Princess Diana glamour, you don't get glamour like that any more, and Callum's mum, bless her, she wore a bright magenta feather. She was a mythical bird. Gorgeous, all the same, and she did great on the day.* Holly imagines that this is what she'll say, even though she hasn't yet seen Rosaleen today, and it remains to be seen whether she will do great or not. She's unwell. More so than ever. Holly is worried.

Callum, on his wedding day, attempts to tie a cravat. He can't do it, gets frustrated, says, 'We've got the wrong ones, it doesn't work,' and his dad, patient, does it for him.

He pats Callum on the shoulder, says that he looks good.

Rosaleen downstairs, asks Phil to confirm that her fascinator looks alright. He adjusts it slightly and says 'Perfect.' She has been pacing around all morning, muttering the words to her speech under her breath. She is terrified, manic, sick to the stomach. But when she rehearsed it last night for Steve and Phil, they both stood up, applauded, cried a little bit.

Ed, in the Catholic church next to Phil. Fellow groomsman, matching navy cravats.

Callum and Holly are seated before them at the altar. Already today, Ed has had to mediate in an argument between Callum and the priest. Holly had wanted to walk down the aisle to a pop song, but the priest had insisted on a strict policy of religious music alone. Callum was furious; he said it was his wedding, which he was paying for, and the priest was overstepping the mark. Privately, Ed found Callum's position to be ridiculous (he had wanted a religious service – what did he expect?) but understanding his duty as best man was to support the groom no matter what, he told Callum he was right; the priest *was* a prick.

Rosaleen and Steve sit across from them, and Ed's mum is behind. Maggie and Keith are somewhere here too, and afterwards they'll all go to a reception at a hotel in town.

The priest reminds the congregation with a big laugh that this is God's house, not a football stadium. At the beginning of the ceremony, he told a joke. He said: if you don't turn off your mobile phones, the floor will open up and you'll all be swallowed by the fiery infernos of hell. It's not the only joke he's told, but it's certainly the most memorable.

Now, he's saying something about Christian love. Ed is an atheist, out of convenience more than anything, but recently he's become open to the guidance of spiritual leaders, and celebrity chefs, and people who make videos about crypto-currency on YouTube. Ed's life is amiss. The only time of day he feels OK is the two or three minutes after he wakes up, because that's the only time he doesn't remember where he is or what's happened.

Where he *is* is his mum's house.

What's happened is his world has crumbled over the course of a few days.

Only weeks ago, there had been a future ahead of him, a little person he could have kissed on the forehead. He could have asked them questions, learned about horse riding or dub-step or PlayStation or whatever children like now – he would hardly know, he hasn't met a child in years – and he could have told them about his own life too, so that after he died, they wouldn't be left at a loss, realising that they had never known their own father at all.

He's grieving for the dad he could have been, and the dad he never had, and the dad that he *did* have, and his ten-year relationship, and his life in London, and his entire sense of identity. Ed is grieving for so many versions of himself that it's hard to look at the Ed that does exist; the Ed who's depressed, lost, broke, living at his mum's house at thirty years old.

Still, it's nice to be here today. It's nice to be seated beside Phil, who has been visiting Rosaleen most days after work, and on the same trips he calls in to see Ed. Phil has continued to refuse any attempt from Ed to apologise for what happened when they were teenagers – 'It's fine, I forgive you, please stop talking about it' – and when they walk around the park, they're too immersed in their own pools of grief to speak much anyway.

And it'll be nice to talk to Maggie, he hopes. They moved out of their flat the Friday after the abortion and he hasn't seen her since then, but they've been texting every day. He cranes his neck to spot her, sitting three pews behind, catches her eye and smiles.

She holds his gaze but doesn't smile back.

The priest says that love isn't a feeling. It's not the butterflies in your tummy you get in the giddy early days of a relationship. The butterflies don't last, he says. Love is something you deliberately decide to *do* through repeated actions of care. Love is something you make.

After the ceremony, Callum and Holly stand at the front of the church.

'Mother of the bride,' calls the photographer. 'Mother of the groom.'

Rosaleen and Holly's mum arrange themselves on either side of the happy couple. Friendly woman. She has a packet of mints in her purse that she's been doggedly trying to share with everyone. *Anyone fancy a mint? No? Well, they're here if you want them!*

Rosaleen thinks about her speech. After the meal, she is going to stand up and address all the people here. Almost unthinkable. Makes her want to flee the scene and never return.

Ed hovers. He feels shy. Is he supposed to be in the photos? Hard to say.

He turns around to see Maggie.

She's wearing a floor-length dress, sleeveless and pale pink, and her hair is down.

'You scrub up well,' she says.

'Oh. Thanks. I'm wearing a cravat.'

'I can see that.'

They both say nothing, then laugh.

'What did you make of the ceremony?' she says.

'I liked it, actually. I'd never been to a religious wedding, but I sort of enjoyed the chance to reflect on love, you know? Most of the secular ceremonies I've been to have been taken up by shit jokes about the groom's small dick and how the bride is mad to marry him.'

'I thought that would have been right up Callum's street.'

'You're not wrong,' he says. 'But he went for the Catholic thing to honour his mum's Irish heritage or something, even though Rosaleen herself is opposed to religion.'

'That doesn't surprise me,' she says.

'I'm glad he did it though. I found it quite poignant.'

'Are you going to convert then?'

'I wouldn't go that far. But I liked the sense of tradition. Feeling the weight of history behind the whole thing. And I liked what the priest said about love and sex being sacred.'

'You've gone very spiritual.'

'I just like the idea that sex can be life-changing.'

'It doesn't have to be though. Nothing wrong with a meaningless shag.'

'Nothing wrong with a meaningful one either.'

She laughs, so he laughs too, though he's not sure what they're laughing at and whether anything is actually funny. He can tell that there are infinite possible subtexts to their conversation, but his interpretation of the subtext could be vastly different from hers.

'It's quite a bold move,' she says.

'What is?'

'Waxing lyrical about love and sex with your recently ex-girlfriend.'

He is dumbstruck for a second, and then says, 'Well, who else would I talk to?'

'Surely Callum is open to hearing your thoughts on the sanctity of love.'

They both cast a glance over at Callum, now glugging freely from an open bottle of prosecco, the froth streaming down his chin and drenching his new navy cravat. Ed laughs.

'Would you prefer it if I stopped talking to you then?'

She speaks slowly then, and smiles while she speaks, emphasising each word.

'I never want you to stop talking to me, Ed.'

. . .

THE WEEK AFTER THE ABORTION, MAGGIE WENT TO Berlin. A friend of a friend wanted someone to sublet their room for the rest of the summer, and Maggie, exhausted and desolate, needed to get out of London. She's been in Berlin ever since, and only came back for the wedding.

She's been living with a German called Deborah and an American called Marco; she barely sees either of them. They both come back to the flat on occasion, hauling their bikes up the stairs and taking big gulps of water from the tap, on their way to and from various parties and never staying home for longer than thirty minutes. Sometimes she joins them at the parties where everyone talks quietly and dances seriously to loud and nondescript techno. She likes it; no one is overly invested in her, and she's not overly invested in anyone else, and on the nights when Deborah and Marco don't invite her out, she finds that she doesn't care.

She has two months left on her sublet, and four weeks until her money runs out.

Since they broke up in an official sense, she and Ed have become better partners to each other in every other sense, if only via the medium of WhatsApp texts. They depend on each other like you could depend on a family member. She often thinks that if some sort of catastrophe took place, her first priority would be to find Ed, and if the two of them had each other, then they would be OK. Sometimes, she dreams of his death, and wakes up distressed. Even though they're devoted to each other, there's no word to describe their relationship. They are, on paper, exes. In theory, either one of them could walk away without recourse, and she is, admittedly, afraid of losing him and ending up alone. Sometimes, she wonders why she and Ed couldn't settle together into a sexless but pleasant marriage. Hadn't that been what their grandparents did, and their grandparents before that? Why was it that her generation had to demand transformation, sex, adventure, comfort, stability, romance, conversation, intimacy, all from the one person? What's so bad about settling?

She rented a city bike that first day, and cycled west to the lakes. They were heaving with people who bunked off work. She walked towards the fenced-off nude section, quieter, relaxed, populated mostly by elderly German couples and gay men who cruise behind the trees. Everyone happily co-existed there; everyone lived and let live. She dumped her things on the sand, took off her clothes and ran straight into the lake. She swam as far out as she could, and then turned around to tread water and stare at the land. The shore seemed so far. The people were specks. She could talk to them if she wanted. She could do so many things with the rest of her day. She was alone in an enormous city, and there were dozens of shapes her life might take. She swam towards the shore, bought a beer, and fell asleep on the sand.

. . .

AT THE MEAL, SHE IS SEATED WITH ED, PHIL, KEITH, Ali, and Holly's gay cousin who works for the civil service. Everyone jokes about how Callum sat all the queers at the same table, and Maggie looks at Ed to see how he responds, but he plays his cards close to his chest.

The meal is in a big hotel with lots of function rooms, and the wedding itself is a big wedding too, with at least one hundred guests in attendance. Maggie recognises people she knew from school and tries to avoid eye contact as she furtively scans the room. She feels like a child in a Halloween costume whenever she wears something formal.

Everyone is drunk. They are all saying what they think about marriage.

'The only good thing about it is the wedding,' says Ali. 'I *love* a wedding. Getting dressed up, getting pissed, dancing with a random granny. But it's all downhill from there.'

'I don't know,' says Phil tentatively. 'I'm sort of the opposite.'

Keith smiles.

'You like the marriage, but not the wedding?'

'Well, yeah,' says Phil. 'There's something very strange about the pantomime of weddings. Like you have to perform your love in front of all your estranged cousins in order for your relationship to be considered real. But I don't know. I like the idea of making a formal agreement to care for someone for the rest of your life.'

'Which is to say: he hates fun but loves pain,' says Ali.

'Such a serious boy,' laughs Maggie, rubbing Phil's back affectionately.

'I mean, it doesn't even have to be a romantic thing,' continues Phil. 'The state doesn't have to be involved, and the church doesn't either. I just want to spend my life taking another person's happiness very seriously. I feel like marriage could be a useful tool for that.'

'What sort of queer are you?' teases Keith. 'Don't you know that marriage is a patriarchal construct designed for nothing more than the protection of private property?'

Holly's gay cousin chimes in, 'I wish! I've been married for nearly five years now and I've not got a stitch of private property to show for it. I feel like I've been scammed!'

Everyone laughs; Holly's gay cousin is a real hit.

'What about you?' says Ed to Maggie. 'What do you think of marriage?'

Everyone goes quiet. She feels Phil and Ali stare at her.

'I don't know,' she says. 'I don't know what I think about anything.'

He nods and smiles and the conversation moves on. A minute later, he gets up from the table and leaves the room by himself, and Maggie, slightly worried, follows him outside.

Across the room, Joan watches her son exit. She watches Maggie follow, and Rosaleen fidget with her magenta feather, distracted, still fretting over the speech which she's resolved to no longer give. *I can't, Joan,* she'd said outside the church. *I'm not able for it.*

Sometimes, Joan feels like an ancient cave mystic, eyes half-closed, half in a trance, trafficking words of wisdom from the spirit world to this one. Her advice to Rosaleen was this: nobody cares. By the time she makes the speech, everyone will be drunk, comatose from eating so much, and they won't mind what she says, *but*, for what it's worth, Rosaleen has a great way with words and could have been among her generation's finest orators given the chance. Her advice to Ed – if he sought it, which he won't – would be that he's younger than he thinks. By the time he dies, his life will change more than he could imagine, and even though this is a particularly hard time – for both of them – they can weather it together.

Joan, for her part, is having a good time. The pork belly: tender. The wine: like a slightly soured raspberry jam. Her husband would have loved it. He would have smacked his lips and relished it. She wishes he were here. It's not right that he's gone. Steve's sister, Sue, is seated beside her. She's telling a story about an error she made on her tax return many years ago. Joan can't for the life of her figure out why she's telling this story.

She allows the woman's words to wash over her. She welcomes the grease of the pork belly which coats the underside of her tongue. She is so comfortable on this softly cushioned chair. She brims, at least, with bodily pleasure. It doesn't matter that the woman's story is boring. Joan is only halfway here. One foot in this world, one foot on another planet entirely.

Callum, next to his wife. Euphoric. He is giddy with the word *wife*. He paws at the word *wife* like a toddler mauls an unsuspecting but tolerant old dog. 'You're my wife,' he giggles in her ear, whispering softly as if it's an obscene joke. It feels like it *is* an obscene joke. The most sexually charged words he's ever said out loud. It's almost unbelievable to him that they're allowed to sit here and be so obviously, desperately in love. Both in their wedding clothes, knees knocking off each other as they eat, they are practically pornographic. But wait: she's distracted. She looks around the room as if she's not in it. He wants to tell a joke so that she might land back in the present, but suddenly it's time for speeches, so he stands, rattles off words – thank you for being here, thanks to my parents, thanks to the beautiful chefs for the beautiful pork belly, thanks to the priest, the prick (he doesn't say this bit out loud) – and then, he looks towards his mother. He nods, as if to say *your turn now*. She looks in his eyes, then looks across the room at Phil, then Steve squeezes her hand, and Joan, alone, applauds. Rosaleen signals with an almost imperceptible shake of the head that she isn't going to give the speech. Callum, understanding, feels sad for a moment but doesn't let it show. He swallows his disappointment for his mother and discreetly moves things on.

. . .

MAGGIE JOINS ED IN FRONT OF THE HOTEL, LEANING ON a bollard, smoking, and staring at the car park. He's untied his cravat and taken off his blazer. Sweat seeps from his armpits.

She says, 'You didn't tell me what you think of marriage.'

He laughs.

'The same as Phil, I suppose.'

'At least that makes two of you.'

He opens his packet of fags and points them at her. She takes one out, lights it, and with a playful sideways glance, she mutters, smiling, 'Maybe you could marry him then.'

He looks at his feet and laughs again.

'Too soon,' he says.

She takes a drag on her fag and leans on the hotel wall beside him. They both stare into the distance, at the sunset, at the articulated lorries crawling down the dual carriageway.

'I'm sorry,' she says. 'I just like that I can joke with you.'

'I like it too.'

'It's weird to see you.'

'Why's it weird?'

'I guess because we still text so much. It's like our relationship migrated from the real world and into our phones, and it's a bit disorientating to be standing beside you again.'

'I've been grateful for the texts.'

'Me too.'

She takes a moment without saying anything. She turns to stare at him, while he stares into space. She says, 'I feel like we're still partners. Like, not in the romantic way. But still.'

He looks at her and smiles. Just now, she notices the hoarseness in his voice.

'I suppose we are,' he says. 'In some ways.'

She takes his hand and squeezes it very quickly before dropping it again.

'I've been going on dates,' she says.

'Oh yeah?'

'No one to write home about. Phil hopes I'll turn out to be a late in life lesbian.'

He nods and blinks and looks vaguely surprised, as if she's just shared a mildly interesting piece of trivia about the Grand Canyon.

'Well, I'm happy for you,' he says.

'Thanks. Have you thought about seeing anyone?'

He smiles sadly.

'I'm not in that sort of place. I don't even know where I'd start. I don't know the first thing about what I want any more. I don't even know if I'm a man, to be honest.'

He closes his eyes and inhales sharply.

'I'm sorry,' she says, and then squeezes his hand for longer this time.

'It's fine,' he says, rubbing his eyes. 'It's just, you know, hard.'

Then they're silent, him leaning against the wall facing outwards, her leaning against the wall facing him, with his hand between her thumb and forefingers. It's very quiet. She can hear traffic in the distance, and the dim clatter of cutlery in the hotel.

Then, the silence suddenly becomes too much and she feels compelled to make a joke.

'Hey,' she says, 'maybe you're a late in life lesbian as well.'

He laughs, perplexed.

'What?' she says. 'Maybe you are.'

He shakes his head, smiling in disbelief.

'I mean, yeah,' he says. 'Maybe I am.'

He looks at her directly then, and she's taken aback by

how playful he looks, the glint in his eye. She smiles then too, and draws him into a hug, and they stay that way for ages.

. . .

THE SPEECHES END, THE BAND BEGINS TO SET UP, AND Phil and Keith leave the wedding. They plan to return soon, but Phil needed a breather. They move down Basildon High Street, smoking.

'I'm sorry,' Phil says. 'Just had to get out of there.'

'Don't apologise, babe. Are you OK?'

'Yeah, it's just that weddings are weird. I don't quite feel like myself.'

'I reckon nobody in there feels like themselves.'

Keith fishes Phil's hand out of his pocket and grabs it.

He strokes Phil's thumb.

Phil smiles. He goes on, 'Maybe it's just that Basildon is weird too. I can feel my adrenaline shoot up as soon as I set foot in this place. I always feel like I'm going to have to break into a run any moment. Whenever I come here, I have this irrational fear that something terrible is going to happen and I'll be stuck here for the rest of my life.'

Keith laughs. 'Don't worry. We'll get you back to London safe and sound.'

. . .

IN JULY, AS PLANNED, KEITH MOVED WITH LOUIS TO Folkestone. He and Phil exchanged long emails every few days, cataloguing their feelings. After months of conjecture and suggestion, now they can't stop explaining themselves, clarifying and re-clarifying over the course of 3,000-word emails, full of sub-clauses and qualifying statements, and phrases like 'a bit' and 'perhaps' and 'I suppose, in some ways, what I'm trying to say is that . . .' always watering themselves down, trying to be nuanced, never wanting to sacrifice the complexity of their feelings for a statement too bold. Louis has become more involved, too, and Phil's feelings towards him have softened into *something*. It's delicate. It's too early to state what it is. If Phil put a word on the *something*, then the *something* would evaporate, become mist, nonchalant and aloof, it would tease: *I don't know what you're talking about. I was never even here.* Suffice to say, Phil has cultivated a newfound interest in making Louis laugh. When he makes Louis laugh, he feels as if he has won a prize, and that prize is increasing in value by the minute. He tries harder and harder to get it. When he's with Louis, it's like being in the last minutes of a football match in which the winning goal is yet to be scored. He is alert and tense and his heart beats in his chest, on the brink of sheer euphoria, looking for openings to make Louis like him, and then (!) the laughter (never forced, from the belly), and Phil thinks: *goal!* He wants to whip his T-shirt off and spin it above his head in a football-style victory dance, which, being shy, of course he doesn't, but lying in bed later the same evening, he thinks back in pleasure at that moment, silently exclaiming to himself *How good was that!*

Still, things are not without their complications.

Phil stayed with Keith and Louis for three days one week, during which they had a sort of summit. Louis and Phil both have moments of jealousy so all-consuming that it spoils days and makes it hard to work or eat or go to the shop. All three of them swam in the sea one morning; Louis and Phil swam vigorous front crawl as far as they possibly could, and Phil felt a pit of humiliation open up; they were literally trying to out-swim each other.

Back on the shore, things were easier.

Since his mum told him about the cancer, Phil has knocked on her door every few days, with flowers or a little teddy bear behind his back, wracked by guilt, thinking of how much more he should be doing. Afterwards, Louis picks him up in the car and they drive back to Folkestone. There, they swim in the sea and eat salty chips. They fuck slowly, very intensely, sometimes just Phil and Keith, sometimes all three. They talk about what it feels like to have a dying parent; Keith squeezes Phil's hand and tells him not to feel guilty.

Still, all Phil gives to his family is his time and his money, and he had to get an overdraft to pay for the gifts that he and his brother pooled for, so it's not even his money at all. They've paid for a patio, garden furniture, an upcoming holiday to Ireland. These gifts seem to make Rosaleen happy, but in the grand scheme of things, they're not nearly enough.

. . .

PHIL AND KEITH CONTINUE DOWN BASILDON HIGH Street, Phil slowly calming down.

'Do you see that big concrete building?' he says. 'That's the town's one gay bar.'

'Did you used to go?'

'Just once. I planned to go every so often when I was a teenager but I walked straight past it every single time. I was petrified. I don't know what I was afraid of.'

'It's cute to think of you at that age.'

'I haven't changed that much, apart from getting more haggard.'

'You're not that haggard.'

'Thanks for the vote of confidence.'

They continue walking and the more they walk, the less anxious Phil feels. Keith keeps asking questions about Basildon and Phil enjoys stepping into the role of a tour guide.

He realises that they're about to go over the dual carriage-way overpass from which you can see the edge of London.

They pause in the centre of the overpass: traffic swarms below. Phil used to fantasise about kissing Ed here (a long, wet kiss, the weight of each other's frames pressed against each other, the swell of each other's bellies). He used to think of that kiss all the time. It was the only thought he had for the whole of his seventeenth year. This overpass had once seemed the height of romance, so high up and its view so spectacular, but now it seems like there's not much to say about it at all; it's just like every other dual carriage overpass. Getting tired, Phil is about to lead them back to the wedding, when Keith grabs him by the wrist and kisses him.

A long, wet kiss.

The weight of each other's frames pressed up against each other.

The swell of each other's bellies.

They pull back. Keith hugs him and lifts him off his feet and they both laugh.

They walk back to the hotel together with Keith's arm around him, and by the time they get there, the band has begun. A group of Holly's aunties dance in a circle. Miscellaneous children, unidentified and strung out on sugar, play hide and seek around the ankles of the aunties. Ed and Maggie half-dance beyond them, leaning in to each other, whispering things which no one else can hear, and next to them Steve chats to Holly's dad.

On the edge of the dance floor, Joan joins Rosaleen for a summit.

'It's not too late to make the speech,' Joan tells her.

'The speeches are over.'

'Everyone else's speech is over, but yours isn't.'

'The band has already started.'

'Do the band not have a microphone? I'm sure they'd be happy to share.'

'It'd be inappropriate. Everyone is already dancing. I'd be interrupting.'

'No one will mind an interruption from you. They'll be delighted with your interruption. Besides, I'll set it up for you. When the next song ends, I'll go up there and say to the band *Excuse me, my friend has something to say. She's the mother of the groom and the finest orator of her generation, so you better listen.* And then, I'll introduce you. I'll say *Ladies, gentlemen, honoured guests, if you don't mind, the mother of the groom would like to say a few words,* and if they're annoyed – which they won't be – they'll be annoyed at me for interrupting the dancing and won't be annoyed at you. They all think I'm mad anyway so I can get away with a little social faux pas. *Typical Joan. Up to her old tricks.*'

This is getting ridiculous, Holly thinks, dancing next to her husband. The day has nearly passed, and still she is experiencing it as if she were observing from the outside. She doesn't feel like a real person. This doesn't feel like a real wedding. It's as if she were on a film set, performing the role of blushing bride, the role of blushing bride having nothing to do with her actual life, as if any second the director with yell *Cut!* and she'll take off the dress and go.

But it is her actual life. Callum is her husband, and he's looking at her. He is saying the words 'What's up?' also holding her waist, also the band are playing 'Dancing Queen' by ABBA, and she finds herself trying to describe to him how she feels, also trying to be kind to his feelings and express gratitude and reiterate that today is just what she wanted, because it was, and it is, she just wishes that she could get out of her head for one lousy second and not think on overdrive, and not get randomly angry at Gemma Hall, her childhood bully, who still skips laps around the edge of her mind, and not worry that she should have pulled a different pose in the photos earlier today and now it's too late.

Callum nods. 'Busy brain,' he says.

'Chaotic.'

'Would it help if I did this?' he says, kissing her neck the way she likes.

She laughs. 'Maybe,' she says.

'How about this?' he says, leaning out and doing a sort of John Travolta disco dance.

She laughs again. 'Not sure.'

'Alright,' he says, coming back and kissing her forehead. 'Well, we can keep trying.'

The music stops.

Joan is at the mic.

'Ladies, gentlemen, honoured guests, I'm sorry to inter-rupt and we won't take much of your time, but if you don't mind, the mother of the groom would like to say a few words.'

Then, Rosaleen steps onto the stage. It takes a few moments, and during those moments, there is silence, and coughing, and everyone wondering what's happening. Magenta feather sticking out of her head, beautiful in her blue dress beneath the pink and green disco lights.

She thinks of Pauline reading her poem in the pub. She tries to deliver it like that.

'Callum,' she says, hands shaking, her legs – oh God – ready to buckle. 'Before I had you, I never knew just how many creatures could live beneath the earth of one tiny back garden.'

Keith grips Phil's hand as Rosaleen begins.

19

STANSTED AIRPORT IS OVERCROWDED. THE QUEUES IN the duty-free snake for miles and it's impossible to walk anywhere without bumping into a hassled parent telling a tantruming child that the giant novelty M&M's dispenser is overpriced and they can't have it.

Rosaleen, Steve, Phil and Callum are seated separately on the plane, but Rosaleen is lucky enough to sit by a window. It's a bright day. Dublin spreads beneath her. They get a taxi to their hotel on Parnell Street, where the tram crawls by every few minutes, and the old Georgian buildings have been demolished for office blocks and Tesco. There's a Chinese supermarket, a Nigerian supermarket, a Polish supermarket, a Lidl. Half the pubs have rainbow flags hanging outside, and the street sweepers roar as they brush cigarette butts and Coke bottles around. The city is different. The light is different. The sun makes new shadows on the pavement.

She takes them down O'Connell Street and points out where Nelson's Pillar was. They don't know what Nelson's Pillar is, so she explains. Steve has only been to Ireland three times; once to meet her parents, and again when each of them died. Phil and Callum have not been at all. They know nothing of it; no one in England does. They get the DART to Bray, past the cliffs and the gorse bushes. Phil gawks at the mansions and asks Rosaleen if she knows which one Enya lives in, which she doesn't, but she's amused that this is the one bit of trivia her son seems to know about Ireland. Dublin Bay is wide and glistening, and even though she understands this to be objectively untrue, she is convinced then that no other body of water in the world is so richly, so vividly, so deeply blue.

They go to the cemetery. Her parents, Auntie Helen, and Pauline are buried here. She brings flowers for each one and tells her family about how her Auntie Helen had been the kindest woman she knew and her son Stephen, who was very creative, became a makeup artist to the stars. She stands at Pauline's grave, which has a lovely headstone; black marble with a gold cross; little flowerpots around it; all the pink and red geraniums bloom beneath the engraving: *Pauline, beloved sister and daughter, 1959–1981.*

It was her sister who called to say that Pauline had died. Rosaleen can't remember what she said in response. There was a particularly Irish mode of discussion that involved saying nothing back and forth until it was time to go home. *Ah sure. This is it. Grand so.* It was one of those conversations. It was like they were talking about the weather. Pauline had died and all they could muster were the most useless of conversational tics.

She stood in the hallway of her block of flats responding to her sister's nothings with nothings of her own, until the lady from upstairs said *Are you quite finished, I need to make a call,* and Rosaleen went back to her bedsit, alone, no longer sure where she was.

She remembers smoothing the bedsheet. She remembers boiling the kettle to make tea, which she didn't drink, and she stared at the tea for, oh I don't know, an hour, saying to herself *You have to drink the tea. Drinking the tea is a normal thing to do.* She remembers saying *There's a good girl now, don't get upset* and she simply stood in the centre of the room, crying, yes, but also trying to breathe slowly so as to not cry, and she could hear London move beyond her window, a man trying to fight another man, two old ladies calling to each other from across the street, and Rosaleen told herself, *This is your world. Dublin is gone, and Pauline is gone too, and you have to get a hold on yourself.*

But she was angry at Londoners who didn't understand. She was angry at joggers on Regent's Canal, and bankers who clip-clopped in the City, and the good manners of the cashiers at the supermarket. She was angry at them for not knowing Pauline. They wouldn't have known her even if Rosaleen described her with the best words she knew.

She decided then you couldn't be a Londoner and a Dubliner at once. You couldn't care so much about Ireland if you wanted a life of your own in England. Still, a man from Hastings once told her that potatoes were bad for your mind. He had a theory that the Irish had been considered to be lazy and dim-witted because they ate too many potatoes, and the potatoes had rotted their brains. When she suggested that this was a colonial stereotype, he became furious. 'Well,' he snarled, 'we're all products of colonialism here, love. Doesn't make you special,' and once, someone at work changed her screensaver to a leprechaun standing on a stack of potatoes and her manager told her to learn how to take a joke. You couldn't allow yourself to be constantly hurt by the ignorance of people in Britain; you'd end up a furious wreck. If you wanted to get along with people who believed your country had no history of its own, you had to forget your own history too.

They leave the graveyard and decide to climb Bray Head. She used to bound up in great leaps, but now she has to keep stopping for breaths, leaning on Steve and draining the last drops from her water bottle. Still, she puts one foot after the other foot. She feels a terrible heat on her face and a wheezing in her lungs. Phil says slow down. Steve says let's stop. Callum says, 'Go on without me, I need a fag break.'

But Rosaleen keeps going. She says nothing at all.

It's very important that they reach the top. Why? She doesn't know why. It just is.

Eventually, they make it. She collapses on the ground beside a rock and takes fifteen minutes to catch her breath. Her heart rate slows and the sweat on her brow turns cool, and when the nausea finally subsides, she looks up to see Dublin city in front of her, right across to the far side of the bay, and the Poolbeg Chimneys as specks in the distance.

She used to hate when people romanticised Dublin. She used to hate being told it was the magical home of poets and ponderers.

She remembers that she had been cruel in that city. She had been eleven years old. She had looked Imelda Barry in the face and told her she was ugly, even though she knew Imelda Barry to be beautiful.

She had been kind in that city as well. She had been twelve.

She had gone to the library on Kevin Street to borrow history books for her mother because her mother felt stupid for not knowing about the past.

She looks at the city, and she wants Phil to know of her mother who lived there. She wants him to know of the curve of her mother's back over the sewing machine, that her father got too close to a deer in the Phoenix Park once and the deer nearly bit him. She wants him to know about jumping into the freezing cold sea, the stench of sewage, the smell of hops, the taste of salty chips. She wants him to know about Dublin on a sunny day.

She huffs. She grows frustrated. She speaks of Dublin as if Phil were a naive American tourist searching for his roots, and she's an enterprising tour guide gunning for tips.

She tries to go deeper.

She wants him to know where she went to school, and which teachers were nice and which were mean, and how at fourteen years old, Sister Concepta wrote on Rosaleen's *Jane Eyre* essay: 'You're a talented writer Rosaleen, don't ever stop' and that was the only teacher to ever call her anything but stupid.

She wants him to know that a person called Pauline had lived there, and in 1977 Pauline said a poem in the pub, and for the only time in Rosaleen's life, she felt part of something beyond herself, and then Rosaleen left, and then, Pauline died.

There's a lot she wants to say.

It's crazy to think she'll ever fit so many words through her mouth.

She says, 'Do you see the two chimneys? If you follow them back from the river, you get to a place called Ringsend.

There used to be these tall colourful houses there. Maybe they still are. Anyway, they were all turned into flats. People used to call them the Legoland Flats because of the bright colours. I knew someone who lived in one. Her name was Pauline, and she was a poet, and she died young. She said her poems in the pub once.'

Phil looks out in the direction where she's pointing, as if he squints hard enough he'll see Pauline herself, towering to the left of the Poolbeg Chimneys, clearing her throat and calming her nerves, poised to finally speak up in the smoke-choked pub.

'I wish I could have heard her,' says Phil.

Rosaleen smiles then, and looks out at the city, and finds that this is enough.

She doesn't have to say everything all at once.

Acknowledgements

This novel was made possible through the support of a Next Generation Award from the Arts Council of Ireland and a Developing Your Creative Practice grant from Arts Council England, for which I am immensely grateful.

Thanks to my phenomenal agent, Liv Maidment, whose diligent and thoughtful stewardship helped to shape the novel and find a place for it in the world. Thanks to my editors, Katie Bowden at Fourth Estate, and Jessica Vestuto at Mariner Books, whose razor-sharp instincts vastly improved my writing. Thanks to Lola Downes, Eve Hutchings, Naomi Mantin, Martin Bryant, Martin Wilson, and the teams at Fourth Estate and Mariner, it's been a dream to work with you.

Thanks to Spread The Word and the London Writers Award, especially Bobby Nayyar, Laura Kenwright and the wonderful writers I met through the programme, especially Lizzie Clark, Nadège René, Ulka Karandikar and Mark O'Brien. Special thanks to Aparna Surendra, for being so generous in your feedback on a full draft.

Some elements that went on to form part of the text originally appeared in a play script I developed with the brilliant support of Sam Curtis-Lindsay and Nina Lyndon at Hackney Showroom.

Thanks to everyone who gave invaluable feedback on drafts of the novel: Niamh Campbell, Huw Lemmey, Avril Corroon, Georgia Anderson, Sofia Connors, Ed Webb-Ingall, Eoin Fullam, Cat O'Shea. Special thanks to Felix Macpherson for your feedback, support and many drives down the A12, and to Bekah Sparrow, for being very wise and very kind. Thank you to David Evans for taking my picture, and for being a lovely friend.

Thanks to the peers and mentors in Ireland, who helped me to feel capable, valued and like writing was a possibility for me: Lynnette Moran, Una Mullally, Vickey Curtis, Oonagh Murphy, Niamh Beirne, Sian Ní Mhuirí, Stephen Quinn, Darren Sinnott, Anna Clock, David Doyle, Dan Colley, Kerry Guinan, Ruth McGowan, Colm Summers, Erin Fornoff, Aisling Murray, Áine Beamish, Lisa Crowne, Niamh McCann, Ian Power, Tricia Purcell and Shane Daniel Byrne.

Thanks to the friends who I spent time with while working on this: Rosi Leonard, Claire Murphy, Edward Thomasson, Evelina Gambino, Holly Loftus, Siobhan McNamara, David Doherty, Carl Harrison, Lyndon Harrison. Thanks to everyone I lived with at Wild's Rents: Jess, Liam, Nicky, Darragh, Lettice, India, Hannah, Alicia, Florence, Paul, and those already mentioned above, and to the other housemates I've had during this time: Georgia, Lewis, Maite and Jovi.

Thanks to Aoife Frances and Edel Martin, who I'm lucky to have grown up alongside. Thanks to my brilliant, inspiring teachers, Trevor Downey and Irene Nolan at St Mary's Diocesan School, Moynagh Sullivan at Maynooth University. Thanks to Matthew Mulligan, for being kind and dependable, for your impersonations of politicians. Thanks to my love, Michael Walker, for making me laugh, for making me feel at home.

Thanks to my grandad, Teddy McKenna and my siblings, Daragh and Sarah. Most of all, thanks to my parents, Fiona and Ricky, for the many years of love and encouragement, and for always making sure I had books to read as a child.